A REALM OF FEAR & FURY

MIRANDA JOY

For permission requests, email the publisher at authormirandajoy@gmail.com

ISBN: 979-8-9859148-5-6 (Paperback)

First edition, 2024

Formatted by Miranda Joy at Spellbound Souls - Instagram: @authormirandajoy

©Cover designed by Maria Spada - www.mariaspada.com - Instagram: @mspremades

Map by Cartographybird Maps - - Instagram: @cartographybird

Spellbound Souls

www.authormirandajoy.com

CONTENTS

CONTENT WARNING

Please be advised that this book has elements intended for mature audiences. It does not portray real life or healthy relationships and is intended as purely fictional entertainment.

Content warnings include but are not limited to references to abuse, nondetailed references to childhood abuse/SA, violence, nightmares, grief, anxiety, panic attacks, manipulation, bullying, descriptive/detailed sexual content, and more.

Please email the author at authormirandajoy@gmail.com if you have questions or concerns.

This one is for the damaged little girl inside you—the one who feels broken, forgotten, or lost.

May you make peace with your darkness and know that you are whole.

You are *indestructible.*

"And the day came when the risk to remain tight in a bud was more painful than the risk it took to blossom."

-Anaïs Nin

ONE
SOMETHING TO FIGHT FOR
ALESSIA

You can't ignore me forever. My shadow-self mocks me from within, an echo of my own voice.

"You are an absolute pain in my arse." I scrunch my nose in exasperation, weaving through the Umbra Court's gardens.

The resounding dark laughter within me rattles my bones, confirming I'm doing the right thing. Once the high of the possibilities wore off, reality closed in. Apparently, my shadow doesn't want to listen to me. Using it for good won't be as easy as I had foolishly thought.

Perhaps you *aren't listening to me,* it says exasperatedly. It sounds just like me but more fierce. And decidedly more frustrating.

I ignore it, sucking in a lungful of fresh, dewy air.

Hidden amidst a dense mass of clouds, the sun attempts to reveal itself. It's not quite enough to wash away the shadows of Umbra Court. The flowers, with their vibrant colors, bring life to the otherwise dull and unsaturated world around them.

As I walk through the endless gardens, the scent of roses fills the air. They cluster in shades of deep ruby red to light cheery pink. Even some whites, purples, and yellows pop up in between.

Amid them, the stone castle stands tall—an imposing, weathered edifice that never fails to leave me breathless. I strain my neck, searching the maze of flowers for Rainer.

Instead, Ezamae steps into my line of sight. He seems out of place with his knee-high metallic boots, collared shirt, and navy coat with oversized, glittering silver buttons. His hair is the color of moonlight, the curls settling in ringlets around his sharp ears.

Seeing him makes my heart ache for the owner of these gardens—the prince I'm distancing myself from so I can focus on *myself* without distraction—a male who is just as handsome but wild.

I wanted to say goodbye one last time before leaving for my court, but he's nowhere to be found. My shoulders sag, but I can't fault him for not wanting to see me off.

Ezamae watches me sharply, his porcelain face bearing no expression. He's waiting patiently for me to say I'm ready.

But I won't ever be ready.

Leaving Rainer—and Umbra Court—behind is a hard choice, but I must do it. Everything is different now that I have this shadow within me. Now that I'm *the* princess of Spiritus Court. Returning to my court is my duty, and learning to make peace with my new-found magic is necessary.

Good choice, my shadow-self says. *Love makes you weak.*

"I'm not leaving because you're right," I mutter. "I'm leaving because you're *wrong,* and I will prove it."

I need to get myself together and learn how to control this all-consuming darkness before it causes harm.

"Are you talking to *me?*" Ezamae asks, lifting a pale brow. His forehead stays smooth even with the movement.

I shake my head, striding toward him.

A dark storm cloud rolls through the sky overhead, exponentially dimming the already overcast sky.

Ezamae glances up, then tilts his head at me. The first few raindrops fall, and he swipes at his jacket as if they've personally offended him. There's an edge to the Aer Prince, but it's different from Rainer's raw brutality. Ez possesses more of a mystique—his shimmering silver eyes hold endless depths of secrets. He might not be tortured or hardened like some of the fae I've met, but he's no less powerful.

And he will never stir up lust and longing like Rainer does. My eyes flit around the gardens, still searching for the Umbra Prince—to etch one last look into my mind before I leave him.

"Are you ready, darling?" Ez offers me a calming smile, and I force one back. The rain picks up, and he reaches a hand out, wiggling his fingers. "The storm is coming."

I frown, turning to the sky and letting the cool drops prick my skin. "It's not my fault you didn't dress for the weather."

He chuckles, and I sigh, tipping my head back down and accepting that it's time to go.

Over Ez's shoulder, movement snags my attention. Rainer's intense stare locks with mine, his jaw firmly set and his body stiff. His hands are shoved into his pocket, and he toes the dirt with his muddied boots. I fixate on his frosty, blue eyes, waiting for them to soften. But they remain sharp—the rest of his expression unreadable.

I offer him a small smile, hoping to break the wall between us. But when he doesn't make a move to come toward me, a sensation of pins and needles shoots down my spine, leaving me with an unsettling guilt.

Without breaking the stare or shying away from the heaviness between us, I slowly reach for Ez's outstretched hand. There's plenty of time for Rainer to speak, to make a move, but he remains rigid.

Until, at the last second, his face falls, and his mouth opens as if he's going to call for me.

But it's too late.

My skin meets Ez's, and the world tumbles away from my feet. Colors and lights blur past me as we're shot into the ether, leaving Umbra Court behind. I squeeze my eyes shut, but it's over before I can suck in my next breath. The world returns beneath my feet. I stumble, but Ez grabs my arm to steady me.

My head spins briefly with the disorientation, but my balance quickly returns, and I open my eyes.

The sight of Spiritus Court steals my breath. It was known as Shyga, a place of death and decay for many years.

Gone is the dull, haunted swamp filled with shadows and skeletal trees. Gone is the stench of death and sulfur. Now, the land is as abundant, teeming with the chitter of insects and tweeting birds. Hazy morning fog carries a sweet, fresh scent on the breeze.

Also gone is the male with half of my heart tucked beneath his ribs. A heaviness sits on my chest, and for a moment, regret swallows me.

Did I do the right thing?

How does anyone ever know if what they're doing is the *right* thing?

"Spiritus Court is underground," Ez says softly. "That's the entrance." He points.

The once waterlogged bog has transformed into a flourishing landscape, unveiling the long-lost entrance to Spiritus Court. Previously bare tree branches are decorated with leaves and vines in various shades of green. In the heart of it all, a tree of remarkable width stands as wide as a carriage. At its base, a beautifully carved door is nestled into the trunk. The door blends almost seamlessly with the tree, made of the same rough, brown bark.

Had Ez not pointed it out, I might've missed it entirely. However, on closer inspection, I notice the wooden knob protruding like a tree knot. Despite the tree's size, the door is barely wide enough for one to enter at a time.

Staring silently, I wonder what lies below the ground.

I long for Rainer's grounding presence beside me. Doing this without him feels like a mistake. As the seconds tick by, my head grows weightless, and a sharp ache spreads through my chest.

I take slow, deliberate breaths, but my lungs are starved for air. I left him behind.

After everything we've been through to make it back to one another, I left him in Umbra Court.

My body is empty as if all my bones were carved out, leaving only a hollow husk of pining. Every nerve ending in my body screams at me, begging me to make my way back to Rainer.

"Please, gods, don't let this be a mistake," I whisper.

The heat of Ez's body fills the space beside me, replacing some of the emptiness.

"You saved everyone's lives by resuming your role at the Spiritus Court, princess," he says kindly. His eyes sparkle with fondness as he studies me. "There's no mistake in that."

I don't have the energy to correct him—to clarify what I mean. The mistake is not about stepping into my new role. It's about whether or not I should be doing it alone.

Perhaps I'm overreacting, and the tumultuous shadow I carry isn't *that* bad.

Ez must read the turmoil on my face because his shoulders soften, and his arm wraps around my shoulder, pulling me to him. Panic flares to life. Even though Rainer's not here, and he's been cordial with Ez, I don't think he'd appreciate him touching me.

My vision darkens as Ez wraps his other arm around me, pulling me in for an innocent hug. A wave of heat consumes me. My palms vibrate, giving me practically no warning as a dark shadows explode from them. The long, tentacle-like wisps of darkness shove Ez, knocking him straight onto his back in the grass.

He makes a sound of shock and raises himself to his elbows. His lips part as if he's going to speak, but a wisp invades his mouth. Fear spreads across his face as he gags, trying and failing to pull the shadow free.

"Stop!" I yell, my head pounding in alarm. I claw at the shadows, desperate to pull them back to me. With each swipe, pain blossoms on my arms.

It's like in the Cave of Reflection when I tried to harm the shadow and only hurt myself instead.

Ezamae's face turns an alarming shade of blueish-purple as he sputters, eyes wide.

"I will never forgive you!" I scream at the darkness, wholly unsure of how to stop this. "Fight back, Ez! Fight it!"

I grab him by the arm, trying unsuccessfully to drag him away from the shadow. At the last second, the darkness withdraws, slinking away into my skin arrogantly slowly.

A breeze rushes past me as Ez presumably calls upon his air magic to fill his lungs. He sucks in breath after breath, staring down at the ground with a blank expression.

Slowly, he plants his hands on the ground and presses himself up. He carefully brushes his hands off, then inspects his outfit, plucking off pieces of leaves and dirt.

"This is velvet," he says hoarsely. He forces a smile, trying to lighten the mood, but it does nothing.

My heart pounds erratically as I stand there trembling.

"What just happened?" I ask, staring at my palms.

"You tell me." He tussles his curls, trying to appear unfazed as he fixes his hair, but his eyes stay locked warily on me.

I can't voice it, but I know exactly what happened—the same thing that keeps happening and why I left Umbra. My shadow-self is out of control. The magic—the urges inside me—are dark, demanding, and dangerous. It's as if my shadow knew I needed a reminder of *why* I'm here alone: to protect those I care about.

"Why didn't you fight back?" I mumble.

He narrows his eyes at my arms, pointing. Red, stinging lines crisscross my skin. "*That* is why. I know what happened in the cave. I would rather not risk harming you."

"You could've died!" I say, backing away from him. I wrap my arms around myself, trying to avoid his scrutiny. "I'm fine."

Love makes you weak, my shadow-self says. *Not only romantic love but* all *love.*

"Shut up," I say. "*You* did this, and I will never forgive you." Ez flinches at my words, and I give him a look of apology, shaking my head. "No—not you, Ez. It's my..."

I'm not sure what to say. Instead, I begin to pace.

"I'm worried about you," he says softly.

"You shouldn't be here. You need to go."

"It'll be okay," he says, stepping toward me.

Blackness wavers in the edge of my vision, and the thrum beneath my skin grows stronger.

"Just *go,*" I demand, terrified that my shadow will explode out again and hurt my friend. "I need space."

He stiffens and then slowly backs away to put space between us. The emptiness in my heart grows as he tries—and fails—to hide the worry in his expression. He swallows heavily, his throat bobbing with the motion.

"I should get back to Yvanthia before she drags me back," he says quickly. "I'll return to check on you, of course."

There's no way I can risk hurting anyone else. I need to learn to control this damn *power.* I almost scoff at the notion. This isn't something I ever anticipated, nor have I ever wanted. The darkness within me is uncontrollable. It doesn't listen to me and it threatens those I care about.

"It's better if you don't," I whisper to Ez, swiping my shaking hands on my leggings. "Come back, I mean."

"What?" His mouth tips into a frown.

"I need space from all of you." *Please*, I almost say, to soften the blow. Hurt flits across his face, but a look of understanding quickly replaces it.

He hesitates, but I don't waver. I wave a hand at him, telling him to shoo.

Finally, he sighs and nods.

"As you wish, darling." He places a hand on his chest and offers me a quick bow. Leaves kick up in a flurry of wind, and he's gone without another word.

My body crumples, and my knees hit the dirt with a thud. Sobs rip from my throat as I clutch the grass, hating this.

I'm not weak. I'm strong.

I'm not weak. I'm strong.

For a second, I think it's my regular mantra, but then I realize it's that unwelcome voice coming from my depths. It's almost as if it's mocking me.

"Leave me alone," I cry out.

I'm not weak. I'm strong.

This time, it sounds more like me, but I know it's still the shadow. Or *is* it me? I can't tell anymore—I can't even trust my thoughts.

It is you. It is me. We are one.

I clutch my head. "Stop," I beg. "*Please.* Stop."

Forcing myself to a stand, I aggressively wipe the tears from my face and suck in a deep breath. Letting the voice control me might be easier—but it's weaker. Succumbing is not an option. I have too many people relying on me to let them down.

I must learn how to stifle the voice and get my life back.

The weight of the realm seems to rest on my shoulders as I trudge wearily toward the entrance of my court. With each step, the burden grows heavier, threatening to crush my resolve.

This is my *home*.

I am not a victim.

I am not a prisoner.

And I refuse to be either of those things in my own skin.

This is *my* choice. Not my shadow's. Not Rainer's. Not anyone else's. This is what *I* want—to create a home while I learn to master my internal darkness.

"You hear that?" I whisper to myself. "You won't break me. You won't win this."

The scratches on my arms sting, reminding me that my shadow isn't only a liability to others. But to me as well.

I know that I can't hurt it—I only hurt myself. But what if someone else hurts it?

If it acts as an extension of my flesh, and if I take the brunt of the injuries, does it mean I could be *killed*?

The prospect causes me to shudder. If I had solidified my soul-bond with Rainer, and our fates were tied, would *he* be killed, too?

Anxious thoughts fill my mind, rattling me. It's too complicated, too risky, to mess around with. I need answers and solutions. This *thing* inside of me must be dealt with as soon as possible.

Reaching the tree door, I square my shoulders and fill my lungs with a long breath. Whatever awaits me down there can't be any worse than what lives inside me. Even if it is, I'll persist.

I've overcome worse, and I'll overcome this, too.

There is no overcoming; you must embrace me.

"Never," I mutter. There *must* be a way to overcome it. There's too much I have to do. I need my wits so I can free the Tradelings from Dovenak. I need to awaken Spiritus Court and make it a home for the broken and the lost, as promised. I want to let Rainer in—safely.

Gritting my teeth, I grip the doorknob and slowly open the door to my court, ready to face what lies below.

If love truly made me weak, as my shadow implied, I'd surrender. Instead, I will fight to ensure I'm safe around others. Love empowers me. It makes me strong.

That voice inside me is wrong—love gives me something to fight for.

Two
The Darkness Within Me
Alessia

With a steel spine and great resolve, I enter the court that was always meant to be my home—the land that the Lírshadows cherished until we were pushed from the realm because of Yvanthia, the fae queen.

Even without knowing my family or the story of my ancestors, I can *feel* their history here with me.

Thousands of years of magic shimmer in the soil around me, stirring as if awakening from centuries of hibernation.

I suppose that's not a far stretch from the truth, considering the Spiritus Court seems to be welcoming me back with open arms.

The air is stale, pitch black with the promise of secrets.

I should've brought a lamp—I can't even see my hand in front of my face.

Allow me, my shadow-self says.

"No!" I warn. "Don't touch a thing."

But it doesn't listen.

There's a rush through my veins as the darkness surges through me. It bursts from my skin, stretching out. I can feel it, like an extension of me, as it reaches for the wall. There's a soft *whoosh*, then another, as nearby sconces flare to life one by one. I gasp as the space brightens and comes alive around me.

The shadow lazily recoils into my skin, and my breath catches in my throat as my eyes adjust to the lighting.

"How did you do that?" I murmur, resigned.

Magic, my shadow deadpans.

The lights continue to flicker to life around me, highlighting the grandiosity of the space. Part of me is awed by what the sentient shadow is capable of, while the other is deeply annoyed.

A light titter of laughter rings out inside me. *If you light the first sconce at the bottom of the stairs, the rest light up in response—matches are stored within the stone recess beside it.*

Planting a palm against the rough, cool stone, I search for a groove beneath the sconce. When my finger brushes an indentation that feels different than the rest, I insert my finger, and a small compartment flips open, revealing a few dozen matches that sit in waiting.

"How did you know that?"

No response comes from my shadow. I exhale dramatically to express my annoyance and push the questions aside. The irritation is short-lived, however, because I'm distracted by Spiritus Court waking from its slumber.

The pillars in the entrance hall resemble dark, wispy trees that twist and reach upwards. Many open thresholds and corridors shoot off in every direction, resembling a crypt-like labyrinth. My mouth drops open as I take it in. The walls are made of dark stone covered in moss, matching the path underfoot.

A sudden burst of light overhead makes me jump. My head tilts back, studying the looming ceilings. Chandeliers made of tree roots dangle above. Instead of real leaves, they're adorned with glowing green crystals cut in the shape and style of leaves.

"Wow!" I gasp, spinning around in awe.

Squinting, I try to see how far the main hallway stretches, but there's no discernable end. The biggest indicator of being underground—besides the endless stairs I descended—is the lack of windows. But otherwise, I never would've guessed I'm beneath the earth.

"It's beautiful," I whisper in awe.

It's mine.

All mine.

This time, I can't tell if it's the little voice deep inside me or my thoughts. Either way, it's right. This is *my* home.

With a disbelieving laugh, I twirl around, stretching my arms out. My boots kick up the layer of dust and dirt, sending grey specks swirling through the air. I cough, ceasing my celebration.

How long has the court sat empty?

The prospect of cleaning it all by myself is daunting.

Perhaps I was too quick to demand my independence and send Ez away. It suddenly hits me how hauntingly silent it is down here. Unlike Umbra Court, there are no bustling kitchen hands baking sweets or busybody servants laundering linens.

No Das Celyn grumbling at me.

No Ken and Viv clanging steel.

Worst of all, there's no Rainer tending to roses or brooding over tea.

You don't need them, my shadow-self says with a hint of snark. *All you need is yourself.*

My chest tightens, and my heart feels heavy. The loneliness hits me hard and fast. I hadn't anticipated this. I'm alone for the first time in my life. Instead of peaceful, as I had expected, it's an inexplicable emptiness—an ache deep inside me.

You are stronger on your own.

"Stop," I whisper, hating the deceptive assurances it continues to spill.

As I gaze around the endless structure stretching out before me, my joy deflates, and I feel overwhelmed by its magnitude. Each breath grows strained, like I'm struggling to get enough air, and a lightheadedness washes over me.

I can't breathe.

I need fresh air.

What was I thinking trying to do this alone?

My feet move before my mind can catch up, and I blow toward the stairs, ascending to the morning sun as if I can outrun the darkness within me.

THREE

IT'S A LIE

RAINER

Leaning casually against the threshold of my father's office, I inspect my nails. There's something satisfying about picking the dirt clean from them while I wait.

The pixies alerted me to the Aer Prince's arrival moments ago. Sure enough, Ezamae comes speedwalking down the hall, his footsteps swallowed by the crimson runner. I've never seen the fecker move so quickly.

I push off the doorframe, ready to make a snarky comment about how he's back so soon, but the tightness of his features makes me pause.

My blood goes cold as I take in the streak of dirt on his cheek. It's unlike him to be so careless with his appearance. My vision flickers, dimming, and a dozen terrifying thoughts flit through my mind—all of them revolving around *her*.

"What happened?" I growl, marching toward him.

"She's fine." His voice is slightly hoarse, and he rubs his throat. "Are you aware she's struggling with her power?"

My pulse picks up, pounding in my temples. "Elaborate, Ezamae, right now."

His frown deepens. He holds an arrogant palm toward me, and I'm tempted to bend each slender finger back until they snap.

"I am not fond of the way you're looking at me right now," he says, with no tinge of fear in his tone despite how he takes a step back. "I simply offered her a hug—"

I growl, lunging toward him. "Touching her was your first mistake."

His eyes widen, the whites appearing almost comical. "Now, now, it was merely a platonic show of reassurance and affection. Her shadow made its perception of touch perfectly clear."

I stare, unblinking, as I wait for him to go on.

"It tried to suffocate me to death."

As his words settle in, humor bubbles up. "A little deserved, no?"

"Suffocation seems an odd punishment for a *hug*—an attempted hug," he quickly amends. He adjusts the neckline of his velvet cloak. "It didn't appear she was in control. She was rather shaken by the circumstances and—"

"If you hurt her, I swear to the gods above and below I will peel your skin back layer by layer while you—"

"For fae's sake! I didn't—forget it." He scrubs at his forehead. "You two are rather impossible at times. Yet I hold you both dear."

"Take me to her," I command.

A faint pink dusts his cheeks. "Afraid that's not possible. I'm rather depleted at the moment, and I need to return to Yvanthia before she drags me back by the testicles."

My nostrils flare as I take in the Aer Prince. As violent as I'm feeling, I can't take it out on him. He's been an ally to both Alessia and me. In fact, some might say I owe him for looking out for my bond while I was incapacitated.

"Tell me: is she okay?" I ask, working to keep my voice steady.

He nods. "She demanded I leave. Appeared quite rattled. I expect she might push us *all* away, fearing the implications of unchecked shadow magic." He hesitates, shifting his weight. "It's a dangerous power, Rainer. While I don't think isolation is the answer, she's right to see herself as a risk."

I scowl at him, clenching my fingers into a fist.

His eyes drop to my hand, tracking the movement. He raises another hand, attempting to appease me.

"Remember *why* Yvanthia cast away the Lírshadows in the first place? Unchecked darkness spells destruction. Alessia is not going to want your help... but she's going to need it."

"Don't tell me what my bonded needs," I spit, even though he's not wrong.

I take another angry step toward Ezamae, but he's gone in a dramatic puff of shimmering air.

The fecker. I punch the air where he was a moment ago.

I spin on my heel, practically bolting through the hallways to find Kenisius.

Moments later, his booming laughter reaches my ears. I burst into the grand entryway, ignoring the workers milling about, and stalk toward him.

"Rai Rai!" my old pal hollers, oblivious to the stress pumping through my veins. "Sennah and Uriel sent word they're—"

"We're leaving *now*," I say. "But we're stopping at Spiritus Court first."

Kenisius chuckles, scratching at his beard. "Little hu—demon just left. Shouldn't we give her some time to settle in before—" The words die off as he studies my face. "Oh no. Oh no, no, no. Don't tell me she got herself into trouble already. If that no-good brother of yours—"

"It has nothing to do with Tynan," I grit out. "I need to check on her. She won't even know we're there—unless she needs to."

He gives me a swift nod and strides purposefully toward the oversized front door. "Let's go."

We blast out into the late morning air, the doors clanging shut behind us. The vibration reverberates through my bones. I pick up my pace, heading toward the iron gate leading toward the Cursed Wood. Damp, dewy grass kisses my boots with each step.

Kenisius cracks a joke behind me, but I barely hear it over the roaring in my skull.

"Fair warning," I call over my shoulder. "I am not in the mood for feckery today."

Shoving the iron gate open, I hold it to allow my pal to pass. Wordlessly, he begins his shift. His body shakes and cracks, submitting to the earthquake within his bones. He contorts, falling forward as tendons and ligaments snap and reshape. His bearded face morphs, growing hairier and rounder. Beaded eyes and a soft black nose punctuate the appearance.

As much as I never wanted to ride the damn bear again, I don't think I have a choice. With a hefty sigh, I grip his neck and hoist myself onto his back.

"*This* is the last time," I mutter. Although we both know it's a lie.

Four

Too Much to Handle

Alessia

As I walk through my land, the sights of blooming flowers and melodies of birds clear my mind. Nature and sunshine have a comforting effect on my soul. The air is refreshing, a welcome change from the stifling atmosphere of the court. My budding panic attack has been quelled—at least for now.

I suppose I was overzealous in my desire to tackle the court. It's been empty for so long. What did I expect? Perhaps a magically restored environment, bustling with life. But reality has a way of humbling my expectations. Even magic extends only so far.

And now, thanks to my shadow-self, I have no choice but to face the daunting task ahead. The weight of the responsibility is an anchor pulling me under, but it's a challenge I must confront.

With my wits about me, I can think clearly again. And I'm not selfish enough to let my loneliness put my friends at risk. My love for them outweighs my need for companionship.

I admire the gnarled and twisted trees standing tall and noble, exuding a sense of ancient wisdom. Their roots flow underfoot like thick veins, bulging from the earth.

One of the distinguishing features of my land is the presence of those black roses, their velvety petals offering a sense of elegance and mystery. The dark flowers can be spotted in various locations, but they form an obvious barrier at the merging point with the

Cursed Wood. Beyond, where the roses no longer appear, the trees are denser, but their trunks are slimmer.

I have no intention of leaving my court's land—I'd rather not venture into the Cursed Wood and lose myself to Rainer's fearcaller magic. Having visual boundaries offers me a sense of safety.

I sit outside, resting against a boulder and listening to the sweet birdsong. It's decidedly less lonely up here with the woodland creatures chittering about.

The tranquility is abruptly interrupted by branches snapping and leaves rustling in the distance. Adrenaline surges through me as I jump to my feet. My eyes dart in all directions, trying to pinpoint the origin of the commotion.

"Little demon!" Ken comes crashing in from the north. A goofy grin lights up his face as he tramples over a section of my midnight roses, oblivious to the destruction. He carries an oversized wicker basket with a lid. "What a pleasant surprise!"

Waves of relief wash over me, but then my hackles quickly raise. I'm a danger—why can't he see that?

"What are you doing here?" I squint past him, secretly searching for Rainer. I'm mixed with relief and disappointment when I don't see him. At least he's smart enough to keep his distance. It's safer that way, especially with my shadow considering him a threat.

The bear shifter comes closer, his old, worn boots crunching over leaves and twigs as he navigates around flowers. He's in his typical brown leather garb, equipped with daggers. His brown hair is tied into a bun at his nape, and his untamed beard covers the lower half of his face.

"What am I doing here?" Ken repeats, frowning at me. "Friends aren't allowed to visit?"

Studying him, I try to understand why he'd show up like this. "I've only been gone a few hours."

"Well, I was in the area and figured I'd stop by and say hi."

"I told Rainer—and Ez—that I wanted to be alone," I say, scanning the forest again. Even though I didn't see Rainer, I swear I can sense him out there. There's a tug at my heart. "You shouldn't be here."

He rocks on his heels, and a sheepish look crosses his face. "If ya think a threat will get rid of me, you're full of shite."

"It's not a threat—I am *asking* you to respect my wishes and leave me alone."

His merriment melts into a frown. "You know we'll help you with whatever you're going through, right? You don't have to push us away."

A twig snaps in the treeline, and I jerk my head up in search of the sound. Although I know the answer, I ask, "Who's *us*, Ken? Who's with you?"

Darkness creeps into my vision, causing me to panic slightly. An unsettling pressure builds beneath my skin—a silent warning from my shadow.

Ken scratches the back of his neck, glancing toward the sky. "Eh, we just wanted to make sure you're okay. The wind prick told us about—"

"Why can't anyone listen and just leave me alone?" I whisper, my voice cracking instead of harnessing the bravado I'd hoped it would. They need to go before it's too late—before my shadow attacks them like it did Ez.

"Because I've seen what happens when fae shut down and push others out," Ken says softly. "You never saw Rainer at his worst, but I have. I've also seen him come back to life after meeting you."

"So this is about him?" I cross my arms. It's an unfair accusation, but I need to cut this meeting short.

"Yes. It is. And about you. And me." He waves his arms around him—and the contents of his basket tinkle like glass jars knocking. "About *all* of us. We're all in this together, little demon, like it or not."

A lump forms in my throat, and I can feel my resolve weakening. "It's not forever," I say through the thickness. "I just need some time to figure out my life."

Ken nods, but his gaze catches on my arms. Leaning forward, he squints and lowers his voice. "What're those?"

I shift, trying and failing to hide the many dried cuts. "Nothing."

He glances over his shoulder. I follow his gaze, not seeing anyone.

"Rainer's in the woods, isn't he?"

"Yep." Ken rocks on his heels, clapping his hands awkwardly. "If he smells that, he's gonna lose his shite."

Despite the situation's absurdity, Rainer's silent support and watchful eye bring me a glimmer of hope amidst the uncertainty. He'll wait for me—I know he will. I need to ensure he won't get hurt trying to be there for me.

The irony of it isn't lost on me. He once pushed me away to keep *me* safe, but the difference is that he had a grasp on his power all along. I don't.

But him waiting for me is all the motivation I need to return to my court and figure my shadow magic out.

"I'm fine. I'm safe," I say, ushering Ken away. "And I'm returning to my court now, so you two can leave." *Please.*

"Let me walk you home at least, m'lady?" He strides toward me, holding out an arm. "Help me pacify the pissed-off prince hiding in the shrubbery?"

I chuckle, then go still, waiting to see how my shadow responds. Its presence simmers just below my flesh—as if waiting to strike. But the pressure doesn't grow, and it doesn't speak, so I take a risk and accept Ken's arm. At least it's the one male Rainer wouldn't murder for touching me, either.

"Where the hell is your feckin court anyway?" Ken asks, squinting. His head whips left and right as he scans the trees.

"Over there." I point toward the largest tree, sitting a few paces ahead in a small clearing. Its trunk is easily the widest, with the most filled-out canopy. Its ragged roots reach like gnarled fingers, twisting into a labyrinth network below the ground.

Ken trips over a root and stumbles. I squeal as he jerks me with him.

"Oops!" He quickly rights us, then releases me. He adjusts the basket in his free hand, peeking inside to inspect the contents. "Phew."

"What's in there?" I ask, trying to peer into it.

He shuts the lid and grins, stroking his beard. "Where's the entrance? I don't see a thing."

I let out a heavy breath. "The door is right there."

"Where?" Ken spins, searching. "Is it invisible?"

"In the *tree*." I shake my finger at the door, and Ken follows my line of sight.

"Ah wouldya look at that!" He reaches out and pats the door with a strong palm. "It's a little princess-sized door, but I can duck."

Leave it to Ken to be unfazed by my status as a Lírshadow, spiritcaller, and descendant of Spiritus Court.

A *princess*, I suppose.

That notion seems farfetched and ill-fitting. It's only been a few days since I made the sacrifice—taking the lord and lady's lives—to accept my power and restore Spiritus Court's land to its former glory.

I reach up, letting my fingers hover over the Tradeling tattoo that marks the left side of my face. It feels like just yesterday I was in the lord's estate, being whipped by him for disobeying his orders. But at the same time, it feels like that was a different woman—from a different life entirely.

"I got it!" Ken snaps his fingers and begins gesturing wildly beside the tree. "A naked statue. Right here!"

"What?" I recoil from him, scrunching my nose. "Not happening. I do *not* need a naked statue of myself."

"We can do one of *Rainer*," Ken says, waggling his brows. "He would hate it. The others? They'd love it."

"I think I've had enough naked statues for a lifetime." The amusement gives way to sorrow as the memory of Eoin's statue flashes through my mind.

A lingering sense of guilt remains within me, reminding me that I want to *help* others—not cause harm. It's for this very reason that I need to do this.

Pushing the thought aside, I hesitantly reach for the tree's doorknob. It twists smoothly, and the door opens easily, revealing a hollow trunk with steps that descend downward into darkness.

"I'm going now," I tell Ken. "*Alone.*"

He peers at the tree, then studies me. "Are you sure?"

I hesitate, and then I nod.

"I don't love this," Ken mutters, glancing toward the treeline again. "He doesn't either."

My heart pangs at the thought of Rainer feeling rejected, hiding away in the woods so he doesn't disrespect my boundaries. The thought almost makes me smile. Fae and their damn loopholes.

"Tynan's just over that hill." Ken jerks his head to the west. "Lives in that stinky little shack. Get him if you need anything. *He* can travel to Umbra to get us, but *you* stay out of the woods, you hear?"

His face turns solemn, and I offer a small smile in response.

"I'll be okay," I say.

And I genuinely believe it. As much as a menace my shadow-self is, I can feel the protection radiating from it—deep within my bones. *It* might hurt me, but it won't let anyone else.

"Wait." He hesitates, glancing at his basket before thrusting it at me. "This is for you."

Furrowing my brow, I accept the basket. I pry back the wicker lid. Tucked away inside are various meats, cheeses, breads, and fruits. My eyes water at the thoughtful gesture, and I inhale a sharp breath to keep them at bay.

"Wow, this is…" My voice grows heavy with emotion. Instead of thanking him, I give him a genuine smile.

"It's from Rainer," Ken says softly. "He wanted to make sure you had something to eat."

"I didn't even think about that."

"You don't gotta when you have him on your side." He winks.

Overcome by the tender moment, I clear my throat and shut the lid. "Tell him I said he's not such a bastard, after all."

Ken snorts, letting a hearty laugh out. Gripping the basket tightly in both hands, I glance down the spiral staircase, ready to uncover the rest of the secrets that await me.

"I guess this is goodbye for now, Ken," I say, stepping inside the tree. I hesitate, then turn back. "Oh, and also tell Rainer he's not very subtle. If he's going to stalk me, he should at least get good at it."

Ken barks another laugh. "Little demon princess, if you knew he was there, it's because he *wanted* you to know.

"Well, tell him to stop altogether then."

"Can't." Ken shrugs animatedly. "Like I said before—that arse is quite thoroughly obsessed with you."

As I turn and head down the dark stairwell, a smile buds on my lips. I'm glad they showed up. It reinforced my desire to learn my magic, and it reminded me that even if I'm by myself, I won't truly be alone. My friends will wait for me.

"You're perfect for each other!" Ken calls after me. Though I can no longer see him, his voice echoes through the stairwell. "You are both stubborn, broody, irritating little feckers—always learning the hard way."

Perhaps he's right. Maybe I am making a mistake, but I find solace in knowing that my friends will remain unharmed. That *Rainer* will be safe. While I can bear the guilt of pushing them all away, the thought of hurting them is too much to handle.

FIVE

GRASP OF REALITY

ALESSIA

For whatever reason, my shadow-self is delightfully quiet as I reenter my court. Instead of being frustrated at its sporadic and unpredictable involvement, I decide to take advantage of this time and explore.

Already, my arms are aching from the basket Ken gave me. It's easily packed with a week's worth of food. Perhaps I'll locate the kitchen and start there.

A half dozen hallways branch off from the foyer. The largest one runs straight back, while the others appear to twist and turn as they lead away from the entrance, reminiscent of roots.

First, I follow the main hallway.

Many rooms boast open thresholds, inviting a seamless flow between spaces. I peek into each room, marveling at the grandeur of the great hall, throne room, and ballroom. They're fairly similar in terms of layout and aesthetic, except for a few distinguishing elements differentiating them.

The throne room steals my breath. Up on a dais against the far wall, a tremendous black throne commands attention. Like many of the details down here, it's constructed of twisted roots and fragile roses. It's a dark, beautiful masterpiece that adds an air of mystery.

Who created such a stunning work of art?

Who sat there last?

The questions mount as I back away, readjusting my grip on the basket. Perhaps I should set the food down and come back to it later.

At the thought, a tremor runs through me, settling in my palms. The basket slips just as a dark wisp explodes from my hands, wrapping around the basket's handle.

"No!" I yell on instinct at the sight of my shadow. "Don't touch that!"

No sassy remark comes like I expect. Huffing, I try to tug the basket back out of its grasp, but the tendril only tightens.

"Get back inside of me," I command, yanking harder.

A dark chuckle lights me up from the inside, and the shadow tears the basket from my hands entirely, raising it overhead where I can't reach it.

"Fine." Reluctantly, I throw my hands up. "If you're thinking of messing with my food, we're going to have problems."

As if we already don't.

See? You don't need anyone else, it finally says. *You have all you need*.

"I didn't ask for your help."

I grit my teeth, storming down a side hallway. The shadow follows behind like an obedient dog, carrying the basket. I'm too irritated with its blatant disregard for my wishes to be grateful.

While it may prove useful in the present, it reinforces that my fears are warranted.

The stone flooring amplifies my angry footsteps as I walk toward a set of closed doors further down. I shove them open, and a wave of relief washes over me, dissipating much of my irritation.

The kitchen.

My chest ignites with a comforting warmth, like a gentle flame. With care, the shadow sets the basket down on the stone counter. A swirl of dust rises into the air. I cough, and the dark tendril silently absorbs back into my skin.

"Now stay there," I mutter.

Instead of letting my annoyance win out, I roam the kitchen, taking it all in.

When was the last time someone cooked down here?

Running my finger over the rough wooden shelf, I caress the grooves and imperfections. The shelves seem to be constructed entirely from tree bark, giving it a rustic and gothic charm. The shelves, tables, and cupboards match, all birthed from nature.

Various kitchen gadgets are strewn about the shelves and hanging from hooks. The space has everything I'd need: vintage hand-cranked mixers, cast iron pans, wooden rollers, glass jars, and more—so long as it's all still usable and not ruined by time. I squint as I approach the hanging pans, inspecting them closely. Nothing looks rusted, which is a good sign. Just dusty.

At the back of the kitchen, towering stone ovens command attention. Their sheer size makes me gape. A smaller, more modest hearth sits between them, waiting to be used.

I squeal, clapping my hands with joy.

Even with all of my hopeful daydreaming back at Edvin's estate, I never imagined I'd be in a place like this one day. After serving others in their kitchen for so long, I finally have one of my own.

And it's incredible.

A hysterical laugh bubbles out of me. The irony of the entire situation isn't lost on me. It was killing the lord and lady that brought me here. Fate certainly has a sense of humor.

Does Char know I'm here? She must—she's the one who guided me here. There's a Char-shaped hole in my heart, and deep down, I hope she'll come visit one day.

Cleaning up the kitchen took longer than expected. By the time I finish and eat, I'm exhausted by the sheer depth of emotions I've experienced in a short time.

Tomorrow, I'll take inventory of the space and decide what needs to be cleaned first. Tonight, I'll choose a room and rest.

After getting lost several times, I go down a hallway I haven't been in yet. It's more intimate and less grand, with various portraits lining the walls between closed doors.

Their eyes seem to follow me as I move, and I shudder.

What were they like?

Were they all my family?

I open the first door, noticing sheet-covered furniture and another door opposite me. This must be the residential wing. Instead of exploring the room's contents, I sweep through the hallway, checking each room.

Outside the final door at the end of the hall, I pause. I glance up at the nearest portrait. My breath catches in my throat as I take in the face staring back. She looks just like me—like my mother even—with a wilder mane of ashy curls and a fierce look in her grey eyes. The artist somehow caught her feminine strength, portraying it in each meticulous brush stroke. There's a distinguishing beauty mark on the side of her chin—a small black dot.

The plaque beneath reads *Enid Liadain Lírshadow.*

"Enid," I say softly, gently touching the painting's cheek. "Who were you?"

The rest of the portraits lining the hallway boast various faces and names, but none caught my attention like *hers*. The portrait emanates a palpable sense of connection.

Before opening the door, I know instinctually these are the chambers I'll claim. Once I open the door, that feeling intensifies. I stride through the sitting room, not bothering with the sheets concealing the furniture. Instead, I head straight through to the bedroom.

Soft candlelight flickers from a lamp on the nightstand. Three other doors shoot off from the room, and I investigate each, finding a bathroom and dressing room in the first two.

But when I open the third, I gasp.

An enormous desk sits in the middle of the room, surrounded by floor-to-ceiling bookshelves.

An old, leather-worn journal rests beside an oil lamp on the desk. My pulse doubles as I rush over to it. The scent of musty old paper fills my nose, but it draws me in rather than repels me.

I open the first page and take in the name written there: *Property of Enid Lírshadow.*

Suddenly, I'm reinvigorated with a second wind. Instead of climbing into bed like I had planned, I grab the oil lamp and plant myself on the floor, sifting through Enid's journal.

Sleep can wait. *This* is way more important.

This is one of the reasons I'm here, after all. What better way to learn about my magic and find answers than to read my ancestor's journal?

Glancing around the room, I wonder how many more are stowed away within these shelves.

And though I stumble at first, struggling to read the handwriting, I slowly find a groove.

"Thank you, Char." I laugh to myself. "For teaching me to read."

I scan the pages until my vision grows hazy with exhaustion. The words on the pages blur together, forming an indecipherable mess. Unable to resist the fatigue any longer, my head lolls to the side.

As sleep takes hold of me, I drift further away from the grasp of reality.

Six
Master My Shadow-Self
Alessia

After a few days of isolation, I head to the topsoil for fresh air. My arms ache from all the washing and dusting I've done, and I've barely made a dent. Granted, I've abandoned the cleaning early each day to read Enid's journal. So far, I haven't found anything particularly useful. Her entries mainly cover mundane tasks in her daily life, yet it's fascinating to enter her mind. It makes me feel a little less alone.

I exit the tree, and my skin softens under the delightfully warm air. Sunlight filters in through the leaves overhead, scattering in bursts across the forest. The peppy bird chirps greet me, provoking a serenity not found below ground.

Following Ken's directions from the other day, I head west toward Tynan's shack. I don't know that I'll interact with him yet, but it could be helpful to know where his home is in relation to my court's entrance.

"You better behave," I warn my shadow-self.

Silence responds. I shake my head, huffing a breath. It's been quiet again, but I know it's only a matter of time before it riles up next.

Trekking up the small hill, I weave in and out of lichen and moss-covered rocks. Sturdy trees blanket the rolling hills around me. At the top of the tallest hill, I can make out a slanted roof in the distance—down in the valley.

The log shack, nestled amidst the ferns, was likely once a beautifully constructed cabin. Now, it stands dilapidated and weather-worn, leaning slightly to the side. However, unlike the first time I saw it, when the land was still a dying swamp, it has a more quaint, whimsical feel.

Tynan's home is a reasonable distance away from the entrance of my court—close enough in case I need him but far enough to avoid any accidental encounters.

To the left of his home, I spy a clump of ink-colored roses clustered together at the base of a spindly tree, marking where I killed Edvin and Nilda.

It's a haunting reminder of the moment that forever changed me.

Squinting, I observe another structure beyond Tynan's, nestled in a thicket of trees further out. Unlike Tynan's shack, this building appears made of stone. It's practically engulfed by the greenery, with a lush coat of moss and ivy camouflaging it. I hadn't noticed it before.

Curiosity tugs me forward. Scaling down the hill and bypassing Tynan's home, I navigate through the sprawling branches and abundant foliage until I reach the semi-hidden structure. Stretching long, the building is a stout, one-story rectangle with a solid presence and no windows.

And it isn't just sitting between the trees—it's a part of them. Ancient, twisting trunks shoot through the building, their branches intertwining overhead.

Creeping forward, I reach for the rough, weathered wood and press the door inward. The air is thick with musk and waste, and I immediately gag, pulling the neckline of my tunic up to cover my nose and mouth. It does little to weaken the offensive stench.

It's eerily quiet inside, and slivers of light peer in through where the trees sprout up and out of holes in the stone roof. Tree branches entangle overhead, creating a skeletal web. Unlike the branches beyond the roof, these ones lack leaves. The ground is dirt, with ragged roots running in all directions.

My nerves alight, and my body tingles with awareness. I leave the door behind me open, allowing extra light to illuminate the space as I stride deeper.

A stuttered breath fills the air, coming from one of the trees.

Swallowing down my apprehension, I freeze, carefully studying the trees. Something wiggles slightly, and a rattling noise fills the space. Slowly, I lift my gaze toward the ceiling.

My heart drops into my bowels as I take in a naked man entangled with the branches. His pale skin is dirty and bruised, and his limbs are almost indistinguishable from the tree's branches.

I gasp, jerking backward until my spine hits cool stone.

"What is this?" I mutter.

He wiggles, his movements dulled as if he's drugged. I scan his body, making out his prominent ribs. His body is riddled with pinprick holes, both old and new.

Scanning the ceiling, I notice at least half a dozen fae strung up, chained to the branches.

My eyes widen, and terror courses through me. Trembling, I whirl around.

"Oof—" I smack into a rigid body. Hands grip my arms, pushing me away.

"As much as I'd love your affections, my little brother won't appreciate you groping me," Tynan says with a sly smile.

"You!" I take another step back, then glance upward at the writhing bodies. Without another word, I shove past Tynan and bolt out the door.

"For the love of fae," he yells after me. He catches up to me quickly, keeping up with a jog beside me. "I take it my delightful little brother hasn't told you about the prisoners?"

My heart continues to race even as I slow my pace.

Rainer hadn't gone into detail about any prisoners, but he had commented about Tynan's food source in passing. I should've put it together—I should've asked what he meant.

Coming to a complete stop at the bottom of the hill, I bend at the waist and plant my hands on my knees to catch my breath. Tynan crosses his arms, looking wholly unimpressed with me. His dark blue eyes hold a hint of turmoil, and the scars on his hands and eyebrow remind me he has an entire past that I'm unfamiliar with.

In response to my fear, my shadow stirs deep within me. I focus on staying calm, not wanting it to erupt.

"Those are the…" I contemplate my words.

"Guilty of heinous crimes," Tynan supplies. "I keep them alive only to feed."

"What did they do?" I whisper.

Tynan sets his jaw, and fury blazes in his eyes. "You sure you want to know?"

I nod, desperate to ensure they deserve such a fate.

"Well, the newest bastard was found with two faeling in his home—so used and abused that the littlest one couldn't even walk without—"

"Stop!" Tears prick at my eyes as I turn away. "I don't want to hear anymore."

"You asked," he says flatly.

"I changed my mind." I swallow the painful lump in my throat. "The others? Similar crimes?"

"All the same—abusing younglings. Unforgivable, even by fae standards."

I don't know what to make of this. I don't want these types of horrible beings on my soil near my court. It's how Tynan staves off his bloodlust—I get that—but it doesn't make the situation any better.

Except... those fae deserve a fate much worse than becoming blood bags for Tynan.

They don't deserve to live, the voice inside me whispers.

No, they don't, I agree.

The thought might've once shocked me, but not anymore.

Allow me to cleanse the court. I can purge their souls and deliver the sentence they deserve.

Restless, my shadow twists and wiggles within me like a serpent preparing to strike. An indescribable need floods my veins, engulfing me in a dark, intense heat.

"No," I whisper. I can't let myself be influenced by my dark counterpart. But when an influx of unfamiliar faces of small, innocent faelings overwhelms my mind's eye, my stomach clenches painfully. It knocks the breath from me with a powerful punch.

They were just children—faelings.

"Stop," I croak. Pressing my palms into my eyes. "You can't possibly know who they were."

Does it matter what they looked like? It could be any one of these children. It could've been you—it was you.

I shake my head, desperate to make the thoughts stop. I'm vaguely aware of Tynan speaking to me, but I can't hear him over the shadow's voice filling my mind.

Not all of them made it out alive. And the ones who did? They lost their youth and innocence. They are forever broken—

"Don't say that!" I turn around and dart back to the small prison.

This time, the wrath of my bloodthirsty shadow fuels me. Bursting into the prison, I release a roar. I don't know if it's directed at my shadow-self or at the prisoners—the *abusers*—but the anger causes the inside of my skin to itch.

My chest heaves.

"They are *not* broken," I snap.

My body trembles as the frenzy within me pitches, reaching its peak. I combust with a shriek. Dark, cloudy ink bursts from my skin. It unfurls from my body, splitting into half a dozen wispy tentacles as it lurches for the various bodies entangled with the branches overhead.

Snapping and cracking fills the air as the evildoers are ripped free. One by one, their bodies hit the ground like sacks of potatoes, thumping into the dirt.

They're too silent. Why aren't they crying out?

I want to hear them beg for mercy. I want to hear them suffer.

Tynan appears beside me and I swivel to face him. "Your glamour—remove it." I remember Rainer and him discussing it previously. He glamours them to keep them quiet and complacent.

"Now!" I scream when he doesn't comply quickly enough.

One of my shadow tendrils lashes out, wrapping around his throat and squeezing.

"Okay," he gasps. "Let me go."

Placated, the tendril releases him. He stumbles back, coughing.

"You feckin psycho." He rubs his neck, eyeing me warily. "Just like my brother."

He widens his stance, a glossy look overtaking his face. His navy eyes flicker light, paling to an almost-white blue similar to his brother's eyes, before darkening again. His body shudders as he sucks in a sharp inhale, drawing the breath into his lungs for an extended period.

The air around me grows heavy, taut almost, and then, like a rubber band, the spell in the air seems to *snap*.

Screams of agony fill the air, and my shoulders relax as I drown in them.

My shadow continues its onslaught, snapping bones and torturing the bodies. Their cries are like a savage symphony, and I drown in it, allowing my darkness to feast on their torment.

It's only a fraction of the pain they caused those little faelings.

They *still* deserve worse.

"What the feck am I going to eat now?" Tynan asks, staring at me with a hint of distress on his scarred face. "Can you maybe… not kill them?"

I bare my teeth at him. "They deserve it."

"They deserve a lot worse," he agrees, putting his hands up to appease me, "but I'm still a full-blooded vampyr. Unlike Rainer, I *need* blood to live."

Icy awareness washes over me. The sound of Rainer's name grounds me, and the anger dissipates enough for me to understand the implications logically. If I kill these prisoners, Tynan will need to feed on others—innocents—to survive.

Shite.

"Stop," I reluctantly call out.

Closing my eyes, I focus on pulling the tendrils back into me. But they won't budge. The shadow tendrils stay hooked into the various bodies, and it's like trying to reel in a fishing line caught on a boulder.

This time, rage fills me for a new reason—for the shadow-self trying to influence me and disobey me.

I can't lose myself to the darkness.

I promised myself.

Channeling that rage toward my shadow-self, I mentally focus on prying the shadow's metaphorical hooks from the bodies. Then, I picture them returning to my skin, settling against my bones.

At first, there's resistance, but then it starts to work. The shadows waver, melding into one dark figure before fading into my flesh. My arms go limp, and my legs threaten to buckle as fatigue settles alongside my shadow-self.

You should've let me finish them—their souls would fuel us, the shadow hisses within me.

Gritting my teeth, I desperately attempt to drown out the relentless voice in my head and the piercing screams of agony reverberating through the air. As my ears ring, the cacophony of overlapping noises merges into a single, piercing frequency.

I cover my ears, wishing I hadn't asked Tynan to remove the glamour in the first place.

"You can... fix it," I say to Tynan. "Glamour them again. Get them to stop screaming." *Please.*

My human nature wants to apologize for causing such mayhem, but instead, confused and embarrassed by the ordeal, I flee the prison, leaving Tynan to clean up the mess.

Violence is incredibly out of character for me, and though I don't want to place blame on my shadow-self, I would've never done such a thing without its influence.

This is why we're better together.

No.

They deserved it. Let us feast on the souls of the wicked. It's a benefit for us both—

"Leave me alone!" I yell, drowning out the voice.

My body quivers as I struggle to navigate the stairs. I feel like I was run over by a carriage.

All because of my shadow-self's expenditure?

I'm not sure how it works yet, but I'm terrified of what I might become by my shadow's guidance.

At first, I felt empowered to have darkness on my side, bending to my whims. But now I see the truth—I am not in control. No. Like iron bars, my bones confine the voracious darkness within me, but what will happen when it decides it no longer has patience for a cage?

Will it violently claw its way out, destroying me in the process?

I am trapped in my skin alongside it, fearful of the beast I harbor. If I struggle to maintain control, everyone around me is at risk. It's already made unsavory comments about Rainer—and, previously, Eoin. It's tried to convince me I'm stronger without everyone else.

What happens if it decides it doesn't like someone in my life? What happens if I continue to disagree with it?

I had planned to go to Dovenak with Rainer to steal the iron so that Seraphina can break the curse on the woods. I want to help Fern break her addiction. And most important to me, I want to free the Tradelings. But how can I do any of that successfully or safely when I'm fighting with myself?

I'm dangerous.

I have no choice—I need to protect myself and those around me by learning to master my shadow-self.

Seven

Ban My Bloodline

Alessia

Two Months Later

The candle next to my bed flickers as I flip through one of Enid's journals. It turns out that she had many from throughout the years stashed away in her private office.

Though they haven't revealed anything useful about my shadow-self, I'm engrossed. I'm still not sure who Enid was to me, but it doesn't matter—I have her blood. We're connected somehow, and her writing makes me feel close to family I'll never know.

I should be sleeping or cleaning my court to prepare for an official reopening, whatever that looks like, but instead, my eyes are wide as I scan the pages.

Finally, I've arrived at entries chronicling more about our bloodline. The curly script draws me in as I read about *spiritcaller* power.

—all Lírshadows are spiritcallers. Our magic quells the spirits, allowing them to merge with the Soultrees. The trees recycle the deceased's magic back into the land and then deliver the soul to its final resting place—the Otherworld. Soultrees roots reach the Otherworld, the Realm of Resting—

My eyes widen as I devour information about my family's magic.

—without a spiritcaller to tame the spirits, they might refuse to merge with Soultrees and cross over. The spirits and their magic

would be stuck in a state of purgatory, eventually killing the trees and the surrounding land—

—spiritcallers also serve as keepers of death ledgers, marking the names of those who pass and keeping records in the muniment room. It is believed to be a request for good luck in their next life—

Little by little, things start to make sense. Explanations for my magic and the dying court make the last couple of months of scouring books and journals worth it, but it's still not exactly what I'm seeking.

Everything I've read about spiritcaller magic is passive—not violent like my shadow-self. Now, I've begun to accept that it's like Rainer being a vampyr and a fearcaller. I'm a spiritcaller *and* I have a shadow-self. Primary and secondary magic, perhaps?

Flicking through the journals, I search for something about a shadow-self. Finally, my eyes lock on the phrase.

—Lírshadows are all but spiritcallers; for some, the magic is secondary to something… different. Something darker. It is said that in rare cases, Lírshadows might harbor the power of a darker energy deep within. Strengthening the magic is said to be done through sacrifice…

My heart drops as the passage ends. I sift through the following pages, but when I don't see any other mentions, I slam the journal shut with a disappointed huff.

The price of my magic *is* murder. It's why the voice grew stronger and louder after I sacrificed the lord and lady.

The realization sits in my stomach like thick rot.

All this time down here, and all I've found is this painful confirmation that I am destined to be a monster.

Plopping backward, I nestle into the thick quilt. The flickering candle casts soft shadows across the high ceilings. I watch them dance, and my mind whirls—processing the journal, my bond with Rainer, the Trade in Dovenak, and everything in between.

I don't want this to be my life. It's been weeks since I've seen anyone, and I miss my friends. Rainer has left a weekly food basket at my tree, but he's been exceptional at honoring my request for space.

I'd be lying if I said I didn't hope to run into him one day.

I'm no closer to opening my court's doors. I promised Sheila—the Tradeling Rainer rescued—she would have a place in my court. But I refuse to bring her here unless I know she'll be safe… from me.

Fern, Das Celyn, Ken, Viv, Ez… all their faces flit through my mind, each one a chain wrapped around my heart. My heart is so heavy that if I were in the sea, it would sink me. The weight of loneliness is suffocating, dragging me down into an abyss.

Leaning over to the side table, I blow out the candle with a forceful exhale and draw the quilt up to my chin. It's the purest darkness I've ever experienced—eerily silent as if the court exists in a void.

How can I help secure the iron, break the curse on the woods, free the Tradelings, and run a whole court if I can't even manage myself?

For the first time, I start to wonder if Yvanthia was right to ban my bloodline.

EIGHT

COST MY SOUL

ALESSIA

*D*on't make me beg. The voice fills my mind. *It's been too long. You can't keep ignoring me.*

"Shush," I mutter, my annoyance building. "It's your fault we're stuck down here."

You'll feel so much better once we—

"La, la, la, la," I sing obnoxiously, drowning out the noise.

I'll be quieter if—

My boots slam heavily against the stone as I stomp, purposely trying to be loud. The louder I am, the less I have to listen to that infuriating little voice.

The shadow roils, protesting against my skin. It wants out. It craves more sacrifices to fuel its strength—it's growing desperate.

After reading confirmation in Enid's words last night, I'm rattled: strengthening the magic is said to be done through sacrifice.

Focusing on my own thoughts instead of the nagging little voice inside me, I make my way purposefully through the main hallway of Spiritus Court. I've yet to clean the many rooms and labyrinth-like halls that lead away from the main space and my bedchambers. I should branch out and clean the rest of the court, but it's a daunting task. It overwhelms me. Plus, I don't need all this space. I've mainly stuck to my chambers, the kitchen, the study, and the libraries.

Today, I'm headed to the muniment room. I've been there before, but I hadn't made sense of the documents I found on my first visit. But now, after reading the journal, I know they're death records of Avylon's fae.

My shadow simmers down, and the silence grows deafening, broken only by the echoes of my footsteps as I stride deeper through the corridor.

The high ceilings resemble a cathedral, giving the court a hauntingly majestic quality. Tree branch sconces with half-melted candles light my way, casting long shadows that dance along the stone. A chill caresses my neck, and I wrap my arms around myself, sinking into my sweater.

In times like these, when I haven't been above ground for a few days, the loneliness seeps in extra. The quiet cuts deep, a reminder of what I've lost rather than the peace and *freedom* I've gained.

I miss Rainer. I want nothing more than to see that secret dimple he reserves for me, to feel his slender fingers caressing my skin.

My flesh pebbles at the mere thought.

At first, I genuinely believed I needed to discover my true identity before fully committing to him. But instead of learning myself, I'm fighting not to lose myself.

My shadow-self lashed out at Ezamae and choked Tynan without my will. It refuses to return to me when I call. It openly seeks destruction—death. And that's not something I will allow to be around my friends.

Unfortunately, I can't even risk seeing Rainer in my dreams, considering his bite once lingered beyond the dreamscape. If my shadow-self lashes out and hurts him, I worry it'll be *real* in waking life.

If it hurt him, it's not something I can live with. My experience with lucid dream has come in handy, allowing me to craft my own dreamscape without running into him. If only controlling my shadow was as easy as manipulating my dreams.

The corridors twist and turn, eventually narrowing and sloping deeper into the earth. Finally, the path comes to an end. A sturdy door stands before me, built into the stone. It's different from the ornate wooden doors lining the other halls—this one lacks a handle and detailing.

It tempts me, begging me to open it. I step forward, and my skin heats. A zing of magic surges through me as a dark tendril seeps out from my pores, lashing forward and shoving the door open with a loud creak. I jolt, surprise smacking me. For a moment, I freeze. But before I can react, the shadow recoils back into my flesh, curling inside me like a dog near a cozy fireplace.

I swallow the lump in my throat, unease trickling down my spine.

"Stop it," I command weakly, exhausted from fighting with it. "Stay inside of me."

It doesn't reply, but it doesn't need to. I know it won't heed my request. It never does.

It's a reminder of why I'm better off down here.

Alone.

With a heavy exhale, I forge forward.

The muniment room boasts an array of private records and artifacts. The air is thicker here as if weighed with the memory of thousands of souls.

I wonder if Eoin found peace, tethering to a Soultree and sinking into the Otherworld.

It won't bring him back. I can hear your thoughts—it's not your fault he's dead. Let it go.

"Leave me alone," I mumble.

He deserved it—

"Hush!" I focus on my breaths, blocking out the nagging voice inside me—an uncanny imitation of my voice.

My vision locks onto the small drawers built into the wall, floor to ceiling, before me. The sconces flicker, a soft, ethereal light allowing me to see the room's contents. Though much of my new home is still in disarray, having been abandoned for gods know how long, it's easy to see the intricate beauty in every nook of the court.

A stone table sits in the center of the room, with ink pots and quills scattered atop it. Glass cabinets stand opposite the drawers, showcasing various items like vases, jewelry, weapons, and what I presume are other family heirlooms.

I approach the wall of drawers. Each is a delicately carved rectangle about the length of my forearm and only a fist high. I've explored many of them. Inside are parchments that document deaths from the past.

Locating a specific drawer on the right-hand side, I gently pull it open and reveal a collection of yellowed parchment. A plume of dust wafts up, and I cough, waving it away.

The ink on the paper is fading, but it's still legible.

These are the death ledgers mentioned in Enid's journal—records of the fae who have lost their lives and passed through Spiritus Court.

My eyes roam the pages, taking in the list of names, dates, courts, and magic. I flip through the records until I find one with open space. I carry the parchment to the table, use my arm to wipe away the filth, and set it down, smoothing the curling edges with a deep inhale.

Maybe I should've done this sooner. Perhaps it would have helped me move on and make peace with my mistakes.

I'm not a murderer.

But I've directly taken two lives, and even more have indirectly lost their lives because of me.

My hand trembles as I reach for the ink pot. I blow off the dust and twist the lid open. Surprisingly, the ink hasn't dried out even after all this time. I peer into the pot, studying the murky, viscous liquid. The way it appears is exactly how I picture my insides—a thick, inky sludge coating my organs, threatening to spill out of my skin and stain everything around me.

Eoin previously stated that Rainer's magic stained Avylon. He was mistaken.

It's *my* magic that stains Avylon.

Tears prick at my eyes. I blink them away, plucking a quill from its resting jar and gripping it tightly.

I'm angry at myself—at my shadow-self.

I'm afraid of making more mistakes—of hurting others. Even if it's not malicious or purposeful, it doesn't matter. Intentions don't matter to the dead.

Carefully, I dip the quill into the ink pot. Then, steadying my hand, I scribe a new record: *Eoin Glenn Orion, Prince of Terra Court, Empath.*

Guilt and sorrow blossom in my chest, spreading like muck through my veins. I blow gently, helping the ink dry.

Once it's no longer wet, I numbly trudge over to the drawers, tuck the paper safely inside, and shut the drawer.

"Rest in solace, Eoin," I whisper, squeezing my eyes shut. "I hope your spirit finds peace in the Otherworld."

The reminder that Eoin died without magic weighs on me. Did the tree still absorb his spirit even without magic? Was he able to cross into the Otherworld and find peace?

Suddenly feeling too heavy—too stifled in my skin—I rush to the door and blow back into the hallway. Let this be the first and last name I will be personally responsible for adding to the ledgers.

I'm *not* a murderer.

Yet, I am conscious that my shadow-self will continue to claim lives if I don't control it.

And Eoin will be just the start if I let it. The lord and the lady will pale in comparison of what my shadow is capable of.

The two souls satisfied my shadow's thirst, but it's clear it won't last forever. Already, the damn thing is begging for more.

Tilting my head up, I let out a roar of frustration. My hands ball into fists, and I slam them down my thighs. Pain blossoms there, giving me an external sensation to focus on. Tears free fall, cascading down my cheeks in troves.

"I can't do this forever," I whisper.

A light breeze ruffles my hair. The faint, familiar scent of fresh air and pine hits my nose. My head jerks up, and I quickly wipe my tears away, blinking my vision clear. But there's nothing and nobody.

Glancing down at myself, I take in my wrinkled clothing.

Gods, I'm a mess.

I'm losing my mind. When was the last time I bathed and changed my clothes? My mission has utterly consumed me despite getting nowhere. Perhaps I should eat and wash up before continuing my explorations.

There *must* be an answer somewhere down here in one of these journals. There has to be.

Otherwise, the price of using my magic is to be a killer. But that's not the only cost. If I continue down this path, tempted by the ease and power of the magic inside me, I fear it will cost my soul.

Nine

Times Up, Alessia

Rainer

*W*arm sunlight caresses my skin as I stand among my gardens, holding a blue rose by the stem. My other hand is stuffed into my pocket as I wait like I have every night since Alessia left me over two months ago.

She never indicated we couldn't be friends, except the door to her court remains locked. Tynan told me about her incident at the Shyga stockade with his blood sources. Between that and her request to be alone, I'm antsy, desperate to see her.

But I also want to respect her desire for space.

It feels like we've been here before, and I hate it.

Overhead, the sun flickers, and the world around me stutters into darkness before brightening. My shoulders slump as I realize she's not coming—again.

This means I only have seconds before the nightmare slithers in, consuming the cozy dreamscape around me and replacing it with a medley of my fears and pain.

I twirl the stem between my fingers, watching a cobalt petal fall, fluttering gently to the ground.

The blue coloring doesn't exist in my gardens—only in my dreams. It's a rarer breed than the sunset rose; not even Terra Court has them. The blue rose symbolizes an undying, unwavering, unre-

quited love that is both impossible to achieve yet impossible not to yearn for.

They represent unattainability.

Alessia is my blue rose.

She is unattainable perfection and beauty. I could devote my entire life to cultivating her, only to be left empty-handed and longing at the end, much like gardeners of the blue rose.

But it doesn't mean I won't stop hoping for a miracle. Any day now, she will surprise me, making a rare appearance in the garden of my heart.

Thunder cracks through the sky, and the world darkens into an immediate night. The flower wilts, its petals wrinkling and turning grey. Then, they turn to ash and blow away.

The gardens around me shrivel, the vibrancy wasting away into the colors of broken dreams and lost hope.

My body goes rigid as the air around me thickens. I release the stem, letting the flower tumble to the ground. I run a hand over my tense jaw, preparing to bolt as soon as the screams start.

And these days, they always do.

"Sleep like shite again?" Kenisius asks, gently kicking my boot with his own.

I grimace, squatting down beside my roses. "I'm used to it."

"You slept better with the little demon."

Don't I know it.

Grunting, I don't deign to reply. Obviously, I did everything better with Alessia, but that would be incredibly selfish reasoning to refuse her request for space. I know she'll return to me when she's ready.

Digging a finger into the soil, I inspect the moisture level. It's still moist from yesterday's rains. I almost wish the dirt was dry so I could busy myself with watering the flowers.

But to my dismay, my gardens have been perfectly tended to. Without me.

Like Alessia, the roses don't need me, either.

Anger surges through me, and I clench my jaw. In this mood, I'm better off training with the shifters than caring for my flowers.

I'm not feeling particularly nurturing at the moment.

Standing, I wipe the dirt off my hands and roll up my sleeves. There's new ink on my right forearm amidst the various lines. It stands out with dark, fresh detailing: a black rose with bleeding thorns. The small splashes of red are the only color permanently marked on my skin.

A devotion to Alessia that's representative of our relationship—the one I will never give up on.

She might not need me, but I need *her*.

"Aren't you supposed to be scouting the Gleam?" I ask Kenisius flatly, unamused by him following me like a lost puppy today.

I stride toward my castle, shoving the door open and entering a side hallway.

"There's been no movement in weeks—since they moved in. Viv's watching the estate." He clucks his tongue at me, slamming the door shut behind us. "We can proceed whenever you're ready."

An influx of soldiers have taken up residence in the house Alessia grew up in. Every so often, one crosses the Gleam. It's clear the men have no training. It's laughable how pathetic their efforts are. I'd say they're being sent to their deaths.

But why?

There's something I'm missing. But for now, we play the game, destroying them and sending their carcasses back, all while spying and gathering information.

"No," I correct. "We wait for *Alessia* to proceed."

This is *her* vindication—her salvation—after all.

"We can't wait forever, Rai," he says softly.

"Speak for yourself." I pick up my pace, shuffling toward the stairwell.

"And risk losing our advantage? We need to move before the humans do."

I sigh, knowing he's right. Pausing, I rub my forehead aggressively. Before I can turn to him and reply, a pixie blasts into my line of sight.

"Fear Prince," she squeaks. "The Aer Prince has arrived just beyond the gate."

I nod, and she flits away. My heart fills with hope, beating a little faster and matching my pace as I quickly navigate toward the foyer. If Ezamae is here, he has free time from Yvanthia's demands. I can send him to check on Alessia without overstepping her request for space from me.

Loopholes.

"We'll resume this later," I tell Kenisius.

"I'm hungry," he calls behind me. "Gonna go eat."

We part ways, heading in different directions.

When I reach the foyer, Ezamae stands in the center, underneath the bone chandelier. His shoulders are stiff, his navy clothing pretentious and stifling. Blue gems glitter in his ears, the deep color contrasting with his washed-out complexion and hair.

"Prince of secrets and seduction," I greet sarcastically. My tone is flatter than his lips, which tug up as he spots me.

"Prince of fear and feckery," he retorts. "Still clinging to your wards, I see."

I scowl. "Still an irritating arse, I see."

He laughs, and it's a short, surprised sound. Stepping toward me, he opens his arms.

"What is this?" I grunt.

"A hug." Then, he embraces me in a half-hug. I return it, stiff and awkward, then quickly pull away.

Affection isn't my strong suit, but the Aer Prince has grown on me. By some definitions of the word, dare I say, I even consider him a friend. He's been keeping a close eye on Alessia—able to enter and leave her court undetected.

Eventually, I'm getting her damn placed warded.

But for now, I take advantage of the opportunity.

I lead Ezamae through the hallway between the double staircase and take a sharp left into a parlor. Gesturing toward the many seating options, I choose a crimson settee for myself and perch on the edge.

"How is the wretched hag?" I ask, referring to Queen Yvanthia.

Ezamae sits on an armchair facing me. He crosses his ankle over his knee and gives me a long look. "Healthy as ever."

"Unfortunate."

She only visited us once, shortly after I returned from her dungeon. It was merely to deliver a warning, showcase her power with its returning strength, remind us what she's capable of—and remind everyone that both Ezamae and I are nonconsensually bonded to her lest anyone try to harm her.

If she is harmed, so are we. It's a clever trick to keep control over those who care for us.

"She's a cunt," I mutter, crossing my arms.

Ezamae's smile returns, bigger this time. His silver eyes twinkle with amusement, but he lifts a finger to his lips in a shushing gesture. I shrug, knowing the queen has him glamoured into telling her any ill-speak about her.

"You can tell her I said she's a cunt." I scowl. "Although that shouldn't come as much of a surprise."

He laughs and then clears his throat. "Alessia still hasn't come out from that crypt."

"You visited?" I sit up a little straighter.

"Admittedly, I'm rather surprised you haven't stormed in and brought her back yet, you possessive brute."

"I'm tempted," I say.

Very tempted.

I try not to worry about her. She's very capable, especially with the added protection of her newfound magic—as scared as she is of it, it won't harm *her*, and that's what I care about.

At least, in theory, it shouldn't. The magic is tied to her essence; if Alessia is wounded, the shadow-spirit would be as well.

Beyond that, Tynan still resides in his shack on the grounds. He has his faults, but he's been sober—reliable.

The pixies frequent Spiritus Court, too. They might not be able to enter Alessia's court—her door has remained shut—but they at least can keep an eye on my brother, who can keep an eye on the grounds.

It's a very roundabout way to monitor her, but it eases my mind enough to prevent me from barging into her court.

Though, admittedly, I drop off food for her weekly, hoping to catch a glimpse of her in the flesh. It's hard not to feel abandoned when she no longer appears in my dreams.

I run a hand through my hair, replaying everything that built up to me and Alessia being apart. "This shite is all my fault," I mutter. "All because I was insecure."

If I hadn't made the mistake of snapping on Eoin, of giving into my bloodlust, we wouldn't be in any of this mess.

"Yvanthia would've gotten what she wanted either way," Eza-mae says quietly, reading my turmoil. "Don't blame yourself."

My eyes narrow.

He chuckles, adjusting his velvet sleeves. "Don't project your annoyance onto me for being *right*, either."

"I am regretting sharing my feelings with you."

He laughs again.

"How is she?" I ask, unable to tiptoe around it anymore.

His features pinched, a strained expression crossing his face. "She's... alive."

"How *is* she?" I repeat with a growl, jolting forward and leaning into his space.

He raises his hands. "I didn't talk to her. She was doodling on some old documents in a musty room." He pauses, and my hackles raise. "I couldn't stay long."

"You don't need to *talk* to her to know how she's doing. Don't make me ask you a third time."

He shakes his head. "Fine. I really do not want to worry you, but… there's an unusual air of melancholy about her."

"Unusual, how?" I ask with deathly calmness. I hold my breath, waiting for his response.

He glances down, fingering the buttons on his jacket. "She's not as lively or active as she has been previously. With each visit, the light is fading from her eyes. I don't think she's bathed. And she hasn't bothered with anymore tidying up."

A heavy exhale rips from my lungs, and I jump to my feet. I shouldn't have left her alone. I only wanted to heed her request for space.

"The place was…" Ezamae pauses, giving me an apologetic look. "Well, as unkempt as you'd imagine a crypt to be. She's living in squalor."

"It's not a crypt," I mutter, narrowing my eyes.

"It feels like one."

Alessia must be exhausted after a lifetime of cleaning up after others.

I round the settee and face away from Ezamae. Dark waves fall into my eyes, and I push the strands out of my face.

How much time is enough time?

And at what point is she pushing me away not to find herself but to run from someone who cares for her?

Her pattern is recognizable. I've been there. After what happened with my mother…

It took me a long time to trust myself again, and I continue to work on that. If it weren't for Alessia, I might never have allowed myself to *love*.

She could use help, but I don't want to overstep and intrude. The last time I went after her—at Eoin's—look at what a mess I made. Even so, I'd never consider my previous actions a mistake because it brought us to the present. And despite what she thinks, Alessia is stronger than ever now.

But she doesn't see it.

She should be flourishing, and she's not.

She's wilting.

At some point, intervention is required to keep her from rotting. If she hates me for overstepping, so be it. But I can't witness her refusing to live after everything she's done to earn a life.

Perhaps if I send the others instead of showing up myself, she won't see it as me disobeying her request for space and time. Seeing familiar faces like Kenisius, Das Celyn, Ezamae, and Fern might do her well.

This way, she's not alone, but I'm still respecting her need to be away from me. And if she sends word that she's ready, I'll be there in an instant.

We can help her whip her court into shape. I can update her on the plans to invade Dovenak and secure the iron because, as Kenisius said, we can't wait forever.

Or maybe these are all excuses to justify my burning desperation to see her. To touch her.

Feck it.

Alessia wanted her freedom, and instead, she's become a prisoner of her own making.

"I can't wait a moment longer," I say, spinning around to Eza-mae. Leaning forward, I grip the back of the settee. "I need your help."

His shoulders relax, and he smirks. "I thought you'd never ask."

I'm a patient male, but even patient males hit their limit.

And I've hit mine.

Times up, Alessia.

TEN

COULD IT HARM ME?

ALESSIA

The following day, my fingers itch to flit through more journals, but I fight the urge and instead force myself to eat and change my clothes first thing. I've been neglecting self-care, wholly consumed by my obsession with taming my shadow-self.

Fresh air will do me good, and hopefully, it will stave off the loneliness just a little longer. So, I reluctantly trek up the winding stairs. As I emerge from the tree, the door cracks shut behind me, and I lean against it. Turning my face to the sun, I suck in a deep breath and let the worries melt away.

At least for the moment.

Then, the worries intensify. I'm exposed and vulnerable. I could run into Tynan or, worse, Rainer. It's almost time for him to drop off a new food basket. And as much as my heart yearns to see him, I'm terrified of what might happen.

It'll be too easy to give in to him and fall into our pattern of seeking comfort in one another. But what happens if I allow him in, only to lose control of my shadow-self? What if I hurt him?

You don't need him, the shadow says.

It's listening, always listening.

My stomach pitches, and I fear I'll be sick. I place my hand on the bark, allowing it to ground me. It's rough beneath my palm, reminding me that hundreds of thousands of years of magic shimmer in the land around me. Even without knowing my family or the full story of my ancestors, I can *feel* them here with me.

Closing my eyes, I take a few soothing breaths. When the nausea passes, I reach for the door, not wanting to stay up here any longer.

"Please," a faint voice calls. "Please."

My hand pauses on the doorknob.

It's probably another trick of my shadow-self—a last-ditch desperation to get me to bow to its whims.

"Help, please!" The masculine voice is hoarse with overuse and desperation. "Anyone? Help!"

My spine tingles.

Stepping away from the tree, I cock my head to identify where the sound is coming from. Trees stretch out sporadically around me before thickening into rolling hills and forests in all directions.

"Help!"

I whirl around, drawn toward the sound.

I should kill him.

The thought is so sudden that it nearly topples me over. *That* one was undoubtedly my shadow. And it's all the confirmation I need that the damned thing is as alarming as I fear it is.

"What?" I hiss, furrowing my brow. "No!"

Kill him—fuel our magic.

"Hush!" I grit my teeth and tamp down the vicious—and terrifying—urge in favor of jogging towards the tree line.

"Please…" the call grows weaker.

Something about the desperation draws me forward despite the threat inside me. I pause, trying to discern where the voice is coming from. It seems to come from the east—Spiritus Court property rather than the Cursed Wood. And the voice sounds frail, not threatening.

It should be okay to investigate.

Perhaps I'm stronger now—it's been two months. I can test the waters and see if I can keep my shadow-self inside. If I can do this, then maybe I can see Rainer and my friends again.

I shudder, shooting into the thicket just as another feeble plea rings through the afternoon air.

"Please—don't leave me here." The voice cracks.

And it hits me.

Fae do not beg.

The voice belongs to a *human*.

The wailing grows louder. I slink toward the noise.

They are dying anyway, my shadow-self says. *Assist them. Put them out of their misery. Let us grow from it.*

"Shut up," I mutter, my hands trembling.

The urge to give into my shadow's whims builds. It's a rotten little seed, festering and growing inside of me.

I can't let it take root.

Squeezing my eyes shut, I focus on anything other than the dark desires. I envision Rainer's gentle touch, his adorable dimple, and the way he says my name like it's the sweetest prayer.

I let my mind wander, replaying the moments we've had together. My cheeks heat as I replay our intimate moments, watering down the violence inside of me.

"Please!" Another hoarse cry rings out.

My eyes flip open, and I perk back up, feeling more in control.

Confident I've conquered my darkness for now, I emerge from the brush, quickly locating the source of anguish.

A man lies wounded on the ground, with a deep gash on his forehead. Blood trickles out, staining his pale skin. His ankles are twisted in horrifying directions, and I avert my eyes.

I won't be able to help him back by myself. Glancing over my shoulder, I try to calculate how far Tynan's shack is from here. It's beyond my court's entrance, on the far side of Spiritus land.

This man needs help *now*. He's losing a lot of blood—blood that might tempt the vampyr.

Ripping off my tunic, I make quick work of wrapping it around his head to staunch the bleeding.

He cries and moans, pleading for help.

"Quiet," I say softly. "Save your energy. I got you."

I think back to how my shadow-self became sentient, heeding my command to untie Seraphina. It could do the same, helping me with this man.

But... that's dangerous. It wants to kill him.

I can't risk it.

I study the man. His face is pale, and his lips are dry and purple. His eyes flit shut, and his breaths grow shallow.

Shite.

He's going to die.

He needs me.

I can do this.

"Help him," I murmur to my shadow-self. "If we don't help him, he's going to die."

I can help him die quicker.

"We're not killing him!" I yell through gritted teeth. "Stop suggesting that."

The man squeaks, weakly raising a trembling hand above his face. "Please—no."

Pity squeezes my chest, and I take him in, trying to gauge his injuries.

"What happened?" I ask, trying to distract him. My calm tone is at odds with my frantic heartbeat.

"I—" He squeezes his eyes shut, sucking in a sharp breath. "I can't explain it. But my ankle…" He gestures toward his lower half, covered by leather trousers and dirtied boots. There's a hunting knife attached to his waist."It's broken, I think."

I don't bother telling him they're *both* broken.

With a groan, he tries to sit up but falls limply onto the decaying leaves.

"You can't get up at all?" I wince, already knowing he won't be able to.

"My head." He whimpers, clutching it. "It hurts."

Biting my lip, I glance around, searching for something that might be able to help.

Something slithers beneath my skin, like a dozen snakes trying to escape.

"*Help*," I demand, speaking to the darkness inside me. "Heed my command."

The man on the ground groans out a reply, but I ignore him in favor of tuning into my mind.

I can handle this.

With a sharp nod, I fill my lungs and focus on the man. I imagine the darkness exiting my skin as I exhale, envisioning the shadows lifting the man and carrying him.

After a few silent, discouraging moments, an adrenaline rush takes me over, and the pressure builds. It shatters like glass, and two dark tendrils explode from my palms, surging toward the man. He screams, his voice cracking with terror.

"It's okay," I murmur.

The dark lengths wrap around his neck. I hold his gaze, a tickle of satisfaction coursing through me as his eyes begin to bug out and—

"Stop!" I scream, reaching for the shadow tendrils.

My hand slices through nothing but air, doing nothing to stop the assault.

Clenching my teeth, I focus on the darkness inside me—the one controlling the voice and the shadows.

Stop this! I scream internally. *Help him! Don't kill him!*

To my shock, the shadows recoil, releasing the man's throat. Instead, they wrap around his limbs, hoisting his body a few feet off the ground.

Sweat beads on my forehead. With shaky hands, I smooth my hair back out of my face. I can't trust my shadow-self... my control over it is feeble and unpredictable. But this is worth the risk. If he stays here, he will die.

The shadow wavers as it cradles the man. The man screams and thrashes, tearing into the dark tendrils, but they don't react.

My arms and legs tremble as I lead the way back to the entrance to my court, with my shadow close behind. I'm too on edge to find relief in the fact that it's obeying my command for now.

I worry about what might happen if I don't have the energy to command the shadow back inside me. The damn thing has a mind of its own.

And as valuable as it pretends to be, it's dangerous. But if it wanted to, could it harm me?

ELEVEN

BOW TO THE DARKNESS

ALESSIA

W e enter the tree, slinking down the stairs. I lead the shadow to the infirmary. Sconces flare to life the moment I push open the door.

The scents of antiseptic and mildew linger in the air. Dried herbs hang in rows on the stone walls. Once fragrant and vibrant, the colors have long faded to shades of crusted brown and sickly grey.

Tarnished silver instruments and cracked ceramic bowls sit abandoned on various shelves. Cobwebs adorn the corners, exposing the years of neglect. Dripping water echoes through the room, coming from the sink to my left.

In the center of the dimly lit chamber, a single medical bed sits, its metal frame rusted and worn. Tattered linens drape it, but at least they're clean. My first few weeks down here, I washed all the bedding in the court.

I'm glad I did.

My shadow dumps the man on his side atop the cot, and he yelps in pain.

The relief in my muscles is immediate. I soften as the cloud of darkness invades me, curling back into my depths. My head spins, and I grip a nearby counter to keep from tipping over.

I need to feed.

Pushing the unsettling comment aside, I quickly search through the cupboards of old herbs and ancient-looking medicine jars. I find alcohol, a clean rag, and yellow gauze. It'll have to do. I snatch it, and dust swirls up, causing me to sneeze.

I rush back to the man's side and pry my tunic from his head. It did a fine enough job of staunching the blood loss, but the wound needs to be cleaned.

"This might sting," I warn him, dumping some liquid onto the cloth.

He hisses when I press it to his gash, his eyes rolling back into his head. Tears streak down his face, and his voice is hoarse as he moans. A boulder sits in my chest as I work, hoping I'm doing enough to save him.

Once the blood is cleaned up, it's easier to see the cut. It's not nearly as deep as I assumed. He needs stitches, but there's not much I can do about that. Instead, I use the gauze to bandage him, hoping it'll be enough for now.

Between the blood and sweat caking his skin, I fear he's close to dehydration. He needs water—likely food, too.

"Can you help?" I ask, intending the words to be for my shadow-self. "Or will you kill him?"

"I'll do anything…" The man whimpers. "Please don't kill me."

"I'm not going to hurt you."

His wide eyes are filled with tears and terror. My heart skips a beat when I realize it's *me* he fears.

He thinks I'm fae.

I *am* fae.

My pulse pounds in my temples, racing from the adrenaline. He thinks I'd kill him.

A dark tendril bursts forth from my skin, extending toward a cupboard. It retrieves a glass cup, fills it in the sink, and then places it in my hand.

What is he doing here? On your land, near your court?

I pause, contemplating the questions.

"Please," the man's throat bobs as he eyes the cup. He reaches for it, wincing. His eyes flutter, and muscles pop in his throat as he tries—and fails—to lift his head.

He wants to hurt you, yet you are helping him.

It's enough to keep me from handing him the water.

"What are you doing here—in Avylon?" I ask, keeping my face blank to not betray my sympathy for him. I might as well do what the fae would and find out information.

He whimpers.

Guilt roils inside of me as I realize how disgusting my actions are—withholding his care to glean information from him. It's manipulative, harmful, horrible… but I can't stop myself.

I hold the cup out of reach, trying not to hate myself. "Who sent you?"

His glazed eyes zero in on the cup. "I volunteered."

"You need to give me more than that," I say softly.

"Queen Wyetta paid my family handsomely." A sob bursts from him. "I have two young boys at home, and the offering was—"

"She's hiring people to cross the Gleam? Why?"

What reasoning could the human queen have for paying people to enter Avylon? She, of all people, knows how dangerous it is.

He curls in on himself. "I don't know."

"Give me more than that," I demand.

"My family—" He sobs. "They want nothing to do with me anyway. Figured they'd at least be set up for life this way. Figured I'm good as dead either way."

"You need to give me *something* if you want my help," I say, working to keep my voice stern.

For a second, I almost consider summoning up my shadow-self's cruel hardness to take control so I can shut off my sympathy, but no. I need to feel this. *This* is what will keep me human—my empathy, my guilt, my *heart*.

I need to feel the repercussions of my actions.

"I don't know what else to give you!" The man's voice cracks and tears streak down his grimy face. "Rumor says she's announcing something big at her Revival Fête in a few days."

I squint. "Her what?"

"Revival Fête. Celebrating the return of her health."

There was speculation the queen was sick. I can't say I'm glad to hear she's doing better. "What was wrong with her?"

He blows out a breath and hangs his head, eyes fluttering shut. "I… no one knows…" he mumbles. "She's old. Thought she wasn't gonna make it."

Not wanting him to lose consciousness, I tap his cheek. When he glances at me, I lean forward with the glass of water, helping him hold it up to his lips and drink.

"Thank you," he says between sips.

The door bursts open, and someone blows past me, nearly knocking me off my feet. They pounce on the man, and searing-hot fear brands me from the inside.

"Tynan!" I scream, recognizing his sheared hair and stocky frame. "Don't!"

Something clatters to the ground. It slides across the stone, stopping near my feet.

The hunting knife.

A sickening squelch fills the air, followed by slurping.

My breath stutters, and panic floods me.

Sensing my terror, my shadow rises up around me like a half-wall, forming a barrier between me and the vampyr, who is currently bent over the man, drinking him dry.

"Move!" I try to rip through the inky wall to reach the man, but the dense fog is impenetrable this time. My heart races as I try to breathe slowly and settle my panic. "Return to me! Now!"

The shadow doesn't budge.

I bang my fists against the darkness, irritated that it's holding me back from saving the man. This was a mistake—I knew it.

"Don't let Tynan kill him!" I yell. "Stop him!"

Yes. You're right. He is mine to kill.

The wall of inky darkness explodes away from me, wrapping itself around the unpredictable vampyr. It yanks him from the human, sending him flying across the room. My eyes widen as my arms shake with the ghost of exertion.

I don't know whether to be terrified or impressed by the ease in which he was tossed.

Too late, I turn my attention to the human to see one of my murky tendrils holding him down. He thrashes in the bed as the dark fog covers his mouth and nose.

"No!" I surge forward, grasping at the tendril.

It refuses to heed my command to stop.

I frantically claw at it, my heart pounding in my chest with each desperate swipe. The solid surface feels rough and unforgiving as my nails scrape against it. In response, fiery pain shoots through my own arms. With each scratch I make at the shadow, my skin grows more raw and delicate.

Red lines blossom on my arms, crisscrossing and marking my skin as if I'm clawing at myself. Blood beads up, dripping from the deeper cuts.

I stop my attack, stunned by the sight.

When the man clawed at my shadow, nothing happened. How come when I do the same thing, I'm wounded? It's the second—no, *third*—time I've fought against my shadow only to injure myself.

I'm distracted by the thought until the man's body falls limp.

Lazy and contented, the sentient fog soaks back into my skin. The weakness in my limbs subsides, and a newfound energy bursts through me, the aftermath of my shadow being *fed* a soul.

I sink to the floor beside the bed, trembling like a leaf in a storm. If this is how we recharge our power, I want nothing to do with this magic.

"Tynan?" I call, taking slow, deep breaths to keep my pulse steady. "Are you okay?"

He stands, rubbing his arse as his head snaps in my direction. As if it can feel the intensity of his dark gaze, the black smoke spews from my pores again, wafting like steam as it rises around me.

Tynan cracks a smile, blood dripping from his fangs.

"Holy shite." His gaze flicks to the limp body on the bed. "That was…" He shakes his head, his smile growing. "Wanted the kill for yourself, eh?"

"I—no!" My legs quiver with shock and fear. "You had no right to barge in here like that. This is *your* fault."

His brow furrows. "The pixies summoned me. Said you were in danger."

"They didn't need to get you. I had things under control," I say through gritted teeth.

"Our definitions of under control differ." He huffs. "They did the right thing—I *am* the commander of Spiritus Court's army," he says, lifting the brow with the scar through it. "Or was that a crock of shite meant to placate me? Give me a false sense of responsibility—like my brother's done for years?"

"What? I—no, of course not," I mutter, my face growing hot at Tynan's confrontation.

A bitter laugh leaves him. "There's no army. I fell for it again."

Striding forward, he reaches for the dead man's hand, prying a second weapon free. He holds up a dagger with two fingers, cocking a brow, and then he points to the ground where the knife lies abandoned.

Irritation and embarrassment flit through me. How did I miss that? Worse, why did I not remove the hunting knife when I first saw it in the woods?

I was too distracted with my own inner turmoil to use my wits—that's why. Instinctually, I want to blame my shadow, but *I'm* the one who let it get to me in the first place.

"Dunno who's more of an idiot, this guy or—well, I don't know if I can say *you* without my brother pummeling my arse," he says with a bemused expression.

"I'm not an idiot," I mutter.

"You didn't think to check for weapons before bringing a play-thing home?"

I frown, clenching my teeth in irritation. "I made a mistake."

"Mistakes get you killed."

It's not worth explaining myself. He's right. I've gotten too confident in my few measly months away from the lord's estate. But it doesn't replace the fact that I've spent most of my life imprisoned.

There's a lot I missed out on learning. Clearly, common sense is one of those things.

All the more reason to keep myself cooped up away from everyone else—especially Rainer. If we had had sex... we'd be bonded right now. If I got myself killed, I'd get *him* killed.

It reinforces the walls I've erected. This is exactly why I'm staying away from him.

"Why did the pixies get you instead of just telling me?" I ask quietly, trying to distract myself from the harsher realities. "They didn't need to involve you."

Tynan shrugs coolly, and his arrogance reminds me so much of Rainer for a moment that I almost feel at ease.

"You slammed the door in their tiny little faces," he says. "Cruel."

His gaze locks on my bleeding arms. I stiffen, expecting him to charge me for a moment. He must notice the change in my demeanor because his fangs retreat with a slick *pop*. My eyes widen at the exhibit of control, and my shoulders soften just a hair.

"Oh, don't look at me like I'm terrifying. I'm not gonna eat you." He gives me a smug look. "Sobriety has been great for my self-control."

"Surprisingly, you're one of the least scary things in this realm," I say, sighing. Especially now that I know he wasn't losing control—he was trying to protect me.

Based on my observations of Tynan, he's not as crazy as he portrays himself to be. Yeah, he killed Felix, but to be fair, he was drunk, hungry, and tasked with murdering the assassins who venture into his territory. It's hard to criticize him for acting in accordance with his instincts and responsibilities.

Honestly, he's much more like Rainer than either of them will admit.

My eyes flick to the deceased man on the bed, and I cringe. He's slumped forward with his head hanging. A smudge on the base of his neck steals my attention.

I stride to the bed. Carefully, I lean closer to the marking.

A number identifying him as a prisoner is tattooed on the base of his neck. I've heard Edvin's pals talking about it before.

This man is not from the Trade—there's no lightning bolt marking. But his words about Queen Wyetta paying him to do her bidding make sense now. If he was imprisoned and desperate, the promise of support for his estranged family likely sounded worth the risk. He *knew* he would die coming here, but still, he did it.

"Have all the humans you've encountered had similar markings here?" I ask Tynan, pointing out the tattoo.

His smile drops, and he grips the man's hair, yanking him forward better to see the skin at the base of his neck.

"I'm normally focused on the front of the neck, not the back." He snickers. "I've seen it before, though. Yeah." He releases the man's hair.

I can't suppress my surprise, and my mouth drops open. If Wyetta is sending prisoners—not actual assassins… she *is* sacrificing them. She must know they won't return, which means it's all a setup.

If there's anything the fae have taught me, it's that not everything is what it seems.

What trick is she pulling?

"Why is she sending prisoners?" I ask, appalled.

Tynan shrugs, rubbing his jaw.

"The Revival Fête," I say under my breath. "We need to figure out what the announcement is."

"No," Tynan scratches his stomach. "I'm starving. *You* can figure that out. I'm going to get breakfast."

I scowl. "It's afternoon. And you just ate." I point to the man.

Tynan chuckles. "That was barely an appetizer. Your greedy little shadow stopped me."

I cringe at the reminder, not wanting to acknowledge that I've added more blood to my hands.

It makes me even more hesitant to see Rainer, but I need to warn him about this. Something isn't right here. I worry Queen Wyetta is purposely provoking the fae... but why? To get *us* to strike first so she can have a reason to declare war?

A boulder sinks into the pit of my stomach.

Tynan clears his throat. "So, you gonna finish him?"

I recoil. "Wha—no!"

"Can I?" He licks his lips, eyeing the body.

"Absolutely not." I glare at him.

"That's what I figured. Hence why I'm going to get breakfast." He waves and exits, leaving me alone with the corpse.

Great.

The darkness within me stirs, but I growl.

"Stay," I command, balling my hands into fists as if I can keep the shadow from seeping out. "You've caused enough trouble."

But despite its persistence, I refuse to lose myself. I will not bow to the darkness.

TWELVE
I FEAR THE IMPLICATIONS
ALESSIA

With shaking hands, I drag the man down the hall by his feet. Crimson streaks the stone behind him, his bandage having come undone. Between the wound on his head and the one on his neck, it's only a matter of time before he's drained entirely.

Maybe I should've let Tynan drink the rest of his blood.

My stomach roils, and I clamp my lips to keep from vomiting.

What a mess.

So much for learning how to control my power. It's shaping up to be a disappointment and a colossal waste of time.

I can carry him, my shadow says.

It fills me with a sense of dread. It would be too easy to give in and let it help, but after it proved uncontrollable, I'm not taking any risks.

"No!" I say through gritted teeth. The anger burns hot inside me. "Not again. I'm never letting you out again."

We'll see about that.

After a few more steps, I drop the man's feet. They slam onto the stone with a sickening thud, and I cringe.

My hands tremble viciously, and I blink away the forming tears. I can't do this.

The air enters my lungs in short, quick bursts, and my head grows dizzy. Planting my hands on a nearby pillar, I close my eyes.

The rough bark bites into my palms, and the sensation grounds me, distracting me from the budding anxiety.

A soft breeze rustles my hair, startling me. I jerk away from the pillar, searching for the source.

Ezamae materializes in front of me with Das Celyn at his side. He adjusts the thin, silky blue headband holding his pale curls back, and a smile lights up his glass-like face. Das Celyn stares blankly, then lifts a single brow.

The sight of them is enough to undo me.

Tears burst free, and I surge toward them. "Thank the gods!"

"I take it you missed us, darling?" He chuckles.

Sniffling, I throw myself at Das Celyn.

"Oh no." Das Celyn's dry tone fills my ears. Their bag thumps to the ground, and they grunt as they catch my hug. I squeeze them tightly, and they gently pat my back.

"Now get off me," they whisper, shoving me away.

A smile tugs at my lips as I use the back of my hand to wipe the tears from my eyes. Das Celyn's familiar brown trousers and eggshell apron feel like a piece of home. They smell like dough and brown sugar, making my eyes water all over again.

"Had I known we'd be received so well, I would've—" Ezamae's eyes widen, and his head tilts to the side as he stares past me to the body on the floor. "Well, that's messy."

Das Celyn groans even louder this time, then swats my arm. "Of course you're making my life harder. Record speed this time, too."

The flicker of joy I felt snuffs out as the shame and trepidation return. "It was an accident," I whisper.

"Well, I know we agreed to help clean, but I must admit, *this* is not quite what I expected." Ez squats beside the body and pokes it with a finger, grimacing. "Rather fresh…"

Curiosity dances in his silver eyes.

Das Celyn makes a noise of disdain and brushes past me. They stride over to the trail of blood and scowl.

"Horrible," they say with a sigh. Immediately, they roll up their sleeves, tuck their dark, chin-length hair behind their ears, and begin repositioning the body. "We can't bring anyone else here until this mess is sorted."

"Agreed," Ezamae says. "This is rather unwelcoming."

"Help me then, pretty boy." Das Celyn glares at Ezamae.

To my surprise, he smiles and takes his blue-and-white jacket off, handing it gingerly to me. "It's suede and cervelt."

"Okay." I take it from him with two fingers, eyeing it with a furrowed brow. It's heavy but doesn't look any fancier than what he usually wears. My mind replays his previous words. "What do you mean?"

"It's rather expensive and hard to clean."

I gape at him. "No, what do you mean you agreed to help?"

"Rainer sent us." His lips press into a thin line. "I hadn't anticipated cleaning a murder scene, though."

My face flames and bile churns in my stomach as I glance at the body. "It wasn't like that," I whisper. "It was an accident."

"Not the worst accident I've seen." He shrugs, rolling up the sleeves of his silver undershirt. He faces Das Celyn, who rolls their eyes.

Das Celyn gestures toward the body with annoyance. "Grab the legs, pretty."

"You think I'm pretty?" he teases, touching his chest.

"Pretty useless. Now help me out."

Ez chuckles as he squats down to assist.

I'm numb, stuck in place, watching the two bicker lightheartedly. "Rainer sent you?"

Ez nods. "Rather good timing, if you ask me."

A thank you blossoms on my lips, but I swallow it down. "Yeah, good timing," I repeat in a whisper. "But you shouldn't stay long," I add weakly. "It isn't safe."

"The plan is for me to windwalk the workers from Umbra Court over here," Ez says, totally ignoring my warning.

"What, why?" Nervousness blossoms in my gut.

"Because they can't travel safely through the woods."

"No—I mean *why* are you bringing them here?" I squint down at him as he inspects the body up close. "Look what I did…"

He grips the ankles and then hoists the body up. Das Celyn grunts as they grip the upper body. Their strength surprises me.

"Like you said, it was an accident." His eyes twinkle as he winks at me.

"Ez," I say seriously. "You know firsthand how dangerous I am."

"All the more reason not to leave you alone."

"I could hurt you—*again*."

"So dramatic," Das Celyn says dryly. "You act as if you're special—the only one around here gifted with strength and power."

"Hush, you." Ez waves a hand dismissively at Das Celyn, then turns back to me. "The foundation of an authentic friendship is built during difficult times."

"You're a buttock fungus I can't get rid of," Das Celyn mutters, shaking their head.

"Attempting to scare us away is futile." Ez gives me a pointed look. "We're here to help establish the court, at the very least."

"I don't need help," I say exasperatedly. "Really, you're not safe here."

Das Celyn snorts. "Okay, in that case." They drop their end of the body, and the man's head cracks into the stone.

I recoil, my hands flying up to my eyes. "*Gods!*"

"Gods is right, you frustrating creature! We can take care of our damn selves." Das Celyn practically growls at me. "I'm no pansy-arsed muffin."

"Fine! I take it back." I whirl away from the body. My shadow stays quiet, and I wonder if it's appeased now that it's feasted on a fresh soul. "You're right—I need help."

Ez makes a disapproving clucking sound with his tongue while Das Celyn chuckles.

They shuffle around behind me.

"What, no thanks this time?" Das Celyn says sarcastically.

"Nope." I stare at the ceiling, focusing on one particularly gnarly root, wondering if they're real roots from the tree up top.

I'm grateful for their appearance. Admittedly, I'm disappointed that Rainer didn't come himself. I know I told him I needed space, but perhaps deep down, I'm still waiting for him to show up and rescue me.

From what, though?

Myself?

"Is Rainer coming?" I finally ask.

"Do you want him to come?" Ez asks coyly.

Hesitating, I contemplate the implications. I'm getting nowhere down here alone. Perhaps my friends are right—it's time to accept help.

"Yeah," I whisper. "I think I do."

"Finally—she's stopped being an imbecile," Das Celyn mutters. They grunt, presumably hoisting up the body.

"I will send word for him," Ez says. "I may have made him make a deal with me in exchange for my help."

"What?" I whirl around. They stand, holding the dead body between the two of them. The man's head is lolled to the side, his arms dangling lifelessly. Blood stains the floor where his head was. I recoil and turn away. "What did you do, Ez?"

He chuckles. "I was unsure if his presence would make things worse. You already appeared distraught enough without his—"

"Distraught?" My nose wrinkles in confusion. "You haven't seen me in months." Not since he dropped me off.

He clears his throat. "I was concerned he might upset you further. I agreed to assist him with his plan by bringing the workers from Umbra here under the condition that he visits only if you invite him."

His thoughtfulness catches me off guard. "I'm surprised he agreed."

"He's fairly selfless when it comes to you," Ez says.

"Can we move our arses?" Das Celyn interjects. "Glad we're all sappy and shite, but I can't hold this lump of flesh forever."

"Invite him," I tell Ez, my back still to them. "Your help—it means a lot. I suppose I owe you both now."

Das Celyn sighs. "You never learn."

Behind me, the pair get to work, throwing barbs at one another as if cleaning up a body is a typical afternoon occurrence.

Blowing a heavy breath, I hurry down the hall without looking back. I appreciate my friends' help, but I'd rather not spend another second with the body of the man whose life I took.

As I pass a row of closed doors, I carefully hang Ezamae's jacket on one of the doorknobs. He'll find it later.

A surge of anxiety courses through my belly.

After all this time, I'm going to see Rainer again.

I can't take being separated from him any longer. Perhaps it's not wise—still unsafe—but I'm going to hope for the best. Now that the shadow's hunger has been temporarily appeased, hopefully, it won't cause problems. It's seemingly quiet again.

There's got to be a better long-term solution, but for now, I hope this works.

I'm gradually adapting to the various sensations the shadow stirs within me. Unfortunately, feeding it souls is the only method to tame it so far.

The anxiety sits in my stomach, tangling into a big knot.

If that's truly the *only* way to quiet the shadow... I fear the implications.

Thirteen
Kill Them Again
Rainer

I *need* Alessia.

Unfortunately for me, she doesn't feel the same.

My heart calls to her, but *her* heart calls to independence. She's craved her freedom, and she's finally getting it. Though, ironically, she now imprisons herself.

Kenisius gallops toward Terra Court, successfully outrunning any hallucinations that threaten to plague me in my own forest.

Gritting my teeth, I grip the bear tighter as the world whizzes past us. My arms and legs wrap around his back, and my chest stays plastered to him. I wince as I'm jostled around. Each bounding stride crushes my manhood, and I tug Kenisius' fur harder in retaliation.

If I'm not mistaken, I can feel the damn bear rumbling a laugh beneath me. It's different than the jerking and jolting of his running. Instead, the vibration comes from within his furry body.

"You fecker," I grumble, spitting when I accidentally consume a mouthful of his hair.

Instead of fighting the experience, I clamp my mouth shut and continue thinking about Alessia.

I'd much rather be heading to Spiritus Court right now, but since she originally asked for space from *me*, Ezamae took it upon himself to protect her. The deal was that he'd help her so long as I stayed behind—only going if and when she invited me.

I'd love to punch the Aer Prince in the mouth, but how can I when he's looking out for my bond?

As frustrating as it is, he's right. She doesn't need me hovering over her and overstepping boundaries.

These past couple of months, we've been like stars shooting past each other in the night sky. Close, but never colliding.

After everything that transpired with Yvanthia—and Eoin—I want Alessia in my sights at all times. I will never trust the faerie queen's intentions, and though she might've slinked back into the hole she crawled out of, it's only because we're currently benefiting her. If something arises and she no longer needs us where we are?

Well, then, she's a threat.

It's another thing Ezamae is right about, even if he can't voice it openly—the faerie queen must go. We need to break our bonds with her so we can kill her.

But one problem at a time. First, I need Alessia to be okay. Then, we can visit Dovenak and steal the human's iron together. After that, we will figure out Yvanthia.

Hopefully, Ezamae and Das Celyn's visit will be successful. They're doing more than just cleaning her court. It's my hope that this visit from all of her friends will break the shell of fear surrounding her and that she will free herself and let me in again.

Once the pixies send word of whether or not I'm welcome, I'll head there immediately. For now, I'm distracting myself—trying to be a responsible faerie prince and tend to other business.

It's been nearly impossible to get anything done lately.

Soon, the trees break, giving way to sandstone cottages and farmland. We whir past, and the residential area grows more dense. Kenisius doesn't slow his pace as we enter Terra City. He expertly navigates the crowds of fae who scream in surprise, shooting past the shops and heading straight down the main cobblestone path.

Finally, he jolts to a stop. My front slams against his back, and I hiss through my teeth at the impact.

I waste no time jumping off him. My legs tremble for a moment, making peace with solid ground again. I take in the conglomerate of hills sitting before us. We've stopped at the base of endless stairs leading to Sennah's court.

The palace sits nestled about halfway up the hills, with gardens blooming around it. A waterfall cascades from a taller hill beyond the structure, pooling around the palace and trickling down alongside the stairs into twin rivers that border the city. One fuels the city, and the other runs into Laguna Fortuna further south.

Beside me, the giant bear's fuzzy body begins to tremble. Rather quickly, the black-nosed snout recedes, and the round head and ears shrink. His body shifts, bones cracking and tendons popping until he's locked into his upright, bipedal fae form.

Bless the gods, he's dressed in his bespelled leathers today, sparing me an eyeful of his pride and joy.

"Fun ride, eh?" He snickers, giving me an amused look as he shakes out his dark brown tresses and reties a thick bun.

I grumble, plucking a piece of bear fur from my mouth and flicking it away. "I'd rather windwalk with Ezamae than ride you again."

"Hey," Kenisius says, feigning offended. "I resent that."

"At least he doesn't smash my testicles."

A laugh reaches my ears. "At least *I* don't fondle them."

I balk. "He doesn't… forget it."

Turning from my pal, I head toward the palace. No matter what retort I come up with, Kenisius will always have another. Instead, I stay quiet and suppress my amusement so I don't encourage him.

We trudge up the excess of stairs, leaving the city behind as we ascend toward Sennah's palace. With its earth-toned trims and friezes, the white building looks almost like a blossoming flower, with the hill serving as its stem. And it smells horridly floral.

My roses have a distinctly sweet aroma, but it's nothing like this overwhelming catastrophe. I stifle a sneeze, picking up my pace.

"No wonder these folk have the best arses in all the land." Kenisius strains his neck to watch a couple of passing fae over his shoulder. He turns back to me, elbowing me as we ascend. "You saw his bum cheeks?"

I glare at him from the side of my eye. "No, Kenisius, I did not."

He exaggerates his steps upward, with his hands on his hips, taking them two at a time as he passes me. "It's a nice burn! If you focus on squeezing the glutes and—"

I tune him out all the way to the top, where a guard swiftly greets us.

"The princess has cleared the Umbra Prince for entry," the guard says, pointing at me. "She's expecting you."

"Just me?" I ask, frowning.

"I need to find Uriel anyway," Kenisius says, stroking his beard. He grins slyly at the guard. "Any chance you have a moment to show a fella around?"

The guard spins on his heel, striding away wordlessly. Kenisius shoots me a double thumbs up, then follows him, presumably to find Uriel—one of Sennah's commanders and one of the few remaining Angelli in Avylon.

After Eoin's death, Sennah extended an official offer for Umbra Court to borrow her army when we leave for Dovenak, so the Gleam won't be left unattended. Uriel and Kenisius are responsible for coordinating said protections.

"I'll find you after," he yells over his shoulder. "Give the peppy princess a hug for me!"

Rubbing my forehead, I follow after another guard who leads me to Sennah's quarters. I steady myself before knocking on her door. With a deep breath, I rap on the wood. A few long moments of silence stretch on, so I knock again, harder this time.

There's a thump from somewhere beyond the door, and then it whips open.

Sennah's honey hair shimmers in waves around her shoulders, perfectly done, but her amber eyes are red and blotchy. She sniffles, barely sparing me a glance before striding through her sitting room, then her bedroom, to her dressing room, where she proceeds to stuff garments into a travel bag.

I follow, contemplating how to start the conversation.

It's been months since Eoin's death, but that's barely a passing second when it comes to grief. When you lose someone you love, every moment without them feels like an eternity. They're gone, yet the ghost of their memory remains in all the places they frequented.

And even though I didn't like Eoin myself, he was Sennah's brother.

"I'm not going to ask if you're okay," I say, shoving my hands into my pockets and hovering awkwardly near the threshold to her dressing room.

Everything is so *bright*. Her flower-shaped area rug is bright pink, and all of her clothes are pastel, neon, or gold. It's blinding.

"I'm fine," she says flatly, keeping her back to me as she rips clothing down from their hangers.

"We both know you're not."

"I. Am. *Fine*," she repeats, each word punctuated by her aggressively thrusting items into her bag.

"Sennah…" I trail off, hating the tension between us but understanding it, too.

"Enough." She whirls toward me, her lips pressed into a thin line. Her chin tilts up in pride. "I don't want to talk about *feelings*."

I nod, my shoulders softening a bit. "That makes two of us."

Finally, the tension cracks, and she forces a smile. "Why are you *really* here, fear princeling?"

I blow out a long breath, cupping the back of my neck as I try to think of how to phrase my next few words.

How do I tell her Alessia and I plan to work with her brother's murderer?

"I don't like that look." She pauses her packing and crosses her arms. "I can handle whatever shite you're afraid to tell me right now."

I scoff. "I'm not afraid."

"Mhm." A single brow flicks up as she stares me down.

"Fine. We found a way to break the curse on Crescere Forest."

She exhales, untangling her arms and dropping them at her side. "I haven't heard you call it that in… it's been a while." A light blazes in her eyes. "This means you truly found a way?"

"I think so." I hold her gaze, not cowering as I relay the rest of the information. "The sorceress—Seraphina—possibly has a way to nullify the magic, but—"

"*That* wench?" Any curiosity in her expression is snuffed out as pure rage roars to life instead. Her eyes narrow, and her cheeks flash with red-hot heat. "She is dead to me, Rainer. Dead to the realm, soon!"

"I understand." I'm careful to keep a conciliatory tone with her, allowing enough emotion to seep into my words that she can pick up on my empathy, while keeping enough distance to let her know I mean business. "I share your stance here."

The sorceress had intended to kill Alessia. That's not something I will ever forgive. However, without the Cursed Wood standing between our courts, Alessia and I can visit each other freely. Safely. Once she lets me back in, of course.

So it's a risk I'm taking.

"It's strictly a business transaction," I begin, "I don't want you to—"

"This is hogwash." With a disbelieving head shake, she returns to her aggressive packing.

"I understand your anger," I say firmly. "However, we've tried everything, Sennah, you know it. This is an opportunity to rectify the mistake we made." I pause, running a hand through my hair as I suck in a breath. "Alessia has already made a deal with the sorceress to—"

"Of course she made a deal." A sarcastic laugh bursts from Sennah. "She can't help but insert herself and make a bigger mess—"

"Watch what you say next, Sennah," I growl. My vision dims as my eyes flicker, my unruly fury blazing through my veins. "That is my soul-bonded you're talking about."

Her body goes stiff and she slowly glances at me over her shoulder. "That makes a lot of feckin sense." She hums contemplatively. "Soul-bonded." A short laugh bursts from her. "Regardless of your agreements, when I return, I *am* coming for what the sorceress owes me."

I nod. Seraphina is responsible for Eoin's death, after all, and fae deaths are not taken lightly. Especially not the death of a prince. That's between her and Sennah, and the sorceress will likely pay the price with her own life.

Not my problem.

"We have an understanding?" I ask, wanting to ensure this doesn't change things between us or impede the army access.

Sennah narrows her eyes at me. "You better work quickly if you want her assistance. The dead aren't as helpful, I hear."

"How long do we have?"

"I'll be back in a couple of weeks."

"Where are you going?" I look between her and her multiple bags, skewed across the dressing room floor.

"Males," she mutters, tossing her hair over a shoulder. Her many golden bracelets clank and jingle with the motion. I hate the sound. It's sharp in my sensitive ears. "*Now* you ask?"

I shrug. "We were talking about more pressing matters before."

"It's almost summer solstice," she says. "I'm visiting Ignus Court for Litha."

The Litha celebration occurs atop Mount Mors—Avylon's only active volcano—in Ignus Court. The fire symbolizes purification and transformation. The court is a good distance away—straight across the Illustris Sea, north of my court. It's not often I visit or see Laisren, their prince. He encourages violence and bloodsport out of entertainment, and I never thought that would fare well for a vampyr.

"Give Laisren my regards," I say flatly.

A tiny glimmer of excitement shines in her eye, and the tension in the room breaks just a hair.

"I'm glad you're going," I tell her, meaning it. It'll be a good distraction for her.

"Viv is joining me," she says, her eyes hardening in challenge.

"Good."

"Really?" she asks, lifting a skeptical brow. "You're not going to fight me on it?"

"Why would I?"

"Wild guess, but maybe because of your issues with the humans? And a particular Spiritus Princess who is a stone's throw away from the Gleam."

"I can handle it." *She* can handle it—even without me.

"Viv decided to stay in your court, and now she's leaving during a time of need," she challenges.

I sigh, rubbing a hand over my face. "Yes, but I trust Uriel can handle it. And you could use a friend after—"

"Gross—this pity thing makes me itchy." She scrunches her nose, inclining her chin to somehow manage to look down on me despite being a similar height. "Forget I said anything. I need to finish getting ready."

"Okay, but about the reason I came—"

"My issue is not with you, Fearcaller, nor is it with your bond." Tossing her hair over her shoulder, she spins on her heels.

"So, we're okay?" I call after her.

"As long as you're okay with me taking Viv for a while." She flicks a hand over her shoulder without looking back, attempting to dismiss me.

I chuckle, glad to see her spark hasn't totally dimmed.

"And the sorceress—"

Sennah scoffs, jolting to a stop and turning to me. "She's dead. As soon as I return, and she's no longer of use—*poof.*" She mimics an explosion with her hand, sending a gust of hot wind at me.

It blows my hair out of my face, sending me back a step. Then, it dies as quickly as it started.

Sennah stomps out of the dressing room, and with each step, the world beneath me trembles, her anger manifesting as infant earthquakes.

I grimace, understanding her rage, but hoping she can keep it under control until we're done with the sorceress. As the floor beneath me trembles and the portraits on her bedroom wall rattle, I sigh. The last thing Avylon needs is a seismically induced eruption.

It's the perfect time for her to visit Laisren and Ignus Court. At least there, she can take out her feelings with all the violence her little heart desires.

"Kenisius said to give you a hug," I call after her as she heads to her bathing chamber. "I'll refrain."

The door slams in response.

I tap my thigh, exhaling in relief. It could've gone worse, I suppose.

At least Sennah is feeling her anger rather than trying to stuff down her feelings. That's a good sign, right? But magic, anger, and volcanoes don't usually mix well. Hopefully Laisren prepares himself.

Actually—hell, the bastard is the prince of fire and furor, he'll thrive on her rage.

I stride out into the hallway, my boots clicking on the marble as I go in search of Kenisius.

A whizzing reaches my ear moments later, and I whirl toward the source eagerly.

"Prince!" The teal-winged pixie appears before me, its wings an iridescent blur as it hovers.

Relief sings in my chest.

"Word from Spiritus Court?"

"She was attacked," it squeaks out.

The relief shatters, replaced with a hollow sense of doom. "Explain," I growl.

Without waiting for an answer, I break into a jog, heading for Kenisius. We need to go *now*.

"She found a man in the woods!" The pixie flits beside me, keeping up effortlessly. "He tried to attack her!"

The pixie moves into my line of sight, flying backward as it stares at me.

I swat it away. "Move."

"She's okay!" It zips to the side of my head. "We tried to help her. But really, she didn't need the help. She has a darkness inside her, and it came out and it—"

My ears ring. There's a small flicker of returning relief, knowing she's okay, that her new magic protected her, but it's not enough to slow my pace.

"I was going to come earlier, but I couldn't get out—I was stuck in the tree and—then the Aer Prince showed up—"

Annoyance flares to life as I turn a corner and spot the shifter speaking to a tall, bald Angelli covered in tattoos—Uriel. "Kenisius!"

His head snaps to mine, his body going rigid when he takes in my expression. He's on his feet in an instant. I don't have to say anything else, and we're out the door, flying down Terra Court's steps. He morphs before we hit the bottom, his tendons snapping and bones cracking as they reshape themselves.

I jump onto his back, gripping him tightly as he takes off toward Spiritus Court.

Whoever tried to lay a hand on her is *dead*.

And if they're already dead? Well, I'll find a way to bring them back to life just to kill them again.

FOURTEEN

I DON'T TRUST MYSELF

ALESSIA

Hours later, the hallways are bustling with busy hands. I didn't ask what Ez and Das Celyn did with the body. I don't want to know. It'll haunt me more than it already does. Afterward, true to his word, Ez windwalked between Spiritus and Umbra Courts, bringing over helping hands.

I trudge away from the main hallway, where many Umbra folk begin attacking the filth.

Even with my shadow's contented quiet, I'm on edge. It's only a matter of time before it becomes unsettled and lashes out again.

Already, I'm questioning my decision to agree to help.

What happens when it wakes up again?

Shuddering, I wrap my arms around myself and trek further away from the main space, wanting to put distance between me and the fae cleaning the massive rooms.

I told Ez that Rainer could come. Why isn't he here yet? Is there a chance he doesn't *want* to see me?

Down the hallway, light seeps out of an open door. A soft, repetitive tapping sound, like two stones smashing together, reaches my ears. With a furrowed brow, I stride closer and peer inside.

Weathered wooden shelves line the walls, adorned with jars of dried leaves, powders, and roots. The air is thick here, not yet cleaned out. A workspace stretches beneath the dried herbs on the far wall, and a wooden table in the center of the room with old tomes.

The apothecary, I'd guess.

Herbs and spices tingle my nose, reminding me of the very sorceress standing at the counter with her back to me.

Dark braids—decorated with small yellow flowers—reach her middle back. Her dress, interwoven with ivy, has an asymmetrical hem resting just above her knees.

"Seraphina," I say flatly. "What are you doing here?"

She turns, giving me a confident smile. "Making more healing salve for you."

I hesitate before striding over to her. If my shadow-self acts up, I'll just run. But then again... could I blame it if it got mad? Seraphina's previous actions warrant wrath.

Pausing, I suck in a deep, slow breath.

Nope—no. Those thoughts are dangerous. I won't entertain them.

Once I calm my mind, I approach her and eye the ingredients on the counter.

"It's made of moonberries, beeswax, yarrow, comfrey, tea tree oil, and calendula oil." She points to each ingredient as she names them. "Peppermint for scent."

On the counter beside her, a ceramic pot holds a colorful mixture of half-mashed berries. Various jars are filled with a thick, purplish-brown goop.

I wrinkle my nose. "I thought it was white?"

She laughs, tapping a sack on a shelf overhead. "Cloudroot powder. I add it at the end. It helps with absorption." Her smile falters, and she glances down at my arms. "I heard what happened."

I wrap my arms around me, wishing I had worn long sleeves.

"Here." She reaches into a cupboard below, pulling out a familiar jar of white salve. "This one is finished."

Eyeing it skeptically, I slowly accept it from her. It'd be wise to heal before Rainer comes. I give it a sniff. A wave of longing overcomes me as the soft peppermint smell takes me back to Char.

Feeling more at ease, I open the jar and liberally apply the cream to my cuts. They're superficial, nothing serious. The skin stitches together, closing up before my eyes. I use a rag to wipe away the dried blood.

Seraphina continues to work, paying me no mind.

My eyes dart around the workspace. The area where she's working is clean, but a heavy layer of dust sits on the table and much of the other shelves. Cobwebs cling to the corners, stringing overhead.

She follows my line of sight. "They'll make their way here to clean eventually. I didn't want to wait. I wanted to get to work... doing what I'm good at." She half-laughs, waving her arm over the assortment of ingredients on the surface beside her.

I don't reply. She nibbles her lip and leans a hip against the counter.

"I brought my own supplies just in case," she says, pointing to an oversized burlap sack at her feet. "But you're stocked to the gills."

Squinting, I scan the shelves, skimming the labels on glass jars and tin cans. There's a variety of herbs and dried flowers, poultices, tinctures, syrups, and salves. "Everything is so old."

"It's usable." She shrugs a shoulder as she mashes her berries. "They were enchanted to last, it would appear."

"If you say so," I murmur.

She sighs, sets down the pestle she's holding, and turns back to me. "I understand you don't trust me, but I won't harm you. We want the same things."

My attention snaps back to her, my throat thickening. For the first time, I pause to take her in. Her brown eyes glitter with specks of gold, and her rich brown skin is smooth and blemish-free. She's wearing the patience and kindness of the Sera I befriended in Terra Court, but she's also the stranger who tried to kill me—who killed Eoin.

Perhaps I'm better suited to stay here with her rather than near the others. I'm not wanting to be alone, but I don't want to risk hurting anyone else. But I'm not afraid of hurting Seraphina. She hurt me first.

I pinch the bridge of my nose, my eyes flitting shut. *No.* This exact way of thinking is a slippery slope. I'm not one to seek revenge or justice, and it's more important than ever now to stay in touch with my own kindness.

Returning my gaze to her, I try to focus on the bits of the *Sera* I know—the female who sat with me in Terra Court and spilled information about the courts. The one who laughed with me while I was drunk on faerie wine, intoxicated by Eoin's magic, and the one who befriended me when I was feeling lost and alone.

"I… forgive you," I force myself to say. The words come out reluctantly, as if my shadow-self is trying to tug them back down my throat instead of allowing them to spill out. "I want to move forward, Sera."

The darkness rattles my bones like prison bars, begging to be released. Not even Seraphina deserves the harm it could cause.

And I refuse to add another tally to my list.

"I shouldn't be here." Turning, I take a step, but her soft hand lands on my upper arm.

"Wait," she says quietly.

Exhaling, I smooth out my expression and turn back to her. She drops my arm and studies me for a moment.

"I know what it's like," she says.

"I'm not sure what you're referring to," I say emotionlessly. "I really should be going now."

"The guilt. The regret. The grief." She fiddles with one of her braids, tossing it over a shoulder. "His face is etched in my memory—vivid and tormenting. And not just in death, but in the echo of his smile. It's the essence of his life that lingers. I feel it, a palpable responsibility clinging to my soul," she whispers, her voice quivering with the weight of her emotions.

She places a hand on her chest, her eyes glinting with honesty. "I made a mistake that cost a piece of my own soul. I can't do it again. I won't."

My chest tightens in response. "Good," I whisper. The very emotions she speak of clog my throat, and I hate that of all folk, it's Seraphina who gets it.

"I won't pretend to be something I'm not, though," she says. "If my plan had worked—if Ez would've been freed from Yvanthia's horrible clutches—it would've been worth it. I wouldn't have an ounce of regret." She dips her chin, giving me an apologetic look. "I'd do anything for him."

The weight of her words is a blow to my chest. I step back. "Even if you had killed *me*?"

She chews her bottom lip for a second, then releases it. "All I can give you is my word that right now, with how things have turned out, I recognize I made mistakes, and it won't happen again."

My mouth opens, and then I close it, unsure what to say. Her loyalty to Ez is admirable, but it worries me that she'd go to extremes to protect him.

Wouldn't I do the same for Rainer though?

"You shouldn't carry the guilt of the Terra Prince's death," she says, drawing my attention back to her. "*That* was not your fault."

My first inclination is to separate our actions by justifying my own—to convince myself that we are two entirely different beings. But I *would* do the same thing if it came to Rainer. Technically, I already have—accepting my power to spare his life and taking the lord and lady's lives. If they hadn't been easily accessible, whose life would I have taken to assume my court?

Deep down, I know the truth: *someone* was going to die that day. I would've done *anything* to keep the realm from suffering, to keep Rainer and my other friends from facing a lethal fate.

"How do you go on?" I wave to the various herbs and concoctions laid out on the counter. "Like everything is fine. Like you're not different now?"

Seraphina sighs, wiping her hands on a towel and planting her hands on the counter with her back to me. Then, she slowly turns toward me and tilts her chin up. "If I don't, then it's all for nothing. If I let my mistakes and regrets hold me back, I'm only taking another life—my own." Her eyes harden. "That would be a waste of potential. There is so much else to be done in this world, Alessia."

My features pinch together with the conflict of feelings inside me.

"You should know," she says softly. "I can read auras—energy and intention." Her eyes roam my body as if tracing an invisible outline. "Yours is one I seldom see. It's like Ez's. Which is why I fight for him the way I do."

I look down at my hand, trying and failing to see the aura she's speaking of. "And what is Ez's like?"

She smiles, but it's tinged with sadness. "Beautiful," she whispers with a sigh. "You both are much too good for this world."

My eyes water as the words strike me. She's wrong—I'm not good. Not anymore. My insides are rotten, spoiled by the power I never wanted.

My throat tightens. "I should go."

She nods, her lips pulling down on the sides. "If you want my advice? It's time to accept that you *are* different now, Alessia. There's no going back—you can only move forward."

I nod, quickly leaving Seraphina and the unexpected comforts she offered me behind. Although her input wasn't what I sought, her words were precisely what I needed. They stir a deep resonance within me.

But still, I don't trust myself.

FIFTEEN
THE BLISS OF HIS KISS
ALESSIA

T *hat was not your fault.*

Seraphina's words replay in my head with each step I take through my court. Opting for one of the abandoned side corridors, I put additional space between me and the clamor and commotion of the cleaning fae. I need breathing room.

The hallway gradually slopes downwards, delving further into the earth. Eventually, the twisting hallway comes to an end, dumping me in a library.

The air is saturated with the rich, earthy scent of parchment and ancient wood. Stone ceilings soar above me, wooden beams crisscrossing like the ribs of a mighty beast, while the library stands as the pulsating heart protected within. Soft, dark rugs cushion my steps, creating a cozy contrast to the coldness of the stone floor.

Towering bookshelves filled with leather-bound stories surround me. Each wall of shelves boasts a rolling ladder to access the higher shelves.

The far corner of the library beckons me. I stride toward it, finding an intimate setup of leather chairs in a nook. Its entrance is lined with a tied-back velvet curtain. I enter, pulling the cord. The drapes swoosh closed behind me, creating a private sanctuary.

I sit in one of the chairs, and it lets out a gentle creak as I sink into its worn cushion. Soft, flickering light from the sconce beside me dances across the walls, creating a warm atmosphere.

It's as if I've discovered a secret refuge to spare me from the chaos beyond. Or perhaps it's protecting the world from *me*.

Closing my eyes, I lean back in the chair and breathe.

That was not your fault.

Eoin's death was not my fault.

I want to believe Seraphina's words. Unless she's a phenomenal actress, she isn't heartless—perhaps a little lost or conflicted, but not cruel. We have much in common—we're both trying to navigate a complicated world while looking out for those we care about.

I admire her ability to bounce back and find her strength. Perhaps I wish I were more like her.

But right now, I don't feel strong.

"You're not weak; you're strong," I mutter, blinking back the tears.

This is not who I want to be—this self-pitying person who runs away and hides. But it's better than being someone who harms others. And unless I can figure out how to properly restrain my shadow-self, I'm a threat.

We are *strong.* The responding voice comes from inside.

"Yes," I whisper. "But we are dangerous."

Being dangerous is better than being in danger.

"Alessia!" Rainer's voice echoes through the library, deep and dominant. It reverberates deep within me, summoning a flood of emotions. Warmth blooms in the center of my being and spreads throughout my body, like rays of sunlight piercing the clouds.

The world seems to hold its breath as if frozen in time—I'm suspended here, caught between the feeling of being lost and found.

His hurried footsteps grow louder with each passing second. Breaking the spell, I sit up and gaze towards the curtain, brimming with anticipation.

A moment later, he darts through it in a flurry of unchecked rage.

His dark hair is smoothed back out of his face. Bits of dirt and leaves are stuck to his boots, and his clothes are riddled with fur.

With a sudden surge, the floodgates open, unleashing a torrent of pent-up emotions. The indescribable sensation drowns me, leaving me at a loss for words.

"Rainer," I whisper. Every fiber of my being exhales, eagerly taking in his presence. My face scrunches as he storms over to me.

With a thud, he drops to his knees, his strong hands tenderly caressing my cheeks. His touch ignites a pulsating deep in my core, bringing me fully to life.

He scrutinizes my face, wearing a mixture of concern and fury. His irises flicker between icy blue and deep cobalt, indicating he's fighting his protective, animalistic instincts. Time has flown by, and it's hard to believe it's been a couple of months since we last saw each other. My heart spasms in my chest, ready to burst free.

"Rainer," I repeat on an exhale, unable to say anything else.

"Where is he?" he growls, his voice filled with a fierce determination. He drops his hands from my face, gripping my arms gently and flipping them over as he inspects my skin. "Did he hurt you?"

I gape, unsure of what he means. The scent of sandalwood and rose mixed with his natural musk hits me. My insides melt. It's a fragrance with the power to melt away my worries, leaving me immediately comforted.

His presence is grounding, an anchor holding me down. It's that sensation of coming home that I've been seeking for so long. I've been mistaken in thinking the court could provide that feeling of home I've been seeking—it's been *him* the whole time.

I'm overwhelmed with relief and joy, but it's tinged with regret and fear. Regret of denying my connection to him and being apart for so long. Fear of the truth of our bond and what it means if we're truly together. Fear of what might happen if I can't control my shadow around him.

Suddenly, the gravity of those feelings makes sense to me: it's not that I fear losing control and hurting someone or losing myself... I fear hurting *him*, losing him.

He shakes me gently, knocking me from my stupor. "Alessia. Where is he?" he repeats, the ire hardening his eyes.

"Who?" I wrack my brain, trying to decipher if he means Ezamae, or perhaps Tynan.

"The *human* who attacked you."

Oh.

I stay quiet for a moment, letting the words settle. As I gaze into his eyes, I see a reflection of my own longing and vulnerability. A silent understanding flows between us. With each passing second, the realization solidifies within me: he is my home. *He* is my sanctuary.

I close my eyes briefly, taking a deep breath.

He growls, jumping to his feet. "Tell me, now!"

His command is jarring, and it causes a tear to slip free. I shake my head.

"He's—he's dead," I stutter out.

"Are you hurt?" His scowl is sharp and violent as he takes me in. When I shake my head, he begins pacing. He runs a hand through his hair, but his fingers get caught in the knots, and he frowns harder. "I shouldn't have left you alone. I should've stayed."

Choking on a sob, I wipe my tears away. "I'm fine," I whisper. "I promise. I'm not hurt."

He pauses, studying me. "Then why are you crying?" His tone is much softer this time. His shoulders relax, and the rage evaporates.

"I—" *I missed you*, I want to say. Instead, I swallow it down. "How do you even know about the man?"

"The pixies," he says flatly. "I was at Terra Court. I would've been here sooner if they…" He sighs, stroking his jaw and glancing toward the curtain. "It doesn't matter. I wasn't here, and that's all that matters."

"It's okay. I can handle myself," I say quietly, working to keep my voice steady and confident.

"I know you can!" He throws his hands up in exasperation, his eyes finally mellowing back to their normal pale coloring. "That doesn't mean I won't worry about you."

"Your brother was here anyway, and I don't—"

"*Tynan* was involved?" Rainer's voice turns stony again.

He sucks in a sharp breath and schools his expression. Stiffly, he walks to the chair a few paces across from me and carefully lowers himself into it. He watches me, his fingers tapping out a controlled rhythm on his thigh. Amber light glints off his rings.

I want to reach for him, curl my fingers through his, and feel the coolness of those metal rings as they bite into my skin. I want to nestle into his side and let him wrap those strong arms around me. It would be so easy to get lost in his touch—to forget everything else.

Suddenly, he goes still. His face melts into a grimace, and he leans forward, resting his forearms on his legs.

"I can't take this anymore, Alessia."

My chest hitches as I take a shaky breath. "Take what?"

He springs up from the chair, his eyes locked onto mine with an icy intensity. Before I can fully comprehend the situation, he swiftly leans forward, gripping the armrests of my chair and caging me in. With each deep breath, his chest heaves. He clutches the armrests tighter, and the muscles in his forearms flex as if he's fighting to hold himself back.

"Can't take what?" I whisper meekly, finally drawing my gaze up to his. He hovers a mere breath away, a conflicted look pinching his features.

"Feck it," he mutters, eyes flicking to my lips. His hand finds the back of my head, and he weaves his fingers through my hair. "*This*," he says breathlessly. "I can't take *this* anymore."

Then his lips are on mine, and I'm losing myself to the bliss of his kiss.

Sixteen

Let Yourself Blossom

Rainer

The muscles in my stomach tighten, and pleasure zings through me as she presses her lips to mine in response. She reaches up, wrapping her arms around my neck to pull me closer.

I groan into her mouth, nibbling her bottom lip.

"Alessia..." I mutter, my lips drifting to her jaw, then down to her neck. I leave a trail of gentle kisses in my wake. "I've missed the way you taste."

She grips my neck, tugging my mouth back to hers. I want to devour her, ravage her until she's a writhing, screaming mess beneath me, but instead, I take it slow. I've mastered my beast—or rather, *she's* tamed my monster.

And it's the first time she's kissed me since finding out about our bond.

She's choosing this.

She's choosing *me*.

About gods-damned time.

"Mo róisín," I whisper against her lips. "My little rose."

I pull back just enough to take her in. My hand slides to her cheek, carefully cupping it. The ragged tattoo running from her temple to her jaw looks harsh and angry compared to how sweet and soft her face is.

She gazes deeply into my eyes, allowing me to see the vulnerability she hides from the rest of the world. It's a sensitivity reserved solely for me. Her grey eyes sparkle with hope and pain, and… fear.

It's all too recognizable, and it lances my heart.

"I can't," she says, thrusting that invisible blade deeper into my chest and bleeding me out. "We can't."

She turns her head, chewing the inside of her lip as she fixes her gaze on the wall. Slowly, so as not to scare her, I kneel before her. Then, I reach up, gently grip her chin, and guide her gaze back to mine.

She's been through so much in such a short time. She's learned, loved, and lost more in a few months than most others have in a lifetime. Though I refuse to let her waste away into self-pity or sorrow like I once tried to do, I also don't want to overstep or scare her.

I choose my words carefully before clearing my throat and breaking the silence.

"I can't ignore that my heart beats for you," I say. Her frown deepens, and I hate seeing such an expression on that heart-shaped face. "Even if you won't let me have all of you, at least let me have a piece."

My plea hangs in the air, heavy between us. Despite the sincerity in my voice, I can tell by the rigid set to her shoulders that she's hesitant to give in, prisoner to the insecurities she won't let me see.

I stand, returning to the chair to distance us so she doesn't feel cornered by my presence. I'm aware I can be an intimidating male, and I never want her to feel threatened by me.

"I just... I need time." With a sigh, she scoots deeper into the chair and tucks her knees to her chest, resting her chin on them. Curled in on herself and shrunk down, she appears so small... so lost. "How did we get here? I'm home, but I'm all alone, Rainer."

The words cut through me like my favorite pruning shears. "You're never alone, mo róisín."

The pain in her eyes is so recognizable. It's a chronic pain I recognize all too well—it's the very reason I loathe mirrors. I don't like to see my reflection because the pain is a permanent sickness without a cure. It's a shadow that never leaves my eyes, no matter how brightly they shine.

And I'd drain the last dredges of my happiness, pouring it into the cracks of her pain if only I could.

"I'm going to let everyone down." Her voice wavers, and I ball my hand into a fist on my lap, fighting the urge to reach out and comfort her. "I'm a liability."

She wears a haunted look that turns my heart to ash. She's the purest being to walk this land, and that's precisely why we need her. But telling her that is a pressure she doesn't need. Instead, I tell her the more important truth: "You don't owe the world anything, Alessia. You're worthy as you are. You could never do or say anything to change that."

"I can't do anything right. It feels like there are two parts of me, and they're at odds. One wants to do the right thing but only makes mistakes, and the other doesn't care at all. It craves chaos and destruction. What does that make me?"

"It makes you... *human*," I say with a soft smile. "And fae." I pause. "It makes you you. You've looked true evil in the face and put their fire out before it could burn anyone else. That's a strength few can brag about.

She blinks rapidly, as if holding back tears, and her fingers pluck mindlessly at the hem of her shirt.

I lean back in my chair, watching her carefully. Something is going on with her. It's more than the desire for space and time. She's not figuring herself out or finding her confidence down here—she's losing it. The fight in her eyes is diluted as if it's slowly fading.

A wave of anger washes over me. Anger at the pixies for taking so long to retrieve me, anger at myself for leaving her alone for so long, anger at anyone and everyone who contributed to that sad look on Alessia's face.

"No. Enough with this," I say with fierce determination. Even the smallest piece of her is worth more than anything else, because even the smallest cuttings someday bloom into full plants. "I'm not going anywhere. I'll give you time, but I won't give you space. I'm waiting right here."

She shakes her her head. "I can't ask you to wait for me, Rainer."

"You're not asking me. I'm telling *you*."

Her body softens, but then her eyes widen. She shakes her head almost imperceptibly and then becomes rigid again.

I study her, wondering what internal battle she's fighting.

There's no way I'm returning to Umbra Court—or worse, leaving for Dovenak—while she's in this state. I successfully provoked her fight before, and I can do it again, so help me gods.

"I'm afraid, Rainer," she whispers.

My fingers tap my knee mindlessly, staying busy to avoid reaching for her. "What is it exactly that you fear?"

Fear is my jurisdiction. Not only do I dole it out to others, but I experience my own in troves. My fears plague me in the form of nightmares. If anyone understands how crippling the terror can be, it's me.

"Sometimes I wonder what the point is," she says. "All I do is cause pain to others by existing. My magic thrives on harming others. I can't live like this. I've been searching and searching for answers, a way to rid myself of this burden, but there aren't any."

My eyes flicker with darkening heat as I hold her stare. "No," I growl. The muscles in my jaw tighten. "Don't talk like that."

"You don't understand…" She plucks mindlessly at a tear in her leather armrest. "The *thing* inside me—" she says it with disgust, shuddering and sucking in a breath.

"You worry it'll consume you—destroy that soft heart of yours," I say softly.

She blinks in surprise, her hand stilling. "Yes… how do you know?"

I chuckle softly, my eyes crinkling at the corner. "Little rose, you know me better than that."

As her face softens in recognition, the line etched into her forehead smooths out. Her lips, previously set in a firm line, curve upwards ever so slightly.

"You're the one who made me realize I wasn't the monster I feared I was," I tell her. "You showed up out of nowhere, threw my world into chaos, and reminded me that I'm more than my past mistakes—more than my bloodlust. And I'm here to show you that *you* are more than your magic, too."

"It's not just losing myself that I fear." She swallows heavily. "What if it hurts *you*?"

My amused smile grows. "What's love without a little pain?"

She scrunches her nose, trying to give me an annoyed look, but it doesn't work. It morphs into a smile, and it lights up her face briefly before melting. "I wasn't very kind—with what I said before. About loving someone else when you don't love yourself." She flushes. "I'm sorry for that."

Her human niceties tickle me. "It was true for you when you said it, and I don't resent you for it. I became a better male because of you, and I can admit that I wasted much time hating myself. I don't want the same to happen to you."

"What if I can't control it?"

"Then you embrace it."

"But my shadow-self is… violent. And messy." She sucks in a sharp breath. "It's *scary*. I'm afraid of it."

"Stop pushing me away. Let me help you learn it."

She shakes her head. "I can't. Not until I get better at controlling it."

I tsk. "You don't need to be flawless to be loved. You're worthy, even on your worst days—especially on your worst days, because those are the hardest, yet you persevere."

A tear slides down her cheek. "I've wasted so much time." She leans her head back, staring up. "I've tucked myself away, isolating from all of you, and I've only backslid."

"Stop pushing me away, and let me help you. You are my soul-bond, after all."

"Oh, I'm aware." She laughs humorlessly. "I need a *lot* of help right now, Rainer."

"That's the point," I deadpan. "The point of a partnership is to have another pillar to support your load. Some days, you pick me up; some days, I pick you up, but no matter what, we have each other to lean on."

She bites her lip, looking at me nervously. "I don't know about—"

"Get the feck up." I stand, reaching for her. "Now."

Her eyes widen and her mouth parts slightly as she gazes up at me with shock. I know she's probably stunned by my sudden brashness, but I can't stand to see her in this fragile, self-pitying state a second longer. This isn't her. Ironically, the fear of losing herself to her magic is the very thing that is causing her to lose herself.

"Get up," I repeat, cocking a brow. Then, I smirk at her. "*Please*."

She finally snaps out of her stupor. Decisively, she places her hand in mine and entangles our fingers. I squeeze her and watch in delight as she melts beneath my touch.

I lead her out of the library and into the hall.

Ezamae is right again—it is reminiscent of a crypt down here. This surely can't be healthy for Alessia.

"Where are we going?" she asks as I turn toward the main corridor.

"I want to show you something, but I'm also going to tell you something on the way."

"Oh?"

"When I was little, I found out about my bloodlust in the worst of ways. I was just a faeling, and I didn't know what was happening until I was attacking my father. Seamus was beating my mother—not for the first time—and it triggered my bloodlust. It was too much emotion for a young fae, especially one who didn't know he was half-vampyr. And after I killed Seamus, the bloodlust wasn't satisfied, and I turned on my mother…"

"Rainer," Alessia breathes, tugging me to a stop. "You don't have to share this."

I release her hand, running it through my hair. Then, I force myself to meet her gaze. I expect to see pity there, but instead, she just looks so damn sad.

"I don't tell you this to bring you down, Alessia. I tell you this because if you can look at me and see anything other than the monster I am, then why can't you give yourself the same grace?"

She closes her eyes and takes a stuttering breath. "It's not the—"

"If you dare say it's not the same, then you're being a hypocrite." My tone is kind, not wanting to insult her. "I want you to realize that you shouldn't punish yourself for being what you are."

Her eyes reopen and she nods slowly. "It's hard not to."

"I know." I reach for her hand, and we continue strolling as I talk. "After, I spiraled. Very much like you, I hid myself away, thinking I was better off alone. I was afraid of hurting others—of not being able to control my bloodlust. But Kenisius was there for me without judgment. The relentless fecker refused to leave me alone. He practically forced me to feed on him to stave off my bloodlust. And eventually, I learned to control it well enough.

"But when I met you, I worried all my work on self-control wasn't enough. You provoked such strong emotions in me that I pulled away. I might not've ran physically, but I did mentally. I doubted myself until you showed me I shouldn't."

"But you still lost control at Eoin's," she whispers, wincing. "Not that you hurt me of course," she hurries to add. "But your fears were warranted."

"Maybe, but that's life, little rose. We can't hide ourselves away to spare ourselves from making mistakes. We need to get out there and *live*, regardless of our fears. Don't let life pass you by because you're afraid of being imperfect."

"You make it sound so simple," she mumbles. "Except my shadow-self wants to *kill* others, Rainer. I'm not a murderer."

"Then don't be one. Don't cling to that identity. It's not what—or who—you are."

"What if I hurt someone, though?"

I shrug. "I'd say they probably deserved it."

She laughs at this, and I smile, relieved she's softening.

We reach the back entrance to the kitchen, and I move behind Alessia, gently gripping her shoulders as we take in the scene.

Das Lulu, one of Umbra Court's kitchen maids, chats animatedly with Sheila, the rescued Tradeling, as they slice vegetables at one of the long stone counters. The human girl towers over the fae, gangly and awkward as if she's still learning how to use her body. Thick, black braids run down either side of her head, giving her a youthful appearance despite her height.

Leaning in close to her ear, I keep my voice soft. "What do you see?"

Alessia turns to me, giving me a confused smile. "Why is Sheila wearing that? I swear if you are messing with that poor girl—"

"No." I chuckle. "She *chose* to wear that dress. It's her favorite."

I study the horrid purple ensemble that Sheila's wearing. It's the same one Alessia once wore to brunch with Eoin and Sennah. Only this time, it's not a faerie prank.

"Das Celyn altered all of the clothing to fit Sheila properly—she has a variety of choices, but she wanted to wear *that*."

"Why?" Alessia asks, clearly baffled. "It's hideous and inconvenient."

"Because she likes it for whatever reason." I shrug. "Either way, the girl is finding freedom in the small things. She expresses herself through clothing, baking, and painting—"

"She paints?" Alessia turns back to me, eyes lit up.

"Not well, but she does."

Her smile grows.

"She's a lot like you in many ways," I add. "Now that she can be safe, she's thriving."

"Because of you," Alessia says resolutely. "You saved her."

"No." I shake my head, my eyes softening as I gaze at her. "She's here because you refused to forget about her or leave her behind."

She tuts, shooting me a skeptical look. "You didn't leave her either."

I shrug a shoulder, stuffing a hand in my pocket so I don't mindlessly reach for her and scare her away. "I might've rescued her from Dovenak, but *you* saved her."

"I didn't do anything," she says.

"You gave her hope. You inspired her. And she's not the only one." I squeeze her shoulders, hoping she picks up on the meaning behind my words. "You give us all hope for a better future, Alessia."

For a second, it feels as if she isn't breathing as she ponders this.

"I didn't realize..." she whispers.

I move beside Alessia, leaning a shoulder against the doorjamb as I study her. "She asked to come here. She wants to stay here, Alessia—live at your court."

Sheila laughs at something Das Lulu says, tipping her head back. Once the laughter subsides, she shakes her head. Her gaze snags on us. A wide grin stretches across her face. She lifts a hand, waving vigorously at Alessia. Then, she reaches up and traces the dark jagged ink on the left side of her face. Alessia sucks in a sharp breath, and she mirrors the movement, reaching up and doing the same.

Her eyes glint with unshed tears, and for a second, I fear I've done the wrong thing and provoked more sorrow. But she blows out a shaky breath and turns to me, grabbing my hands.

"Thank you, Rainer," she rushes out. "She looks so healthy. So happy. *You* did that."

I shake my head. "No, little rose, she did that herself. She gave life a chance and allowed herself to find her joy because she thinks *you* did the same. She looks up to you."

"She barely knows me," she whispers.

"It doesn't matter. It's what you symbolize."

The *hope*.

Growing up in the Trade, surviving the humans' abuse, braving a new realm, facing the fae's mischief—Alessia has done much without it fazing her.

She can't let a hiccup with her power be the thing that stops her.

I place a finger under her chin and direct her gaze to mine. "Tap into your strength, little rose. Tap into your strength, embrace all versions of yourself, and let yourself blossom."

Seventeen

Already Betrayed Me

Alessia

Seeing Sheila dredges up a mixture of old emotions. The joy on her face showed me a different future—one where little girls like her and past me are safe, healthy, and *happy*. The dark ink marking her cheek stirs up palpable anger at the people in Dovenak who stand by and let the Trade happen or, worse, people like the lord and lady who take an active part in it.

I watch Sheila work, catching a whiff of something sweet. My stomach rumbles, and I yearn to join her and Das Lulu. Even in my darkest moments, baking in the kitchen has always been a comfort. It's a form of stress relief for me. My heart softens as I realize Sheila finds solace there just as I do.

Rainer squeezes my shoulder, and I smile genuinely at him.

He and Seraphina are right—my mistakes do not define me, and I'll likely make more in the future, but that shouldn't stop me from *trying* to do the right thing.

Like the visions I saw of myself in the Cave of Reflection, perhaps my shadow-self is only one alternate version of me. But it isn't my entire identity.

I am more than my guilt, fear, and fury.

Despite my imperfections, I, Alessia Lírshadow, am determined to protect the goodness within me, but I will no longer run. Anytime the lord or lady punished me, I faced them without cowering.

I may have been meek before, but I never hid out of fear. I cried and trembled, but I never broke.

I might never learn to overcome the darkness fully, and every day that passes is another day others continue suffering needlessly. Rainer is waiting for me to head to Dovenak. Not only is he waiting patiently to get the iron he needs to break his woods' curse, but he's also willing to help me stop the Trade and free the Tradelings.

Once we succeed, many beings on both sides of the Gleam will have better lives. We're bringing greater freedom to people *and* fae.

But we need to get started.

"Rainer," I whisper, turning to him. He watches me with rapt attention, ready to cling to anything I say. "We shouldn't wait any longer."

He kicks off the doorframe, standing tall. "Dovenak?"

I nod. "I'll never forgive myself if we miss our chance." Before he can reply, I continue. "The man that I found—he wasn't an assassin. He had a prisoner marking on his neck—tattooed numbers."

Rainer strokes his jaw, eyes glazing over as he focuses on the wall beyond me. "I know." He clears his throat. "I've sent Kenisius and Viveka to spy. A group of soldiers is taking up residence in your old house just beyond the Gleam. We've gathered that they're prisoners who were offered a chance at freedom from Queen Wyetta."

"What does it mean?" I ask.

"She's using them. It's a sleight of hand. We're looking over here, distracted, instead of seeing what's happening there." He gestures obscurely into the air.

"Distracting us from what?"

His eyes darken as he narrows them into slits. "Her preparations for war."

"What are we going to do?"

"Avoid said war at all costs." He runs a hand over his face. "I need to talk to my brother."

After Rainer sets off to find Tynan, I decide to practice trusting myself around others. Seraphina and Rainer have both instilled in me a sense of empowerment. If no one else is afraid of me, maybe I don't need to fear myself. Perhaps desensitizing myself to my shadow-self is the answer.

As I move through the court, I appreciate the diligent effort of the visiting fae. I smile at everyone I pass, letting them see my gratitude. Words cannot express the immense amount of appreciation I harbor for what they've done here.

I turn a corner, and a gust of wind sends me flying backward. I stumble, almost losing my balance.

"Oops," Ez says. "I didn't see you there."

I shoot him a playful glare, my eyes narrowing in jest. It quickly turns into a chuckle. I can't be mad at the male after everything he's done—bringing all these fae here to help clean.

He delicately flicks his wrist. A gentle breeze encircles him. Skillfully directing the wind, he stirs up dust from the corridor's nooks and crannies. His magic creates a tornado of dust, whimsically demonstrating its usefulness. He rotates his wrist, directing the funnel into a trash bin and settling the mess.

Once the air settles, he lets out a long, low breath and plants a hand on the wall to hold himself up.

"How is it going?" I ask, taking in his pallor. A thin sheen of sweat lines his face, beading on his brow and upper lip. "You look ill."

"Very kind of you," he says. The smile he gives me is forced, his eyes revealing a glimmer of pain.

"You need to recharge."

"Ah, yes, I probably should."

"Come on," I say. "We need to get you some food."

"It's not *food* I'd like to eat right now," he murmurs, wavering on his feet.

"Oh gods." I rub my temple. Apparently, he's never too weak to make sly jokes. "Should I fetch Seraphina?"

Taken aback, his face contorts into bewilderment. "Why her?"

"I—" I almost say because I know she'll help him, but I think twice. If she were an option, he would've mentioned her, surely. "Well then, who? Can't you just... do it yourself?"

His response is a breathy chuckle. "Not how it works."

"How does it work?"

He licks his lips, glancing away, but he doesn't answer.

"It's irresponsible to overexert yourself like this." Frowning, I place his arm over my shoulder and attempt to keep him steady as we traverse the hallway.

"I'll be fine," he says quietly.

"Damn you, Ez."

His weight is heavy as he leans on me for support. The shadow fidgets beneath my skin, pent-up energy begging for a release. It would be so easy to let the darkness out to help me carry Ez...

No.

That's how it starts. The lines will blur if I start relying on my shadow-self for little conveniences.

Grunting with exertion, I carefully guide him down the hallway. His weight slows me down. After a few steps, my hair dances in a gentle breeze that quickly fades away—Ez's pitiful attempt at using his magic to help, but he's exhausted his reserves.

He makes a noise of frustration.

"Can you die from this?" I ask, morbidly curious.

He emits a short, stifled laugh that turns into a sharp inhale. "Of embarrassment, yes. Arguably worse than death itself."

We barge into the kitchen a short while later, nearly colliding with one of the workers. My breath escapes me in ragged gasps as I assist Ez to a chair. Gripping the counter, I steady myself and take a moment to regain my composure.

"I assure you, food is not what I need," Ez mumbles, lifting a brow.

"No, I know—I figured we might find someone to help." The kitchen serves as the central meeting place for everyone, where they gather between tasks.

"This ought to be interesting."

I quickly scan the room, counting at least two dozen fae. They stay busy by engaging in a range of cooking and cleaning duties.

Blowing out a frustrated breath, I turn back to Ez. "Who should I ask?"

He chuckles again, slumping down in the chair. "Whoever is willing, darling. If *you* are willing to reconsider—"

"Hush up." I purse my lips and shake my head. "Do I just approach someone and ask if they'll make love with you?"

A slow smirk spreads across his face. "Making love isn't exactly what I'd call it."

"Ugh." I rub my forehead, groaning. Deciding to get this over with, I clap my hands, instantly grabbing the attention of the bustling crowd. An awkward moment of silence stretches as they peer at me curiously. Mustering up my courage, I clear my throat and yell, "Would anyone like an orgasm?"

The resounding silence is so awkward and sharp that I want to crawl into a hole and hide. Perhaps I should've thought about my approach.

Recoiling, I scrunch my nose and glance at Ez, giving him an apologetic look.

His eyebrows flick up as he tilts his head, appraising me. "I find your method quite fascinating."

I turn back to the various onlookers, clearing my throat. "The Prince of *Pleasure* could really use some assistance."

With hungry anticipation, their eyes begin to light up as they draw closer to him.

"Well?" I ask, shifting impatiently.

Without delay, the fae erupt into chaos, each one desperate to be chosen to share a bed with the Aer Prince. I flush, wanting to extricate myself from the commotion.

"Have your pick," I say to Ez, shimmying out of the crowd.

His eyes twinkle in delight as he watches me leave.

I whirl around to exit the kitchen just as a familiar face enters. She looks past me, gaping at the uproar. I double-take. Her burgundy hair flows in soft waves around her shoulders, matching her lipstick. A thin layer of cosmetics smooths her peachy skin and complements her brown eyes.

"Fern? It's nice to see you."

She turns her attention to me, giving me an unsure smile. "It is—isn't it?" Her button nose scrunches, and she glances down at her flats, toeing at the floor. I'm glad to see she's not in those neck-breaking shoes again. "I mean, good to see *you*."

"Yes," I agree.

A light laugh spills from her lips as she looks back up at me.. "I'm not good with small talk." She waves her hand toward the crowd gathered around Ez. The various fae vie for his attention, and he smirks, eating it all up. "What's going on, anyway?"

"He's... hungry, and they're arguing over who can feed him," I say suggestively.

"Another arrogant prince." She rolls her eyes, and then she sucks in a sharp breath. An apologetic look crosses her face. "Not that *your* prince is arrogant, of course. At least not these days."

Gently, I touch her shoulder. "It's okay. I get it."

And I do. Rainer *was* arrogant when I met him. He still can be, although he's softened a lot. Beneath that arrogance is a softer interior that not many see. I'm privileged to know the pieces he hides away, but Fern doesn't know him like that.

Her lips quirk. "Are you thirsty? I need a drink."

"No." I grimace, knowing she means faerie wine. It's nice to see Fern sober. But I know she *needs* the magic she's addicted to. Rainer said withdrawals can kill her, and it breaks my heart. "Do you ever wonder what life would be like—without the dependency?"

She gives me a sad smile, tilting her head. "I try not to."

"Why not?"

"It's too late for me, Alessia. It's a waste of time to hope for the impossible," she says softly. Her face drops, and she blinks rapidly, glancing away. "I'm lucky for the luxuries I have. It's no big deal." Her voice cracks.

Not for the first time, I glimpse the woman beneath the confident aura and beautiful makeup. She reminds me so much of me when I was Lord Edvin's Tradeling. I wavered between holding onto hope and considering it a waste of time to *wonder*. This is another reason why getting the iron is so important—so Seraphina can make a viable concoction to help break Fern's addiction to magic. The human woman deserves a life of her own, free from her addiction.

I make a silent vow not to let her down.

"I will say…" Fern leans toward me, plastering on a broad grin and brushing aside the heavy moment. "The silver-haired prince makes my lady bits tingle. Maybe I'll put him to use—make a faerie prince work for *me* for once."

We both giggle. Ez glances up as if sensing we're talking about him.

Slowly, he stands from the counter. He drags his eyes up and down Fern, then smirks, straightening up before sauntering toward us. She turns her back to him, flicking her long hair over a shoulder and whipping him in the face.

"No," I say, shaking my finger in warning. "Not her."

Fern turns, narrowing her eyes at Ez. A slow smile spreads across her face when she glances back at me. Her eyes twinkle with mischief.

"Fern," I groan, feeling oddly protective over her. "Have you taken anything today? Drank at all?"

She shrugs a shoulder, flipping her hair again. "Not yet."

My muscles loosen a bit, and some of the tension dissipates. "I swear to the gods, Ez, if you hurt her..." I glower at him. My shadow churns like a storm beneath my skin, sensing conflict.

"I assure you, Alessia, any pain is mutually consensual," he says, winking, before holding a hand for Fern. She grips it, giving him a coy look.

A collective groan of disappointment rises through the kitchen as the fae realize the Prince of Pleasure has chosen someone to assist him. They scurry to their various stations, returning to work as if there had never been an interruption.

Ez leads Fern toward the exit at the far end of the kitchen.

"The bedrooms are that way!" I yell, jerking my thumb over my shoulder in the opposite direction of where they're navigating.

"We don't need a bed," Fern yells back, casting me a sly grin over her shoulder. She takes the lead, tugging Ez out of the kitchen.

A weird feeling niggles in my stomach—not jealousy, but something else I can't name. They're both consenting adults, and Fern doesn't appear to be under the influence of anything. On top of that, Ez is someone I'd consider a friend—I trust him. But I worry about her.

She deserves joy, though, and I hope she finds it.

"I don't like her," Sera says sternly, appearing beside me with crossed arms. She stares in the direction Fern and Ez left with narrowed eyes.

"Be nice," I admonish, scrunching my nose at her. "You don't have to like her, but if you try anything, we're done for good, Sera."

She turns to me with a frown. "You don't need to threaten me. You need me as much as I need you."

"I don't *need* anyone." I incline my chin, and my shadow-self thrashes against my insides, begging to come out and play. "I mean it. If you harm any more of my friends, everything is off."

"Okay, okay." She puts her hands up placatingly. "I won't harm anything—not even a pixie."

"You better not hurt a pixie," I say, appalled. "What are you even doing here?"

"A gal's gotta eat." She shrugs. "Join me?"

The last time I joined her for a meal, she tried to kill me. Like wafting steam, a faint, dark fog begins to expel itself from my skin. A bolt of terror crashes through me.

I don't want to harm anyone else—not even Seraphina. The terror must be written on my face because Sera reaches out, gripping my hand to keep me in place.

She sighs, clearly unconcerned with the darkness hovering around me. "Wait."

I count my breaths, trying to quell my shadow's unease. "I need to go."

"I came to find you, to give you this." She reaches into her pocket and pulls something small out, but I don't move to take it. Instead, I eye it suspiciously. It's an amber-colored jar and dropper. "What is that?"

"For your monthlies." Stepping forward, she shakes it gently, urging me to accept it. "And for... you know. Avoiding faelings. Unless that's what you—"

"Got it." I quickly accept the tincture to quiet her. Pregnancy is decidedly *not* something I want right now. Maybe not ever. I'm not sure, but I know I want to be ready for such a massive commitment if it happens.

I unscrew the top and give the liquid a sniff. It smells like the one Char used to make for the lady, which eases my nerves. Slowly, the dark smog begins to thin out, absorbing back into my skin.

"It's safe." Sera touches her chest. "You have my word. Take it once per month. I take mine with each full moon."

Nodding, I say, "Okay."

Her eyes shine with emotion as she holds my stare. "You can trust me."

"I know, Sera, and I said I forgive you. I'm trying."

"Then why does it feel like you hate me?"

"Because rebuilding trust takes time."

She nods. "I understand. And I appreciate you trying at least."

With a heavy sigh and a heavier heart, I tuck the small vial in my cleavage for safekeeping until I can put it away.

It'd be much easier to trust the sorceress if she hadn't already betrayed me.

EIGHTEEN
THE POWER OF FEAR
RAINER

I burst through the shack's door, not bothering to shut it behind me. A feminine gasp rings out as the lump in the bed shifts. A female with light brown hair and a face full of freckles pop up, wrapping the sheet around her bare skin.

"Tynan." I curse, pinching the bridge of my nose as I whirl around. My eyes focus on a spot of rotting wood above the door.

"Guess we're done here," my brother says lazily. There's a soft slap sound and the female gasps. "I'll find you later."

There's rustling behind me as someone dresses, and the female brushes past me, dressed in a drab brown dress. She turns and pauses on her way out, glancing at me before shifting her gaze to Tynan. Her brows scrunch together as she opens her mouth, but she quickly sighs and shuts it. I recognize her from the Umbra halls, but I do her a favor and avoid eye contact. Instead, I turn, taking in the small space.

Dominating two walls of the room is a kitchenette and its cupboards, leaving only a sliver of space for a tiny table, a single chair, and an unlit fireplace beside the door. The bed occupies almost the entirety of the remaining wall.

Tynan sits on his mattress, smirking while his bare feet skim the rough wood floors.

After a few beats of awkward silence, the female scurries away, slamming the door behind her.

The few pots and pans hanging over the kitchenette clatter together with the force, and Tynan laughs, low and deep.

"I like Spiritus Court more than Shyga," he says.

It smells like sweat and mildew in here, and my nose scrunches in disdain. Tynan stands, letting the sheets fall. I glare at his face as he slowly grabs his trousers and dresses, keeping his chest bare.

"This is not a playground for your whims," I say, balling my hand into a fist beside me. He smirks, and I notice there's a small rust-colored stain on the corner of his lips. "You *bit* her?"

The muscles in my neck tighten as I fight to keep myself rooted in spot.

He raises his hands, chuckling. "She *begged* for it."

My blood burns hot as my mind flicks to an image of Alessia begging for me to bite her. It's pure hypocrisy to condemn Tynan for the very thing I enjoyed doing myself. But this is different—reckless.

Sucking in a deep breath, I scowl at him. "If I ever find out your endeavors are *non*-consensual, you're done." Before he can reply, I continue, my voice a low growl. "Not just done with this court, but *dead*, Tynan."

His face grows serious, and his jaw tenses as he turns away from me and rummages through a cupboard. "I'm not that despicable, you arse."

"I don't know what you're capable of."

He throws his head back as he laughs, then glances at me over his shoulder, raising a brow. "That's exactly the thing, little brother. You really don't know me at all."

I clench my jaw tightly, not wanting to give in to the back-and-forth. In some ways, we've made progress over the last couple of months, but we're a far cry from forgiveness, as Alessia would say.

"Why'd you interrupt my afternoon?" He slams a cup down, then opens his icebox and pulls out a glass milk bottle. "You want some?"

"No." I lean against the threshold and cross my arms.

He snags a bag of cocoa powder, adding it to his cup and stirring. My gaze swoops through his shack again, and upon a second look, I realize there are no wine bottles around. I sniff the air.

No scent of liquor.

"You've stayed sober," I say, uncrossing my arms.

I stride to the chair, plopping down to appear casual. Perhaps it'll put him at ease. If he's trying, I'll do the same.

He chugs his chocolate milk, turns toward me, and leans against the counter. "I wasn't drinking because I've got a problem." Pausing, he sets the glass down on the counter beside him. "Scratch that. I was drinking because I have *many* problems—but not because I'm a feckin alcoholic."

I rub the back of my neck awkwardly. "Why didn't you say anything?"

He snorts. "To who? *You*?"

The air around us is stiff with silence, weighed down by our unspoken words. There's no sense in rehashing the past. Not now, at least.

"I'm here because you could be of use," I say finally, circling back to his question from earlier.

Tynan's lips pull into a grim line as he slowly sips his chocolate milk. He polishes it off, slams the cup down beside him again, then wipes his mouth with the back of his hand.

"You want nothing to do with me for years, then you burst into my cottage in the middle of the best sex I've had in…" He pauses, tilting his head as he contemplates. "Doesn't matter. You accuse me of being a degenerate—" A sarcastic laugh filters out of him. "—and now you want my help… because it benefits *you*."

Uncomfortable guilt prods at my insides. I rise, frowning. "Never mind. I shouldn't have come here."

"Wait," Tynan says before I can leave. "Just tell me one thing."

I stuff my hands in my pockets, eyeing him warily. "Go on."

"Whyd'ya let me stay here—alone with your bonded—if you think so poorly of me?" His dark blue eyes flicker with pain before the expression extinguishes.

I sigh, scrubbing a hand over my face. "Because maybe I *know* you're not as horrid as you appear," I mumble.

"What?"

Clearing my throat, I try again, "Maybe I misjudged you, and you're not as… depraved as I like to think."

When I refocus my eyes on him, he's smirking. "That wasn't so bad, eh?"

"The worst, actually," I mutter. He's not wrong. In many ways, I suppose it's easier to see the worst in the people we keep at arm's length. It makes us feel better when we're the ones doing them wrong.

Even if we're blind to our actions.

He's at my side in two strides, wrapping his beefy arm around my neck and pulling me in. "All right, little brother. What do you need my help with?"

Scowling, I push him off me and brush my hair out of my face. "Your glamour."

"You're asking me to use it for once?"

"If you're interested, I'd like to test the limits of it... See just how far it stretches and how powerful it really is."

Tynan's eyes narrow, and he studies me. A few beats pass before his lips curve up into a grin. "Only if you promise not to cry when you realize how much more powerful I am than you, little brother."

I try not to roll my eyes. He might be a rough bastard from the streets of Ethyria, bred in the underground fights, but I could take him. His fists have nothing on the power of fear.

Nineteen

Face My Fears

Rainer

Alessia's voice carries down the hallway. It's soft yet sturdy, loud but controlled. I smile to myself as I stuff my hands into my pockets and follow it. She grows louder until I finally reach the kitchen where she is.

I enter the threshold, leaning against the archway.

Alessia stands barefoot on the counter, her back to me. Her hair is in a long braid, trailing down her back. She wears a plain tunic and leggings, with grime streaking her, and still, my heart skips a beat when she turns. Beautiful is too dull a word to encompass her essence.

Her eyes crinkle adorably at the corners as she addresses the dozens of servants from my court. They pass trays of pastries between them, stuffing their faces as they listen with rapt attention. Witnessing Alessia summon her confidence is enthralling.

Past her, I spot Das Celyn scowling in the shadows across the room. They lift a doughnut and tip their chin in greeting, and I raise a brow in return.

"—and I learned my lesson the hard way, so not a single one of you will hear a *thank-you* from me today—" the room chuckles and titters as Alessia continues, "—but accept these treats as offerings of gratitude."

She gestures across from her, and I strain to see through the crowd. On the counter opposite her, dozens of wine bottles litter the counter.

She hops down, exchanging a few words with folk as she moves through the crowd. Her eyes meet mine when she glances in my direction, and her shoulders soften. A smile blossoms on her lips, and she surges toward me.

"Nice speech," I say, reaching forward and plucking a piece of cobweb off her shoulder.

Her pale neck tints pink, and it creeps up to her cheeks. Her mouth quirks up. "I'm not thanking *you* either, prince."

My lips twitch at the sass, and I don't bother to bring up the fact she's already thanked me recently. "Good." I glance past her at the makeshift revelry in the kitchen. "Interesting place for a formal announcement and a party."

She bites her lip, glancing at her feet. "The throne room is big and cold. It didn't feel right. The kitchen is the heart of any home—it's warm, comforting, and full of life."

"I like it," I tell her honestly. "It's rather unique. Very casual. Very *you.*"

A playful glint shines in her eyes. Already, she's coming back to herself. It confirms that coming here was the right decision. As independent and capable as she is, she thrives with the right care and attention.

"Do you think they'll appreciate the wine and doughnuts?" she asks.

A fae whoops as they run past, guzzling straight from one of the many bottles. I jerk my chin toward them. "Does that answer your question?"

She chuckles. "There's a wine cellar—another level below the court. It's *incredible*," she breathes the word with awe. "This whole place is just... I can't believe it's mine."

I nudge her gently with my elbow. "It's what you always wanted, isn't it? A home?"

Heat crackles between us as she holds my stare, her eyes bouncing between mine. I'm mesmerized by her kind, grey irises. They sparkle with unspoken emotion, growing watery. She blinks rapidly as she glances away.

"Yes," she whispers. "Freedom... a home."

A throat clears, and my head swivels toward the noise. Ezamae stands with an uncharacteristically goofy smile on his face, gripping the lapels of his ornate, blue velvet jacket.

"Can I help you?" I ask flatly.

"Yvanthia has summoned me," he says, looking to Alessia. His silver locks are mussed up as if someone has had their hands running through it.

I sniff the air, picking up on a familiar scent clinging to him... it's an amber perfume that's so unlike the normal crisp, fresh scent of the Aer Prince.

My eyes narrow at him.

He shifts awkwardly, but his smile doesn't fall. "I must heed her call, but I'll return tomorrow to windwalk the fae back to Umb—"

"Don't bother."

His eyes swing to mine, and he arches a brow. "They're staying longer?"

"Yes." I answer Ezamae, though my attention is focused fully on Alessia. "As long as she needs. I want this court up and running entirely before anyone even thinks of returning to Umbra."

She frowns. "But what about your court? Who's going to keep an eye on things?"

I chuckle. That's the least of my concerns. It's not like I even run a court these days—more like I keep a castle and isolate myself from my folk. Plus, Uriel and a handful of other Terra warriors will be around Umbra while I'm gone.

"It'll be fine."

"Are you coming with us?" Alessia asks Ezamae. "To Dovenak?"

He purses his lips together and shakes his head. The twinkle in his eye dims. "Yvanthia relies on me too much to loosen her invisible grip on me."

A tiny pinch of pity sits in my chest for him. But it's immediately followed by a selfish burst of relief that even though she has me forcibly bonded to her for the time being, I am still allowed my freedom. As long as we continue to oversee our respective courts, she's promised to leave us be.

Ezamae is another story, though. Apparently, trying to trick and overthrow the queen will do that. If he hadn't had such useful talents of enchantment, I wonder if she might've tried him for treason. Instead, she benefits from his *power*.

The cunt.

"Once we return, we will discuss…" I pause, stroking my jaw. I don't want to speak the wrong thing aloud, knowing he's glamoured into relaying certain information to Yvanthia. "*Things*."

He nods sharply. "She knows you're going to Dovenak."

My jaw tightens. "I figured."

"And she's okay with it?" Alessia asks, eyes widening.

Ezamae laughs, but it's humorless. "*If* you succeed in eliminating the human queen, it does little to affect Yvanthia. Her biggest concern is her only Lírshadow dying and destabilizing the land again." He tilts his head toward me. "But she knows the grumpy vamp won't let anything happen to you."

I glower darkly at him, and he smiles as if I'm proving his point.

So Queen Wyetta of Dovenak isn't the only one who underestimates us—Queen Yvanthia of Avylon's fae does, too.

Amusement tickles my spine. Let them underestimate us. See how that works out for them.

Ezamae perks up, focusing on something in the hallway behind me; his pale cheeks tinge with color. I glance over my shoulder, but whoever he spotted is already gone. A hint of amber perfume floats into my nostrils, and this time, it hits me.

"*Fern*?" I ask, aghast, whirling back to him.

His smirk grows as he scratches the back of his head. "I have no idea what you're talking about."

Alessia groans. A whisper of air tickles my skin as Ezamae disappears with a *poof*.

"Fern?" I whisper-yell, gauging Alessia's reaction.

She grimaces, shrugging a shoulder. "I know. It's weird."

"Ezamae is messier than Tynan." I grit my teeth. "Absolutely no shame."

"What'd Tynan do now?"

"You don't want to know," I mutter. "If Ezamae can't join us, we're left to journey on foot."

"Can we ride Ken?" she asks, straightening up at the prospect of riding the bear.

"All three of us? There's no way." Kenisius is rather robust in his animi form but not *that* strong.

"Three?"

"Me, you, and… Tynan," I grit out. "His glamour will be useful."

She nods, tapping her chin. "What about Seraphina?"

My eyes narrow. "What about her?"

She grips my wrist with her delicate fingers, tugging me out of the kitchen. We walk a little way down the hallway until we reach a closed door. Alessia opens it, and the candles in the chandelier flare to life on their own, illuminating a study carved of stone like the rest of the court.

She yanks me inside and closes the door behind her. It shuts with a *thwack* that echoes off the high, arched ceilings.

"I figured it's better to talk in private." She bites her lips, blushing.

The wooden desk in the middle of the room sparkles, its wood recently polished. The matching shelves around the room, boasting various artifacts, appear well cared for. My crew put in work today. I'm glad Alessia recognized that and treated them to a party to celebrate their efforts.

Who am I kidding?

Alessia would be the first one to do so.

I snicker to myself, shaking my head.

"What's so funny?" Alessia asks, perching on the edge of a carver chair behind the desk. She runs her hand over the smooth wood, eyeing the many drawers.

"Just thinking of how lucky your folk are to have you as a ruler."

Her face pinches as she tugs open a drawer. "I don't *have* court-folk." She ruffles some papers, tugging out what looks like an old journal with a leather cover and sloppy binding. "They were all exiled, too, apparently. I guess it's good I don't have a full city to oversee like you and Eoin—er, Sennah do."

She glances at me, eyes filled with sorrow and her lips tight. Then she drops her gaze to the journal on the table, carefully opening it.

Stuffing my hands in my pockets, I stride to her, leaning my hip against the desk. "You realize your underground abode is nearly triple the size of my castle, right?"

She mutters something under her breath. I raise a brow, waiting for her to reply.

"Yeah," she says absentmindedly, flipping the page.

"I believe the folk of Spiritus Court resided down here—directly within the court—alongside your family."

She pauses her perusing, scrunching her nose and giving me her attention. "Why underground?"

I sigh, stroking my jaw. "I assume it has something to do with stronger magic. Aer Court is atop a mountain, high in the air. Ignus Court is near a volcano, flourishing near the lava and fire. Though the magic comes from nature, each court sources it differently."

"And Umbra?" Her brows draw together.

I chuckle. "My court is gloomy, thriving in nature's shadows—where nightmares and fears thrive."

Her brows flick up. "Interesting. And Terra has all the hills, water, and flowers... But Spiritus?"

"Spiritus magic is... different than the other courts."

"Darker, you mean?" There's a challenge in her tone and a sparkle in her eye.

"By some accounts. It does come from spirits—which requires death."

She bites her bottom lip, gazing up at me with rapt attention.

"They say the Otherworld—the Spirit World—is deep inside the Spiritus land," I explain. "That's why the spirits tether to the trees here. The trees' roots run deeper than normal, reaching to the Otherworld. The trees absorb the spirits and recycle their magic—"

"Depositing their souls in the Otherworld. I know, I read all about it in a journal…" Something seems to dawn on her because she gasps quietly and sits up straighter. "Maybe that's why my shadow-self is louder down here."

"Does it still want to do wicked things to me?" I tease, my voice low.

"Perhaps," she says, smiling softly. "Or perhaps I'm the one who wants to do those wicked things."

The sass she hits me with sinks into my stomach, turning it over excitedly. I work to keep my expression neutral, not wanting to influence her any further than I already have. She chuckles softly, returning to the book without noticing how much she affects me.

But by the gods, the newfound confidence she wears unravels me. The tenacity with which she employs it is admirable. The only thing that makes her sweetness better is how she perfectly balances it with her darkness—not letting the latter consume her.

I know firsthand how easy it is to lose oneself to the roiling power within. She's battling herself—no denying it—but she's not letting it dismantle her tightly-wielded decency.

I clear the thickness from my throat, trying to focus on anything other than the way her words have me half hard already.

A harsh exhale snaps me from my thoughts.

I arch a brow, amused by her avoidance of me and the conversations we need to have. "Alessia, would you like me to leave you to your… reading?"

"Ah." She glances at me, lips slightly parted as if searching for words. A faint flush colors her cheeks as she downcasts her eyes. "No, sor—I haven't looked through everything in here yet, and I was looking for anything that might give me answers."

She holds an old book up, showing me the weathered covered with grease stains marring the leather.

"Anything interesting?"

A flash of excitement lights up her eyes. "Very, actually." She sets it down on the desk, and then she positions her small frame toward me. "But it isn't what I'm looking for. I can read it later."

"What if you stop seeking answers and just embrace yourself?" I ask softly.

She pulls her bottom lip between her teeth, leaning back in the chair. "I know you love it when I'm violent, Rainer, but I am afraid of my shadow-self. It's not who I want to be."

The grin stretches across my face as a low chuckle leaves me. "It's not violence I'm drawn to, my little rose. I'm turned on by *you* being yourself—without apology or doubt."

"Oh." She shifts, her hands fiddling with the hem of her shirt.

I slide between her chair and the desk, perching atop it. I reach for her, clasping her hand tightly as I pull her to her feet. Widening my legs, I pull her towards me, locking her between my thighs. Our bodies are so close that only a breath separates us. I ache to be engulfed by her essence from now until forever, losing myself to the soft touch of her hands on my waist.

"It's not the violence," I repeat, wanting the words to sink into her bones. I place a hand on her chest, finding comfort in the warmth. It rises and falls rapidly beneath my touch. "It's the fight inside of you. I admire how you possess a heart full of kindness and compassion despite the many ways the world has tried to shatter it. At the same time, you are unflinchingly capable of ferocity when it's warranted."

She stiffens and seems to hold her breath, waiting for what I'll say next.

I smirk, reaching up to twirl a lock of her hair between my fingers. "Your ability to switch between tenderness and brutality commands my deepest respect. Your skill in choosing the right moments to be gentle or when to stand your ground is something I find truly remarkable."

Her lips tighten as she glances down at the meager space between us. "No. I have terrible control over my darkness, and I've made plenty of mistakes."

Placing a finger under her chin, I gently tilt her head up, until she focuses on my face again.

"The only ones you've caused harm to are the ones who've inflicted it upon you first. You've exercised impeccable self-control." I think of how reckless I was when I first came into my bloodlust. I know our powers differ, but Alessia is new to Avylon, to freedom, *and* to her power, yet still, she rises. "You never cease to amaze me, mo róisín."

"What if I hurt someone?" she whispers. "What if I hurt you?"

I study her. The waver in her voice, the way her shoulders begin to curl inward, and that wet glimmer in her eyes tell me everything I need to know. She feels deeply for me, even if she doesn't voice it. But she's scared to keep me close. Afraid of hurting me. Afraid of losing herself.

I draw her closer to me, until our chests brush.

I expect her to push me away or shrink down, but instead, she surprises me and tilts her mouth toward mine. She hovers there. Her warm, chocolatey breath grazes my lips as her eyes flit between my mouth and eyes.

"Don't start something you won't finish, Rainer," she warns.

My smile grows, crinkling my eyes at the corners. Gone is the meek, timid girl I once interpreted her as. Granted, that perception was short-lived. I witnessed her unwavering inner strength long before anyone else did, even herself.

I reach up, running my thumb over her bottom lip. "I will gladly ensure you finish, my sweet rose." My voice is husky, and her breath hitches in response.

The door whines open. My head snaps toward the sound, and Alessia jumps backward as if I've burnt her.

Kenisius enters the room with a grin.

"There you two ar—" He pauses, tilting his head to the side and sniffing the air. His grin morphs into a look of mischief as he wiggles his brow and slowly backs away. "I'll come back."

"Wait," Alessia squeaks out. "We were just discussing our next steps. For Dovenak."

He rocks on his heels, his brows flicking up. An awkward silence stretches in the room.

"Come in," I growl, hopping off the desk.

He scratches the back of his neck before shrugging and kicking the door shut. It slams, and Alessia flinches at the sound.

"Oops," he says, chuckling.

I discreetly adjust my pants before turning around to face the room. Alessia sits back in the chair and Kenisius throws himself into an armchair by the bookshelves.

I sigh, gritting my teeth. I'm annoyed at the intrusion, but part of me is grateful. There's only so much self-control I have when it comes to Alessia. It isn't wise to lose myself to my feelings for her, but there's little keeping me from ravaging her.

If she says the words, I'm hers. In any way she wants me. On my knees, on all fours, tied up, tied down—

The images flit through my mind, and I scrub a hand over my face.

"So, about Seraphina," Alessia says, pulling us back to the conversation we came in here to have in the first place and effectively watering down my lust. "I think we need to keep her close. Her skills could be of use."

"No," I say harshly. "I want her nowhere near you."

She groans. "I don't want to leave her here, though."

"Excuse me." Kenisius waves a hand, fighting a smile. "She's cute. I don't mind keeping an eye. No fur off my back."

"No. *Ezamae* will keep an eye on things. Including her." I can't believe I'm saying the words, but the Aer Prince isn't as awful as I thought. "He is an adept ruler. He can handle things."

She chews her lip, mulling it over. "I trust Ez." Her face softens. "Call it a feeling, but I know he has good intentions. But Seraphina is coming with us."

I clench my jaw, not wanting to argue with Alessia. What she wants goes, and her reasoning isn't horrible. I'll have to work harder to keep my emotions in check, considering I despise the selfish sorceress.

Kenisius slaps his thigh. "Does this mean you're finally ready to storm the human realm, little demon?" He doesn't bother to hide the excitement in his voice.

She nods. "Yeah." Her eyes lock onto mine, and she gives me a soft, private smile that's just for me. "I'm ready to face my fears."

TWENTY
GROW INTO YOUR THORNS
ALESSIA

"**W**hat the feck is this shite?" Tynan scrunches his nose as he sniffs the flask.

Two days later, we stand in the main hallway of my court, preparing to head to Dovenak. Tynan and Ken are dressed nearly identically in dark brown leather armor sets with reinforced chest panels and broad-shoulder pads. Both outfits are adorned with metallic studs and intricate stitching, and a wide belt cinches their waists. Their boots are worn and long broken in.

Daggers are strapped discreetly to their massive thighs and forearms, ready for swift action. I swallow nervously.

"It smells... kind of good, actually," Tynan says, taking another deep inhale.

"It's a mixture of deer blood and human, with a tinge of magic to make it more... flavorful," Seraphina says.

Like me, she wears leather pants with knee-high boots and a lightweight black tunic with an asymmetrical hem, cinched waist, and hood. We're dressed like warriors prepared for battle, although I hope it doesn't come to that. Dressing the part is one thing—being able to actually fight is another, and I'd rather not go there.

"It should tide you on your journey." Sera's eyes flit toward Rainer, and she shrinks slightly. "At the very least, it should keep both of your bloodlust at bay."

"Ah, to keep me from draining all those tempting humans?" Tynan tilts his head back, lifting the small metal square above his mouth. A viscous crimson liquid pours out, and he catches it, swallowing it in one go. Then he runs a hand over his sheared hair, staring at the flask with a pinched expression. "Not bad."

On the other side of him, Ken's gaze meets mine. He rolls his eyes dramatically, gesturing at Tynan.

"*This guy*," he mouths to me.

I chuckle.

"Whose blood did you use?" Rainer asks, voice cold.

"Fern. She offered," Seraphina says. "I didn't take more than a few vials—just enough to replicate the flavor of human blood, but it's mostly deer blood."

Rainer makes a low noise in his throat, like a mix between a scoff and a growl. He stares Seraphina down, clearly not impressed with her assistance.

Like his brother and friend, he's dressed for battle. However, his leathers are the color of the midnight sky and without embell-ishments. It's sleek and functional—snug to his skin. My eyes are glued to his frame, hungrily taking in the cuts of his muscles. A sliver of his skin peeks from the top of the collar, adorned with whirling ink. His ears glint with gold studs, matching the rings on his fingers.

I stare as those slim fingers tap out a rhythm on his thigh. It's the only movement from his otherwise rigid body. A memory of those fingers inside me lights up my mind, and I'm forced to look away before I get too… excited.

When I look up, I accidentally lock eyes with Ken and he gives me a sly, toothy grin. My cheeks flare, and I grimace.

Luckily, he turns his attention back to Seraphina instead of picking on me for what he obviously scents. "So, fake human blood?"

"It tastes pretty real." Tynan rubs his sheared hair, his scarred brow flicking up, impressed.

I blink in surprise. I'm not sure what's more shocking, that Fern willingly offered her blood, that Seraphina can manipulate it in such a way, or that Tynan isn't being a cocky arse for once.

Seraphina stretches out her arm, offering a matching flask to Rainer. "Drink your fill now if you need. I've batched a barrel in the apothecary and can top them off before we leave."

"A barrel?" Ken's eyes widen. He glances around the group, gauging our reactions. "A whole *barrel*? Is no one going to comment on this?"

"*You* just did," Tynan deadpans.

Rainer's arm snakes around my waist as he pulls me flush to his side. He eyes Seraphina's offering warily, his brows low, and his features pinched with disgust.

"Rainer," I whisper, elbowing him gently in the ribs. "Just take it."

"No," he growls. "Don't accept a thing from her." He doesn't bother trying to hide his words from the sorceress.

Dejectedly, she drops her arm. Her mouth turns down, and her forehead creases. "I understand." She takes the empty flask from Tynan. "Let me refill this at least," she mutters. "The more we have, the better. Just in case."

She places the flask in her knapsack, throws it over a shoulder, and scurries away. The metal clinks together as she goes.

Tynan snickers, wiping his mouth with the back of his hand. "Not bad, really."

Kenisius watches her go with a frown. His mouth opens like he's going to say something, but he shakes his head and strokes his beard.

I turn to Rainer.

"You can lecture me all you want, mo róisín, but I refuse to be *nice* to the one who tried to harm you." His voice his flat, his eyes narrow.

I shake my head. "Fair enough. Nice isn't a word I'd use to describe you—but can you try for me?"

Ken and Tynan chuckle.

"Should I be offended?" Rainer asks, gently tugging the end of my braid.

"Of course not." I muffle a laugh behind my hand. He turns to me, his sharp eyes softening like rose petals. His lips twitch, but he keeps his stoic mask on.

"But in all seriousness, I've already chosen to trust Seraphina for the time being," I tell him, inclining my chin slightly in a challenge. "I drank a preventative tonic from her, and everything is fine."

He squints in confusion. "A what tonic?"

My cheeks burn with embarrassment. Ken and Tynan fidget, both having the foresight to turn back to their previous conversation to at least pretend they're not listening in.

Stepping closer to Rainer, my heartbeat doubles as his soft sandalwood and rose scent hits my nose. The heat from his firm, lithe body caresses me, welcoming me. I grit my teeth and lean up toward his ear.

"Preventative," I whisper. "To prevent… pregnancy." He shudders ever so slightly as my lips graze the shell of his ear. "And menstruation," I rush to add so he doesn't get the wrong idea.

When I pull back, his eyes darken and he takes a deep, slow breath.

"Do you plan to partake in activities that require such a tonic?"

I bite down my lip, giving him a coy smile. "Of course not. It's mostly to avoid the monthly bleed and its undesirable side effects."

"Good to know." His voice is strained.

I step out of his space, but his body remains rigid. He keeps his piercing eyes locked on mine, but with each breath, they slowly fade back to their usual pale blue coloring.

"Okay, I'm ready," Seraphina says, interrupting the tense moment as she rejoins us.

Tynan kicks off the wall, and he and Ken grab their bags. We head toward the spiral stair exit.

"So, who's riding me?" Ken smirks. He glances at Seraphina, offering her a wink.

She flips one of her braids over her shoulder. She turns away, but not before I catch a hint of a smile playing on her lips.

I exchange a look with Rainer. He rubs his forehead, shaking his head.

He leans in toward me. "Last chance. Are you sure you want these three to accompany us?"

"I can hear you, little brother." Tynan stops as he reaches the stairs, glaring at us. "I haven't done shite. I'm sober. I drink artificial blood now. I'm a good vamp."

Ken gives Rainer a toothy smile. "I'll be greatly offended if you don't let me join in on this adventure. Little demon already kicked me off of the last one."

"Hey!" I scowl at him. "That's not how it happened and you know it."

He tilts his head back, chuckling.

One by one, we ascend the stairs and exit the tree. The bright sun assaults me. I squint, holding a hand up to defend my sensitive eyes. It's always a transition returning to daylight from below the earth.

We head to the northeast treeline, where the Cursed Wood begins. At the black roses standing guard, we come to a halt.

"The Gleam isn't far," Rainer says, running a hand over his jaw. "Me, Tynan, and Kenisius should be okay. We'll move quickly, and we'll protect you."

"And Seraphina," I say, reminding him I'm not the only one susceptible to the woods. Then again, even *he* is affected now that he has a fear: losing me.

A warmth spreads through my chest, mingling with guilt.

Rainer's expression darkens as he stares into the trees. "You might be better off riding Kenisius—just in case, Alessia."

"What about me?" Seraphina waves her hand awkwardly as she looks around the group. "Should I be concerned?"

"Yes," Rainer says flatly.

I nudge him with my elbow, but he continues to scowl.

"She tried to kill you," he says.

"Stop bringing that up."

He's right, my shadow-self says. *Who cares what happens to her? Let her face her fears.*

"Sera, you ride Ken," I say, ignoring my shadow-self and the truth behind its words. Mustering up my courage, I add, "I have my... power to protect me."

Rainer's lips twitch with amusement. He arches a brow at me. I incline my chin and shrug.

"There she is," he murmurs. "Fearless."

"Trying to be."

He likes me. My shadow-self purrs, preening at his attention. *Yes, yes, yes, let's show him how fearless we can be.*

The impulse sends a heady vibration of desire through me. It's short-lived, though, because Tynan grunts, surging past us. He crashes through the trees at his usual pace.

"How isn't he affected?" I ask, squinting in the direction he went. "Does he have no fears?"

"Of course he does," Rainer mutters, shoving his hands into his pockets. "We all do."

Ken chuckles. He reties his hair into a messy low bun. "The bastard is a born and bred fighter. He doesn't go down easily."

"*I* can take him down just fine," Rainer says. "But he's used to the woods and their tricks. It doesn't faze him as much as my direct magic. Just as Kenisius and I have learned to fight through it, so has he. We've built resilience."

I can take his cocky arse down, too, my shadow-self says.

My insides spasm as my vision dims. In a quick burst, cool darkness shoots from my palm. It stretches like a long tendril all the way to Tynan, shoving him in the back. He yelps as he's thrust forward. He faceplants on the muddy trail, and the darkness recoils back into my skin before he can get up.

I gape in shock as I slowly comprehend what just happened.

"The feck was that?!" Tynan yells, whirling toward us with narrowed eyes.

Even from this distance, I can see the mud all over his leathers. He brushes himself off aggressively.

Ken cackles openly while Seraphina stifles her laughter in the crook of her arm. I glance at Rainer, wanting to gauge his reaction to the incident. He watches me with a smirk that grows and grows until his dimple pops out. Tynan curses at us and continues storming off.

I stand there shaking and staring at the hands that betrayed me.

"Naughty little demon." Ken shakes his head as the laughter tapers off. "Come on. Let's get our tails grooving."

Ken's body shakes as his bones snap and crack. Seraphina recoils, her mouth gaping as she watches his tall, broad body contort and bend into a new shape. Thick, brown fur spurts out, and his kind, rugged face morphs into a snout with a black nose and beady eyes.

"Well, shite," she says, blinking rapidly. "You're even cuter than before."

Ken, unable to talk in his bear form, snorts and stomps his front paws excitedly. She pets him, crooning in his face.

"Get on him," Rainer says coldly, his previously kind expression fading. He narrows his eyes at Seraphina, pointing to Ken. "Lest an unfortunate accident befall you in the woods."

I sigh, torn between scolding him or laughing at his savagery. Not long ago, his brutal, beautiful scowl was directed at me.

I love it almost as much as I love his dimple.

"Can you at least try not to actively be an arse." I settle on the half-hearted admonishment.

Rainer smirks at me, shrugging a shoulder. "At least *I* didn't push her."

My cheeks flare with mortification. "That wasn't me," I mutter.

We are one, it reminds me.

Though I must admit, there's a great relief that my shadow-self's outburst was playful this time instead of violent. Maybe Rainer is right, and I need to embrace it as part of me instead of separating it so harshly. Perhaps getting away from Spiritus Court—and Avylon—will do us some good.

Sera gracefully climbs atop Ken, gripping the fur around his neck. As she adjusts the hem of her tunic, she slides slightly to the side and gasps before Ken shimmies to help her level out. They take off into the woods, with her muscular thighs flexing around his furry body and her braids whipping out behind her.

"You sure you don't judge me," I ask Rainer nervously once we're alone. "For having this… darkness inside of me?"

His eyes crinkle at the corners as he takes me in, contemplating his words. "No, Alessia, I don't. The only reason your shadow appears so dark is because of how bright your light shines." He holds out a hand for me, and I accept it instinctively. "The stark contrast between the self you show to the world and the self you stuff down is highly entertaining."

See, he likes me. Let me out.

"Shush," I mumble. "Stay inside me and stay out of this."

Rainer makes a noise in his throat, turning toward me with a curious look. "'Shame lies not in the possession of darkness, but in the refusal to master it,'" he mutters, a faraway look in his eyes. "It's something I heard in the Ephemeral Dungeons. It applies to you as well."

"I'm not ashamed," I say, but the words are tar in my mouth.

Am I ashamed of my power? Of my ancestral magic?

Of myself?

I shake my head. I'm not going to *master* my shadow-self any time soon. That much, I know. I can't even keep it inside of me.

"You can do it, Alessia," Rainer whispers, keeping his voice low and steady. "You once believed in me, now I need you to have that same belief in yourself."

Chewing my lip, I let his words sink in. "But I can't control the shadow. I don't know *how*."

He shrugs casually, his eyes sparking. "That's the beauty of it. You try. You learn. You make mistakes. You try again."

"Those mistakes are deadly."

"Not learning how to manage your magic is deadlier," he says, lifting a brow in challenge. "You already know the worst that can happen." He takes another step closer. "Now let's find out what the best that can happen is."

As I absorb Rainer's words, a mixture of emotions surges through me—first, a wave of doubt, an inner quiver confirming my lack of confidence. But amidst the doubt, a flicker of determination ignites. It's as if a fire has been kindled within me—that same spark of hope I wish Fern would hold onto.

I can't let it die out.

Rainer steps closer again, cupping my cheek. "I believe in you, mo róisín."

My gut constricts, nervous about the risks, but I nod anyway. Instead of following the fear, I allow myself to become *fearless*, like Rainer thinks I am.

"I need your help getting through the Cursed Wood unaffected," I whisper, directing my words to my shadow-self. "Let's work together."

A taunting laugh rises from inside me. Focusing on the scent of damp earth and musk, I stand tall and proud, not letting the shadow's restless writhing unsettle me. A quiet hush fills the air, along with a sense of anticipation. As if it's a living entity of its own, the shadow begins to expel itself from my skin.

Rainer watches in awe, his face softening as it roams the dark cloud pouring from me.

It expands around us, rising like a wall. It contracts, forcing Rainer and me closer and blocking us from the world. His pinky brushes mine, and for a second, all I can see is *him*.

The rest of the world has faded away, keeping us safe from all the bullshite out there.

The wall shimmers, thinning out in front of us until it's translucent. Now that we can see our path, reality crashes back in.

"We should get moving," I say. Instead of allowing myself to be distracted by the handsome, tortured fae prince, I focus on my shadow. "And *you* behave yourself, or you're going back inside of me."

Rainer's lips twitch in amusement. "If I'm naughty, does the same fate befall me?"

"Hush," I tell him, blushing furiously. "You're not helping matters."

He smirks, and I exhale, allowing myself to relax into the safety of his presence—and my shadow, I suppose.

"I'm *trying*, okay?" I mutter, tucking my braid into my hood.

A quick, quiet laugh slips from his lips. "You are delightful, little rose. It's about time you grow into your thorns."

TWENTY-ONE
BURN THAT FECKIN HOUSE DOWN
ALESSIA

"**W**hy are there so many people?" Ken whispers.

Ken, Sera, Tynan, Rainer, and I huddle in the trees at the edge of Edvin and Nilda's property, having made it through the Gleam without incident.

I had expected tiredness to overcome me from using my shadow. Instead, I'm filled with vigor, frantically awaiting the next leg of our journey.

Deep down, I know it's because that man's death fueled it. A sickening sludge sits in my stomach, and I try to push it aside. Dwelling on that does none of us any good. At least now, my shadow-self is contented and ready to heed my orders. But for how long?

The thought sends a trickle of fear down my spine. What happens when it's no longer appeased?

Squatting low to the ground, I stay behind a fallen log, peering over its moss-covered surface.

This time of year, Lyson's forest is filled out, concealing us within its dense foliage.

Last time I was here, the woods were frigid and barren, kissed by winter. I ran frightfully, burdened by grief's baggage and fearing for my life. The icy forest symbolized my heart at the time—cold, still, and lifeless.

Now, upon my return, the symphony of bird chatter and lush vegetation represent my renewal. Like the forest, I have thawed.

But a closer look reveals the forest floor is carpeted with decaying leaves and scattered, dead branches, creating a natural mosaic of decomposition. It embodies the hidden depths of darkness within me, kept well-hidden beneath my exterior.

People spill out of Edvin's old house, milling about the yard. The stables sit adjacent to us, halfway between the woods and the house, slightly off to our right. Just beyond the stables is the pasture, with horses lazily grazing.

Despite the warm midday air, a bonfire stretches between the house and stables, bringing scents of charred meat to our noses. A loud voice cracks through the air, and hearty laughter follows.

From what I can hear, their accents are thicker and less refined than Edvin's usual company.

"They don't sound familiar," I say, squinting. Old, uncomfortable emotions bubble up at being back here.

They will never hurt you again. They're gone.

I nod in agreement, swallowing down my unease. Things are different now. *I'm* different now. That old house is nothing more than four walls and a roof, and I won't let it haunt me.

"Are you doing okay, mo róisín," Rainer whispers, gently squeezing my hip.

His presence immediately settles me. Between him—and surprisingly, my shadow's reminder—everything will be okay.

"In the ways that matter, yeah, I am." I smile up at him, and he subtly nods back. His attention stays locked on me, and I know he won't let anything happen to me ever again.

I *won't let anything happen to you*, my shadow-self adds.

I refocus my attention on the distance. Although they're a little too far away to make out all the details of their faces, they wear matching deep green leather tunics and black trousers. Silver accents on their buckles and arrowheads, slung in pouches, catch the sunlight as they move.

A few of them wield bows, shooting at a target attached to a hay bale beside the house.

Soldiers.

"I count sixteen men," Tynan grumbles.

"No females?" Seraphina whispers, looking at me with her brow drawn tight.

We're so close our shoulders brush, and I'm surprised Rainer hasn't ripped me from her proximity yet with the way he's watching us with sharp eyes.

"The men and women don't really... share hobbies," I say, trying to communicate the human's pointed differences between genders.

"That's weird," Seraphina says, huffing. "Makes our job easier."

"How so?" My nose crinkles.

She chuckles softly. "Men are idiots."

Tynan, on Seraphina's other side, elbows her. "Hey."

Her head snaps in his direction. "I said *men* as in hu*man*—not faerie males." She turns back to me, rolling her eyes.

"Look," Ken says, pointing at the ground nearby.

The field, neglected for the past few months since Edvin and Nilda's deaths, lies between us and the house's maintained yard. Weeds flourish in the transition from spring to summer. A well-worn path cuts through the knee-high grass, a trail from the house to the woods.

How long have these men been here? *Why* are they here?

"Bet they've been scouting the Gleam," Ken says. He goes still, cocking his head and straining. "They're talking about a party. At the queen's. In just a couple of days... oh, delightful. No one is coming to check on these feckers until afterward—they're awaiting further instruction."

The bellowing voice carries across the field again. I can barely make out the voice.

"...used to live here. Little Tradeling with a tight arse." More laughter.

Rainer balls his hand into a fist, and his back goes ramrod straight. He and Ken share a look, and I know they heard whatever the man said.

"What is it?" I ask.

Rainer's eyes flash dark, and he stays deathly quiet, focusing his lethal gaze on the distant house. He leans closer to me. "Was anyone else you cared for left behind?"

His head turns toward mine, and suddenly, our faces are only a breath apart. His eyes flit to my lips, then slowly drag up my face.

"N—no," I stammer, my hands growing clammy. "You would've known about them."

He sets his jaw. "Good. Just checking before I..."

I wait, but he doesn't go on. He turns forward, closing his eyes.

"Before you what?"

A chorus of deep screams slices through the air. Tynan and Ken both chuckle, lurching to their feet. They reach for their weapons as they break out into a run, seemingly working in tandem to advance on the group. The sun glints off their blades, and I squint, looking away from the brightness.

"My mama always told me not to run with scissors." Seraphina sighs. "I'd imagine a dagger is even worse."

Rainer stands, holding a hand out for me. I put my hand in his, and he pulls me to my feet. He trembles slightly, before releasing me and focusing forward.

I watch him storm toward the house in awe. The entire group of men have erupted into chaos. Some run in circles, clawing at their hallucinations. A few have dropped onto the ground, curled into fetal positions.

But just like Eoin's ballroom not too long ago, every single man is affected. My stomach tickles at the sight. It's easy to forget just how powerful the Prince of Fear is since I don't often see this side.

"He's terrifying," I say breathlessly to Seraphina.

She breaks her stare on the distant scene to study me. "That's nothing compared to what *you* can do, you know."

I pause. "What?"

She gives me an assessing look, then shrugs, heading toward the house. I take my time catching up, not wanting to rush after anyone.

When I reach the scene, their screams reverberate through my skull. The tall grass gives way to a maintained section of the yard. The men thrash about, roiling in the grass. Ken and Tynan stand amidst them, humorously taking in the sight. Rainer stands off to the side, near the bonfire.

"What if someone hears and comes to investigate?" I ask Rainer over the ruckus.

He rests a foot casually on a nearby log, and his hand taps out a lazy rhythm on his thigh. His eyes narrow as he stares into the flames contemplatively.

"No one is coming." He points to Ken as he passes. "These are the soldiers sent to protect the Gleam, after all. There's no one left to protect *them*."

Ken doesn't even break a sweat. The brutish male drags two men by an ankle—one in each hand—as they writhe and cry out behind him, their hands clawing at the grass. He throws us a grin as if he's having the best time of his life. Tynan passes a second later, dragging *four* men behind him—with two ankles in each of his massive grips.

"Show off," Ken says, barking a laugh.

They make it to the stablehand's quarters and toss the forms inside before trudging back to the group, presumably to repeat the action.

Soon, many of the screams are muffled, and the rest have morphed into whimpers.

I swallow the thickness in my throat, drawing closer to Rainer and lowering my voice. "You're not going to kill them, are you?"

I freeze at how dark blue his eyes are when he looks at me. His lips carve out a mischievous smile, and he laughs lowly as if the question amuses him.

"Of course," he says. "The things they were saying..." His face hardens, and he strokes his jaw, glancing away. "I refuse to let them think another thought of their own. They belong to their fear until they perish, deservingly so, mo róisín."

Bile rises in my throat. As Ken and Tynan pass again, I turn away, not wanting to remember any of the faces.

"What if they're innocent?" I ask quietly.

My shadow thrashes around inside me. *You know they're not.*

Rainer laughs dryly. "Those weren't the words of *kind* men."

Seraphina stands off to the side, her face void of emotion as she watches Ken and Tynan drag the fear-drugged men into the stablehouse.

The dark energy within me pulses, but I fight to stay focused. I need to keep it contained. It takes all of my effort. My head grows light, and my limbs become heavy, but the voice stays quiet.

Rainer reaches up, gently cupping my chin. He tilts my head back to him. "Look at me," he whispers.

His eyes are so dark they're almost black. A tremor courses through his body again, and I wonder how hard he's fighting to use his fearcaller magic like this and stave off the obvious bloodlust threatening to take over.

I stand firm, refusing to cower in the face of his power. Oddly, my shadow settles down.

"If we don't do this now, they will only cause problems later. We are sparing the truly innocent."

"You're not afraid?" I ask him, searching his face for any sign of struggle. "Of losing control?"

He chuckles again, that dimple briefly popping out before he swallows it down. "No, mo róisín, I'm not afraid of that anymore."

"Why not?" It comes out in a breathy whisper, betraying my disbelief.

"Because you showed me I don't have to be afraid. *You* don't fear me." His dark eyes scrutinize every detail of my face, and he's slow to continue speaking.

He releases me and turns back to the fire. A bead of sweat trickles from his temple down the side of his face. He makes no move to wipe it away. I can't tell if it's from the heat of the fire combined with the armor he's wearing or if it's from the mental focus he's using to wield his power.

"They're easier to control than the fae," he says without looking at me. "Don't worry about me."

"I always worry about you," I say softly.

Not wanting to disturb his focus further, I back away and join Seraphina.

"They're not innocent," she says, wearing a hardened stare. "If that makes you feel better."

"How do you figure?"

"I can read their auras—energy and intention." She faces me, arms crossed in front of her chest. "That's the real reason why Ez sent me to your side in Terra Court—to find out if you were as innocent as you seemed."

I nod, turning away from her. Tension coils in my jaw as my attention flits from the wretched house where I was raised to Tynan and Ken, who drag more men into the stablehouse, to Rainer, who stands rigid beside the fire, and back to Seraphina—the female who tried to kill me.

Never would I have envisioned being here, *free*. Working alongside the fae. Being fae myself and causing destruction.

"Could you feel my darkness?" I whisper. Did she sense what was inside of me before I did?

She nods, grimacing. "But you have a light about you, too. Your intention is pure. Just as Ez's is. We need a leader like him, and I hope you'll support him. He would do great things for our realm."

"You really care about him, don't you," I ask softly. With her opening up more, I'm starting to see a new side of the female. I don't think she's a threat at all, honestly. At least not to me. Not anymore.

She doesn't reply at first, but then she nods slowly. Her chin juts out as she stares at the scene before us with a hard expression. "Your darkness is different from theirs—I want you to know that." She gestures toward the stablehand's quarters, where all the men have been locked away. Rainer, Tynan, and Ken stand beside the door, murmuring amongst themselves. "Theirs is... vile. Wretched. Similar to the energy that was dissipating from that couple you..."

"Edvin and Nilda?" I offer before she can say *killed*.

"Yes."

Warm relief trickles through me, and it helps me feel slightly better about who I am and what I've done. There might be a bloodthirsty shadow within me, and I might be a demon, but at least I'll never be *evil*.

With a new sense of confidence and self-acceptance, I roll my shoulders back and stand tall—like Sennah once taught me to do before she knew I was a princess, too. This time, I don't avert my eyes as Ken and Tynan grab whiskey bottles and return to the stablehouse.

My muscles tense in anticipation as they hurl them at the door.

Glass shatters. The liquid stains the wood, saturating it with the pungent smell of alcohol. They snag a couple more bottles from the ground beside them and launch them through the windows.

The horses in the pasture buck and neigh.

"Wait!" I yell. I bolt toward the pasture. Gripping the latch, I pull it back and throw open the old wooden gate. It creaks as it swings open. The horses pause for a moment. "Come on!"

A couple edge forward curiously, and then they pick up their pace. Their hooves hit the ground in tempo with my frantic heartbeat, and they kick up dirt as they bolt past me.

They'll likely wander to another pasture nearby or a farm, or maybe they'll run wherever they came from initially. Wherever they go, it's better off than trapped here with these wretched men.

Dead men, soon.

I jog back to Sera's side, and she claps my back, and we share a mutual look of understanding. Rainer turns, meeting my eyes. His expression is entirely blank, void of external emotion. Instinctually, I give a soft, quick nod. He returns it, turning back to the building. Without hesitation, he scoops a kerosene lamp from the ground and chucks it through the shattered window.

The liquid ignites instantly, erupting into a brilliant, violent blaze. Rainer must drop his power because the screams ripping through the air suddenly change. The men begin pounding on the door as flames leap up the walls, consuming the building with an insatiable hunger.

A few of the men scramble towards the open window, climbing on one another in an attempt to escape. Tynan hisses, baring his fangs and prowling forward. He chucks a brick through the window, and it slams into someone's face.

I recoil, turning away as my stomach churns. The heat licks my skin and I back up to put space between me and the blaze.

Ken, Tynan, and Rainer stride toward us, unhurried. Tynan wears an impish grin, Ken strokes his beard, and Rainer's demeanor is casual—unbothered. The flames shoot up behind them, creating a gruesome backdrop—a reminder of what they are. What they're capable of.

Despite their kindness, they are not to be underestimated.

"We should go," Rainer says when he reaches me—my dark, beautiful nightmare. His eyes are still nearly black, and sweat beads on his brow.

"Wait," I whisper.

The main house captures my attention as it holds the weight of my most painful memories. The scars from the horrors I endured as a child have stayed with me, casting a long shadow over my life. Leaving it standing feels like a betrayal to the little girl who lives on within me.

"Go ahead," Rainer tells the group without taking his eyes off me. "Stay out of sight. We'll meet you at the tree line in a moment."

He reads me like an open book because he whirls on his heels, striding over to the bonfire, snatching something up. The small fire looks innocent beside the roar of the stablehand's quarters.

Felix's old home.

The image of his face crosses my mind. At last, his memory no longer burdens me with guilt. I realize now that he was fully aware of what was happening in that house, but he chose not to assist me. The more I reflect on it, the clearer it becomes that he used me. He knew that I seldom ventured outside, had never truly lived, and hadn't had the opportunity to develop, mature, and find my own identity. I was enslaved—abused—and instead of protecting me, he took advantage of me for his pleasure.

Ultimately, his worthless and belated apology led to his downfall. He died trying to appease his own guilt.

That is not my fault.

Burning these buildings down allows me to release any lingering responsibility I might harbor about Felix, Edvin, and Nilda's deaths. They crafted their own paths in life—all I did was protect myself.

Release it all, my shadow encourages.

It had stayed quiet much of this time instead of thirsting for the souls, which surprises me. It's almost like it's defaulting to Rainer's magic—letting *him* protect us.

I can't make sense of it, but honestly, I don't care as long as it doesn't cause problems for us.

Rainer returns a moment later, handing me a bottle of whiskey and another kerosene lamp. He pulls a box of matches from between his knuckles, pulling out a small wooden stick and striking it against the box. It bursts to life, and he lowers the flame into the glass chimney, lighting the lamp.

No words pass between us, but he walks with me as I turn toward Edvin's main house.

Adrenaline surges through me, my heart pounding so hard I can feel it in my throat. I feel like I'm moving in slow motion as I launch the whiskey bottle through the kitchen window. The shattering sound is barely audible over the crackling and popping of the other fire. With a trembling hand, I pull back, then hurl the lit lamp through the broken window.

As soon as it collides with the alcohol, the flames roar to life, quickly grabbing hold of the wooden walls and furniture. Intense heat blasts my face, and I quickly turn, jogging a good distance away.

I bend over, resting my hands on my knees and catching my breath. It comes in quick, shallow pants.

Rainer appears beside me, and rubs my back in small circles, remaining silent.

Other than the fire's hiss and the sound of debris crashing down as both houses burn, I realize my mind is entirely silent. There's no little voice there trying to coerce me.

No shadow-self pressuring me to commit such a violent act.

I did this myself.

I *wanted* to burn that feckin house down.

Twenty-Two

My Newly Darkened Soul

Alessia

A hysterical laugh bubbles up, and my eyes water. Rainer's hand quivers against my back. I straighten, turning to him, concerned. His face is pale, sweat lining his forehead. I meet his glossy eyes, instinctually knowing what's wrong.

"You need to recharge," I say.

"I'm fine, mo róisín."

"When is the last time you fed?" I know he hasn't touched Fern, and he denied Sera's juice-blood. "You're clearly drained, and we're just starting our journey."

I pull my hood back, moving my braid from my shoulder and baring my neck to him.

"Drink," I order.

"No," he says in a strained voice.

He turns, moving away from me, but I grab his wrist. Even in his weakened state, he's strong enough to pull free, but he lets me tug him back to me.

His eyes blaze to life as he narrows his gaze on me. "I don't do well with being told what to do."

"And I never thought I'd light the lord's house on fire, but here we are. People—*fae* change."

He smirks at this, firmly gripping my chin. His eyes flit to my lips, then drag up my face. "I am not drinking from you."

I hold his stare, refusing to cower under his intense gaze. Sweat prickles at my spine from the infernos not too far away. "We need to go, but I'm not moving until you refuel yourself."

He sighs, his lip curling up at the side. "You beautiful, stubborn creature."

"Drink from *me*, or you drink Seraphina's concoction." I raise a brow in challenge.

He drops my chin, running that hand through his hair. "I'm weak against you, mo róisín."

My heart flutters as he steps closer.

"Who is stubborn now," I murmur, fisting his hair and drawing him closer.

The flames behind him rise higher, skimming the sky. There should be a sense of urgency as if we should hurry before we get caught, but I only feel an unexpected peace. Even with the disturbing, sickeningly sweet odor of burnt flesh and the symphony of screams, I'm unbothered in Rainer's presence.

Rainer drags his nose up the column of my throat, inhaling greedily. "I refuse to taste anyone but you."

I go still, releasing his hair. But I don't move away.

He pulls back, giving me an apologetic look. "Your blood is much too decadent. Incomparable to anyone else's, if I'm being honest."

I chuckle, pulling him back to my neck. "Just drink, you bastard."

He draws closer again. His hand wraps around the back of my neck, but he pauses, his lips tugging downward.

"What is it?" I say, growing impatient with the want for him to touch me—to take his fill.

"There's no Eoin here to heal your wounds."

"We have Sera and her healing salve."

"It's a limited supply," he says flatly.

"I'll be fine."

"I'd rather not give the humans fodder for gossip. It could unravel our disguise."

"What disguise?" I laugh, touching his pointy ear. "You're very clearly fae—all of you. They don't make humans with quite the same beauty."

A low growl builds in his throat. "You better be referring to me, not my brother—or Kenisius."

I smirk. "I meant what I said. *All* of you have ethereal beaut—"

He pounces on me, descending into my sensitive underarms with his supple fingers, tickling me. I screech, wiggling until I'm breathless, and he finally pulls back.

"Fine. You're the most handsome of them all," I whisper when I finally catch my breath.

Color floods his cheeks as he turns away, as if not wanting me to see how my words affect him.

"We'll need disguises later," he says, clarifying what he meant a moment ago. "And the less Tynan has to change with his glamour, the better. It costs him a great deal in blood consumption."

"So what do you propose?" I ask, my voice growing husky. "If biting my neck is too… inconvenient."

His expression grows intense as his eyes drag down my body, landing on my inner thigh.

I squirm, remembering the feel of him between my legs. Slowly, I reach up to undo the button of my pants. He watches wordlessly as I pop it open. Then, I lean back into the grass, looping my fingers in the waistband.

"Wait," he growls, eyes flickering. His hand lashes out to stop mine. "Are you sure?"

I feign confusion. "It's just a little bite to help out a friend. Of course, I'm sure."

"Friend," he repeats hoarsely.

His grip loosens, and he pulls back, allowing me to wiggle my pants down to my knees. I lie back, presenting myself as an offering.

A few tense moments pass, and I prop myself back up on my elbows when he doesn't move. "What're you waiting for?" I gesture to the roaring fires behind him. "We don't have all day."

A dark chuckle leaves him. "This isn't going to work."

My nose wrinkles. "What's not going to—ahhh—"

He grips my left boot, yanking it off in a swift motion. Then he does the same to the other, and my body jerks with the force. A disbelieving laugh pops out of my mouth. Once my feet are free, he tugs my pants down around my ankles and then effortlessly plucks them clean off my body.

Reaching up, he plants his hands on the inside of my knees. His eyes stay locked on mine as he gently presses down, spreading me open in front of him.

"Just friends," he growls.

Before I can respond, he dives between my legs, plunging his teeth into my fleshy inner thigh.

I gasp, letting the euphoria of his bite sweep me away. After a few gentle suckles, he pops free. He wipes his mouth, pulls back, and takes me in.

"You're not the same girl you once were, Alessia," he says, running his finger across the small wounds I know are now on display. He stares at them with reverence, then dives back in for more. I whimper, roiling in the grass beneath him. He places his palm on my stomach, his fingers splayed out. It's less of a demand not to move and more of a claim. I'm his to feast on.

"I—sorry," I say meekly, my chest rising and falling vigorously with the adrenaline. "If I've been too feisty."

He pops free, narrowing his gaze on me. "Don't apologize, or I'll punish you for that."

I suck in a sharp breath. Before I can ask what the punishment would be, he descends on me again. This time, his mouth hovers over my underwear, his warm breath heating my neediest part. The heat of his lust is incomparable to the fire roaring behind us.

I squirm, desperate to draw closer to his skin, wanting friction.

"Just friends," he whispers, his lips grazing my underwear. He hovers there momentarily, just breathing, with each exhale teasing me. I wiggle, begging for him to lean forward and add pressure.

Instead, he shakes his head and laughs sarcastically. Then, he stands, storming off.

For a second, I lie back stunned, with no pants on and two tiny bloodied holes in my thigh.

A rage floods me, dragging me under. I push myself to a seat. "You will *not* leave me like this, Rainer Rohan Iorworth!"

A blast of my anger shoots out—in the form of a shadow strand. The dark wisp stretches toward Rainer's retreating form and wraps around him like a fist. Effortlessly, it drags him back and plants him in front of me.

His expression is unlike anything I've ever seen, his mouth agape and his brows practically touching his hairline. He seems to shake it off, quickly reverting to his usual scowl.

"You're playing dirty," he says, eyes flickering with intrigue.

"You are going to help me clean up, then you're going to help me lace up those damn boots." I point to said boots, unimpressed with the amount of lacing required to get them on and off.

His lips curve slightly at the ends, and he bows his head. "Yes, my rose."

He drops to his knees, heeding my requests. First, he licks up the tiny bit of blood trailing from my wound, then he locates my pants and helps me slide them on.

I grin at the top of his head as he pulls my boots on, lacing them with tender care.

The shadow recoils deep inside me, pleased and purring like a cat as it snuggles against my newly darkened soul.

TWENTY-THREE
WHAT LIES AHEAD
ALESSIA

We join the others in the woods, moving away from the wretched, acrid scent of charred wood and flesh. I wait for that horrible prickle of guilt to claw at me from the inside, but it doesn't come. In its place is a steady acceptance—not necessarily a numbness nor a disappointment.

It's a closure. It's what I was hoping for when burning down the lord's home.

Perhaps I am genuinely changing, becoming like the fae around me. Months ago, all of this cruelty and death would've devastated me, but I've learned to make peace with the grey area of life. Not everything is as simple as *goodness* or *evil*.

I'm tired of constantly being torn apart. Instead, I'm acting against those who cause harm, dismantling their ability to hurt others.

Ken gently punches my shoulder. "You will never stand in that vile house again, little demon."

I turn, watching the structures burn. I wince at the brightness.

Tynan sniffs the air, his gaze dropping to my thigh. I glance down to make sure I'm not bleeding through my pants. Rainer was gentle with his bite, tidy even, and the wounds quickly stopped bleeding.

"I'm shocked you're not fully human. You *do* smell delightful," Tynan says. His looming presence draws closer as he leans toward me.

It's more annoying than predatory. My gut instinct says Tynan is harmless... at least to me.

The air grows tense. Tynan inhales deeply, a groan budding in his throat as he hovers over me.

His body heat disappears instantly, leaving only a cool breeze as he's ripped away from me. A loud thump echoes through the air as Tynan crashes onto his back. A strangled gasp escapes his lips. Rainer's knee firmly presses against his neck, pinning him to the ground.

"Touch her again, and I won't be so nice next time," Rainer hisses in his brother's face.

Ken chuckles. Seraphina watches me. Her eyes crinkle in the corner, and she presses her lips together as if fighting a smile.

Tynan lets out a grunt as Rainer releases him. He extends his hand, only for Rainer to reject it with a slap and turn away.

"I didn't touch her," Tynan mutters, rolling his eyes and pushing himself to a stand.

"Close enough," Rainer shoots back. "Too close."

Tynan cocks a brow. "I thought you were *just friends*," he mimics the words Rainer said to me when he was between my legs.

My face heats with embarrassment, knowing that Tynan—and likely Ken with his shifter senses—heard us. I yank my hood up, desperate to hide away.

Tynan gives a sharp laugh. "Can't blame a male for trying."

Rainer growls. "Try elsewhere. She is *mine*." His voice is low and gravely, brokering no room for argument.

My stomach tumbles. There's something about his possessive-ness that gives me a deep sense of satisfaction.

After being used, abused, and manipulated my entire life, there's something beautifully reassuring about knowing there's someone there who would do *anything* to protect me. He might call me his, but he doesn't own me. Not in the way I'm used to being owned. No. I'm *his* in the purest meaning of the claim. His to protect. His to support. His to live life with.

Perhaps it's the fact that I know he's mine as much as I'm his. Or maybe it's that I know he would protect me at all costs.

The thought nearly stops me in my tracks.

I *want* to do life with him.

I don't want to be just friends.

Ken clears his throat, leaning down toward me. "You look aw-fully smug over there."

I bite my lip, glancing away as my face heats.

"I don't blame her," Seraphina says, dramatically fanning her-self. "That was *stirring*. Can someone claim *me* like that?"

Tynan throws an arm around her. "Sure thing, beauty." He leans toward her neck, inhaling deeply. She laughs and tries to shove him off. "You smell like a snack, too."

Ken snakes a foot out, tripping Tynan.

"Okay, can we go now?" I ask quickly before the males begin brawling.

Tynan jumps up, glaring at Ken, who snickers with Sera.

Rainer meets my eyes, and the tension in his jaw dissipates. He runs a hand through his hair and exhales heavily. Then, he nods.

"We need to head south," he says.

Both the palace and mines are south.

"Ryalle is about a day's ride away," I add. "Longer on foot."

"Yes." He nods. "And a group like us will attract attention. Especially after…" He waves toward the waning flames across the field. "*That.*"

"That wasn't very smart," Seraphina says, giving Rainer a scolding look.

"It wasn't about being *smart*," Rainer shoots back. "It was retribution."

Ken sidesteps to Sera, nudging her with his elbow. She glances at him, and he subtly shakes his head in warning. She sighs and crosses her arms, but she drops the fight.

"This sends a message," Rainer drawls, inspecting his fingernails as if utterly bored with Sera's input. "The humans have been much more measured than we initially expected. I theorize they're not as rash and ineffectual as they want us to think. They'll know this was an attack from the fae. They'll take time to reassess their next steps. We have a few days before retaliation—at the very least."

"How do you figure?" Sera asks. Her tone is no longer challenging. Instead, she sounds genuinely concerned.

Rainer surprises me by not growling at her. Instead, he drops his hand and gives her his attention. "Those were prisoners—not real soldiers but decoys. Plus, the queen is preoccupied with her fête."

Ken snorts. "I bet we'll find answers at her party. Call it a bear-hunch, but whatever she's planning, it has to do with her announcement."

"If we leave now, we'll make the fête," Rainer says.

"You're certain it's wise?" Sera asks. "What if it's a setup?"

Rainer presses his lips together, staring into the trees. "If it were a setup, she'd have a real army stationed in range of the Gleam, ready to attack upon provocation..."

"She can't guarantee we'd travel all the way south for her little shindig," Ken adds. "She doesn't know we want the iron."

Tynan plants his boot on a fallen log, resting his arm on his bent knee. "The owl and the bear have been scouting, keeping an eye on things. We're a mystery to the humans. They don't know shite about us, but they surely shite their pants about us." He laughs.

"Let's go," Rainer says, gesturing for the group to move.

We start walking, trailing along the edge of the forest. Tynan and Ken lead, with me and Sera following behind. Rainer takes up the rear.

I glance over my shoulder at him. His eyes are lowered, focused on my arse. Slowly, he drags his gaze upward until it latches onto mine.

"I like those pants," he murmurs, smirking.

Pixie wings flutter in my stomach as I face forward. I step around a rotting stump, careful not to lose footing on the mossy rocks.

"We should head slightly west," I say to the group. "Rather than straight south." From what I've seen on maps, the forest runs along the perimeter of Lyson. "The trees will offer us cover. If we go far enough, we'll find the Valor Sea. We can follow it south to Ryalle's ports."

"It'll take longer this way, but if you're certain we have time..." Ken says.

"She's right," Rainer says quickly. "It should be less problematic than traveling through the villages."

Ken nods in agreement. "It seemed considerably less traveled when we scouted."

We maneuver through the forest, hidden within the trees. The lord's pasture on the left gives way to another field. In the distance, the village rests down a short hill—all boxy, straw-roofed houses and smoking chimneys.

Distant yells ring out as villagers run through the streets, heading toward Edvin's. Plumes of thick, dark smoke rise into the sky, drawing people toward the calamity.

I return my attention to the group, shaking off any budding sympathy.

"—I'll glamour your pointy-eared arse once we get to the city," Tynan says.

"Why can't you just glamour us now?" I ask.

Tynan laughs. "My power isn't endless. The more I use, the more blood I need. Although, if you let me have a little taste, that would help me." He winks at me over his shoulder, and Rainer growls, stepping beside me.

He gently places a hand on the small of my back, reminding me he's with me. Although he's tender with me, his eyes are sharp as a hawk's as he watches his brother.

"What now, little brother?" Tynan chuckles lowly. "It's true—glamour can last endlessly if I feed on whomever I'm glam—"

Something rustles behind us, like heavy footsteps stomping their way toward us. There's a grunt, and I turn just in time to see a tall, lanky man with curly black hair fall to his knees, clutching his head.

Rainer turns with his arms crossed, peering down in annoyance at him.

The man whimpers, squeezing his eyes shut.

"Stop," he begs. "Please stop. I'll do anything."

"Who the feck is that?" Tynan asks.

"I dunno," Ken replies. "He's been following us since the fire."

I whirl toward the shifter. "What do you mean he's been *following* us?"

Ken gestures toward the forest. "Just watching us by himself."

"Why didn't you do something?"

He shrugs. "Eh, Rainer's got it under control."

I glance at Rainer, who stoops to pick up a knife the man must've dropped after the onslaught of fear power.

"He had a weapon?" I squeak. Seraphina stays quiet beside me. "He tried to sneak up on us!"

"I knew he was there," Rainer says, his lips twitching as he glances at me. "No sneaking occurred."

With a gasp, the man drops his hands from his head. He sits back onto the dirt and scoots away from us. His eyes are wide, his skin pale with terror. The dark zig-zag on his cheek marks him as a fellow Tradeling.

Rainer leans forward, snatching the man by his throat and yanking him to his feet. He looks about my age or maybe a couple of years younger.

Something about him is familiar, but I can't put my finger on it.

"He's dressed like the others," Tynan says, pointing at his rugged, flexible trousers tucked into tightly laced boots. His deep green tunic is snugly fit, reinforced at the chest and shoulders.

Tynan leans forward, patting the man aggressively. He grunts. "No weapons."

Seraphina touches my arm gently, snagging my attention. She leans toward me. "I don't pick up on the same energy from him as the others."

The man wheezes, clawing at Rainer's hand as his face turns from deep red to purplish.

"Rainer," I whisper. "Don't."

Rainer doesn't wait for me to ask again. He drops the man immediately. "I would very much like to end his life."

I shake my head, and Rainer runs a hand through his hair, stepping back.

Ken circles the man, a slight grin on his face. "You're untrained." He chuckles. "Or else you'd know better than to try to sneak up on a group of warrior fae."

"Fae," the man croaks, eyes watering. "Please don't kill me."

Ken squats behind the man, resting his chin on his thin shoulder. "You shouldn't beg the fae."

Tynan steps forward. He hisses, and his vampyr fangs elongate to sharp, deadly points. The man sobs, pleading even more.

"No, no, please." He puts his hands together in a symbol of prayer, bringing them up in front of his face. Ken stands, backing away from him. "My sister—she's in the mines. I just want to get her out."

Rainer shares a look with Tynan, and then he gives him a sharp nod.

Tynan squats in front of the man, locking eyes with him. His eyes briefly flicker pale—almost white—then return to their normal dark blue coloring. "You'll answer our questions with full honesty."

The man's expression melts, his brown eyes glazing over. He sniffles up the last of his tears, wiping his dirt-streaked face. He nods rapidly, agreeing with enthusiasm. "Yes."

"Good." Tynan pats his cheek a few times more aggressively than necessary. He stands and turns to Rainer. "All you, brother."

"Why are you following us?" Rainer asks, his tone low and lazy as if he's entirely unbothered by this turn of events. He leans against a tree beside the man, crossing his ankles as he plays with a dagger, twirling it in warning.

The man stays on the ground but angles his face toward Rainer. "I thought I could use you to get my sister back."

"Dumbest shite I've ever heard," Tynan says with a sharp laugh. "And I've heard a lot of dumb shite."

"Well, you've been hearing yourself talk for years, so I'm not surprised." Ken arches a brow, trying to suppress his amusement.

"Use us how?" Rainer asks, ignoring them.

The man's cheeks flush. "I saw your ears. I saw what you did to those other men." He turns away, swallowing thickly. "The fire." He sucks in a sharp breath and stares at the ground. "I thought if I captured you, I could barter for my sister's freedom."

The silence is so thick I can hear my own breaths. Then, suddenly, a chorus of laughter rings out. Tynan, Ken, and Rainer wear various expressions of amusement as they stare at the man.

"Feckin idiot," Tynan says. "I love me some idiots."

"You do love yourself," Ken adds under his breath.

Tynan glowers at the bear shifter, but he keeps his mouth shut.

Seraphina sighs, wandering off. She investigates some plants growing nearby, paying us no mind. She plucks something, then sets one of her bags down at the base of a tree to stuff the plant inside. Returning to the weeds, she scrutinizes them.

Ken strokes his beard. "I didn't realize the humans fancied bargains."

Rainer kicks off the tree, striding toward the man who flinches, putting his hands up in front of his face. Rainer places his hand on the back of the man's head, shoves it forward, and moves the hair hanging over the back of his neck.

"Same prisoner marking," he says. He releases the man's head. "Why were you released?"

"I should've never been in that prison," he mutters, his features pinching in anger. "All I did was fight a guard in the mines—for touching my sister."

Rainer's jaw tightens. "How old was she?"

"Fourteen."

Spicy anger blossoms inside me, bringing a pounding pressure to my head. The fury isn't to be blamed on my shadow-self. No, it's all mine this time.

"A feckin child," Ken says, voicing my exact thoughts with a growl.

Rainer gives me a long, haunted look. I don't need to ask him what he's thinking to know he feels the same way I do. It takes a specific type of foul to hurt a child.

"When was this?" Rainer asks.

The man sniffles. "A couple years ago."

"You haven't seen her since then?"

He shakes his head.

"Tell me about your release." Rainer's mask slips back into place as he wipes the emotion away and returns to his tree, leaning against it and focusing on the man.

"I don't know what to tell." He swallows audibly. "One day, one of the queensguards showed up at the prison and offered payment in exchange for serving the queen. I had already been imprisoned for almost two years. I was basically awaiting death, so I had nothing to lose."

"What was your payment?"

"I requested my sister be free, and in exchange, I'd do anything the queen wanted. I was promised my freedom *and* my sister's."

"So they let her go?"

His expression shutters. He quickly shakes his head. "Not yet. Not until we complete the task."

Rainer narrows his eyes. "Which is?"

The man points at Rainer. "Go to Avylon and catch a faerie. Bring it back."

Tynan and Ken laugh, and even Seraphina sighs heavily at this, abandoning her herb picking and returning to the group. Rainer and I study each other. That dark, unsettled feeling creeps through me again.

Rainer turns back to the male. "She never freed you. She sentenced you to death in a more creative way."

Tynan's eyes flash with humor. "You sure as shite weren't going to survive crossing the Gleam."

"Then my Sheila would never be free," the man whispers. "I had to try."

I swear my heart stops beating for a few seconds. Rainer remains stoic, but his eyes lock with mine, silently acknowledging the name we heard. He gives me a subtle headshake, and I know instinctually that he doesn't want me to say anything.

But I can't help it.

"What did you say your sister's name was?" I ask softly.

The guy swallows heavily, meeting my gaze. "Sheila. Sheila Victoria West," he says reverently.

"Hey," Ken says gleefully. "That's—"

"What does she look like?" I interject, shooting Ken a stern look.

The man smiles sadly. "She's tall. Sweet. Black hair."

That she always wears in braids.

I fiddle with the end of my own braid, trying not to let my surprise show.

Rainer's silence doesn't give anything away, but I bet he's thinking the same thing: this guy doesn't know his sister was sold from the mines a while ago. More importantly, Sheila is safe now, in my court, protected by the same *fae* he had hoped to kidnap and use as bartering tools.

"I'm all she has," he whispers. "But she likely thinks I'm dead by now."

"Shame," Tynan says sarcastically. "Can I drain him now?"

"What?" The man sobs, and tears run down his face. "Please, no! I can—I can help! I can take you to Ryalle. I can help you get to the queen like you want."

"You don't know what we want," Rainer says with a growl. He steps beside me, the back of his hand lightly brushing against mine. His pinky reaches out, entangling with mine in silent support. It's my new favorite show of affection from him—our private, wordless conversations.

I glance up at him, and his face softens.

"I overheard you earlier... about wanting to attend the queen's fête," the man says. "I can help you! I swear." He clasps his hands together, pleading again. "I need you to help me get my sister. We can help each other."

Rainer stares him down. "No."

"What's your name?" I ask, finding my voice. All eyes swing to me.

"Zephyr," the man says quietly. Then, he quickly adds, "I have a cousin in Wyrville—he's a tailor. He owns a shop. He can help dress you for the queen's event. I promise—I can *help* you!"

I pause, contemplating this. Glancing at Rainer, he gives me an almost imperceptible smile, his eyes softening around the corner as he watches me, letting me lead.

I think about what Tynan said about his glamour—how exhausting it can be and how it requires blood. The less he has to glamour, the better. Having clean, appropriate garments would be incredibly useful. Zephyr might be able to give us insight. Plus, if we keep him close, I can ensure he gets to his sister after.

I might not know him, but Sera said his aura wasn't like the others. And Sheila deserves to see her brother again.

Good call, my shadow-self murmurs. *Now you're thinking like the fae.*

I balk, processing this. It's not the cruel commentary I've come to expect. Instead of letting my shadow's changing temperament distract me, I put the thought aside for now.

"Okay, Zephyr, you're coming with us," I say, working hard to focus on the issue at hand.

"Let me string him up instead," Tynan says to Rainer, flashing his crazy eyes again. "Those brittle bones will snap so nicely."

"For the love of the Mother," Rainer mutters, running a hand over his face. "Listen to my bonded."

Tynan grumbles. "You're not even fully bonded."

"Doesn't matter," Rainer says, his eyes locked on mine. "She will *always* be my soul-bond, and what she says goes."

My body prickles under his gaze and the implication of his words.

"Come on, new little human," Ken says. He grabs Zephyr by his shirt and throws him over a shoulder. The guy trembles like a leaf as he whimpers. "Don't snot on my leathers. I just cleaned them."

We continue southwest, until the air grows humid and heavy with the scent of saltwater and brine. After living here my whole life, I'm finally getting a chance to see the peninsula.

But there's not even a sizzle of excitement at the notion. Instead, only a deep, churning fear of what lies ahead.

Twenty-Four
Unbridled Lust
Alessia

It turns out Dovenak is relatively uneventful compared to Avylon. Other than murdering a slew of people, lighting the lord's house on fire, and picking up a hitchhiking human, of course.

Here, we don't have to worry about cursed forests or manipulative magic like we do back home.

Home.

I smile to myself at the thought. After all of this, I have a home to return to.

Glancing to my right, I look out over the rugged coast. Waves slam against the jutting rocks, roaring with each crash. Now, I understand why the docks and trade ports are further south in Ryalle—the cliffs are much too sharp here to scale down, and the current is vicious.

A slightly cooler breeze wafts in from the west, smelling of seaweed and fish. It's oddly refreshing. The forest meets the cliffs, occasionally becoming sparse before regaining density.

We continue south toward the outskirts of Tyrson—a small fishing village—and it takes us the better part of the day to get there on foot, even without any other interruptions.

Eventually, we make it to a small clearing and pause to rest. The sun melts into the sea, and a breathtaking golden glow washes over everything in sight. Ken and Sera perch on a couple of boulders, gazing out at the sea, while Zephyr dangles his legs off the cliff's edge.

Tynan paces the tree line, inhaling vigorously.

"Village is over yonder—on the other side of the woods." Ken turns on his rock and points towards a cluster of formidable pine trees towering at the forest's edge. "Makes a nice barrier, no?"

"Safe to rest?" Rainer asks, scouting the area alongside his brother.

"This is as good a spot as any," Ken says, spreading his arms wide. He cocks a head, pausing. "I haven't heard anyone nearby for a while."

"No fresh human scents," Tynan agrees.

"It's best we stop for the night," Rainer concludes, stuffing his hands in his pockets as he strides toward me. "We have plenty of time before the fête begins. We'll continue our travels in the morning."

Tynan grunts his agreement and tosses his bags down in the clearing. He unclips a larger bag and rummages through it.

Sera leaps off the rock, snatching her bag. Crouching beside Tynan, she begins searching through it. She emits a thoughtful noise as she locates her desired item—a tiny vial with a dropper.

"The tents are in your bag," she says to Tynan.

"Here." He pulls out two dark cloth cubes the size of my fist. "Where do you want them?"

"Tents?" I squint, trying to figure out what's happening.

Rainer steps forward, taking one of the cubes. He strolls around, finding a nestled spot between two trees, situated halfway between the forest and the cliff but discreetly hidden from the open area. He tosses the lump down, satisfied.

Meanwhile, Ken snatches the other cube and tosses it up into the air. It tumbles to the ground and rolls like an unpredictable die before halting in a random spot in the clearing. Amused, he bursts into laughter.

"No," Tynan says. He rushes forward and snatches the cube. "At least put it somewhere it's protected." Deliberately, he places the cube in the tree line, pressed against a robust trunk and concealed by bushes at its back.

The males and Sera continue to bicker about the placement of the cubes while I find myself utterly perplexed. I turn, making eye contact with Zephyr. He's at the cliff's edge, with his back to a boulder and his knees tucked to his chest. His mouth and eyes are comically large, betraying his bewilderment. At least I'm not alone in my confusion.

"There's only two tents and six of us," Sera says adamantly. "We should split up three and three."

Rainer groans.

"What *tents*?" I ask, confused, eyeing the little cloth boxes.

In response, Sera walks over to one, holding her vial, and uses the dropper to squeeze a couple of drops onto it. She jumps backward as the cube pops open and expands rapidly.

"Well, I'm relieved that worked," she says, satisfied. "I've never actually used them before, and unfortunately, they're not reusable."

"Holy shite," Zephyr says from behind us.

My eyes widen in astonishment, my eyebrows rising to meet my hairline as I watch the cube expand into a generously sized tent. Whenever I think I have a handle on the fae's peculiarities, they surprise me again.

"I'll stay with Rai and the little demon," Ken says gleefully.

He joins me, patting me on the head as I gape at the now full-sized tent, with plenty of room for multiple muscular bodies to fit comfortably.

"Under normal circumstances, that would be my first choice, too," Rainer says. "However, you should stay with the sorceress and the boy."

"We don't need to be supervised," Sera mutters, squeezing a couple more drops of her concoction on the other cube. It also quietly explodes into a tent, nestling nearly perfectly between the trees.

"You're untrustworthy," Rainer says flatly. "Alessia and Tynan are with me."

Sera sighs, then beckons for Zephyr to follow her. He balks, unsure, but then he hurries over to her. She leads him to the first tent, holding open the flap and gesturing for him to enter.

"Wait," Ken says. Sera and Zephyr pause, turning toward him. "I hear a river over that hill. You don't want to bathe?"

"If we stay in Wyrville tomorrow, I assume we'll find an inn?" Sera says.

Zephyr nods. "Yes, the inn is near my cousin's shop."

"Good." Sera smiles contently. "I'll wait."

"Me too," Zephyr adds.

"No one cares what you want, human," Tynan says.

The human in question flinches. I feel bad for the guy. The fae can mean well, but they're decidedly not *nice*.

"Knock it off, Tynan," I say, rubbing my aching neck. We're all tired, cranky, and hungry. The last thing we need is to start provoking each other.

Sera and Zephyr enter the tent, and Ken turns to us, plastering on a broad smile.

"Great." He gives us a thumbs up. "It's fine. I'll be fine. I've smelled worse things than a tent full of ripe arse."

Rainer swipes a hand over his jaw, and I can tell he's trying to hide a smirk. Once he manages to suppress his amusement, he gives Ken a stern look. "Keep a close eye on them, Kenisius."

The shifter salutes, giving him a crooked grin. "My pleasure." He chuckles, striding to the tent. "No bathing for this guy, either, then. Apologies to your noses."

Tynan eyes me hungrily. "Looks like I'm with you, princess."

Rainer growls, and in the blink of an eye, he's in front of me, blocking me from Tynan's view. "Keep it up, Tynan. The world will not mourn your loss."

Tynan throws his head back and chuckles. He steps forward and pats Rainer on the shoulder. "It's fun to rile you up, brother. Now go bathe—you reek of smoke and sweat. You'll never consummate your bond like that." He winks.

Rainer's jaw tenses. "Knock off your shite." He turns to me, his gaze immediately softening. "Are you okay with this?" he asks softly. "Sharing a tent with us?"

I nod. Tynan only flirts with me to rile Rainer up—there's nothing else to it. As tough as the elder vampyr pretends to be, he's as harmless as a pixie, usually. But I don't voice my perspective aloud, not wanting to instigate anything between the brothers.

As for spending a night with Rainer... *that* will be a true test of self-control. But I'd rather be with him than away from him now, especially after so long apart. It feels *right* to be beside him.

Interestingly, I can tell my shadow agrees. There has been a noticeable increase in its stability. It's as if its view of Rainer has shifted from enemy to ally, and it now finds peace in our friendship.

"I'll be fine." My eyes linger on the soot smudged on his sharp cheekbones. "Go—clean up."

The tight muscles in his face and neck relax slightly, and he nods. "I'll be quick."

Like Sera, I'll wait until tomorrow night to clean up. As refreshing as the river sounds, I'd rather not strip down and make myself vulnerable. Even though I have my shadow *and* Rainer and Ken, too, it doesn't make mean I'm comfortable exposing myself out in the open.

Instead, I hoist my bag onto my shoulder, the weight pressing against my tired muscles as I make my way to my tent. I step inside, and refreshingly light air greets me. Surprisingly, it's not as warm or stifling as I expected. Reaching out, my fingers graze the velvety soft texture of the tent's wall, which is pleasantly cool.

One big room sprawls out before me, furnished with two cozy cots seamlessly integrated into the fabric—one on either side of the room.

I throw my bag down on one, rummaging for a knee-length tunic and fresh underwear to sleep in.

My leather clothes hug me like a second skin, suctioned to me as I pry them off. They've kept me surprisingly cool—likely bespelled like Ken and Rainer's garb—but sweat beads on my neck. Summers in Dovank can get pretty warm, and today has been no exception. The further south we travel, the warmer it grows. At least today, we had the sea breeze working in our favor.

I bring my leathers outside, laying them on one of the boulders to dry out. Laughter seeps from Ken's tent, and I smile, glad the animosity is lessening. He's still in there with Sera and Zephyr because their voices ring out in light conversation.

Tynan and Rainer are nowhere in sight.

Instead of hanging around by myself, I head into the trees and climb a small hill. At the top, I spy a wide river meandering down at the base on the other side.

Staying hidden within the trees, I slowly descend toward the river and find a spot on the bank to sit. At first, I don't see Rainer. A few seconds later, he emerges, facing away from me.

He raises both arms, running his fingers through his wet hair. The jewelry on his fingers and sharp ears glints in the waning sunlight. The muscles in his back flex, and I unabashedly take in his well-defined physique. The water reaches his waist, covering his lower half.

He drags a bar of soap over his body, washing himself. His body is adorned with dark tattoos that form intricate patterns of swirls and whorls. They cover his arms, extending across his back and down to his waist.

Though I can't see it from this angle, I know his chest boasts a scripture in an unfamiliar language. However, the rest of the ink seems to be a collection of random patterns.

The only color comes from the inside of one of his arms—small splashes of red.

I'm in no rush for Rainer to finish as I hungrily take him in. The water drips down his muscles, highlighting his lithe yet muscular body. He isn't as bulky as Tynan or Ken but sharp and efficient.

He turns, and the sun glints off his piercing blue eyes as they meet mine, highlighting the confidence and vulnerability there. His presence captivates me, and it's as if time stands still as he holds my stare.

The sun's fading rays highlight his chiseled jawline and stubble, adding an air of ruggedness to his already striking features.

A subtle smile tugs at the corners of his lips, hinting at a hidden depth beneath his indifferent demeanor. It feels private, like a secret shared between just us.

My heart quickens as he gracefully moves through the water, treading toward the shore. With every stride, the water responds, rippling around him.

He slowly emerges from the water. The sight of him standing there, completely nude, sends a jolt of excitement through me.

Unable to resist, my gaze involuntarily drifts downward. My heart pounds, and my mouth goes dry.

I crave his touch, missing the intimacy we were building before I pushed him away. Even in our dreams, we've managed to put distance between us. He respects my wishes, but I'm questioning whether it's worth it, especially when he wants me as badly as I crave him.

Rainer chuckles. He begins to harden under my perusal, his thick shaft lengthening and standing to attention. I quickly put a hand over my eyes.

"Sorry," I squeak out. "I mean, not sorry, but…" I trail off before I dig myself into a deeper hole.

He sighs, and I can hear him stepping closer.

"Mo róisín," he says softly. "Look at me."

I shake my head. "I didn't mean to invade your privacy."

He chuckles again; this time, he's so close I can feel his body heat wafting off him.

"Look at me," he commands, more sternly this time.

He reaches up, gently caressing the hand obstructing my view. Slowly, I lower it and take him in. The fading sun and warm air have already begun to dry him. Only a few stray droplets remain. His wet hair is pushed back out of his face, allowing me to see every bit of his ethereal face. The only thing he wears is that tempting, taunting ink.

"What do they mean?" I ask softly, my eyes tracing the dark lines on his body.

He sighs, rubbing his jaw and glancing away. "Ever since I was a young faeling… I'd see the shadows in my nightmares. Sometimes, they'd help me escape."

I go still, trying to process. This time, when I look at his tattoos, I view them less as random shapes and swirls and notice how the abstract designs look similar to my shadow's essence.

I gasp.

"They look like…" I can't finish. It must be a coincidence. But is there such a thing? Or is it another message from Fate?

"I know." His gaze latches onto mine, the tight edges of his eyes softening. "I never knew what they meant, or why they meant so much to me, until recently."

My fingers caress the tendrils along his shoulder. "It's as if your subconscious knew before you did."

"I always belonged to you and your shadows, my little rose."

I blush furiously as my fingers trail below his collarbone to his chest, where the unfamiliar script sits. "What does this mean?"

He bites down his lip as if fighting a smile. "Na tromluithe is binne," he says softly, in a beautiful accent. "The sweetest nightmares."

"Oh," I exhale. My fingers trace the cursive lettering. "It's beautiful."

He gently taps the bottom of my chin, causing me to look up at his face as he takes me in with an intense, unreadable stare. "*You are beautiful.*"

I can't help the smile that blossoms on my face, alongside the curiosity rapidly beating in my heart. "Why did you choose that phrase?"

"It's in my nature to have nightmares, so a plea for sweet dreams would be too much to ask for."

"So you asked for sweet nightmares instead," I whisper.

"The *sweetest*." He nods. "Until I met *you*. Now I pray for *our* sweet dreams every night."

A deep, raw kind of sorrow bleeds from him, and it strikes me just how much I was hurting him by taking my space. I wasn't only searching for my freedom—I was abandoning him and stealing his peace. My heart clenches tightly as I come to the painful realization of my selfishness.

So many words perch on the tip of my tongue, but I'm not sure they can convey my complex emotions. The feelings intertwine with each other deep in my core—love, affection, guilt, apology, *need*.

As he studies me, his lips tilt up, and that soft dimple of his makes an appearance. I trace it, my thumb lingering on the edge of his lip. He playfully bites down, pretending to nibble on my finger and breaking the tense moment. I giggle and pull it away.

"What's this one?" I reach for his right arm, where I saw a hint of red, and flip the inside of his forearm toward me. I gasp as I take in the sight of a bleeding rose.

Finally, he turns those icy blue eyes back to me. "You know what that one is, mo róisín."

It's me and him. *Us.* A rose and her thorns.

All of his tattoos, in a way, represent *us.* But this one is brand new based on the vibrancy of the ink.

"I thought the soul-bond was platonic?" I whisper. "Why would you get this if we aren't together."

His glacial stare softens. "This has absolutely nothing to do with the bond."

"Then what does it have to do with?"

He reaches up, tracing a finger carefully over my Tradeling tattoo. "*You.*"

My skin heats beneath his touch. "Why do you think we're bonded?" I ask. "I mean, there has to be a reason for it, right?"

"There's a reason for everything if you look closely enough," he says. "As for us? We were meant to be, Alessia."

His fingers linger on my jaw, caressing the skin there before he drops his hand. Neither of us pulls away, but we don't move closer, either.

"I know you're the one for me," he says. "I'll wait as long as you need me to."

My heart flutters. I swallow the lump in my throat.

"What if I only want to be friends?" I ask quietly.

Lies, the voice inside me says. *You lie to us both.*

A dark, low laugh escapes him, and I feel it deep in my gut. It distracts me from my shadow-self's voice.

"We both know you want more than that, mo róisín. It's not a matter of *if* you'll have me, but when. And I assure you, I am a very patient male."

Without thinking, I reach out and trace one of the swirls on his ribs, tracing it lower. His manhood jerks, standing proud and hard only a hair's breadth away from my hand.

I caress his pelvic bone, trailing to the dark tuft of hair framing his hardness. His hand flashes out, wrapping around my wrist to stop me.

"You don't want me to touch you?" I ask, voice husky with desire.

He closes his eyes briefly, swallowing a pained groan. "I want nothing more."

"Then let me," I whisper.

"I can't," he croaks. "Even patient males can only take so much before losing it, Alessia. I need you to help me out here."

A palpable silence settles between us, the weight of his words pressing against my chest. The air around us grows thick and heavy, making it hard to breathe. The lines on his face tell a story of vulnerability, allowing me to see his fear and longing.

When our gazes lock, the intensity of our desires collide, reigniting the smoldering flame between us—the one that never died out. It's so powerful that it sends a shiver down my spine.

"You're right," I whisper. *Finally*. "I don't want to be *friends*."

His grip tightens slightly, then he sighs and relents, loosening his hold on me. I tug free of his hand, reaching for his length. My fingers curl gently around him, seeking his warmth. He's silky soft, yet hard at the same time. I work my hand slowly up and down him, amazed at his girth.

"If we aren't going to fulfill the bond, at least let us play," I whisper nervously.

He groans, his hands working their way into my hair. "This is anything but playful—I take it quite seriously."

"Then let us *seriously* enjoy each other," I tease.

With a gentle tug on my hair, he pulls my head back, forcing me to face him. "I can make you scream my name without ever being inside of you, little rose." A mischievous smile dances on his lips, and it spurs me on.

A rush of fiery heat overwhelms me, causing me to dissolve into a puddle of lust. All my reservations melt away, and I surrender completely to the intoxicating mix of love and passion I feel towards him.

Gripping his erection harder, I make my intent clear. "Me first."

"Alessia," he hisses, his fingers winding deeper into my hair.

It boosts my confidence, and I shift my weight forward, resting on my knees before him. His breath quickens with certain motions, especially when I swirl my thumb around his mushroom tip, licking the underside lightly.

I smile around him and take him deeper into my mouth. He hisses, and his hips jerk forward until I'm choking. He holds me in place, sliding in and out of my mouth. Tears stream down my face, but they only turn me on. I grip his arse, letting him know I'm okay with this.

"Gods, you naughty girl," he mutters darkly. "You take me so well."

Keeping a steady rhythm, I work him until he goes rigid.

A loud, low groan comes from him as he shoots a thick, salty stream down my throat. Swallowing it all, I lean back on my heels and wipe my mouth.

Before I can say anything, Rainer leans down, pressing his mouth to mine. He kisses me with enthusiasm, unfazed by the taste of himself on my lips.

He pulls away, cupping my face tightly. "Gods, you beautiful, wicked woman. How did I get so lucky?"

Without giving me time to reply, he scoops me up in his arms and plants me on the soft grass, hovering over me. His lips descend on mine again, and I giggle, squirming with delight.

It fuels his desire, and we continue to explore each other with unbridled lust.

Twenty-Five

I Want to be Hers

Rainer

A *sweet, romantic scent fills my nostrils. It doesn't take long to realize I'm dreaming. As soon as I spot the whimsical blue roses, I groan. I looked forward to my dreams for a short period, expecting to see the grey-eyed girl who gave me a reason to sleep and dream.*

Lately, sleeping has been a genuine nightmare.

I'm tired of it, but I'm used to it at this point in my life.

Instead of fighting it, I lie back on the ground and close my eyes. The sun warms my skin, but it's only a matter of time until the illusion shatters.

Sure enough, the sun fades out moments later, and shadows blanket my eyelids.

"Rainer?"

"No," I groan. The worst nightmares are always the ones with her.

"No? Am I interrupting?"

My eyes flick open. Alessia stands over me, glancing down with a confused smile. The sun hovers in the blue sky behind her, casting light like a halo around her curly ash-blonde hair.

I blink a few times, unable to speak.

"What are you doing down there?" she asks.

Instead of judging me, she drops down beside me.

"It's been a while since I've seen you here," I whisper, taking in the beautiful sight before me. My breathing stalls, and suddenly I'm afraid to move—as if I'll scare her away and be left alone again.

She's here.

My heart skips a beat, fluttering in my chest.

We lie with our arms brushing, gazing up at the sky together. Fluffy white clouds skim across the sky in various shapes.

"I know," she says quietly. "Have you slept okay?"

Not one bit. "Well enough."

"You're lying."

"I'll sleep great tonight," I say in quick rebuttal. "You're here now."

"I'm here." She reaches for my hand, interlacing our fingers. I turn to face her, wanting to memorize this moment. It's been too long since we've had time in our dreamscape together. She watches the clouds, her face lighting up. She points with her free hand. "That one looks like a cat."

"Mhm," I agree, without bothering to look at it.

She glances at me shyly and scrunches her nose. "Why are you staring at me?" A light pink dusting coats the apples of her cheeks.

I can't help but chuckle. She had my cock in her mouth not too long ago, yet something as innocent as me looking at her makes her blush.

She sits up, swatting playfully at me. "You make me nervous. Knock it off."

"Make me," I tease.

Her bashfulness morphs into a coy smile, and she lifts a brow in challenge. In one swift move, she throws a leg over me, straddling me in the grass.

Immediately, I'm taken back to the time she indulged in moon-berries and expressed her desires aloud for what seemed to be the first time.

Her eyes sparkle with lust as they lock onto my lips. I can't help my body's natural response, and I'm instantly aroused, my cock hardening beneath her. I reach up, gripping her bare thighs. She's only wearing a thin nightgown, which rides up with the movement.

I glance down, catching more skin than I expected. The air whooshes out of my lungs, and all the blood in my head shoots downward.

I groan, lifting her skirt a little higher to reveal her bare beneath the fabric.

"You're not wearing underthings," I say hoarsely.

She giggles, pushing me back down and leaning in closer to my lips. "Do you like that?" Her voice is husky, thick with lust.

I'm seconds away from undoing my pants and freeing myself. I want nothing more than to nestle into her slick, tight opening—to feel her clamp around me as I pump into her. I've envisioned it far too many times, abusing my hand these past few months.

My chest rises and falls violently as I battle to keep my wits about me.

"I love that," I growl. My fingers tighten around her thighs, biting into the flesh there. She gasps, squirming against me. "But we can't—not like this."

Her brows flick up in surprise, and her mouth drops open. "Rainer… really?"

"The first time I have you, Alessia, will not be in a dream. It will not be in a tent with my brother lying less than a stone's throw away."

Her blush returns, this time in embarrassment, as she mutters a non-apology and pushes herself off of me.

"Wait," I reach for her, pulling back into my lap as I sit up. I pull her back to my chest and wrap my arms around her. Fighting to ignore my painfully hard and demanding erection, I focus on the scent of her—sweet and tempting.

Feck.

It doesn't help.

I close my eyes, taking a few steadying breaths. Think about anything else—Kenisius's fur in my mouth, Tynan's sweaty balls, Yvanthia bonding me—

That does it. The blood returns to my brain as my cock deflates, the desire calming down.

"You kill me," I groan into Alessia's ear, resting my chin on her shoulder. She giggles, settling into me. It's a battle not to get excited all over again.

But the thoughts reminded me of something—the bond.

"You realize if we have sex in our dreams, it very well might complete the soul-bond," I tell her. "When I fed on you in my dream..."

She exhales long and slow. "It carried over into waking life."

"We have to be careful, mo róisín."

"But what if we do complete it, Rainer. What if we just give into the—"

A gust of wind blasts into us, sending our hair tangling around our heads. Alessia screeches as the world goes dark. Thunder crashes around us, and the dreamscape erupts.

I shoot out of my cot, ready for violence. Whatever interrupted such a beautiful feckin dream is going to pay.

Ezamae stands before me with a manic look. His usually styled silver hair is askew, and dark bags line his wide eyes.

"What are you doing here?" I roar, glaring at the one responsible for waking us.

Alessia yawns, sitting up and looking at us. The early glimmers of dawn peek through the tent, highlighting the flush on her cheeks. Tynan's cot is unmade, and he's nowhere to be found.

"What's going on?" Alessia asks, frowning at Ezamae. "What *are* you doing here?"

"I figured it out," he says quickly. His hand cups his mouth as he stifles a short laugh. When he releases it, he smiles widely at us. "I know how to break the bond to Yvanthia."

The world around me fades away as I lock onto his words. "How?"

His smile grows, highlighting his uncharacteristically wild appearance. "Soul-bonds trump magically placed bonds. It doesn't matter if she's queen, Yvanthia's bond isn't as powerful as *yours* will be." He points to Alessia and me.

"Explain," I demand.

"I don't have time. Yvanthia doesn't know I'm here. The fecking cunt." He laughs, shaking his head. "She's a *cunt*. Wow, that feels delightful." His laughter grows, and he does a gleeful dance, waving at us. "I must go now, but I'll return."

The air wavers around him, and he's gone as quickly as he appeared.

"What was that about?" Alessia asks, wide-eyed as she clutches the blanket to her chest. "Is he high or something?"

That was a rather strange interaction, yes, but I don't think he's under the influence of anything. I scratch the back of my neck. The fact that Ezamae windwalked all the way here… across the Gleam and through another realm. It's a sign of great power—as in he's accessing the full spectrum of magic he hasn't been able to.

On top of that? He spoke poorly—freely—of Yvanthia.

Her bond and glamour no longer restrict him.

Curious, indeed.

"What are you thinking?" Alessia asks. She tugs on my arm. "Rainer, talk to me."

I chuckle, swiping a hand over my face. "I think…" My amusement grows as I process the pieces to the puzzle, and I chuckle harder, plopping down on the cot beside Alessia. "I think Ezamae is soul-bonded."

"*What*?" she yells, her hands flying up to cover her mouth. "How? To who?"

"I don't know." I snort, finding the whole thing rather absurd, but how else would he so confidently know that a soul-bond overcomes a magic-bond? How else would he have been able to windwalk all this way unless *he* broke his bond with Yvanthia?

"Rainer," Alessia says softly this time. "You know what this means?"

Her voice has an air of hope, but it instantly brings me back to reality. There is absolutely no way I'm consummating the bond with her now. Because I know her, and I know she'll do it before she's ready, just to free me from Yvanthia's clutches.

The thought sends a searing pain through my chest.

Good hell.

"It doesn't mean anything," I say coldly. Carefully, I pry myself from the cot and stand. I run a hand through my hair and shake my head. Walking toward the tent's exit, I pause, looking back as

I say, "It doesn't change anything. We are not going through with it."

Her face falls as she blinks at me, trying to get a read on me. I turn away before she can.

There's no way I'm letting her do this now—not if I'm worried she's making this decision for anything other than her own pleasure. I won't let her tether her life to mine to spare me from Yvanthia's clutches.

As I storm away from the tent, a violent anger courses through me. Fecking Ezamae. I want to punch him again—bruise his pretty face—for breaking the news in front of Alessia.

But then again, she has a right to know. It involves her, after all.

And as much as I want her to be *mine* forever, this isn't what I meant. This is us being forced into something, and it feels awfully like stealing a bit of Alessia's freedom, which I abhor.

Furthermore, I can't risk tethering her life to mine. If something were to happen to me… *no.* I refuse to increase the risk to Alessia's life.

No matter how desperately I *want* to be hers.

TWENTY-SIX
ALL OF HIM
ALESSIA

I stare at the tent's opening long after Rainer leaves. Part of me isn't surprised that he went cold and stormed off again, but the other part of me thought we were past it by now.

He's not running from me—he's running from his emotions. It's not easy for him to open up, especially after stifling parts of himself for so long. Part of caring for someone is accepting their flaws. And as he accepts mine, I embrace his.

He was there for me, and now I'll be there for him.

See? I told you that love makes you weak. You shouldn't be distracted by this—

"I thought you liked him," I say, exasperated by my shadow-self's everchanging temperament.

I run a hand over my braid to smooth down the flyaways, then stand from the cot and begin folding up the blanket.

I like him when he serves our needs.

"You're just as wishy-washy as Rainer is," I mutter, shaking my head.

Behind me, the entrance to the tent rustles open. I turn.

"You think I'm wishy-washy?" Rainer says as he ducks, entering through the tent's flap, holding my clothes from yesterday. There's a half-smirk on his face, and his dark, wavy hair falls across his forehead in the most alluring way. He's ridiculously gorgeous, even when he's incurably frustrating, and it steals my breath.

"Yes," I say, not cowering under his intense stare. Then, I clear my throat and force a stern look onto my face. "You can be incredibly emotional and open, but other times you're so cold you freeze me out."

His smirk fades into an embarrassed frown as he hands me my garments. "I'm not emotional."

"Okay." I shrug, but this time, a grin creeps onto *my* lips.

"I'm not." He scowls, and it causes me to chuckle.

"But you *do* admit you're freezing me out?"

He glances away, runs a hand through his hair, and sighs. "I'm trying not. It's why I came back."

I toss my clothes onto the floor and drop to the cot, patting the space beside me. He sits, legs stretched straight out, and his body angled forward as if facing me is too hard for him.

"I know I pretend I'm not, but I *am* afraid, Alessia," he says quietly. "I've been afraid of hurting you from the moment I met you. I've finally gained confidence that I won't hurt you with my bloodlust, but now…"

"But now what?" I drop the blanket I'm holding and turn my body toward him, pulling my legs up to my chest.

"Now, I'm afraid if we complete our bond, I'll do something stupid to get you killed."

I can't help but laugh softly. "If anyone would do something of that nature, it'd be me. In which case, you should fear being stuck with *me*—not the other way around."

I realize he's genuinely struggling with this when he doesn't show signs of amusement.

Reaching out, I interlace my fingers with his. "I'm glad you came back to me," I whisper.

Finally, he shifts to face me. "Admittedly, I regret reverting to my arsehole tendencies. I don't actively *want* to push you away and avoid my feelings, but Ezamae's words don't change anything."

My nose scrunches. "That's not only up to you."

"We're *not* consummating the bond." His eyes harden, and I swear I see a flicker of darkness there.

"Think about what you're saying, Rainer." I've only just admitted to him that I want more than friends. I'm ready to take the risk and be with him—give myself to him. But now... now he's saying we can never fully have each other.

"I'm saying that I refuse to put that pressure on you. I won't let you make that decision just to free me from Yvanthia's bond."

"So you'll force me into another decision that assuages your fears?" I challenge. "You don't think I'd want to complete the bond if I chose to? You think so little of me?"

"No." He shakes his head and glances down, his dark hair falling into his eyes. "I think so *highly* of you."

"Give me a feckin break, Rainer."

Before he can reply, I allow the gust of courage to pull me to my feet. Shoving him backward, I straddle him, letting my nightgown ride up around my thighs.

I raise my brows. "Just like our dream."

"Alessia," he warns. His eyes darken, shifting from the pale blue to a darker shade, settling at cobalt. "Now is not the time to tease me."

"Who said anything about teasing?"

I lean forward, pressing my lips to his. He groans, wrapping his hand around the back of my head and holding me in place as he devours my mouth. His length hardens to steel in record time, and I grind against him.

Something about him undoes me.

No—

Everything about him undoes me.

"Rainer," I whisper as I break free from his lips. "I need you to know that everything I feel for you is real." I bring his hand to my chest, planting it against my heart. "The external distractions have no bearing on what I harbor *here* for you."

Nor does it tamper down my craving for him. My center aches with the desire to feel him bare against me. Reaching for his pants, I work the button. I expect him to stop me, to slow us down, but he tilts his head back to the cot and watches me with a predatory hunger.

A soft rustling noise permeates the air, followed by a loud "Well, shite!"

I squeak as Rainer shoots forward, tugging my dress down.

"Don't stop riding the steel eggplant on my account," Ken says, smiling from ear to ear.

The tent flap rustles again, and Tynan steps in behind him, carrying a couple of bowls.

He glances at me and his brother and narrows his eyes. "Yeah, feck this, I'm out." He thrusts the bowls at Ken and turns, and leaves.

"Stew?" Ken asks, lifting them in an offering. He hovers awkwardly above us, his massive frame looming as we stay planted on the low cot.

The smile on his face grows despite me not thinking it could possibly get any bigger. He makes no move to leave.

My cheeks heat even though I'm fully covered. Technically, we were only kissing.

"Steel eggplant?" I repeat, confused.

"Yeah, the ol' tallywacker. The petrified garden snake." He snickers. "The single-legged horse. The good ol' concrete carrot—"

"Kenisius!" Rainer yells, his hands tightening around me. "Out!"

The bear shifter laughs harder, unfazed by Rainer's annoyance, as he sets the bowls on the ground before us and leaves.

My attention shifts back to Rainer, whose cheeks are red. At first, I think it's anger he's wearing, but when he closes his eyes and sighs, I realize it's embarrassment.

"That was for the best," he mutters. "I'm proving my incompetency by letting it get this far."

Gently, he stands and tugs me to my feet. I freeze, waiting to see if he's going to revert to his previous demeanor and leave again, but his face softens. He cups my cheek, leaning in to plant a chaste kiss on my forehead.

"I'm not pushing you away again," he mutters against my skin. "I'm inclined to, but I'm trying very hard not to."

He bends and snatches up my clothing, handing the garments to me. "Now, get dressed so we can eat and leave."

Or get undressed so he *can eat*, my shadow-self says coyly.

The words are so shocking that I gasp and almost drop my pants.

That's of use to us.

"Hush," I mutter, appalled that this *thing* can see and hear us.

This thing *is you*, it says dryly.

"Stop talking," I say through gritted teeth.

Rainer gives me a strange look, and I shake my head, brushing it off. As soon as I reach for the hem of my dress to change, his eyes fill with heat again. But instead of ravaging me, he puts his back to me in a respectful manner.

Disappointment courses through me, which is entirely unfair. He's trying to make my life easier.

And we want to make his *harder.*

A snort of laughter escapes me. At least the damn voice is being harmless, albeit annoying.

I change quickly, pulling on pants and boots, and then we each grab a bowl of stew. He sits on Tynan's cot across the tent while I sit on ours. We quickly slurp the meal down. My attention is firmly locked on Rainer the entire time, remembering how beautiful his naked skin glowed in the sun yesterday. My stomach tightens, and the overwhelming urge to pounce on him builds.

"We should get going," Rainer says. "We slept well past dawn."

Forget the journey. We have everything we need right here. The darkness vibrates through my veins, preventing me from forgetting its presence. It pools low, in the exact space I crave Rainer most, tempting me with a slight pressure.

I take a deep breath, trying to quell the lust. "I'm not sure that's a good idea right now."

He cocks a brow. "Why not?"

Let's have some fun, first.

I wince, embarrassed by the desire consuming me. "My shadow is a bit… riled up. I'm afraid I might lose control when it's in this state."

"What state is that?"

Warmth creeps up my neck. "There's this unrelenting *need*—and I don't know if it belongs to me or my shadow-self, but it won't quiet down."

His eyes turn steely as he rakes them over me. He's quiet as the seconds turn to minutes. Then, his lips tilt up in a mischievous smirk.

"What are you thinking?" I ask.

He chuckles softly, his eyes crinkling at the corner as he drops his hands to his thighs. "You sure you want the answer to that?"

"Always," I say softly.

"It might shatter your illusion of me—my thoughts are rather depraved at the moment."

I give him a small, reassuring smile. "I never had any delusions about you, Rainer."

His eyes flit to my lips, then slowly drag up my face. "I want nothing more than to see you lose control."

My spine tingles, taunted by his words.

"In *this* regard, I mean," he adds quickly. The timbre of his voice prickles my skin. "You never have to hide who you are with me; I hope you know that."

My darkness roils as if responding delightfully to his words. *Listen to him. Embrace yourself.*

"I thought you didn't like him," I mutter to the dark voice within me.

Rainer arches a brow. "Sounds like it likes me plenty."

I sigh, plopping back down on the cot and waving a hand toward myself. "My shadow-self doesn't know what it likes. It tries to convince me to do… things."

"Bad things?"

"Yes," I whisper.

His face softens as he stares down at me. "To me?"

I nod. "Sometimes." My nostrils flare as I turn my head away from him. "Or—it used to. Now it wants me to do the good kind of bad things to you. Which is much better, but still a pressure, and I don't know which thoughts and feelings are actually *mine* and which are—"

"Look at me," he commands softly.

I cease my rambling. My head lifts on its own accord as if my senses are tethered to him by an invisible string.

He quietly and gracefully drops to his knees and plants his hands on the ground. Like a quiet, graceful predator, he crawls to me.

My heart thumps erratically. When he reaches me, his hands wrap around the back of my calves, his touch scalding me through my pants. With a wicked smirk, he bows his head, resting his forehead on my knees.

"I am *yours*, Princess Alessia Lírshadow of Spiritus Court, spiritcaller, and captor of my heart."

It's sexy but also so corny that I can't suppress the giggles. His head lifts at the sound, his icy gaze piercing me. His mouth is in a tight line, his face free of humor.

"I am *yours*," he repeats, unfazed by my response. "I belong to your light and your dark—to your sun and shadows—completed bond or not."

Yes, yes, I like him, my shadow-self says, practically purring.

I bite down my smile as Rainer leans forward and kisses each of my knees.

"I thought *I* was *yours*?" I smirk shyly. "Your little rose."

"Don't you know me better than that by now?" He stretches out, still resting on his knees before me. Reaching for me, he gently grips my neck and brings our foreheads together. His warm breath flits across my lips. "The roses never truly belonged to me. They own me, as do you. I exist to serve them—as I do you."

My eyes close, and I breathe him in. He smells like sandalwood and roses, tinged by sweat and earth, but I like it. It's wholly *him*. He murmurs something I can't make out, his mouth brushing mine with the barest of touches. My stomach tumbles with the promise of his kiss.

Then he pulls away.

The emptiness is a harsh contrast to the fullness of his presence. My eyes flick open to catch him on his feet, facing away from me.

His dark waves fall around his decorated, pointed ears. He stretches his hand out, reaching for mine. "Whatever happens, we face it as a team. I will do *anything* for you." His cheek muscle twitches. "Anything other than complete the bond."

My smile falters. My eyes flick to the floor before meeting his. "Yes, of course."

Disappointment swells in my chest.

Rainer shifts his weight, his hand still hovering in the air before me. I place my palm in his, allowing him to help me to my feet. We interlock our fingers as he pulls the tent's flap aside, allowing me to exit.

I expect him to drop my hand once we step through, but he grips it tighter.

"I meant what I said, Alessia," he whispers in my ear, pushing the hair off my shoulder. "I will always be yours—in any way that you'll have me."

All the ways.

I want him in all *the ways*.

And I can't tell if it's me or the shadow-self this time, but we agree for once.

Except I can't have him in all the ways. He made it clear: we will never be intimate. Not fully and completely. And that should be okay—sex isn't everything—but I've never craved anyone like I do him. The thought of never having him in that way floods me with a river of sadness.

I will never truly have *all* of him.

TWENTY-SEVEN
SAVED HER LIFE
ALESSIA

"At this rate, we won't arrive at Wyrville until sundown," Tynan grumbles. "Can we go any faster?"

"If you save energy on complaining, you might be able to," Ken says.

Sera walks between them, openly laughing at the barbed exchange. They've been at it for a good hour now.

We keep a steady pace, journeying further inland, away from the coast, through Bear Valley. The landscape is a breathtaking mix of hills and rivers winding their way around us. Farmland stretches on the horizon to the east. There's less tree coverage here, though, and the summer sun beats on our backs, slowing us down. It's borderline unbearable without the cool sea breeze, even with bespelled leathers.

"There are no bears here," Ken says, disappointment lacing his tone. "Why name it such a lie?"

"Because humans." Tynan grunts. "It's probably named after a man—not a bear."

"A man named after a bear?" Ken asks, confused.

The two continue to debate the origins of the valley's name while we press onward. Zephyr follows behind us, his hair drenched with sweat.

"Arriving after sundown is preferable," Rainer says, leading the group alongside me. "Less people, less light, less attention."

"Yeah, yeah, you and your feckin logic," Tynan mutters. "I wanted to get there earlier."

"Why?" Rainer takes a chug from the flask hanging from a leather strap across his chest. He offers it to me after and I accept, doing the same, even though I have my own water.

"Maybe I wanted to explore now that I'm away from the damn bog for once," Tynan says.

"The less time we spend in town, the better," Rainer says.

"It's not even a bog anymore, actually," Ken adds, perky as ever. "It's a really pretty place now."

He grins at me, slowing down to plant his hand on a trembling Zephyr's head. I snicker to myself, knowing exactly what the human must think—because I was also afraid of Ken when I first met him until I got to know him.

"Doesn't mean I want to stare at the same few trees the rest of my damn life," Tynan says.

"If you weren't such a liability, maybe you'd have more freedom," Rainer deadpans.

"You wanna go there, little brother?" Tynan's voice hardens, and he wipes the sweat from his brow. "You're not my keeper—I stay in Shgya because I take my responsibility seriously. I stopped drinking because I don't want to be like our piece of shite father—"

The males continue to bicker, so I fall back and match Seraphina's pace, zoning them out. She forces a smile, and adjusts her grip on the bag she's carrying.

"The heat is getting to them," I say, sighing.

"It'll take the rest of the day to get to Wyrville, and another whole day to get to our destination?" she asks.

I nod. "Ryalle. Yes."

"Have you ever been?" she asks.

"Never." I'd spent most of my twenty-three years with the lord and lady, puttering around their estate. "Even trips into town were rare, let alone traveling out of Lyson."

She glances upward at the sky, and I follow her gaze. We've been walking for hours, and the sun is barely cresting over the midpoint, beginning its descent. We must be about halfway to Wyrville by now.

"I can make something to help," Seraphina says. "With the heat."

My gaze whips to hers so quickly that I stumble over a rock. A hand wraps around my arm, steadying me, and I blink up into Rainer's face. My heart skips a beat.

My brows shoot up. "How did you...?"

"Quick reflexes." He winks, then releases me and darts back to his brother, a scowl in place as he seamlessly integrates into their conversation.

My arm tingles where he touched me, as if my body is begging for him to come back.

Seraphina smiles as she keeps her eyes straight ahead. "I'm jealous," she says. "Of your bond."

The air whooshes from my lungs as a small piece of my heart breaks off. "Don't be," I mutter. "We're not completing it."

"No. Not that bond—your bond in general. Your relationship." She jerks her chin toward the males. "He *really* would do anything for you."

My cheeks heat. She's not wrong, but the fact she can see that so easily refills my deflated heart with a touch of joy. "You can see auras, right?"

She nods, glancing at me from the side of her eye. "Energy and intent, yes."

"What does his say about him?"

She chuckles, shaking her head. "You already know what's in his heart, Alessia. You don't need my insight on the matter."

"Not as pure as Ezamae, eh?" I tease, knowing damn well that Rainer has a good soul, regardless of what Seraphina reads of his energy.

She bites her lip and a look of longing flashes across her face. "I wish he looked at me the way Rainer looks at you."

"Who... Ez?"

Silence hangs between us until Sera lets out a long, defeated sigh.

After her words sink in, I realize two things: one, she's definitely in love with the Aer Prince. Two, she will be utterly devastated when she learns he's soul-bonded to someone else.

Shite.

Now isn't the time to tell her. Especially since I'm not entirely positive that's the case.

Instead, I refocus on what she said a few minutes ago. "If you can make something to help with this heat, why not do it earlier?"

She sighs. "There's no nefarious intent—I simply hadn't realized it would be so warm here." She points at a thicket of trees cascading down the hillside ahead, past a wide river. "We can stop there for lunch—it's fairly hidden away, and I'll whip up a cooling salve."

After crossing the river, we spend nearly thirty more minutes going uphill, then descending on the other side, until we're nestled deep within a serene, wooded area. The trees offer tangible relief, blocking the harshest of the sun's rays. We keep moving until we come upon a small stream.

We collectively let out a chorus of sighs as we toss down our belongings, all needing a break.

Ken shifts into his bear form and secures us fish from the river for lunch in an impressive manner. Tynan sets up a fire, and the two work to skin and debone the fish, cooking it on a makeshift spit. Rainer scouts the area, trekking to the top of the hill to gather intel. Sera and I forage for berries and fresh herbs to complement our meal. I follow her lead, allowing her to teach me which plants are edible and which should be avoided.

Honestly, I don't remember a single thing. As much as I love the beauty of flowers, plants aren't my thing.

It makes me respect her that much more. It's a skill, being able to identify them with ease.

We gather fresh rosemary and bring it back just in time for Ken and Tynan to put out the fire.

"Done!" Ken booms, a broad smile on his face. "Get your sweet, sweaty arses over here and eat up."

Rainer descends the nearest hill expressionlessly. "Still no sign of anyone as far as I can see or hear."

"Is that normal?" I ask Ken since he previously scouted the Wessex Peninsula with Viv. For some reason, I expected the entire realm to teem with soldiers, searching for escaped Tradelings to drag back to their owners. I'd always harbored that fear, instilled by the lord and lady.

"From all the recon we've done the past couple of months, yeah," Ken says as he hands me a flat rock with a chunk of fish on ir. Sera reaches over, ripping the rosemary and sprinkling it across the fish.

"I wish we had some lemon," she murmurs.

"Be grateful you have fish," Rainer hisses.

Sera rolls her eyes, flicking a piece of rosemary at him, then stomps away. I giggle, finding enjoyment in her sassy attitude. Rainer seethes, but he quietly folds into a cross-legged seat on the ground instead of giving her shite back.

I know it's for me that he keeps his attitude tame, which doubles my joy.

We eat, relieve ourselves, and refill our waters.

"Sera can make a cooling salve," I announce as the males pack up.

This grabs their attention. I half expect them to complain about her not doing it sooner, but instead, Ken fist-pumps the air with a whoop.

"Gods love me!" he says. "What do you need?"

She bends over, rummaging through her bag. "I have everything I…" Suddenly, she goes still and peers into her bag with a frown. "In my other bag."

With a furrowed brow, she drops her cloth knapsack to the ground and begins searching through our bags.

"Where is it?" she murmurs.

Concern prickles along the back of my neck. "Sera? What is it?"

She hesitates, dropping the bag she's holding and meeting my gaze. "My other bag… it's not here."

At the start of our journey, she had two bags. I hadn't even noticed one was missing. When I think back, I vividly remember her placing one down to gather herbs in the Lyson woods.

"I think I left it," she confirms, her face falling.

"What was in the bag?" Rainer asks, stepping forward with a stony look in his eyes.

Sera shrinks down, her natural confidence withdrawing as she suddenly looks scared. "Some ingredients… healing salves…" Her voice lowers. "The blood."

"The blood," Rainer repeats flatly. "You just so happened to lose the most important thing you were carrying."

I glare at him. "Rainer—"

"On *accident*," he says, raising his voice. "Despite knowing that Tynan needs it to glamour us." He scoffs, narrowing his eyes. "It wasn't an accident."

Ken remains quiet, his lips pressed into a tight line.

Shame creeps onto Seraphina's face, and I know she didn't do this on purpose.

"Rainer," I say carefully, not wanting to challenge him in front of the others but also wanting him to understand that it *was* an accident.

But he doesn't look at me. Instead, he keeps his icy scowl pinned on Seraphina, crossing his arms arrogantly.

"You're pissed about Ezamae being soul-bonded to someone else, and now you have no real reason to help us," he says. "Is that what it is? You're taking it out on *us* now?"

"Rainer!" Concern blazes through me, and my mouth drops open. "She didn't even know about that!"

I turn to Sera, bracing for her reaction to the news. But instead of shock or fury, she wears a blank expression, holding Rainer's stare.

"Ask her, Alessia." Rainer inclines his chin at her. "Ask her if it's true."

"Sera?" I whisper, looking at her.

"No," she says quickly. "Of course it wasn't on purpose."

I shift, glancing at Ken and Tynan, who wear expressions matching Rainer's irritation.

"You knew about Ez?" I ask her.

"She was eavesdropping at our tent while Ezamae was there—I sensed her," Rainer responds, not giving her a chance to. "She knows."

"But…" My features scrunch as I focus back on her. "The conversation we just had about him…? You lied?"

This time, Sera presses her lips together in anger and meets my gaze. "Lied about what? I *do* wish he looked at me the way this bastard—" she waves a hand at Rainer "—looks at you. That wasn't a lie. I never *lied*. And I didn't lose the gods-damned bag of blood on purpose." Her confidence returns as she squares her shoulders and snags her single bag from the ground. "I never meant to eavesdrop. I heard Ez's voice and was coming to say hello…" Her voice cracks, and a tear streaks down her face. "Forget it. I don't owe *you* a single thing, Rainer."

A sob breaks free, and the strong female cracks. But before we can see her crumble entirely, she turns the way we came and takes off into the trees.

My mouth drops open as I stare at her retreating form.

This isn't good. She's upset and alone in an unfamiliar realm, far from the Gleam.

Let her go, my shadow-self says. *She can handle herself.*

I shift my weight, feeling uneasy about the situation.

"Good thing we got this guy," Tynan says, snagging my attention. He pulls Zephyr to a stand, placing an arm over his shoulders. The guy practically buckles beneath Tynan's meaty bicep.

"You can't drink *Zephyr*," I say, appalled.

The man in question squeaks, his eyes popping open almost humorously. He pales, his body going rigid.

Rainer sighs, rubbing his forehead. "Unbelievable."

Tynan smirks. "Whaddya say, flesh-sack? Pay your dues for the journey?"

"Sh—sure," he stutters, flinching when Tynan tugs him closer.

"No," I growl. "He's innocent."

"I never said he wasn't," Tynan repeats.

"Alessia," Rainer says softly, stepping closer to me. His expression is still stern, but the wrinkle in his forehead smooths out. "The fresh blood might be better for him—stronger glamour. We might need... Zephyr's help."

"Not you, too," I say, shaking my head in disbelief.

He's right, my shadow-self adds.

I groan, pressing the heels of my hands into my eyes. "*Now* you side with him!?"

Tynan is a full-blooded vampyr in a realm full of humans. He needs to feed. Especially if he'll be using his magic. It's better this way than the alternative.

"What's the alternative?" I ask, fearing the answer.

Rainer sighs, running a hand through his hair. He glances at his brother.

Felix, my shadow-self says, reminding me of the ex-lover of mine that Tynan killed. *We're all the same. You, me, Rainer, Tynan. We all have needs. Stop standing in our way. You're making it harder for everyone by pretending you're better than them.*

"You pick the best times to become chatty," I say sarcastically.

We're the same, it repeats, *you and me.*

"I get it!" I yell, growing increasingly irritated.

Gritting my teeth, I glance up at the canopy of leaves overhead. Then, I turn back to Zephyr. Sheila's face flickers through my mind. This is her brother. He doesn't deserve this. The Tradeling mark on his face mirrors mine, filling me with a sense of kinship.

These are the very people I'm trying to look out for.

I won't agree to this.

"No," I finally say. Then, without looking back, I jog in the direction Sera went. Something tells me she didn't lose the blood intentionally, and she's been through enough.

Despite her heartbreak, she was suppressing her misery to continue helping us. Adding to her pains is the last thing I want to do.

She deserves it for—

"Shush!" I say exasperatedly, increasing my pace. "Shut the feck up already."

I don't care if she *deserves* it. I'm not going to be the one who adds to her troubles—just like I won't allow Sheila's brother to be harmed.

Up ahead, I catch sight of Sera, her back to me as she storms away in the direction we came.

"Sera!" I call. "Wait!"

She turns around, and I catch the surprise—then relief—flashing across her face. It dawns on me how similar the two of us truly are. We both understand the importance of making sacrifices for those we hold dear, often risking our hearts.

The difference is that her heart has been thoroughly crushed—her hope smudged out.

And leaving someone alone when they're utterly devoid of hope is the cruelest thing we can do to another.

She takes a step toward me, but before she can take another, a dark blur bursts from the trees, tackling her to the ground just as an arrow shoots through the air where her head was a moment ago.

A scream rings out, and it takes a moment to realize two things:

One, the person screaming is me.

Two, it was my shadow that just saved her life.

Twenty-Eight

Tied to Her

Rainer

Alessia's scream pierces my heart like a needle, aspirating every drop of blood in a split second. The sound barely registers in my mind before my feet instinctively start moving.

With her essence still in my system from yesterday, my vampyr senses are heightened. I inhale, quickly catching her scent in the air.

A growl bursts from my throat as I pick up speed, shooting through the trees so quickly my lungs are seconds away from bursting.

Up ahead, the treeline breaks, and just beyond, I catch sight of a dark shadow the size of a carriage sitting at the base of a small hill.

I abruptly come to a halt, my hackles raising.

The shadow wavers slightly, like a dark, thick fog, obscuring whatever lies within it. I close my eyes, listening carefully.

Thump. Thump-thump. Thump.

Two overlapping, frantic heartbeats reach my ears.

Alessia.

I know one of them is her. I can't explain it in words, but I'd recognize the sound of her heartbeat anywhere. But I don't immediately run to her because she's safe within her shadow shield.

I detect a couple of faint, remote heartbeats, followed by the distinct fragrance of *human*.

Crouching to plan my next move, I scan the valley. Movement atop the hill to the left catches my eye. A couple of men dressed in hunting boots and green leather tunics move swiftly, descending the hill. They use the few sporadic trees there for cover.

An arrow zips through the air, hitting Alessia's shadow and bouncing off without piercing it.

Panic sluices through me. My legs coil with tension, ready for me to spring free. But I stifle the urge to move.

She's okay.

Her heartbeat stays steady, and her shadow doesn't budge. I don't smell any hint of her blood spilling.

She's okay.

I repeat it to myself, reminding myself not to be rash. If we were bonded, and I acted impulsively—running to her side and recklessly exposing myself to the enemies—it would put her doubly at risk. Risking my life would be risking hers.

So, instead, I steady my gaze on the men trickling down the hill. There are three of them. They crouch low, keeping their bows raised and arrows knocked.

I squint, my heightened eyesight allowing me to make out the details of their weaponry. They each have a quiver at their back and a dagger at their side, and they're in matching harnesses with finger gloves.

They're undoubtedly soldiers.

It would be easy to unleash my fearcaller power to make them cower and beg, but Alessia's scream from earlier echoes in my mind, dredging up my bloodlust.

I'm not afraid they'll hurt her—not with her shadow power at her side. However, I *am* concerned that her lack of control could lead to three fatalities, for which she would feel personally account- able. She has only recently begun to accept and reconcile with her inner darkness. I want to avoid the possibility of her regressing and withdrawing again due to guilt.

Staying in control during a high-stakes situation is a win she needs. It'll serve as proof that she is the one in charge. The shadow does not own her.

I must get to them before her shadow can strike and kill them.

Another animalistic growl bubbles in my throat. My vision flick- ers as my primal urge grows, further enhancing my senses. The sweet, tempting scent of human blood draws me forward a few steps.

Unlike Alessia, I feel no remorse in ensuring the safety of my loved ones—no matter the cost. I want to look these adversaries in the eyes as I kill them. I want them to beg me as I tear open their thin, pathetic flesh with my teeth and drain them dry.

I track my prey with steady, quiet steps, maneuvering unseen through the trees. As I edge closer to the men, my nose prickles with a familiar scent.

Tynan.

He's somewhere close behind me, but he's wise to stay out of my way—unseen and unheard.

The three men reach the base of the hill.

The moment their feet hit the valley, the shadow in the middle of the clearing convulses. It shifts from the box-like covering into a massive tentacle in the blink of an eye. The dark arm lashes out, sweeping the men's legs and taking them all down swiftly.

All three of them hit the ground, groaning.

Alessia and Seraphina stand in the tall grass, exposed. My rose is stiff, her jaw slack with disbelief, and I quickly realize her fear is warranted—she isn't in control of her shadow-self. It'll kill these men, and in the process, it'll destroy another piece of her heart.

Run.

Her gaze swings in my direction as if she can sense my presence. I'm unsure if she can see me, but her body goes limber as she relaxes. In the next breath, she's grabbing the sorceress's hand, and they're bolting toward the forest's cover.

My attention jerks back to the men now rising and nocking their arrows. I don't give them a chance to succeed, nor do I give Alessia's shadow another opportunity to attack them.

I explode from the trees in a fury, my body trembling with a potent mixture of rage and primal instinct. The air crackles with tension as I succumb to the bloodlust coursing through my veins. My vision narrows, the darkness encroaching from the edges and the rest of the world fading away, leaving only the savage desire to *feast*.

Bursting forth, each second dissolves into a blur of frenzied motion. My snarls echo through the air as I pounce. The first man's face contorts with fear and disbelief. Trembling, he reaches for an arrow, but I knock it loose, wrapping my fingers around his throat and squeezing.

Another man jumps on my back, clobbering me in the temple with his fist. Unable to breathe through my grip, the first man slumps to the ground unconscious. With relentless ferocity, I whirl around and tear my teeth into the second man's throat. The sound of flesh ripping and bones shattering fills the air, blending with a gurgling scream of agony as I tear him apart.

I'm not drinking—I'm annihilating. Using my fangs, I tear into his limbs, ripping the flesh from his bones. A thick, metallic tang fills my mouth, and I roar. As soon as the ivory bones come into view, I snap them with a satisfying crack, casting them aside without a second thought.

With the man now a grotesque heap of torn flesh and shattered bones, I turn my focus back to the first man. He remains unconscious, his body limp and pitifully sprawled across the grass. With a sudden lurch, I pounce towards his neck, piercing my fangs into the tender flesh. I tear through it like paper, feeling the warm blood coat my lips as I consume him like a crazed beast.

With each swallow, I feel my vigor expanding and my power growing stronger. My senses sharpen and intensify.

I mercilessly deplete him of all vitality until he's a dried-up husk. Then, I forcefully snap him in half, leaving him with his friend.

As abruptly as it began, it ends.

Except… where's the third man?

My head snaps up, and I catch him stumbling up the hill. He trips over his own feet as he flees in a panic. Growling, I bend and snatch up one of the abandoned bows. With ease, I nock an arrow and aim. Closing a single eye, I lock onto my target, pull the string taut, and release.

The arrow whistles through the air, finding its mark exactly where I aimed. It penetrates the back of his neck. His body convulses violently, causing him to collapse to his knees and slump over.

Slowly, the adrenaline subsides. The dark haze lifts from my vision, and a sense of satisfaction swells in my chest. The surrounding forest and hills stand tranquil.

My lungs heave with my ragged breaths. I use the back of my hand to wipe the blood from my face, but it only smears it further. Glancing down, I take in my red-stained hands and arms.

I'll have to bathe again before continuing.

"I'll take care of them," Tynan says, licking his lips. He bolts past me, quickly reaching the dead man on the hill. Dropping to all fours, he yanks the arrow free. Then, he bends and latches his mouth onto the man's wounded neck, greedily consuming the remaining blood.

Even in my state of bloodlust, I subconsciously left one of the men intact so Tynan could feed—so he could leave the boy we're traveling with alone. Even my monster would do anything to make Alessia happy.

Turning, I prepare myself to hunt her next, but I'm surprised to catch her running toward me. Her ashy curls bounce behind her, having freed themselves from the braid she usually wears.

She picks up her pace when she meets my eyes, lunging for me the moment she's close enough.

I catch her with ease, planting one hand under her arse and cupping her head with the other. She wraps her legs and arms around me, clinging to me.

"Are you okay, mo róisín?" I murmur into her hair, squeezing tighter.

"Me?" she says on a heavy exhale. Her heart thumps relentlessly against my own as if desperate to break free from her ribs and mesh with mine. "You saved me."

I can't help but laugh, feeling lighter despite the weight of her body in my arms. "You would've been just fine without me."

And I believe it. Even if she didn't have complete control over her shadow-self, it would've protected her. She was afraid, but it's because she hasn't yet learned to trust herself.

"I didn't leave you," she says, pulling back to look at me. Her wide, grey eyes roam the mess I've made, but she doesn't balk. She keeps her hands wrapped around my neck. "I couldn't. I was watching from the trees. You…" Another big exhale bursts from her lungs. "You *protected* me."

The way she says it tells me she knows why I stepped in. Not to save her life but to save that tender heart of hers.

"Always, little rose," I murmur.

Her eyes sparkle with unshed tears as they bounce between my eyes. Her fingers slide up to the nape of my neck.

"My only regret is that you had to see that," I say, using my thumb to wipe away a clump of blood on her cheek.

Her gaze flits to the ground behind me, then to the distance, where Tynan slurps from the body. She pales, and I angle us around so she's no longer facing them. Then, I carry her toward the trees.

"Let's get you cleaned up," I say, hoisting her up to adjust my grip as I stride away from the scene. She doesn't deserve to be stained by their filth.

She's much too precious, too perfect to be tainted.

"Rainer," she whispers. Gods, I love how my name sounds when it falls from her lips. "My shadow was shot at—with arrows."

My feet stop moving, and fear licks my spine. I pull my head back, quickly inspecting her for any signs of a wound. I hadn't seen—or smelled—an injury on her.

A tired laugh spills from her. "No—I'm not hurt. That's the thing, though. I'm *not* hurt." Wonder lights up her face. "It's like only *I* can hurt my shadow."

Leaning forward, she wraps herself tightly around me. I let her ponder the implications in peace, grateful as hell that she's unharmed.

"I'll never let anything hurt you, mo róisín," I mutter into her hair. "You're mine to protect."

We make it back to where we stopped for lunch. Kenisius sits with Zephyr—exactly where I told him to stay. My pal's brown eyes flash with the fight, and his leg bounces. I'm sure he's *thrilled* about being left behind to watch a human. Seraphina sits on the ground beside our belongings.

"You," I snarl at Seraphina. "You could've gotten her killed, pulling that shite."

The sorceress's mouth stays in a grim line, and she nods. "I shouldn't have fled."

Kenisius glances up at me, and he must read whatever is on my face because he quickly jumps to his feet.

"Hey!" He tugs Seraphina's braid playfully. "There's something over here that I wanted to show you." The two of them swiftly move away, giving us privacy.

Zephyr stares at me, his body trembling like a leaf. He jumps up, darting after Kenisius and Seraphina. "Wait for me!"

I place Alessia on the ground, gently guiding her to sit on a rock. Then, I locate a canteen and rag, wetting it to wash away the droplets of blood on her arm and face.

"You need that more than I do," she says softly, trying to pull it free of my hands. I don't relent, wiping her down carefully before I bother to analyze my own unfortunate state.

After a stretch of silence, she sighs.

"Rainer… I could've gotten you killed. If we were bonded, I mean," she whispers. "Doesn't that scare you?"

I go still, lowering my arm. "No," I say honestly. "But living in a world without you does."

Her breath stutters, and she gazes at me with a question. Those grey eyes of hers soften, flitting across my face.

Much like myself, she had contemplated the consequences of the bond. Neither of us would've entertained the possible implications unless we were considering it. The fact she worries about how it might affect me indicates that she's giving it serious thought.

A gleeful warmth fills my guts, radiating through every inch of my body.

We shouldn't complete the bond.

We have so many reasons not to.

But none of them are stronger than my reason *to* complete it: for her. The thought of losing her and living on without her is worse than dying at her side. There is no life for me without Alessia.

I *want* to be completely and irrevocably tied to her.

Twenty-Nine
Indestructible, Demon
Alessia

M y mind spins, struggling to process the whirlwind of events. Rainer obliterated those men. They stood no chance against him as he effortlessly tore them down, showcasing his superior strength and skill. In the past, it would've terrified me. Now, it only deepens my sense of security around him. He was wholly in control the whole time.

It's evidence of how much he's *been* in control—even when he feared he wasn't.

Like when he bit Eoin, that wasn't a gory or lethal attack. It was precise and vengeful but nothing like what just happened.

And when he bites me? He's deliberate and gentle, which re-flects his careful nature.

The Rainer who bites me is hard to reconcile with the one who ruthlessly took down those men.

As we walk, I steal glimpses of him, and my heart warms at the sight of his striking profile. Before we packed up and left our resting spot, he meticulously scrubbed away every trace of blood. The black leathers he wears show no trace of blood—the material is seemingly impervious to stains. Convenient for a vampyr.

His wet hair, slicked back and out of his face, accentuates the in-tensity of his gaze, framed by furrowed brows. He glances my way, and when he catches me staring, the harsh edges of his features soften.

He's your thorns, and you're his petals, my shadow says.

It's not wrong. That's something Rainer once said to me, too. And the other thing my brain is struggling to process is how—*why*—my shadow responds the way it does. Those arrows didn't hurt it or me. So why am *I* injured when I attack it?

Am I the only one capable of causing damage?

I also noticed that my shadow was quieter and more stable, even in the higher adrenaline situation. It wasn't as vicious as it has been. It's significantly tamer. Instead of lashing out, it saved Seraphina's life—and mine. Then it pulled away when Rainer got there instead of taking control like it usually does. It *let* Rainer save me. They both spared me the guilt and pain of having to defend myself.

Something changed between us in that moment—between me and my shadow *and* between me and Rainer.

Shaking away the thoughts, I use my remaining energy to travel onward with the group.

We arrive at the edge of Wyrville shortly after sundown, exhausted and on edge, ready to slumber in a safe bed. Even though the past few hours were mostly silent, I still haven't had time to process everything that happened.

"We should stop here," Rainer instructs the group. We pause at the forest's edge before it gives way to the curved main street ahead.

I gaze at him longingly, admiring the way he confidently assumes control. I'm exhausted, but he excels in anticipating my needs. He instinctively knows when to follow my lead and when to take charge.

My shadow-self was wrong, just like I said from the beginning. Love doesn't make me weak. It makes me stronger because I'm a better version of myself with Rainer by my side. He brings out my strength and protects my softness.

Loving him *makes you stronger,* my shadow-self confirms.

I blink, stunned at the change of heart. It snickers from somewhere deep inside of me.

It's not my *change of heart*, it says. *We are one*.

I brush it off, not wanting to get into conversation with it right now with everyone around.

The lights of the town shine brightly, with flickering shades of orange and yellow dancing in the various windows. Shops and residential buildings line the main dirt-packed street stretching out before us.

Despite its southern location, the village resembles Lyson, featuring old stone and wood cottages. Unlike Lyson, this village is much more expansive, scaling the hills. To the north side of the town, I catch a glimpse of the cornfields. Wyrville is known for its agricultural production, another place Tradelings commonly get sent for work.

"Where are we staying?" Tynan grumbles.

"The inn is that building there—at the edge of town." Zephyr points. "The one with the smoking chimney."

My gaze fixates on the building in question, with its steepled roof and windows adorned with flower-boxes. Oil lampposts illuminate the exterior, creating an inviting atmosphere.

It's a cute town, but it does little to ease my anxieties about staying the night here.

"My cousin's shop is three doors down," Zephyr says. "The red door with the broken sign overhanging it. We can head there in the morning for proper attire."

"Think we can trust him?" Ken strokes his beard, looking to Rainer for an answer.

Tynan smirks. "We can if I glamour him into obeying."

"Please," Zephyr begs. "You don't have to do that."

Rainer sighs, his eyes swinging to me and then back to his brother. "You shouldn't waste energy glamouring the boy."

Tynan presses his lips together and narrows his eyes. "I'm freshly fed. Plus, if I—"

"No," Rainer says, his features hardening. "Not an option."

"What's not an option?" I ask, picking up on an unspoken conversation between the brothers.

Tynan holds Rainer's stare, but he answers me. "If I feed on the subject I intend to glamour, the effect is much more powerful. Even a sip of their blood makes my glamour stronger."

I frown. "So it'd be easier and less work to control him?"

"Yes," Tynan says. "We could ensure he upholds his promises without betraying us. And it would barely cost me any effort." He squeezes the boy's bicep. "Easy prey."

"I'm—I'm not prey," Zephyr stutters. His wide eyes flit between us. Dark, sleepless bruises underline them. It makes the Tradeling tattoo stand out with an even starker contrast, the dark lightning bolt connecting us.

He meets my eyes, his expression morphing into a plead that physically pains my heart.

"No," I say. "We're not doing that."

Tynan sighs. "But he—"

"He won't betray us," I say.

"But—"

"You're not biting or glamouring him against his will, Tynan," I say adamantly.

Tynan opens his mouth to argue, but Rainer cuts him off. "You heard your princess." He shrugs a shoulder, smirking at me with a flicker of pride.

The word *princess* sends a flurry of mixed emotions through me.

Tynan's mouth snaps shut. Annoyance flares in his features, but he sighs again and runs a hand over his face. "Fine. You fixed Shyga, and you've demonstrated your strength, so you've earned my loyalty, but if this shite goes wrong..." He shakes his head. "I advise against it."

"It'll be fine," I say. His sister Sheila is a good girl, and it's not too bold of an assumption that her brother is, too. But if he's not... I meet Zephyr's eyes, forcing the following words out. "If you want to see your sister again, you won't betray us."

The man's eyes flare in shock as if he didn't expect that from me. "I—I don't intend to."

I nod. "Good."

Rainer clears his throat, and all eyes swing to him. "We'll pose as soldiers from the north—stationed in Lyson—who are traveling for the queen's event. We'll stay the night and not a second longer. In the morning, we'll retrieve the clothing for the fête and head straight to Ryalle. Understood?"

Tynan and Ken nod.

"That will explain Zephyr's presence, should anyone recognize him," Rainer says. "Tynan, you'll glamour our clothing to blend in with Zephyr's armor. Keep it simple."

Tynan pats his stomach dramatically. "Like I said—freshly fed. Let's get shite done."

"One problem," I interrupt. All eyes swing to me. "There aren't any female soldiers in Dovenak."

Rainer sets his jaw, taking me in as he contemplates the issue.

"I have an idea," I say, squirming under everyone's scrutiny. "But it's not… great."

My fingers skim the Tradeling marking on my cheek. It's a role I've held much of my life, so I'm familiar with how to act. I can certainly pretend.

Plus, I'm not that little girl anymore.

No, you're not, my shadow-self confirms with pride. *You are indestructible, demon.*

Thirty
I Choose You
Alessia

A short while later, our group bursts through the inn. Tynan has a bulky arm around Seraphina's neck, and she grimaces, her gaze so sharp she could slice him. An inky, jagged line runs from her temple to her chin, matching my Tradeling mark. Though it's glamoured, it looks like the real thing.

We head toward the empty counter at the back of the room, the plank floorboards creaking under our weight. A few people relax in worn sofas, but their conversations fade out and their eyes follow our group.

My night dress skims my ankles, swishing softly when I walk. My boots peek out from beneath the hem, looking out of place. Sera's dress matches my own—because she's borrowing it from me—and it stops around her shins, coming up short. It's much more snug across her chest than mine.

Tynan smirks as he glances down at her cleavage. She scowls harder, adding to the guise.

"Play nice, Fifi," he murmurs in her ear.

"Don't call me that," she growls, trying to pull away from him. He pulls her in tighter, clearly enjoying himself.

Her lips twitch as if suppressing a smile, but she stomps on his toes. A nearby onlooker watches, clearly shocked at the *Tradeling's* misbehavior.

Tynan notices and tugs Sera closer. "You'll pay for that later," he growls in her ear.

Ken watches them with a tight expression. He's uncharacteristically quiet, as if debating whether to intervene.

"I can handle you," Sera whispers to Tynan, a challenge in her gleaming eyes.

With tight shoulders, Ken whirls back toward the counter and approaches it.

Rainer wraps his hand around my elbow, gently guiding me. He leans in toward my ear, eyes darting around. "I don't like this, mo róisín."

Unlike his brother and Sera, he's not having fun with this. The fact he's uncomfortable with my idea of pretending Sera and I are soldiers' Tradelings is enough to put me at ease. Rainer is *nothing* like Lord Edvin. The fact I once considered the enigmatic faerie prince in the same category as that horrible human bastard is abysmal.

I smile up at him. "I trust you," I whisper. "It's okay."

With a tender gesture, he brushes his thumb over the corner of my mouth and leans in, his voice soft against my ear. "Although I adore your radiant smile, my dear rose, you might want to appear slightly less thrilled by my company."

He pulls away, and a tingling sensation lingers on my skin where his touch was.

In an effort to appear more uneasy, I bite down on my bottom lip and allow my shoulders to curl forward—shrinking in on myself.

Ken leans on the counter with Zephyr—who fiddles with his hands, looking unsure of himself—and slams his open palm on the tiny silver bell, causing it to ring out aggressively in the quiet space.

When no one comes, he does it a few more times. The sharp noise makes me wince.

"Enough," Rainer mutters, huffing a breath out.

Ken chuckles, and when an older, bald man with rounded shoulders hobbles out of the backroom, his smile grows. "Ello there, *man*," he says.

Rainer rubs his forehead as if he can smooth out the permanent stress wrinkle there.

"I didn't realize Queen Yvanthia was sending troops through Wyrville," the man says gruffly, scrutinizing our group. His eyes linger on Seraphina, then shift to me, boring into me for longer than I'd like.

Rainer steps in front of me, breaking the stare. "Three rooms," he demands.

Unlike Ken's playful demeanor, Rainer's cold, no-nonsense tone and lethal stare spur the innkeeper into action. He nods, then reaches below the counter to produce three keys.

He looks Ken up and down, frowning. "Why'dya say you're passing through again?"

"We're stationed in Lyson," Ken says nonchalantly. "Passing through on the way to the queen's fête."

The man *hmms* to himself as Tynan produces coppers, slamming them down on the counter.

"A little out of the way, no?" he asks, scooping the coins and counting them.

"My f—family is from here," Zephyr says quickly, surprising me. "My unit agreed to leave early and stop here for a night so I could see them."

The innkeeper turns his skeptical gaze to Zephyr. His features loosen. "You're Mary's boy, no?"

Zephyr smiles at the mention of his mother, and it seems genuine. "Yes, sir."

"Shame what happened to her." Pity flashes across his face, and Zephyr's smile drops. "Good woman, she was. Her sister still lives locally. Shame she didn't take you in. That son of hers runs the shoppe a few doors down, though."

Relief flickers through me as I share a look with Rainer. Zephyr was honest about his cousin's store, which counts for something. However, hearing his mother passed away fills me with sorrow.

The fact his aunt was here the whole time, but she still let him be taken as a Tradeling instead of adopting him herself, makes it hurt even more. I study Zephyr, suddenly wanting to know more of his story.

"Thought you were in the mines," the innkeeper says, continuing the conversation.

"I am, sir. I mean, I was, sir." Zephyr swallows heavily. "I'm stationed in Lyson now, though." He glances at Rainer before continuing. "Queen Yvanthia pulled me for the draft."

"Hm." The man places his forearms on the counter as he leans forward. He meets my eyes over Rainer's shoulder and grimaces. "They drafted whores, too, I see. Wise to keep you boys entertained up there in the north. It's rather dull, I hear."

Rainer goes stiff. I instinctively reach for him, grabbing his arm the moment he steps forward.

The man smiles at Rainer, revealing his missing teeth. "You don't much seem like the sharing type, but I'll refund your rooms if you let me have a go at one. It's been a long time since—"

His legs give out, and he crumples to the ground, quivering. A whimper escapes his lips as he stares at something invisible hovering over him.

"What's wrong, Prichard?" One of the patrons on the couch says, alarmed. They jump up, charging toward the counter.

"Rainer," I hiss quietly through my teeth. "*Don't.*" I wait a beat and add, "*Please.*"

My nails bite into the fleshy part of his forearm as I grip him tightly, silently begging him not to kill the man. Not here, not like this.

The patron rounds the counter quickly, shaking Prichard's shoulder and speaking rapidly to him.

I clutch onto Rainer tighter, and he sighs, finally relenting.

"Call my property a *whore* again, and find out just how much I like sharing," Rainer spits.

The innkeeper stands, his eyes wide and face pale, as he gapes at our group with even more skepticism than before. It doesn't matter if Rainer's ears appear round and he's dressed in soldier garb; if he uses magic recklessly, it's only a matter of time before our cover is blown.

"Tynan—handle this?" Rainer says, waving lazily toward Prichard and the worried patron at his side. He snatches one of the keys off the counter and places a hand on the small of my back, leading me toward the stairs.

Ken and Seraphina follow expressionlessly. The bear shifter pats a gaping Zephyr's head.

"Come on, *man*," Ken says to him.

If the tension weren't so thick, I'd laugh at the awkward accent when he says the word—trying extra hard to sound human.

I glance over my shoulder to catch Tynan glaring at Rainer as he retreats, shaking his head with his arms crossed.

"Waste of energy, brother," Tynan calls. "For us both. But *I'm* the one with no self-control?"

Rainer leads me up an old set of wobbly stairs. "We all have our limits," he says without looking back."

"He's wrong," I say as we reach the landing. "About you not having self-control."

Rainer sighs, hanging his head and shaking it.

"But we *are* supposed to be blending in. This doesn't help."

We all agreed it's wise to be careful with how much energy Tynan uses for his glamour. The less, the better. And now he has to glamour a handful of people into forgetting what just happened.

"No one calls my little rose a whore," he growls, glancing down at me. His pale eyes flicker with a dangerous cobalt warning. "And no—I do *not* share."

He glances back toward the stairs as if he's about to storm down there and make a bad decision. I rip the key from his hand, noticing the number *three* label on it. I hurry toward door three and use the key to unlock it, quickly yanking him in by a belt loop.

As I go to close the door, I meet Ken's eyes across the hall. He nods, and I know he'll handle Zephyr and Sera, but *I* need to handle Rainer.

I shut the door and turn to Rainer.

"He's not leaving this building with his life," he says, eerily calm. And I know he means it.

Sighing, I give him a stern look. "You can't kill him."

"I can and I absolutely will."

"What happened to listening to me and my commands?" I ask, trying to lighten the mood.

"I'll always listen to you, mo róisín," he says, his eyes softening as he gazes adoringly at me. "Except when it comes to scum like that."

Men like Lord Edvin. I shudder.

He's right, my shadow-self says. *If you won't let* me *at the weasel, at least let the prince protect you.*

"The gods have blessed us," he mutters, smirking.

It takes me a second to detangle from my shadow's musings and address his comment. "How so?"

He points. "A single bed."

I follow his line of sight, finally taking in the room. It's small but cozy, with one steel-framed bed occupying most of the room. A weaved, oval carpet matches the brown quilt, and a bedside table with a lit oil lamp illuminates the space. An oak dresser sits across from the bed, and a door leads to what I assume is the bathroom.

My eyes flick to the ceiling, and disappointment courses through me when I notice there's no mirror like there was in Ethyria.

"Why does it matter if there's only one bed?" I ask, confused.

He moves my hair away from my neck, leaning in and inhaling my skin. His tongue whips out, tracing a line from my collarbone to my ear. His teeth skim my lobe, and I shudder, a flood of warmth alighting me from the inside out.

"There's no way you can avoid sharing a bed with me now," he teases.

"As if multiple beds would stop that," I say, turning to him with a coy smile. "And if I recall correctly, *you* are the one who ran away from me after we shared a bed in the tent."

"Yes, *after* we shared." He smirks. "And correction, I fled from my issues—not from you."

"Apparently, I *am* your issue."

"No." He shakes his head, his voice dropping an octave. "You're the solution to all of my problems, mo róisín. The healing salve to my damaged soul."

His eyes darken again, but this time, it's with lust instead of the quiet rage he experienced only moments ago. I adore the intensity of his pale blue irises, but there's an undeniable allure in the darkness that emerges when his bloodlust tempts him.

"You need to drink, don't you?" I whisper. My voice comes out huskier than I expected.

His eyes drop to my mouth, and he nods almost imperceptibly. "If you'll let me." He reaches up, caressing my bottom lip with his thumb. "You're the only one I ever want to taste, mo róisín. Your blood. Your flesh. I want to drown in the taste of you."

The breath escapes my lungs, and for a moment, I can't get it back. The heat in my chest drops low, settling between my legs.

He reaches for my waist, swooping me up into his arms. I squeal with delight, wrapping myself around him as he carries me to the bed. Anticipation courses through me and all I see his him.

All I smell is him.

All I *need* is him.

On top of me, inside of me—I want to be *one* with him.

A light breeze flutters across my skin, followed by the scent of pine and fresh air.

"Feckin hell," Rainer says, his features tightening as he glances at something behind me. Instead of depositing me on the bed like he clearly intended, he sets me down on my feet beside him and quickly adjusts his pants.

"Consummating the bond?" Ezamae says cheerily, from where he's just appeared on the opposite side of the bed. His navy cloak rests heavily on his shoulders, and the velvet-lined hood is pulled up to hide much of his curly moonlight-silver hair.

"Clearly not." Rainer looks less than amused as he addresses the Aer Prince.

My fog of desire dissipates as I take him in. "What are you doing here, Ez?"

"Yes," Rainer drawls, his eyes narrowing. "Do tell."

"I have a plan," he says, his smile growing. "To kill the faerie queen. But I need you to consummate your damn bond."

Rainer's features tighten as he glances at me. "No."

I frown at the quick rebuttal. "But—"

"Rainer," Ez says, the playful demeanor evaporating as he stands tall and holds Rainer's gaze. "You are tied to the queen's life. If I successfully remove her the way I intend, you won't survive."

I gasp, clutching Rainer's arm, but I address the Aer Prince. "You can't, Ez."

"Which is why I need you two—" he waves a hand at us, sending a gust of wind through our hair "—to solidify your soul-bond and break free of Yvanthia's."

"And if you're wrong?" Rainer growls. "If we consummate our bond, and it doesn't break Yvanthia's, then we all die. *All* of us."

He squeezes his fist at his side, working to reign in his fury. "That means *you*, too."

"I'm not wrong." Ez pulls back his hood, shaking out his hair, and rounds the bed. "I'm free from Yvanthia's clutches, and you will be, too."

"Who did you bond with?" I ask curiously, wanting to confirm I'm understanding this situation correctly.

His cheeks tinge with a dusting of pink, but his silver eyes sparkle. "Someone rather... unexpected. She's quite displeased. You're fortunate the two of you have a mutual affection. Completing your task should be a breeze."

Before I can press him, Rainer steps forward until he's chest-to-chest with Ez. "*Stop* pressuring her," he hisses lethally. "I'll find another way to break my bond with Yvanthia."

"There's no other way." Ez's lips flatten as he holds Rainer's stare unwaveringly. "I've been looking for *years*. This is the only way."

"No—"

"I thought you'd be rather ecstatic about this," Ez says calmly. He glances over Rainer's shoulder to meet my eyes. "I must admit, the refusal strikes me as unexpected."

"Rainer," I say, softly touching his shoulder. "I'll do it."

He runs a hand through his raven-colored hair, turning stiffly toward me. His expression is unreadable as he studies me. The tension in the room grows thick as none of us speak for a few moments.

"I can be patient for now," Ez says, his words slicing through the tension like a blade. "But Rainer, the longer we hesitate, the more susceptible we become to Yvanthia's suspicions." Ez clears his throat awkwardly as Rainer stalks toward me, ignoring him. "I need to return. But, one more thing," the Aer Prince says quickly. "If I'm to buy time, I require Sera's assistance—"

"*Go*," Rainer growls.

"She needs to come with me to—"

"Take her!"

Ez gives me a broad smile and winks, and he's gone in a poof of shimmering air in the next breath.

Rainer stares at me with unwavering intensity. "What do you mean you'll do it?" he asks, looking more furious than excited.

"The bond," I whisper. He opens his mouth to refute me, but I put a hand up. "It's not because of Yvanthia, or Ez. It's because I want it. I want *you*." Sucking in a deep breath, I muster up my courage and finally speak the words I know he needs to hear. "Rainer, for now and forever, I choose you."

THIRTY-ONE
YOUR ROOTS AND PETALS
RAINER

F ecking hell. She chose me. She finally chose me.

After everything we've been through. Even though it's been only half a year, it's felt like much longer. And I never want to go another season without her by my side.

After I attacked those men to protect her, she didn't shy away from me. There was no fear or disgust or resentment. She sees me, and she accepts me.

Perhaps I won't let her down. Maybe we can truly do this—become one—and I won't ruin it.

"I will always belong to you," I say quietly, my voice overflowing with need.

I storm toward her, pulling her flush to me. I work my fingers into the back of her hair, cupping her head and directing her gaze to me.

She bites her lip and then looks away. "I need to bathe first."

My grip on her tightens, and a tiny, surprised gasp escapes her.

"Rainer," she whispers breathlessly. "We've been traveling for two days now and—"

"I don't care." I lean down, scraping my teeth against her neck solely to make her shudder. The natural scent of her turns me on, and I press my erection against her, letting her feel how badly I want her.

"Come with me." She pulls free and tugs me along as she heads to the bathroom. "We can *talk* while we bathe," she teases.

She opens the bathroom door, revealing a toilet, shower, and expansive counter that spans the entire wall to our left. Another oil lamp sits there, casting an orange glow around the room.

"I suppose we can talk while we *shower*," I amend, opening the glass door. I reach for the faucet and turn the shower on. The pipes rattle as the water makes its way through the ceiling and out of the showerhead.

She watches as the water shoots out, causing steam to rise. "I've never taken a shower before. Up north, the pipes freeze in winter, so they rarely install them for bathing needs."

"I'm honored to be your first," I say, smirking at her. Holding open the shower door, I gesture for her to enter.

My eyes linger on her arse as she passes, mesmerized by the curves there. Her backside is textured with scars, and her legs are covered in fresh bruises from the journey, but it only deepens my attraction to her. Unblemished flesh doesn't tell stories like textured, bruised, and scarred skin does.

I loathe the fact she has scars—if the man responsible wasn't already dead, I'd kill him myself—but it's a reminder of her survival. She made it out.

"You're strong," I say, nestling my body against hers in the shower. "But I hate that you've had to be."

I can't see her response because she faces the spray, her skin pebbling as the water hits her. But the way she becomes soft against me is all the response I need. She trusts me. She *is* strong as hell, but she knows she doesn't always have to be with me.

That's the best compliment a male could receive.

"I'll always protect you," I murmur. I trace a line down her spine, loving how her body responds to my touch.

She spins to face me, and her breasts brush my chest. I groan as need floods every fiber of my being. Vulnerability shimmers in her grey eyes, and I eat it up like the starved beast I am.

The water washes over her hair, the ashy-blonde darkening and the curls straightening as it becomes wet.

"Turn back around," I order in a clipped tone, wanting more than just her hair wet. My resolve hangs on by a thread.

The way she nods and immediately obliges has my cock hard as iron, nudging against her bare arse. She wiggles slightly, rubbing against me. I groan, tipping my head back. Steam rises around us, and I'm lost to the heat of *her*. Wrapping my arms around the front of her waist, I pull her flush against me, nestling my hardness between her cheeks. She gasps, leaning her head back on my shoulder and allowing the water spray to hit her chest.

I keep one arm locked around her, reaching for her rosy little nipple with my free hand. I caress it gently. It hardens beneath my touch, and her breath stutters.

"You need me as badly as I need you, don't you?" I whisper in her ear. Her eyes flutter shut and she nods. "I'll take care of you, baby."

Reluctantly, I release her, reaching for the soap on the shower's ledge. She pouts, batting her long lashes at me. The way she immediately searched for me the moment I stepped away from her has my cock jerking with need.

Her eyes trail down, filling with heat when they land on my erection. She reaches for me, gently caressing my tip with her thumb. When she licks her lips, I read the intention on her face.

"Don't you dare," I command. "Stay where you're at."

"But I want to—"

"No. Right now, you are mine to take care of."

Her cheeks turn pink, and she nods, putting her back into the water spray and continuing to face me. I use the clean rag beside the soap, lathering it up nicely. Then, I begin at her neck, rubbing small circles against her flesh and slowly moving down.

She tilts her head back, letting the water run through her hair as she gives into my touch, letting me explore her body. One hand works to clean her skin, but the other is a greedy bastard, memorizing every piece of her bare flesh.

I avoid using soap on her most delicate area, not wanting to irritate it. Plus, the savage I am wants her to smell like *her*—not like flowery soap.

When I reach her feet, I gently lift one, placing it on my thigh and scrubbing her delicate toes.

She flinches, giggling when I get to the sole. I repeat on the other foot.

I finish, steadying her as I plant her foot back on the slippery basin. Then, I toss the rag to the side and tap her thigh.

"Open for me," I murmur, kneeling before her like the beggar I am.

Hesitantly, she widens her stance. But it's not enough.

I growl as my vision darkens and my gums ache. "Let me see you." This time, my voice is dark and commanding, leaving no room for negotiation.

Her breath hitches as if she didn't expect the order, but she moves quicker this time, widening her stance so I can gaze up at her tempting center. Gently, I reach up, caressing her.

"You listen so well, baby," I say. I smirk up at her as I lean in, placing a kiss on her thigh. Ghosting my lips over her skin, I continue ascending until I find what I seek.

The way she gasps, practically choking on her breath as I trail my tongue upward, has me almost coming right then and there. It wouldn't be the first time. But I sure as hell don't want to come until I'm done with her.

I ache with the need to bury myself inside of her. But I steady myself and continue to move slowly, trailing kisses up and down her inner thighs.

"You can bite me," she says breathlessly. "If that's what you need." Her fingers work their way into my hair, gripping onto me.

"Oh, I will," I say with a dark chuckle. Then I lean up, swiping my tongue across her wetness. She jerks, her hands gripping tighter. When I'm sure she has her balance and is prepared, I bury my face in her center, flicking my tongue against her clit.

The hot water trickles over her body, soaking us both as I work her to climax. She detonates, tugging my hair so hard my scalp burns. Her hips jerk up, meeting me lick for lick, and she yells out my name.

I chuckle against her, finding satisfaction in the symphony of her pleasure.

We finish cleaning up, then I turn off the shower and scoop Alessia up. Throwing open the shower door, I step out. Water drips from us, leaving a trail to the bed, where I toss her down. She gasps as she lands, her breasts bouncing with the movement. My vision flickers as I take in her dark, rosy nipples.

"The bed—" Alessia glances down at the quilt beneath her. "Rainer, I'm all wet."

I give her a devious grin, gripping her thighs and parting them so I can lick a trail up her delicious flesh. "Just the way I like you."

She shudders, tilting her head back and gripping the blanket as I flick my tongue against her clit. It doesn't take long until she's bucking beneath me, one hand working into my hair to hold me in place.

Her pleasure floods my mouth as she reaches another climax, screaming out my name. I rise to my knees, gripping my thick cock in my fist and smirking down at her.

She's so painfully beautiful. It mesmerizes me. The way her wet hair fans out around her, and those big grey eyes stare up at me with trust and vulnerability.

I open my mouth to tell her how deeply I feel about her, to pour my heart out to her, but the door thunders open behind me, slamming into the wall.

Alessia gasps, jolting at the intrusion. Then she sighs, and annoyance crosses her features. I throw my body over her, covering her with my own.

"Nice arse, brother," Tynan booms out. "I don't mean to spoil your sport and ice your balls, but can you tell me why the scrawny wind prince stormed my room and stole the sorceress?"

"Stole?" Alessia asks, chuckling beneath me. The feel of her bare skin against mine does little to quell my need despite the fact my brother is standing in the room.

Feckin Tynan.

"Turn around," I yell, seeing red.

After a beat, I peer over my shoulder. He faces the doorway, obliging the command. I kiss Alessia's cheek, giving her a look of apology before pushing myself off her. I pull the quilt out from under her, throwing it on her body to cover her. Then, I grab a pillow, holding it over my nudity.

"Should've locked that," I mutter, viciously annoyed. "What's your problem?" I bark at Tynan.

"Can I turn around?"

I glance at Alessia, confirming she's covered. She shrugs, her bare shoulders and collarbone peeking out from the quilt.

I turn back to my brother. "No."

He turns around anyway. I glower at him.

"The pretentious little prick burst into my room and—"

"The way you're doing now?"

"No not the way—" He groans, running a hand over his sheared hair. "He took Seraphina."

"What do you mean took?" Alessia asks, her voice laced with concern.

"Did she go willingly?" I ask.

"Yes, but—"

"Then you should be relieved." I narrow my eyes, seeing through his bullshite. "It's one less burden on your shoulders. Now you get a room entirely to yourself."

"Yeah, well…" His features pinch together as he scratches the back of his neck. "Just don't want him meddling. I don't trust the two of them running off together."

Alessia makes a contemplative noise behind me. I glance at her, and she fights a smile, her eyes crinkling at the corner. Meanwhile, I roll my eyes at Tynan's dramatics.

"Question," Alessia says, humor lacing her tone. "Does your room have one or two beds?"

He pauses, considering the question, picking at a piece of splintered wood on the doorframe. "One, but what does that have to do with anything?"

Alessia giggles harder, and Tynan's brow furrows as he tries to understand the joke. I sigh. He's an oaf if he can't see it himself.

"Ezamae is trustworthy, and I'm incredibly unbothered by Seraphina's departure," I say, striding toward him. One hand holds the pillow firmly in front of my now soft penis, and the other ushers him out of the room.

"But you don't trust anyone." He stays rooted in place.

"Exactly." I don't trust just anyone—it should be enough proof for him to follow my lead.

I plant my free hand on his beefy chest, shoving harder until his feet move, and he stumbles backward. "You're a fool, Tynan."

His brows dip low. "So she's not coming back?"

I frown at him, removing the pillow from my manhood and shoving it in his face. He yells, but I'm too busy slamming the door on him. Moving quickly, I lock the doorknob and slide the chain in place. He bangs on the door.

"Kindly feck yourself," I yell.

"Really? Even after I cleaned up your mess."

I groan, and part of me feels guilty for my dismissal. But for fae's sake, the timing is horrendous. "We'll talk at literally any other time. Now *go*."

He chuckles darkly from the other side of the door. "This is payback, by the way, little brother."

I rub my forehead as if I can work away the wrinkle Tynan has permanently induced. He's not wrong. I suppose it is my payback for barging in on him previously.

Alessia giggles adorably. "Your brother likes Sera."

Rubbing my brow, I shake my head. "He likes anything with a pulse." Perhaps even that's generous.

"He's not so bad," Alessia says admonishingly.

"I don't want to talk about him." And as angry as I am with him, now that the adrenaline, lust, and subsequent fury are dissipating, I can think clearly. I see what I was blind to a moment ago—that I was about to put Alessia at risk by solidifying the soul-bond. "I want to talk about *us*, Alessia."

"Talk?" She lets the quilt fall, baring her breasts to me again.

Instantly, the blood shoots south, and I groan, bringing a knuckle to my mouth and biting down on it to keep from reaching for her.

"Are you sure you want to *talk*?" she teases.

I blow out a heavy breath. "We almost went too far, mo róisín."

She groans, throwing herself back onto the bed. "Not this again."

"We can't yet—not now. Not like this." I glance around the dingy room, taking it in with clear eyes. This isn't *our* safe space. It isn't meaningful to us. We're in the middle of a potentially dangerous journey, and the time isn't right. No matter what Ezamae says.

Alessia deserves better than that for our first time, especially with *what* it means for us.

I stride over to her, slipping beneath the damp blanket. My hand finds her face, cupping it and tilting her head to look at me. Frustration brims in her gaze.

"It's not a matter of *if* anymore, Rainer. It's *when*." Despite the annoyance, she still gazes at me with the moon and stars in her eyes. "I'm sick of letting fear run our relationship."

I chuckle at the irony—I live and breathe *fear*; it will always be a part of our relationship, my life—but she's not wrong.

"I promise you, my little rose, my fear is not stopping me this time." My thumb traces the zigzag ink, softly working its way up and down the left side of her face. "You deserve better than this." I wave my hand around the space. "Better than an inn shower and raggedy quilts that smell like powder, with my brother and best friend just a wall away."

She purses her lips, and then a sigh of defeat escapes her. "I don't *care* about any of this." She reaches up, cupping my face. "I care about *you*."

I lean forward, covering her mouth with my own, whispering, "I know," before kissing her softly. I pull back, keeping my weight on my elbows as I hover over her, giving her a look of apology. "But this means more to me than pleasure. It's a bond for eternity. One I take very seriously."

The light sparks back up in her eyes. "I respect that. I hope you know I feel the same way."

"Then we agree—we shall wait?"

"Not too long, I hope," she says playfully, threading her arms around my neck.

"Once we finish what we came for and return home," I say confidently. "I shall wine and dine you properly, Alessia Lírshadow, and then I shall thoroughly ravage you."

She gives me a coy smile. "You better, Rainer Iorworth. You owe me. And—"

"Iorworths always pay their debts," I finish with a chuckle. "You're not mad?"

"How could I possibly be mad? There's something beautiful about getting lost in pleasure and falling wholly into someone without thinking of repercussions, but it's way sexier to have self-control and be able to stop."

Her words hit me right in the chest, meaning even more than I think she intended. Since the moment I met her, I've second-guessed my self-control and doubted my ability to keep her safe. Not only was I able to control myself through regular lust, but my bloodlust didn't take over—it didn't consume me.

I haven't even bitten her yet, despite her offering herself up to me.

Suddenly, the room is too small, and the emotions are too big. Sweat beads on the back of my neck, and I'm *nervous*.

Fecking hell. What is happening to me?

Pushing off of her, I run a hand through my hair and work to keep my expression neutral so I don't freak her out.

"The blankets are soaked," she says, kicking the blanket off her.

"And whose fault is that?" I smirk, the light playfulness returning.

I reach for her bare foot, tickling the sole. She squeals, trying to squirm out of my hold. I grip her tight enough to keep her in place but careful not to hurt her. Breathless laughter pours from her as she gasps my name, flailing around. Finally, I relent, giving her a smug smile.

I expect her to chastise me or throw some sass, but a dark tendril shoots out from her palm, lurching toward the pillows. Before I can register what's happening, a firm but soft pressure slams into my face, whacking me off the bed.

I land with a thump and gaze up, stunned. Alessia crawls to the edge of the bed, her eyes wide.

"Oh my gods," she says quickly. "Are you okay?"

I quirk a brow at her. "Playing dirty again are we?"

She reaches a hand out for me, and I accept it. But I yank her down into my arms, catching her gracefully before she hits the floor.

Her lip quivers nervously. "I let down my guard, and it just came out and—"

"And it hit me with a pillow," I deadpan. It's intriguing that her shadow, once filled with aggression, has mellowed into a playful companion. I tickle her underarms and make her cry out again. "I can handle your shadow, mo róisín. In fact, I think it likes me."

"Sto-stop!" Tears of laughter stream down her face as she swats my hand away. Her chest rises and falls rapidly as she pants, trying to catch her breath. "It might come back out."

"Let it," I encourage.

"I don't—don't know—if I can control it."

"You can. I believe in you." Just like she believed in me.

"What if you don't like me anymore because of it?"

"It's part of you," I tell her. "I love every part of you—your light and dark, your roots and petals."

THIRTY-TWO

SOMETHING IS GOING RIGHT
ALESSIA

I wake before Rainer and gaze at his sharp, angular features. In sleep, he appears gentle. All the tension has melted away from his eyes and lips, leaving them soft and inviting. Dark wisps of hair stick to his smooth forehead. I reach over, brushing it back and planting my lips there.

He stirs, mumbling something inaudible.

Carefully, I pry myself from his grip and tiptoe to the bathroom to relieve myself. I finish and wash my hands, catching a glimpse of myself in the mirror. My curls are braided back away from my face, sticking up in frizzy chunks, but my eyes capture a new lightness. My lips twitch into a giddy smile as I think of waking up next to Rainer like this every day for the rest of my life.

I dry my hands on a towel and smooth down Rainer's oversized tunic. It comes down to my thighs, swallowing me whole. Pinching the neckline, I bring it up to my nose and inhale. It smells delightfully of sandalwood with just a faint hint of roses.

A soft whoosh of wind chills me, and I glance up, locking eyes with Ezamae in the mirror.

"What are you doing here?" I whisper-yell, whirling around and glancing at the closed bathroom door. As much as Rainer likes Ez, his possessive side would be rather displeased with another male alone in the bathroom with me.

"Checking in." He smirks, his eyes skating over my bare legs. "Your work is completed, I take it?"

I scrunch my nose. "Don't put it like that."

He lifts his hands placatingly. "Ah. Let's try again—is your wonderous, realm-shattering, love-making complete?"

Heat floods my cheeks. I'm no prude, but I also don't appreciate my intimate life being discussed and dissected by others. Even if it's only Ezamae—especially if it's him, actually.

"Not that it's your business," I hiss through my teeth, hoping Rainer doesn't hear us. "But no."

Ez's shoulders stiffen, and he frowns. The excitement he possessed in his earlier visits is gone, and I hope it doesn't mean he's out of patience.

He wouldn't kill the queen with Rainer's life still tethered to her, would he?

We need to kill him first—before he can betray us.

My eyes bulge. So much for the shadow being fully pacified. No. Ezamae wouldn't do that, and I certainly would never harm him.

He's betrayed you before.

"Stop it," I mutter. "We're not killing him."

Ez's silver eyes widen as he tucks a strand of hair behind his pointed ear. "I assume you're conversing with your... less moral half?" He gestures toward the door. "And obviously, I'm not referring to your tormented prince."

Sighing, I scrub a hand over my face. "Yep."

"I'm not here to threaten or trick you, Alessia." He places a hand on his chest, keeping his voice low. "I wanted to talk to you alone, in case you hadn't already gone through with bonding."

"Why?" I ask, nervous prickles dotting the back of my neck.

"Because I know the Umbra Prince. He will drag his feet, hopping from one excuse to the next, prolonging what's inevitable out of fear—"

"Don't do that." I shake my head. "This is important to us both, but we will not be pressured or bullied into it, Ezamae. You'll have to wait—be patient a little longer. That's all I ask."

It makes me feel guilty and selfish to ask him to pretend to stay bonded to Queen Yvanthia even longer, knowing that as soon as Rainer and I complete our bond, he can be free. He can end her life and vie for her throne, successfully ending her rule over Avylon.

But Rainer and I only recently agreed to put aside our fears and commit to one another fully. Ezamae needs to respect that we want to do it right for us. After everything we've been through, an intimate, peaceful bonding isn't too much to ask.

"Things have changed, Alessia." He leans against the bathroom wall, one of his legs bouncing nervously.

He's usually so regal and collected that seeing him so worked up is strange.

"In what way?"

"Yvanthia found an Iorworth in the city—a cousin of Rainer's—with enough blood to sustain Umbra Court."

My heart plummets to the pit of my stomach and I tense up. "What does that mean?"

"She wants to... dispose of him."

"What?" I yell, before checking myself and glancing toward the door. "She can't just..." *Kill him*. The words lodge in my throat.

"She can and she will." He gives me an apologetic look. "Unless you bond."

"How would that help anything? We'd both die!"

"Exactly. You would *both* die."

It takes a second for it to sink in. The whole point of Yvanthia manipulating me into place at Spiritus Court would be null if I died. "She needs me. She can't kill Rainer if it means I die, too."

He nods. "Precisely."

"And you're sure there are no other Lírshadows?"

"She isn't aware of any. If there are..." His lips tighten, and hardness glints in his moonlit eyes.

"If there are, *what*, Ez?"

"If Yvanthia stayed in rule, we would need to find them and kill them," he says carefully, as if it can soften the blow.

"But?"

"When I achieve my goal and secure her position, you will never have to worry about that with me."

The sincerity in his voice is louder than his words. He holds my gaze, allowing me to read all the deep well of emotion there—the fear, the concern, the honesty.

"Okay," I say, swallowing down my own confusing emotions. "I understand the urgency."

"That's all I wanted," he says, "For you to understand the importance of speeding things up. I know it's... asking a lot of you both."

I give him a soft smile, grateful for his consideration despite everything. "Hey, Ez?"

He pauses, cocking his head.

"Are you going to tell me who you bonded with?"

An arrogant smile lights up his face. "Eventually."

"Okay, Prince of Secrets." I roll my eyes playfully. "Just one more question."

"Hm?"

"Are you bringing Sera back when you're done?"

He blinks as if surprised, pushing off the wall and straightening up. "I thought you might be relieved she's gone."

I shrug nonchalantly, thinking about how she's grown on me so quickly. How I'm apparently not the only one she's grown on. "I figured it might be awkward for you and your bonded."

His brows pinch together. "Why? She is one of my dearest friends."

Leaning a hip against the counter, I cross my arms and study him. "You do realize she's in love with you, right?"

His breath hitches, and he pauses, considering my words. Then he bursts out laughing. "It's a mutually platonic friendship, I assure you."

I shake my head. "Idiot," I mutter softly. "She most definitely harbors feelings for you."

His high cheekbones tint pink. "Shite." He rubs his slack jaw. "I left them alone together."

"At least Sera won't kill them," I joke, although heartbreak's not funny. If Sera realizes she's with Ez's bonded... I wouldn't wish that on anyone.

Ez stays silent for far too long. His already pale face looks at least two shades lighter, and my heart drops.

"She wouldn't, right?" I ask, alarm flitting through me.

Ez gives me an exasperated look. "Of course she wouldn't!"

But he quickly disappears into the abyss with a cool puff of air.

I redress in my plain nightdress to reassume my role as a pretend Tradeling, and I comb and braid my hair out of my face. It takes longer than I'd like, and the curls give me hassle. Then, I leave Rainer slumbering peacefully upstairs as I head down to locate food.

Prichard stands in the lobby, glaring down at something. Mid-morning light reflects off his shiny bald head, and I'm surprised the others hadn't come to wake us up at dawn.

A boy, maybe about sixteen, kneels at Prichard's feet, his peach cheeks tinting red and his brow pulled low as the elder man's mouth moves rapidly, giving him a quiet lecture. I move closer, trying to make out what he's saying.

"—and be grateful your arse isn't in the mines, *boy*," Prichard barks.

The boy nods, keeping his gaze downcast. Fury blazes to life inside me, burning my skin from the inside. My shadow thrashes against me, roused by the potent emotion.

The boy bends his head low and then disappears through the door behind the counter.

I don't like that.

"Me neither," I mutter.

Prichard's head snaps in my direction, and some of the violence in his eyes dissipates. Instead, it heats in a new way, dragging up and down my body. My teeth grit and dark spots dance in my vision. I know it's my shadow threatening to come out and *play*, but I take slow, steady breaths, working overtime to keep it down.

"Excuse me," I force myself to say softly, to stay in character lest we attract unnecessary attention. The smile I give him is horribly fake, and I fear he'll see right through it.

His eyes are too busy lingering on the neckline of my dress to notice. "The pretty little whore came to play, eh?"

The air leaves my lungs in a fiery burst. My hands shake, fighting the urge to unleash the gates and let my shadow out.

He deserves it. The bastard is a piece of—

"My... owner sent me to acquire food for his... unit," I grit out, talking over my shadow-self. I pause between words, forcing myself to breathe before I lose control. "To break fast."

"Ah yes, and for payment, he sent you, did he?"

A deep growl rises from somewhere within me.

"No, you grimy spud." The words burst from my mouth as if my shadow had spoken for me.

I gasp. Thinking quickly, I drop my hands and pretend to fiddle nervously with my dress. Outside, I'm the picture of a weak, insecure Tradeling. But inside, I'm a monster desperate to be unleashed—anything but meek or quiet.

I clear my throat. "My owner said to insult you if you proposition me again."

"Again?" he asks, brows pinching together.

Tynan must've glamoured last night's entire interaction out of his mind. *Shite.* I'm making this so much worse.

A tense silence rings out in the otherwise empty lobby as we hold each other's stares. Finally, a rough, scraping laugh leaves him as he flashes his teeth at me—all regular teeth. No incisors.

He's not a vampyr.

Not a *monster*, as some might say—he's only human—but I prefer monsters to men.

His laughter subsides and he crosses his arm, giving me another leery graze. Gratefully, he stays where he is, keeping distance between us. "Well?"

"Well, what?" I try very hard not to sound challenging. I might not be trying hard enough because his mouth tightens.

"I'm waiting for an apology."

I stare at him blankly. No apologies burn my tongue like they once did. I'm done placating the egos of men.

"My *owner* said not to apologize." The words taste like bile. After leaving the lord, I said I'd never heel to another again. "Just obeying my orders lest I be punished by his... brutal hand."

A malicious smile lights up Prichard's face, and he scratches his chest as he lets out another entertained laugh. "A man I understand."

Rainer is no man, you prick.

He turns, cups his hands, and hollers. "Luis!"

The door quickly opens a few seconds later, and the teen boy reappears. He practically bolts to Prichard.

"Yes sir," he says, out of breath.

"The soldiers would like to break their fast," Prichard says, holding my eye contact. "Now, we don't normally serve a meal on demand, but since our *guests* are so kindly serving the Wessex Peninsula, it's the least we can do."

"Yes, sir." Luis quickly flees through the back, likely toward the kitchen.

My stomach pinches with nausea, and I'm left hating myself—hating Prichard—for Luis' treatment.

Prichard returns to the counter, busying himself counting coppers. It takes everything in me to force myself into an armchair while I wait for Luis to emerge. I sit with my back to the wall so I can see the desk, the door to the back, the stairwell, and the front door all from one vantage point.

Prichard hums to himself, and as the minutes tick by, he checks a couple in and greets a few patrons as they head out into the day.

I study him, my anger building as I think of poor Luis stuck listening to his berating day in and day out. My hands tremble with my shadow's promise of violence, so I try to think of anything but the teen Tradeling making my food in the back.

I'd tell Prichard to forget about it if I didn't think Luis would pay for it. If I had known last night that he was a Tradeling owner, I'd never have stayed here. Never would've supported his business with our patronage.

A short while later, Luis emerges, balancing an oversized tray cluttered with various foods. I jump to my feet, surging toward him.

"Can I help?" I ask quietly, hoping it won't attract Prichard's attention.

Luis's eyes widen and he shakes his head. The movement is a little too eager because it throws him off balance, and the tray sways to the side.

We both gasp, and he finds his balance, righting himself before the whole thing topples sideways. But not before a jar of jam crashes to the ground, spilling everywhere.

Instinctively, my gaze jerks toward Prichard. The ire in his beady eyes sends me back to the lord. Suddenly, *I'm* the one who is a teen again, dropping a mug of tea on the hardwoods of his estate.

Prichard charges toward us, and I notice Luis coiling in on himself from the corner of my eye. When the old man raises a hand, preparing to strike, I lose it.

"Touch him and *die*," I spit, my voice propelled by venom. My vision darkens at the edges, and pressure builds beneath my skin.

A split second before his hand makes contact with Luis' face, the pressure dissipates, bursting out of me like a gushing waterfall. My shadow wraps around Prichard's wrist, yanking it backward.

Snapping sounds fill the air, and Prichard screams. Luis pales, and he drops the tray, surging backward.

My shadow is fast, splitting off into a second tendril. It lurches for the food tray and catches it a second before it hits the ground. It places it carefully on the counter, then merges back into itself, winding like a dark vine up Prichard's arm and around his neck.

Everything happens quickly, but somehow, with the adrenaline and shock coursing through me, time feels slower.

"Run," I whisper to Luis.

"Th—thank you," he stutters, eyes wide and glistening. Fear is etched into every corner of his young face, and I can't tell if it's me or Prichard he's afraid of. Until he puts his hand on his heart and says, "Forever thank you. I'll keep your secret."

Then he turns and bolts.

My shadow doesn't waste time. It doesn't play with its prey. It doesn't ask me for permission—because I've already silently granted it.

This time, it snaps the man's neck, swiftly ending his life and tossing his body on the floor. It recoils immediately, silently into me.

Perhaps it's because I didn't fight it this time, but I'm not nearly as exhausted as before. And the shadow must realize something changed between us the past few days, too, because it nuzzles up gratefully against me from the inside and immediately settles down.

At least *something* is going right.

THIRTY-THREE

Time is Running Out

Alessia

I stare at Prichard's unseeing eyes and his wide-open mouth for another few seconds.

"Shite," I mutter. I glance around, wondering how no one heard the ruckus. But when my eyes meet a cool gaze in the stairwell, my heart drops.

"Rainer," I exhale. Warm relief floods me that it's him.

He stands casually with his ankles crossed and his hands in his pocket. His lips twitch as he takes in the body on the ground. He pushes off the wall with ease and arrogance and strides over to me.

"Are you okay, mo róisín?" he murmurs, cupping my cheeks carefully. His eyes roam my face, then drop down my body. He studies me carefully, like I'm the most valuable work of art he's ever encountered.

It's like the first time I met him.

"I think I am," I whisper. My heart races with adrenaline still, and my hands shake with shock, but my mind is clear.

He pulls me to his chest, wrapping his arms around me and hugging me tightly.

I wait for the guilt to hit, but it doesn't come. There's something decidedly humbling about taking a life and not feeling *wrong* for it. Murder doesn't feel like the wrong choice when it comes to protecting someone without the power.

"How long have you been there?" I murmur.

"The whole time."

I pull back, gripping his forearms as I stare into his face, confused. "Why didn't you help?"

His responding laugh is so genuine, giving me a glimpse of that darling dimple, that it catches me off guard.

"You didn't need me this time—*you* were in control," he says with pride tinging his voice. "And you, my little rose, were magnificent."

I run a hand over my braid, exhaling heavily. "I think my shadow likes it when I let it choose violence."

He studies me, searching for anything I might not be saying. His lips pull down, and his eyes lock onto mine. "Are you *sure* you're okay?"

I nod, swallowing the thickness in my throat. "I won't ever be okay," I say honestly, giving him the truth that sticks to my insides like tar. "Not when innocent people are stuck in these lives. Not when abusers walk freely, wielding their power over others." I suck in a sharp breath and stand a little taller. "It's not just Luis I'm thinking of—or Zephyr and Sheila—but all the others, too, Rainer. There are so many out there being…" Emotion clogs my words. "I don't want to be a murderer, but the alternative is worse."

Watching this happen and doing nothing is *worse*.

Fire blazes in his eyes as he gives me an appraising look. "You might be a monster to some, but you are a hero to others."

A tear sneaks down my cheek, and I quickly wipe it away. "I just wish the violence wasn't necessary."

He nods in understanding. "Do you remember when I called you the girl who fights?"

I smile through my watering eyes. "How could I possibly forget that?" It's stuck with me, an echo of confidence amidst all the chaos.

"We wouldn't be fighters if we didn't have something to fight *for*, little rose." He uses his thumb to swipe away another escaped tear, and I shudder, letting my eyes fall shut. His touch lingers, sending a surge of calmness through me. I don't reopen my eyes until he pulls away.

"Is that why you kill the humans and send them back?" I ask. "Because they're... perpetuators of harm?"

He smirks at me. "If I admitted that, you might think I'm *too* soft."

I chuckle. "On the outside, you're all sharp edges and lethal glares—all thorns—but you're soft as rose petals on the inside." My smile grows. "Maybe *you're* the rose."

"Maybe I am." He winks at me. "Let's keep this between us, though. I have a reputation to uphold."

I playfully swat him, but the humor is short-lived. "Where is everyone?" I glance at the stairwell, half-expecting one of the other patrons to appear, curious about the source of the screams. "There are other guests here."

Rainer snorts, eyes darting toward the ceiling. "Yes, Tynan is glamouring them into forgetting everything they heard in the last half hour. And Zephyr and Kenisius left early this morning to gather our garments for the fête."

My cheeks burn with embarrassment at my careless actions. What if Tynan hadn't been here? "Is he going to be okay with using so much glamour?"

Rainer strokes his jaw, apology forming in the corners of his crinkled eyes.

"How exactly does he make his glamour last permanently?" I ask.

"He needs to feed from the source," he says. My mouth drops, and before I can protest, he adds, "Only a few drops. And his self-control is much more than I've given him credit for."

"He killed Felix," I hiss. As much as I've forgiven Tynan and warmed up to him, it's impossible to forget that he killed my first—and only—lover on Ostara.

"He was drunk," Rainer says. "And he thought Felix was like the others."

As in the assassins—the humans caught crossing the Gleam to spy or kill. Deep down, I figured as much. It's why I was quick to forgive Tynan.

"If he hurts any of them, I swear I will let my shadow have its way with him."

Rainer's lips quirks. "And I won't stand in your way."

The front door slams open. Ken strides in, gripping Luis by the back of the shirt. The boy's feet dangle, kicking around uselessly. Zephyr follows behind, carrying a stack of garment bags and practically bowing beneath their weight.

Ken kicks the door shut with a booted foot and then drops Luis.

Zephyr scurries to the couch, dropping his load on the cushions. He sighs heavily and plops into a chair to catch his breath. "This is insane."

"What the hell, Ken?" I scurry to Luis, checking for injury. He swats my hand away, curling into a fetal position on the floor.

This time, there's no mistaking that the fear in his eyes is reserved for us—for me. It curdles my heart, but I'm getting used to it. At least he's alive, spared from Prichard's abuse. He can hate me if that's the cost.

"Found this guy pacing out front," Ken says, pointing at Luis. "His fear reeked for a great distance."

"You told him what happened?" I ask Luis softly, not wanting to scare him.

"No—no. I swear!" he says.

"Didn't have to," Ken says. "I saw him this morning on the way out. Knew he worked for the inn prick, and the moment I smelled him I knew something happened." He snorts, then sniffs the air. He continues inhaling deeply, and follows the scent he's latched onto. He strides to the counter, peering behind it. "Yep. That ain't good."

"We're handling it," Rainer says flatly, cocking a brow at me.

Ken pauses, then looks from Rainer to me. His smile grows into a blinding flash of teeth. "No... *you* did this, little demon?"

Heavy footfalls clamor down the stairs, and Tynan appears. "What the *hell* did she do now?"

Rainer growls, whipping his head toward his brother. But when Tynan offers him a placating grin, his protectiveness is quelled.

"I was only protecting one of my own," I say, inclining my chin.

"Picking up strays again." Ken chuckles, lifting himself onto the counter beside the tray of food. He picks up a piece of bread, dipping it into a ceramic jar of butter, and shoving it in his mouth. "Rawnee likes uhm bruhken end—"

"Chew," Rainer orders. "Swallow. Then try again."

Ken's throat bobs as he obliges, giving us a crooked grin. "Rainer likes 'em broken, and you like 'em pitiful, eh?"

"I'm not pitiful," Zephyr mutters unconvincingly from his place on the couch.

"Stop being mean," I command. "Ken, I was *freeing* Luis. You weren't supposed to bring him back." However, as soon as the words out I realize the flaw in my plan.

There is nowhere for Luis to go.

There is no freedom. Not here.

Rainer steps toward me. "I recognize that look," he says quietly so only me—and Tynan and Ken—can hear.

"Oh, for fae's sake," Tynan mutters. "Let me glamour him and let him go—"

"No," I bark, narrowing my eyes at him.

"Then what the hell do we do? We can't travel to Ryalle with all this baggage." He gestures toward the two Tradelings we've picked up on the way.

Rainer watches me curiously, but he stays quiet. I like that he's giving me a chance to figure things out. He knows Dovenak was my home for so long—and being a Tradeling was my identity. He's wise enough to recognize that this is part of *my* battle to fight.

Ken finishes his bread, then hops off the counter, inspecting the body.

I take in the sight of Luis—coiled and trembling on the floor—and Zephyr, boneless and defeated in the chair. They both represent different stages of my emotions when I escaped the Trade and met the fae. They might view me as a monster right now, but I can spare their lives. I can give them the freedom they crave.

"I'm taking them to Spiritus Court," I say, crossing my arms and facing Tynan.

"You think that's wise with a vampyr on the premise?" he challenges.

"I think sometimes we all pretend to be something we're not." I lower my voice. "And you're no different, Tynan."

Neither of us moves, his cobalt eyes narrow, holding mine. Then, a tiny grin graces his lips. He scratches the scar bisecting his brow, and strolls toward the counter where Ken is. On his way past me, he leans in, his words merely a breath as he says, "Guess my brother was right about you."

Rainer steps forward, ready to intervene if needed. I give him a subtle shake of my head, and he halts.

Tynan chuckles and pulls away. "Guess I'll clean this up. Kinda need it after all that work upstairs."

"Take it to the back," I say. The last thing the human boys need to see after everything they've been through is a feeding vampyr. If they choose to stay in Spiritus Court with me, they might one day, but today is not the day for that.

Tynan holds the door to the back open as Ken hoists up the body, throwing it over a shoulder. The two crack jokes as they stride out of sight.

I grimace, unsure that I'll ever get used to the violence.

My body hums with awareness as Rainer joins me at my side. "They're right, unfortunately." His pinky brushes mine, and it lights me up. "I'm not sure it's wise to bring them to Ryalle."

The fact he waited to question my plan until his brother and pal were out of the conversation speaks volumes. It shows he respects me enough to have my back publicly, but keep me in check privately.

Despite everything going on, my heart melts a little.

"We're *not* bringing them to Ryalle," I say, glancing over my shoulder at the humans.

Zephyr helps Luis up, leading him to a chair. The two talk in quiet voices. Probably planning a way to overpower us and escape. The thought makes me chuckle.

"Then what's your plan?"

"We'll send them back to Avylon early."

I can practically feel the questions radiating from him. "And how exactly do you plan to do that?"

I meet Rainer's pale blue eyes. He watches me with a wolfish intensity, but the slight curve to his lips tells me he's entertained.

"Ezamae," I say.

"You think he'll be back again?"

"Oh, he's coming." I smirk, finding humor in the unintentional innuendo. Ken's humor is rubbing off on me.

After Ez's visit today and after everything Rainer has done for me—all the ways he's shown up for me—I'm confident that completing the bond is the right choice. I need him to accept it, even if it's under less than ideal circumstances.

Soon.

Because our time is running out.

THIRTY-FOUR
SURRENDER TO FATE
ALESSIA

"I *really* wanted to explore town," Tynan mutters, glancing at the village we're leaving behind.

He lugs the small cart he found behind the inn, the wheels bumping over the dirt path. We tossed most of our bags in it, along with the garments Zephyr secured for us.

We quickly trek toward the trees, leaving the quiet street of the inn behind. Once we reach the grass, the sound of the cart's thudding is softened, and Tynan tugs it a little harder to keep it moving.

"I'm not even a risk," he adds. "I'm all fueled up and safe to roam, swear it."

"Visit on your own time," Rainer says, giving him an unamused look. "Perhaps when we're not preoccupied with other matters."

"You know, I'm listening to you out of respect, little brother. Not because I *have* to."

"And I'm tolerating you out of respect," Rainer mimics. "Not because I have to, either."

Ken snickers. He has a thrashing Luis thrown over a shoulder while his other arm rests heavily around Zephyr's shoulders. The shifter shoots me a goofy grin, clearly unfazed by the turmoil of the two humans in his company.

A tinge of guilt flits through me, but it's quickly replaced by the thought of them being brought to safety. They can hate me so long as they're safe and healthy. I intend to free *all* the Tradelings in the Wessex Peninsula, and if all goes well, they can choose to return and build their own lives here. But for now, until that happens, neither Tradeling is safe here on their own.

We make it to the trees without attracting attention and begin our journey west toward Ryalle. If all goes well, we should arrive in the evening, in time for the party.

It's going to be a long day—and night.

"You know, that ain't a bad idea—coming back by myself later," Tynan says, yanking the cart harder to get momentum over a few exposed roots. "Maybe I'll bring the sorceress on a vacation."

Ken's smile melts, and his head whips toward the vampyr. "Why would you bring Seraphina?"

Tynan flashes him a wicked grin. "Use your imagination, bear."

Ken stares blankly at him, and then he bursts out laughing. "You are *not* her type."

"And you are?" he shoots back.

Ken cackles harder. "Probably not, but at least I—"

"You both have horrible taste in females if that's who you're going to bicker over." Rainer grunts, hiking his bag higher on his shoulder and picking up his pace.

"We're not bickering over her." Ken says at the same time I say, "She's not bad, Rainer."

The males continue to toss remarks at one another while I think of the sorceress and all she's gone through in a short time. Maybe it's that she lives alone in the woods or that she was so open and warm with me when we first met, but something tells me she doesn't have many friends.

And the one she does have? Well, she's in love with him, and it's unrequited. And now she's helping him and his soul-bond. It takes a big heart to put her pains aside to do the right thing.

I commend her for it.

I don't know what I would do in her position. The mere thought of watching Rainer fall for someone else while I pine for him afar physically pains me.

"Where did you go, mo róisín," Rainer whispers in my ear.

I hadn't even noticed he slowed his pace to match mine. We fall back, letting Tynan, Ken, and the two humans continue through the forest.

"I was just thinking about how lucky we are," I say earnestly. "To have found one another."

"I *am* the luckiest bastard to walk the realms." He chuckles, reaching for my hand and threading his fingers through mine.

The mere contact of his skin against mine sends butterflies careening through my stomach. I bite down my smile as we continue walking, hand in hand.

We catch up to Tynan and Ken, tuning back into their conversation.

"—and she made me artificial blood," Tynan says to Ken, arching a brow in his direction. "I think that's proof she likes me."

"Nah, it means she thinks you're a sad wittle vamp who can't control himself." Ken snorts. He puffs out his chest, adjusting a squirming Luis higher on his shoulder. "Plus, she rode me already."

"She borrowed your bear for transportation," Tynan corrects.

"And she *liked* it a lot by the smell of her—"

"No!" I groan, rubbing my forehead with my free hand. "Don't go there, Ken."

"She'd rather ride a bear than a vampyr," Ken says, taunting Tynan.

Tynan scoffs. "Wait til she sees what I can do with my teeth. Things no damn *bear* could dream of."

"What? Bite her clit off? I can make that happen if that's what she's into."

"No, you idiot!" Tynan sighs exasperatedly. "I can nibble her—"

"Enough!" Rainer says.

I squeak, my face heating at the vulgar conversation. "Can you two not talk about my friend like that?" Rainer's grip tightens at my words, but he doesn't pester me about calling Sera a friend, wisely opting to stay quiet.

Ken shifts Luis to the ground, allowing the man to walk on two legs now that we've cleared the village. "Run, and we'll catch you," he warns, wagging a finger in the young man's face. "And remember, bears and vampyrs can bite your little human weenie clean off."

I choke on my spit, covering my sudden laughter with a cough.

Luis' eyes widen, and he glances at Zephyr, who quickly shakes his head. The two Tradelings opt to continue walking peacefully, side by side, between Tynan and Ken.

"It's settled," Tynan says. I catch a grin on his profile. "As soon as we're done here, I'm inviting the sorceress on a little getaway. I'll show her a real good time."

"You have real responsibilities now," Rainer says cooly. "Perhaps it's time you take them seriously."

Tynan twists to face me. "It okay with you if I take some time off, *princess*?"

I shake my head, chuckling. As raunchy as Ken and Tynan can be, I like seeing the playful side of the vampyr. The friendship between the two warms my heart, and being sober looks good on him.

"You know what?" I say. "Something tells me you could benefit from a break. Life's short, and you deserve to enjoy the little things."

Tynan's smile grows. "I knew you were wise." He stops walking, reaching over to flick Rainer's nose as we pass. "Maybe you can learn something from her, little brother."

Rainer swats him away, then huffs under his breath, rolling his eyes, but I don't miss how his lips twitch as if fighting a smile. At least the brothers have come a long way, working on repairing their relationship.

I can't help the sense of pride that builds at knowing these relationships are forming—or fixing—in part thanks to my resuming Spiritus Court. Of all the various ways fate could have taken me, I'm glad it's this path I'm walking.

Hours later, halfway to Ryalle, a breeze picks up, sending leaves skittering across our path.

Rainer tugs me to a stop. "You were right."

"About what?" I ask, confused.

A second later, Ezamae materializes in front of us.

"The wind-stalker has returned yet again," Rainer deadpans.

Ez fixes his navy velvet jacket, a coy smile playing on his lips. "I thought we were friends, fear-crier."

"Fear*caller*," Rainer corrects flatly.

"Wind*walker*," Ez mimics. His smile fades into a frown, and he sighs. "Based on your attitude, I'd guess you still haven't completed your bond?"

Rainer grunts. "Not your business."

"Why do I feel like this is my fault?" Tynan mutters, running a hand over his sheared hair. He nods at Ken. "Come on, big fella, let's go set up lunch."

They lead the Tradelings away, leaving me and the princes with some privacy. Not that I'm under any illusions that our conversation is actually private, given the heightened senses of the fae.

"Tell him what you told me," I say to Ez, with my eyes on Rainer.

Rainer bristles, his eyes swinging to me.

The Aer Prince sighs, leaning against a tree briefly. He seems to think twice, quickly pushing off it and rubbing the hints of bark off the arm of his jacket.

"I'm attending tea as Yvanthia's... companion," he sighs. "I don't have long. It's a miracle we've made it this far without her catching on."

"Do you honestly think she isn't already aware?" Rainer asks, narrowing his eyes.

Ez chuckles humorlessly. "By some grace of the goddess, she isn't, which is why I'd like to complete the task. Unfortunately, I am waiting on the most stubbornly abstinent male in all of Avylon."

Rainer goes rigid, his icy gaze locked on Ez. "Not all of us want to get it done and *over with*," he spits.

Ez's moon eyes flash with curiosity, then his head tips back as he laughs. He stops abruptly. "Wait a damn minute."

My brow furrows, wondering what I missed.

Ez strides closer, looking Rainer up and down with an arched brow. He leans in conspiratorially. "Is the Prince of Fear a *virgin*?"

Rainer scowls, his jaw tensing. "That's not what this is about."

Ez's face lights up. My body goes still as I process this.

"But you're so good at…" I say, flushing as the words spill without forethought.

Rainer's gaze meets mine, apology flickering in his tight brow and tense mouth. "Despite the easy assumptions here, I'm *not* inexperienced."

"But you've never…?" I whisper, a new flurry of emotions rising within me. I feel doubly awful for trying to rush things. It's not just the implications of solidifying the bond but also what it means for *him*.

"No—I'm not a virgin," he says exasperatedly as if the words taste like ash on his tongue. "And there'd be nothing wrong with it if I were."

"Oh," I say lamely. As much as I hate thinking of him with anyone else but me, knowing it won't be his first time is a bit of relief. Less pressure, I suppose.

Ez chuckles, his shoulders shaking. "Then get on with it, will you? Yvanthia found your cousin to rule Umbra, which means she has little use for you, Fearcaller." He taps his wrist, where a watch might lie if he was wearing one. "Tick tock, tick tock."

"What cousin?" Rainer frowns in confusion. "*Shite*—it doesn't matter." He shoves a hand through his hair, pushing it out of his face. It highlights the stress crease cutting through his forehead.

"The worrisome thing is that I couldn't tell you." Ez winces. "Yvanthia hasn't been as forthcoming as she has been in the past."

"Even *if* we completed our soul-bond, how do you propose you end her life?" Rainer asks.

Ez taps his chin, looking thoughtful for a moment. "Sera is helping, of course, but I have also recruited Laisren's help."

"How will the Fire Prince help exactly?"

Ez smirks. "Let *me* worry about that."

They have a stare-off, and I glance from one to the other, at a loss for what silent conversation they're having between them.

"Why would Laisren help you? What do you have over him?"

Ez's eyes twinkle. "Wise male. I may have aided him occasionally, fostering a sense of affinity between us."

"Give us time," I cut in. "We'll... complete our bond. But in the meantime, I need your help."

I give him the rundown on Luis and Zephyr, instructing him to bring them safely to Spiritus Court.

"What if they don't want to stay?" he asks. "I truly cannot keep an eye on them right now, amid these... events."

"They'll want to stay—at least Zephyr will. Sheila is his sister," I say confidently. "Maybe keep them away from Das Celyn for a bit—their humor is an acquired taste, and the Tradelings' wounds are raw right now. But Sheila is there, and oh, Fern! She's a little rough around the edges, but she's human—"

I notice Ez has gone still, his cheeks flushing. I frown, studying him. "Fern," I repeat, watching as the red on his pale cheeks deepens.

I gasp. "Holy shite. Your bonded is *Fern*?"

Ezamae shoots his gaze skyward and then blows out a heavy breath. "I'll watch your little friends. Bye." He bursts away in a gust of air, presumably to go find the Tradelings.

They're not that far away, but the casual showcase of windwalking rather than *walking* reminds me that Ez is at full strength now.

Because of *Fern.*

I giggle, a hand coming to my mouth to stifle the noise.

Rainer shoves his hands in his pocket, squinting at the space where Ez vacated.

"What's that look?" I ask.

"It's just…" He scratches the back of his neck. "Fern is human. I haven't heard of a *human* with a soul-bonded."

"Are you sure she's human?" I quirk a brow. "Everyone thought I was… until I wasn't."

He shakes his head. "This isn't like that, Alessia. I've tasted her. She's human."

The reminder, even though it was platonic and solely life-sustaining, sends a niggle of discomfort through my insides. "You're not allowed to feed off her ever again."

Rainer slowly turns to face me, his lips curving at the ends. "Are you jealous, mo róisín?"

I incline my chin. "No," I lie. "If you need to feed, you come find me."

He stalks toward me, his eyes darkening slightly as his eyes flick to my lips, then drag lower to my neck. "Or what?"

Before I can reply, my vision wavers with a hint of darkness. My shadow silently surges from my palms, lurching toward him. It splits into two rope-like tendrils, gripping his wrists and yanking them behind his back. They wrap intricately around his arms, binding them behind his back and shoving him to his knees. Then, another tendril branches off, reaching for his hair and tugging his head back. He gasps, his smirk growing as he glances up at me.

A cloud of dark navy flickers in his irises, eclipsing the pale blue coloring usually found there.

"Well, this is fun," he murmurs.

A ghost of a smirk plays on my lips as I stare down at him. The newfound companionship with my shadow sends a thrill through me. Rather than fear it, and what it's capable of, I suddenly see a whole new world of potential for how we could *play*.

I bite my lip, trying to tame the excitement blossoming.

"You look like you're enjoying this," Rainer says, his voice low and gravelly.

My shadow releases his hair as I step forward. I reach for him, running my hand through his dark waves. His gaze heats with lust as he leans into my touch.

A dark, unfamiliar confidence courses through me, but instead of running, I lean into it. Lowering my face to Rainer's, I lightly let my lips brush his. "My blood is the *only* blood I want filling you."

"Yes, ma'am," he says with a heavy breath.

"Little demon is a *freak*!" Ken's booming voice snaps me out of my fog of desire.

I jump back from Rainer, my shadow unwinding from his body and retreating deep into my skin. I blush furiously as I turn to see him and Tynan standing a few paces away, wearing equal expressions of mirth.

Rainer groans, slowly getting to his feet and grimacing. He doesn't bother to brush the dirt off his knees, rub his red wrists, or fix his mussed-up hair. It only makes him that much more enticing.

My heart flutters as I take in his profile, lingering on his sharp jaw and that full mouth.

Gods, he's gorgeous.

"You two are *never* coming with us again," Rainer mutters, pointing at Ken and Tynan.

"There's a joke in there, but I shall refrain," Ken says, his toothy grin growing. He strokes his jaw, arching a brow.

"Hey," Tynan says, putting his hands up. "*I* wasn't going to interrupt. Not again."

"That's almost worse," I say, trying not to laugh.

"To think *you* judged me for *my* kinks," Tynan says to Rainer.

Ken raises a brow, turning to Tynan. "This I gotta hear."

"Later," I say, clapping my hands to get the males' attention. "I take it Ez found you?"

"Yeah, and he whisked your little humans away," Ken says, making a whooshing noise to imitate Ez's windwalking.

"Tell him to bring Sera back next time," Tynan adds, crossing his arms. His muscles bulge beneath his shirt. "I could kick his skinny arse."

"Not this again," I groan. "Can we just go, for the love of gods?"

At this rate, Rainer and I will never consummate our bond. Not that we were planning to here in the woods, but something tells me it'll be next to impossible with Ken and Tynan around.

As if he can read my mind, Rainer turns his attention to me, his face softening.

"Soon, little rose," he says softly. "Soon."

My skin pebbles as his promise washes over my skin. I've never wanted anything more than to feel Rainer inside of me—he takes up every piece of my head, heart, and spirit, and I want to give him every piece of my flesh, too. It's more than completing a bond. It's completing our vow to one another—wholly giving ourselves to one another.

I'm glad we're both done fighting it.

Instead, we're ready to surrender to fate.

Thirty-Five
It's Party Time
Rainer

I t takes too long to get to Ryalle. By the time we arrive, I am thoroughly annoyed with my brother and my best friend. Their mouths moved faster than our legs, exhausting me early on.

The thought of attending this damn party tonight only drains me further. I stifle an annoyed sigh, working to keep a neutral expression on my face.

My free hand runs the length of my fitted breeches. They're a little more snug than I would've opted for and a brighter red than I prefer. My tailored doublet matches, the color drawing more attention than black would. The gold buttons down the front are ridiculously ostentatious, and the collar is too high around the throat. At least the undershirt is black, and the material is delightfully lightweight and breathable. My movements aren't as restricted as I feared they might be.

Tynan wears a similar outfit in burnt orange and Ken in yellow. They look decidedly less comfortable than I am as they squirm and fidget with their detailing. Like mine, the waist of their doublets are cinched, making their chests and biceps appear even larger than they usually do.

Crowds of various colors move through the port's streets before us like a swarm of bright-colored ants. Apparently, the peninsula's southern cities enjoy flashy garb.

Eyes trail us as we pass. Many of the men and women here are of diverse statures—some frames are thick and curvy, some are lean and lithe—yet none of the nobles possess the frames of warriors as we do.

Then again, we are *fae*. And we are trained in combat. The human nobles have Tradelings to do their fighting—rather pathetic, really, considering it's coerced.

Tynan scratches at a loose thread on his hem while Ken tugs the neck of his top.

"Stop fiddling," I mutter to them.

Like two scolded faelings, they drop their hands in unison. I shake my head, unable to keep from chuckling at the ridiculousness.

My greedy eyes latch back onto Alessia—the only thing keeping me grounded today. She stands regal and thoughtful as she takes in the various docks to our left, and the city to our right.

Her dress is more like a slip than a gown, the purest of white, with a seductively low neckline and a high slit up her right leg.

I watch her quietly as we walk side by side, grinning as she takes everything in with those wide, grey eyes. The dress only makes the whites appear brighter and the greys stormier than ever—a symbol of both her purity and shadows.

It's easy to forget how sheltered she's been her whole life, but moments like these remind me. There's a childlike curiosity to her. And instead of bringing me sorrow or anger like they initially did, I feel relief. There's comfort in knowing she will have moments of wide-eyed wonder over and over again for the rest of her life. She will never be imprisoned or stifled again. I pledge my life to that promise. Instead, I will take her gently by the hand and lead her to experiences beyond her wild imagination.

"I will always provide you with intrigue," I whisper the promise more to myself than her.

She turns to me, a soft gasp escaping her when she catches me staring. She blushes, and it's so cute, almost innocent, contrasted with her boldness around me. The thought of her taking me to my knees with her shadows sends a bolt of heat straight to my cock.

I cough, adjusting myself discreetly.

"Do you see this, Rainer?" She squeals, turning back to the horizon off the shore to the west.

I continue to take in her profile, scanning the bare skin on her cheek where her thin tattoo usually is. As much as I hate the mark, it feels strange to see her without it. It's almost as odd as my ears feel.

My fingers caress the tops, catching on smooth, rounded skin rather than my natural points. It's a great thing Tynan fed when he did since he's working hard to keep our true appearances masked. Instead of posing as traveling soldiers like in Wyrville, we now pose as nobles visiting for the celebration. He's not only working his power to hide my ears but to hide Alessia's Tradeling mark as well.

Alessia catches me staring again and grins, gesturing animatedly toward the water. "You're not even looking!"

"I'm looking at something decidedly more beautiful than any water or trees could ever be, mo róisín," I mutter.

I push my hair off my forehead and turn my attention to the view before us. The thick air is broken up with a light breeze carrying the scent of salt, brine, and jasmine. The city is perched on the edge of a lush, green peninsula framed by turquoise waters. The sun melts into the water off the coast, the water glimmering like a thousand diamonds around it.

Further down the coast, closer to the city, the harbor bustles. Ships of all sizes with colorful sails bob gently in the calm waters. Grand oaks interspersed with palm trees and magnolia trees line the cobblestone streets, swaying gently in the breeze.

We stand and watch the water as fishermen and tradesmen rush past us. When Alessia grows restless, we move toward the city center, lingering at various street shops since the fête doesn't begin until sundown.

I figure it's an excellent way to pass the time, indulge Alessia, and give Tynan the thrill of traveling, so he shuts up long enough to give my poor, fake-human ears a break.

I chuckle to myself, shaking my head.

The deeper we get into the city, the more alive it becomes. String music and flutes reach my ears from a nearby square, where a small crowd gathers to watch live performers.

My gaze doesn't linger for long, though, because I'm drawn to Alessia's face, soaking up how her lips part and her eyes twinkle. She intertwines her fingers with mine, and I tug her closer.

A few nobles pass, dressed in elegant, lightweight garments that match ours. They offer me a nod. I return it with a forced smile, playing the game.

We turn a corner, and the buildings give, offering us a glimpse of the looming palace.

"Holy shite," Alessia says breathlessly.

Perched where the grass meets the sand, the palace stands against the coastal backdrop. It's four stories high and built like a massive, ornate square—a castle disguised as a house. The pale, weathered stone seems to glow softly in the evening sun. Tall, arched windows catch the light, and sloping roofs topped with dark slate add a sense of grandeur. The windows are framed with louvered shutters, a bright blue-green color that matches the sea behind it.

I eye the gardens curiously, taking in the azaleas, camellias, and honeysuckles that add a burst of color against the lush landscape. Towering oaks and willow trees—larger than I've ever seen—and pillars wrapped with trailing moss provide ample shade around the property.

We all stand silently, watching in awe as the sun sets in the distance behind the castle. Once the sun finally sinks into the sea, tiki torches blaze to life around the palace, lighting the paths lining the property.

Guards mill about. Most lean casually against trees, laughing and carrying on, occasionally waving at a passing noble.

Everything appears eerily perfect.

There's an ominous, inexplicable edge in the air, a silent warning that if you do or say something wrong, the friendliness will dry up, leaving nothing but raw viciousness.

A few soldiers pass, offering an animated wave, but there's a sharpness to their eyes as they take us in keenly. I do the same, sweeping my gaze over them from head to toe. My eyes catch on the blades tucked discreetly to their sides, and I relax. It would have the opposite effect on most, but I like knowing what to expect from my enemies. And despite the welcoming façade, these *are* my enemies.

Their casualness is a show. I would know. I might be the Prince of Fear, but I am the king of faking indifference.

Casually, we meander toward the palace's entrance. Our group stays quiet and alert, following the path of the other nobles entering.

The double doors are propped open, and a man in a white jumpsuit and matching top hat stands at a podium. A scroll is laid before him, and he smiles widely at each person, checking their names off with a feather pen.

"Let's wait a moment," I mutter.

We pause, pretending to take in the sights again while the doorman checks in the group ahead of us. Once it's clear, I scan the stone pathway, ensuring we have enough time to do what we need.

"Okay," I say. "Tynan, you're up."

His wicked grin grows, and he strides up to the podium with all the swagger of a male with nowhere to be and nothing to lose. I practically roll my eyes at the display, knowing it's not entirely fake—he possesses a genuine arrogance that would fit quite well with the human nobles.

"Well, hello there," Tynan says, smirking. He leans in, holding the doorman's eyes. "The four of us are all checked in," he says in a deep, demanding tone.

A dopey look crosses the man's face as he smiles wider and nods. "All checked in," he repeats. "Thank you, sir."

Tynan chuckles. "Oh, the pleasure is all mine."

The man reaches into a drawer tucked away in the podium and produces two skeleton keys with little bows tied around them. He hands one to Tynan and one to Alessia.

"You will be on the second floor," he says.

Alessia smiles sweetly, nodding her head in genuine thanks. I know she's dying to say the words, but she's fighting it to break the habit. I chuckle. Her eyes swing toward me and I shrug a shoulder, and offer her my arm. She loops hers through mine.

"Two?" Tynan asks.

The man nods. "For each couple."

Tynan scoffs. "We're not a—"

"Come on, sweetlips." Kenisius scoots closer to my brother, wrapping a thick arm around his neck. "How convenient it'll be to share a room.

Tynan opens his mouth to say something, but Kenisius reaches out and pinches his arsecheek. "Perk up, sweetcheeks."

"The feck!" Tynan's previous swagger fades away as he shoves Kenisius away from him. "Don't call me that."

Kenisius's chest shakes as he chuckles to himself. "Don't ruin it." He pulls him away, saluting the doorman as we enter the foyer.

A hideous glass and crystal chandelier tinkles overhead, illuminating the ivory flooring and glossy wooden staircase flaring out before us. The banisters curl at the side like pulled-back lips—a hungry mouth ready to devour us.

My nose scrunches at the floral runner. "Humans," I mutter. All this wealth and no taste.

"Look," Alessia says, holding up the old key. She tugs the white bow, and it unravels. It serves a dual purpose—not only adding a decorative flair but also securing a small piece of paper with a number. "202."

"*We* are 219," Tynan says flatly, scowling at Kenisius.

"Up we go!" Kenisius leads the way toward the stairs.

At the top of the landing, a small sign perches on a stand. An arrow points to the left with the numbers 200-210, and another arrow points to the right with 211-219. A third arrow points upward, labeled with 300s.

I lock eyes with Kenisius. He tilts his head toward Alessia, then me, and I quickly nod in response. Then, he glances at Tynan and then back to me. I nod again. Confident in our unspoken agreement, we turn and diverge toward our assigned rooms.

He and Tynan will stick together, and Alessia and I will stick together, but we will split up in case anything goes awry.

Because, for some reason, things *always* go awry.

Alessia grips my hand tighter, and I lead her down the hall. We pass doors numbered 200 and 201, quickly locating 202. She inserts the key and turns it. A lock pops and the door creaks as it opens.

We push the door open and acquaint ourselves with the space. It's a fair size, with a large bed, armoire, standing mirror, and large window with a seat beneath it. A flickering chandelier overhead illuminates the space, and I scrunch my nose in disdain at the blue and white florals everywhere.

It reeks of dust and mothballs as if the room has sat unused for quite some time.

Alessia throws herself on the bed with a chuckle, her arms wide. "It's not nearly as comfortable as the beds in Avylon." She sits up, eyes twinkling. "I suppose everything is better there, huh?"

"Tell me," I say, stalking toward her. My gaze rakes up her exposed leg as the slit in her dress rises dangerously high. "What do *you* think?"

"I *know* the males there are better." She gives me a coy smile.

My body jerks to a stop, and I narrow my eyes. "Males?"

She toys with the neckline of her dress, pulling it lower and lower to expose her bare skin, but not low enough to give me what I want.

"*Males*?" I repeat, not succumbing to her teasing until she amends the comment.

She's trying to rile me up.

And fecking hell, it's working. My vision darkens, flickering briefly.

"Perhaps one male in particular," she says, lying back on her elbows and patting the bed beside her.

I open my mouth to retort, but a trumpet resounds through the hallway. Groaning, I reach down and adjust the crotch of my pants.

"What's that?" she asks nervously, sitting up and swinging her legs over the bed.

The blaring of the instrument comes again, and I sigh, rubbing my brow and begging my erection to calm the feck down. "It's party time."

THIRTY-SIX

TONIGHT, WE CELEBRATE

ALESSIA

Queen Wyetta is a horrid woman, and I should hate her palace by default, but it's so darn beautiful. On top of that, everyone is welcoming. All the guards wave and smile rather than standing rigid or stern. The clothing is incredibly vibrant, and the people are so lively. The ballroom isn't as massive as some of the fae's, but it's equally beautiful. Mahogany tables boast an assortment of miniature foods—cupcakes, sandwiches, crackers, and more—and a bar stands beside it, with a butler serving drinks to waiting patrons.

Musicians play live music on a dais in the front of the room. Soft string music floats through the room, mingling with the excited chatter. A space for dancing is cleared in the middle of the space, the pale flooring outlined by ebony tiles. People twirl and dance within it. Unlike the fae, who cheer and move fluidly with reckless abandon, the dancers' movements are all the same. They move in tandem, following the same few steps over and over. I pause, tugging Rainer's hand and forcing him to stop on the outskirts of the space so we can watch the dancers.

A few more couples join in, and soon, the space is filled. The songs change, but the dance steps don't.

"How unappealing," Rainer mutters lowly in my ear.

Chuckling, I playfully swat his chest. "It's not that bad."

It's worse because it's fake.

The comment from within me comes so suddenly that it catches me off guard. My shadow-self has been enjoyably quiet lately.

At least we—the fae—are honest about what we are.

This time, I take in the space with new eyes. Underneath the smiles and polite chatter, I see these people for what they are—supporters of Queen Wyetta and the Trade. My shadow is right. All the beauty is nothing more than a perfume hiding the truly horrid stench of humanity.

The dance moves are too stiff, the smiles too forced, and when I *really* pay attention, I notice how noses are upturned. No one seems like they're genuinely having fun.

Yet they all pretend.

They imprison and sell people of all ages—to the mines, the brothels, the *rich*. Hell, most of these people look rich enough to own their own Tradelings.

My skin blazes as a fire rips through me. I close my eyes and take in a few deep breaths.

I don't want to make a scene here. I have to stay calm—keep my shadow-self contained. We traveled all this way to hear Wyetta's news, and we still need to head to Illynor for the iron after. *That* is the main reason we're here, after all. There's much left to do, and I can't let my emotions and unchecked shadow-rage ruin that.

When I reopen my eyes, I scan the room until my attention snags on a broad form by the snack table. Immediately, I recognize the bright yellow suit and the dark hair tied into a neat low bun. The sight of my familiar friend eases my budding rage.

"There's Ken," I say, tugging Rainer toward the table.

We stride through the room, and suddenly, Rainer growls and jerks me to a stop. I whip my head toward him. His lips pull back into a snarl, and his eyes narrow lethally. I follow his gaze to find a young man standing a few steps away, and his eyes drop down my body, then pop back up to my face. He must notice Rainer immediately because his cheeks turn red, and he hurries away.

A laugh bursts from me. "Did you just growl at that man?"

Rainer shrugs, looking displeased. "He was looking a little too long at something that doesn't belong to him."

"You are incorrigible." I shake my head.

He grips my hand, quickly twirling me around smoothly until my back is pressed to his front. His arms wrap around me, locking me in place against him. He surprises me by swaying us gently to the music.

His breath tickles my ear as he whispers, "I will be *anything* so long as I'm *yours*."

I shiver.

"Cold?" he asks, amusement lacing his tone.

I nudge him with my shoulder. He releases me, and I spin to face him. "Not at all."

"Shame." He grins slightly. "If you were cold, I'd have a reason to keep my arms around you."

"You are rather sly this evening." I chuckle. "You never need a reason for that."

He arches a brow, leaning in. "Are you granting me permanent permission to touch you?"

I shudder at the hidden promise in his words, and his smile blossoms in satisfaction. His dimple appears, sending a flurry of excitement through my stomach.

"Always," I whisper.

He wraps an arm around my midsection, tugging me against him again. The material of my dress is thin, and I plaster myself against him, delighting in the rough, erotic feel of his body, even amidst a crowd of people.

"Gods." He cups the back of my head. "You are the most stunning being I have ever laid eyes on."

My cheeks heat. I wouldn't consider myself shy, but Rainer has a way of continuously lighting the fire in my soul.

"Come on, mo róisín," he says, smirking. "Let's go see Kenisius before we get ourselves into trouble."

I reach up, fingering the soft, round edge of his ear. I miss his ethereal fae ears. It's strange seeing him without a piece of himself. In response, his thumb skates down my left cheek, where my Tradeling mark should be.

He releases me with a disappointed groan, gripping my hand and taking me toward Ken.

The bear shifter stands with his back to us, shoveling tiny muffins into his mouth with one hand, and gripping an overfilled glass of wine with the other.

"Oh! Hello," he says through a mouthful of food when he spots us beside him. Crumbs topple onto his shirt. His long, curly hair is loose around his shoulders tonight, making him appear slightly softer and more handsome than usual.

"Hi, Ken," I say, delighted to see him.

He holds up his glass. "This wine is shite compared to—"

A gasp rings out from a woman beside him. Ken smiles at her. Her eyes drop to the crumbs in his beard, and she smacks her lips in disdain. Then, she quickly scurries away.

Ken shrugs. "The cakes are good, though." He offers us one. "Want?"

Rainer sighs, his expression flat. But despite what his face shows, deep down, I know he loves Ken and his shenanigans.

"I'm good," I say, waving Ken's treats off.

Not too far away, I spot Tynan. He busies himself with a group of women, leaning casually against the wall. His mouth moves rapidly, his expression an arrogant backdrop for whatever ridiculous story he's sharing. They eat it up, leaning in closer to the brute male.

A trumpet blares, and I jump. It renders the string quartet silent, and the chatter swiftly ceases.

"Your attention, please!" A voice bellows through the room. "Her Majesty, Queen Wyetta, Heiress and Sovereign of the Wessex Peninsula, graces us with her presence!"

Guests bow their heads in rapid succession, everyone conveying respect. I quickly follow suit, not wanting to stand out. Rainer huffs under his breath, but he slowly tilts his head down. Loud chewing from Ken snags my attention from my other side. I step closer to him and quickly bring my heel down on his toes, causing him to gulp. He tosses his snack on the table and falls in line—copying us.

The thunder of shoes on tile echoes through the room in a rhythmic cadence. The people stay quiet. I peek through my lashes, catching sight of a small entourage leading what must be the queen to the raised dais where the musicians were previously.

When the nobles begin lifting their heads and clapping politely, we do the same.

The sight of Queen Wyetta catches me off guard. Unlike the fae queen, Yvanthia, who exuded power and wisdom even when she was sick, the human queen is a frail thing. Her bony frame drowns in a cerulean gown, and her face is gaunt and tired. She's not necessarily wrinkly, but her face and neck sag like slabs of raw chicken. A halo of wispy, white curls frames her pink complexion. Her gilded crown sits awkwardly atop her as if it's too heavy for her fragile bones to hold up.

"My loyal subjects," she rasps, lifting a trembling hand. The room sucks in a collective inhale, as if we're all holding our breaths and straining to listen together. "I thank you for gathering before me today—"

Loud chewing reaches my ears again, and I turn to Ken. "Hush!"

He shoves the remaining sandwich into his mouth, swallowing it whole. Then, he raises his hands and shrugs.

I can't help but chuckle. My attention shifts back to the queen, but I've missed what she said. The people around us murmur excitedly. Rainer watches with rapt attention, his mouth tightening into a stern line. His hand tightens around mine, and I pat him gently until he releases it. He flashes me a look of apology, then turns his glare back toward the queen. It takes two guards on either side of her to lower her onto her throne.

Another blare of the trumpet has me wincing. Once the room is silenced again, one of the guards beside the queen stands tall with his hands clasped behind his back. He tilts his chin up and clears his throat dramatically.

"Your sacrifices—paying increased taxes, offering your young to the Trade, and supporting the army—" a whoop rings out, and the guard raises his hand to silence the crowd again. "Thanks to your many sacrifices," he repeats, "we have a new advantage over our beastly adversaries."

Two other guards lift a floral-covered lump onto the dais behind the queen. When Wyetta turns to them—painfully slowly—and nods, they reach up and tug the covering away.

"The diligent labor of our forge has yielded a formidable collection of weaponry, now enhanced with iron," the guard says. "They've been coming to our realm, stealing our babes, feckin' our wives, and killin' us. Now, we return the favor!"

Cheers erupt in the room, the roar deafening.

I lean toward Rainer to ask him what the hell the humans are talking about, but his jaw is tense as he stares straight ahead. I follow his gaze, squinting at the dais as I try to understand what I'm seeing.

Weapons hang on display, a variety of blades and swords. Some are long and thin, some are curved like a farmer's scythe, and some are as small as a steak knife. They're all matte black, as if absorbing the light instead of reflecting it.

I glance around the crowd, gauging the response—various expressions of excitement and intrigue light up the faces around me. Ken stands by the snack table still, his hands empty and his mouth agape.

"We will win this war," someone yells, drawing my attention. They pump a fist into the air, and the people around them clap.

Wyetta is lying to them—telling them we're at war to garner support?

Is *that* why she's sending prisoners across the Gleam? To blame us for attacking when we send them back dead? Meanwhile, she's keeping her real army down here—safe and preparing for a battle with *iron*.

"What're those weapons for?" I ask Rainer slowly, even though I already know the answer. Fear trickles down my spine.

I need to hear him say it.

"She's declaring war on the *fae* of Avylon," he says through gritted teeth. The look he casts me is full of shadowy anger.

The speaking guard strides to the weapons, pulling a dagger free and holding it over his head. The hilt is carved like a wave, curling at the end. "Iron has a detrimental effect on their magic, impairing their abilities in combat. With significant damage, it has the potential to cause fatal harm!"

The crowd oohs at the show as if it's the most magnificent thing they've ever seen. Nausea roils in my stomach.

"We march north to the Gleam soon!" The guard pauses for dramatic effect as the crowd roars to life. When they quiet down long enough, he yells, with a disturbing smile, "But for tonight, we celebrate!"

THIRTY-SEVEN

SUFFER A FATAL FATE

ALESSIA

"Rainer," I say, clutching his arm with both hands. My fingers bite into the soft fabric, aching to rip it away. To tear off this entire façade and show these people we can give them a reason to fear us.

Rainer runs his free hand soothingly down my back. He leans in toward my ear, his voice low. "Not now, mo róisín. Not here." When he pulls back, the promise of danger flashes in his icy eyes, but he forces a smile. "Shall we dance?" he asks loudly.

I frown, studying him.

Dance? Now?

Dark spots crowd my vision, and my veins tingle. I am inclined to agree with my shadow-self's line of questioning. The last thing I want to do is dance.

I want to burn this place down, like the lord's estate. With all of these sickeningly joyful humans inside.

"I can't." My breath quickens, and I narrow my gaze on the old queen sitting atop her throne with a flat expression. She stares out into the crowd of revelers.

The sight of her indifference sickens me. How can someone so seemingly small and harmless cause so much pain and violence across *two* realms?

It's despicable.

Everyone around us hollers and cheers, celebrating the prospect of war—of killing fae. As if harming their own innocent people wasn't enough, they're threatening my kind now, too.

The inside of my skin burns as my shadow grows antsy, begging to burst out.

"Look at me, little rose," Rainer demands, sensing my struggle. Clasping my shoulders and lowering his face to mine. Against my lips, he whispers, "Breathe."

I shake my head, my chest tightening as I hyperventilate.

My vision blackens, and my ears ring as Rainer grasps my hand and tugs me away. For a moment, I think he's taking me out of the room, but we stop abruptly. He pulls me to him, wrapping his arms around me. Swaying us slightly from side to side, he murmurs something low.

Dancing? Why are we dancing?

My body trembles with rage, and it takes everything in me to hold back the dark fog clawing its way out from inside of me.

I will kill them all—

My back slams against a wall, and a warm pressure envelopes my mouth, effectively silencing the shadow's voice. The kiss is not unwelcome—quite the opposite. My lips move back in response, tasting *him*.

All too quickly, he's gone.

My chest heaves, this time with need rather than wrath.

I blink, and my sight clears. I take in Rainer's handsome face. A calmness washes over me. His mouth moves, but I don't hear a word he says at first. Slowly, the sharp ringing in my ears fades away, and string music comes back, along with the chatter of people nearby, followed by his voice.

         MIRANDA JOY

"—not alone in this," Rainer says.

He bends and grips the back of my bare knee, exposed from the high slit in my dress, and hikes my leg up around his waist. Then he leans my back against the wall for support. His lips descend on mine again, tenderly and meaningfully. Unhurriedly, he kisses a path down my chin and then trails to my neck. Goosebumps break out along my skin.

"Do you feel me, little rose?" he whispers into my collarbone, pressing more firmly against me. My cheeks heat in response. His body is warm and hard against mine. "I'm here with you. Right here, right now. We have each other, and nothing else matters."

He reaches for my hand, placing the palm over his heart.

The thud beneath the fabric is a silent melody, our love song.

"I'm with you," I murmur, my eyes dancing across his face as I greedily take in this beautiful specimen who somehow knows how to support me, even when I'm losing myself. "I'm okay."

"Good." He pulls back, skimming my arm with the pads of his fingers. I writhe in response, and he smirks. "I like the way I affect you."

Even with everything around us, I practically melt in his arms. My shadow settles, quieting down.

"You know, I do, too." I sigh with relief. "You help keep my shadow calm and..." I frown as the words trail off.

My eyes widen, and my heart thumps furiously as panic sluices me.

"What is it?" he asks quietly.

I reach up with a shaking hand, trying to cover his sharp ears. They cut through his tousled onyx hair, appearing entirely fae. Gone are the soft human edges he wore moments ago.

His eyes drop to my cheek, and his brow furrows. His fingers come up, caressing the spot where my Tradeling tattoo sits. "Shite."

"How?" I ask, alarmed. Glancing to my left, I search for Tynan. The spot where he was earlier is empty. "Where's your brother?"

Tynan dropped our glamour.

The rigid set in Rainer's jaw tells me he's realizing the same thing. He pulls my loose curls forward until they fall over my cheek. I tilt my head down, attempting to hide my mark. Someone bumps me from behind, and I draw closer to Rainer.

Suddenly, our area feels suffocatingly crowded, with people brushing up against us. There are too many eyes here.

"What do we do?" I ask, trying to hold onto the control he instilled in me. If my shadow-self latches onto the panic and—

"Hey." He cups my face, bringing his forehead to mine. "Look at me. We're in this together. We'll be—"

"Feckin' fae!" someone beside me yells.

Resounding gasps respond, and someone jostles us. I grip Rainer tightly. In the chaos, the crowd around us surges as people begin yelling and shoving in a frenzy. A cold wave of terror crashes over me, and my limbs turn to jelly.

This can't be happening. We need to find a way to get out of here—now.

"Mo róisín," Rainer says calmly, eyes locked on me. He cups my cheeks in his hands. "It's going to be okay. We're going to be—"

Rainer's body jolts, his hands falling limp at his sides. His brow furrows, confusion shadowing his features as his gaze drifts downward, slow and deliberate. The crowd around us pulses, pushing in closer. People scream around us, but I don't hear them.

All I hear is the single, shallow gasp that leaves Rainer's mouth. All I see is the droplet of blood that escapes his lips.

My gaze falls to the hilt protruding from his side, its wave-like carvings taunting cruelly. Blood blooms around it, soaking into his red shirt and darkening it a shade.

"No," I choke out. "Rainer, *no*."

I meet his glossy eyes, which speak loudly enough for me to see the truth.

That this is it.

We fecked up.

It's over.

A roar rips from the room as a bear—*Ken*—crashes into the crowd. He exerts his dominance. His brown fur ripples as he runs, swiftly tearing his claws through bodies. A chorus of ear-piercing screams meets the melody of bones crunching.

Behind him, guards storm the dais with urgency, ripping weapons off the display.

Shock and terror course through me as I watch in what feels like slow motion. The guards yell instructions to one another, and people stampede for the door. Like a force of nature, Ken bolts towards the exit, blocking their path. With the strength of his astonishing weight, he brings people crashing down, their limbs snapping like twigs in his path.

Fear roots me in place, causing my body to tremble uncontrollably.

Rainer coughs, breaking my stupor. His legs give out, and I catch him right before his knees hit the ground. Cradling him in my arms, I carefully lower him.

"What do I do?" I cry, functioning in a haze as I situate him on my lap.

My hands tremble uncontrollably, hovering over him helplessly. A hollow ache spreads through my chest as the truth crashes into me: there's nothing I can do. My view narrows to the faint rise and fall of his chest, and the world around me crumbles.

"I love you, mo róisín," he mutters, eyes fluttering shut before whipping open again.

"No," I growl, gently slapping his cheek to keep him awake. "What do I *do*, Rainer? Tell me!"

A scream of desperation builds in my throat, raw and animalistic, but all I can do is choke on it as I watch his face pale. My heart shatters, splintering into jagged shards that pierce through my breath. I'm suffocating. No matter how hard I try, I can't catch my breath.

His thumb reaches up, attempting to wipe away the endless stream of tears from my face. He sucks in a shaky breath. "I'm s-sorry I failed you—that I failed *us*."

Darkness claws at the edges of my vision, dragging inward until only a pinprick of light remains—and then even that is gone. Reality crumbles into a void, but the terror within me explodes, ripping through the blackness.

I throw my head back, allowing the scream to erupt from my soul. The noise is deafening, and my throat grows raw as I let out my rage. The silky, snake-like shadow spills out of me, carrying my cries to each corner of the room.

My pain saturates the space, flooding the ballroom with the weight of my anguish.

No. I am *not* helpless—I refuse to ever be helpless again.

And this time, the perpetrators will suffer a fatal fate.

Thirty-Eight
Realm of Fear and Fury
Alessia

A tidal wave of darkness engulfs me as a lifetime's worth of rage, grief, and regret finally breaks free. The outburst is never-ending, pouring out of me relentlessly. The suffocating shadow engulfs everything in its path, blinding me along with everyone else.

The screams thicken, polluting the air.

My shadow's ravenous hunger pitches, driven to a frenzy by my fury. I brace for the screams to falter as my voracious beast swallows them whole.

But something in the shrieking changes.

The combative cries shift into that of fear—pleas laced with desperation.

The blanket of darkness begins to recede, relinquishing its oppressive grasp. The fog thins, winding into a single tendril as it swirls around me.

I blink, letting my eyes adjust to the returned light in lieu of my darkness. Nobody is clamoring to the exits. Instead, they stand frozen, their eyes wide with terror, their bodies quivering as they desperately grasp at the empty air around them.

I recognize the scene—they're fighting illusions of their worst nightmares.

The horrifying moment unfolds as many of them frantically claw at their faces, ripping their eyeballs out. Blood pours from their sockets, staining their extravagant clothing. I avert my gaze in disgust, unable to bear the sight.

Their anguished screams gradually dissipate to faint sobs as their movements grow more sluggish, losing intensity. Exhausted to death, people begin to collapse, crumbling around me. Their skulls hit the ground with a sickening thump. Some seize up until they go still, others lie unmoving.

An eyeball rolls past me, and my stomach heaves. I squeeze my eyes shut and swallow the bile.

A dark, weak chuckle reaches my ears, and my attention snaps back to Rainer.

He stares at me, his eyes the color of the night sky. A silver twinkle reflects back, my image, as if I'm a single bright star in his dark sky.

"Rainer," I cry out, reaching for him.

"I'll always—" he coughs, and the rattling noise sends an alarm through me "—take care of my little rose."

"You have to, Rainer." My voice cracks. "I know you think I'm strong, but I only am because of your love. You are the lighthouse guiding me to my strength."

He sucks in a sharp breath, wheezing. "Not even death can weed the love for you from my heart."

"Don't you dare!" With tears streaming down my face, I cling to him, relishing his warmth and strength.

My fingers brush against his side, coming into contact with something firm and sticky. My eyes quickly scan downward. The distinctive carved hilt juts out from his torso, taunting me with his impending doom. The iron on the blade is coursing through his veins at this very moment—poisoning him—but removing the blade would risk him bleeding out.

It's not a question of *if* he will die, but rather, which death will bring him the least amount of pain.

"I can't do this," I rasp out between sobs. "I can't lose you."

"You must."

"*How*?" I cry.

There are a thousand desperate questions in that single word: How is he using so much magic—and with iron in his blood? How can he love *me* so fiercely? How do I deserve him?

How do I decide which death is the easiest for him?

How can I possibly be okay with losing him?

And it's the last question that has me burying my face against his chest, clutching his arms so tight that my fingernails threaten to bend. It's as if I can hold him tightly enough, and then perhaps I can keep him from teetering off the cliff into death. Knots tighten in my stomach as I weigh the impossible decision.

I can't do this alone.

I lift my head briefly, searching for Ken. He's nowhere to be seen. Neither is Tynan.

The bodies continue to drop around us, a symphony of skulls cracking against the marble. Blood runs in rivulets through the cracks on the floor.

I feel nothing when I look at it.

All my empathy is used on the male who lies on death's doorstep beside me.

Rainer smiles weakly at me, his dark eyes flickering. They slowly grow lighter and lighter, back to their pale blue coloring—as cold as my heart at this very moment.

Then, as those beautiful eyes shut, my frozen heart crashes to the ground, shattering into a million irreparable pieces.

The last bit of hold his power has on the remaining humans lifts, and they resume scrambling for the exit once more. They pass by in a blur.

I don't see them.

I don't hear them.

It doesn't matter.

Nothing matters.

Quietly and calmly, I extend my arms and let my shadow explode from every pore. The rage is palpable, my body vibrating as the darkness bursts forth again, ready to claim all the remaining souls.

They deserve it—every single one of them.

For encouraging the Trade, for supporting Wyetta, and for killing my gods-damned soul-bond.

"Feast," I cry, my tone lethal. "Take them *all*."

A chilling silence blankets the ballroom as my words hang in the air. My shadow twists and dances, its inky tendrils lashing out and encompassing those who remain standing after Ken and Rainer's onslaught.

An unusual sense of power courses through me. There's no pride or joy—only an intense disappointment that it's come to this. The weight of responsibility settles heavily on my shoulders, and I'm all too aware of the consequences of my actions.

I *am* a monster—a demon—a destroyer of souls because they made me one. My shadow-self carries out my vengeance with ruthless efficiency. As the cacophony of anguish and terror fills the air, I stand silent, witnessing the destruction I've wrought.

It might be my doing, but I didn't choose this. I didn't want this.

I wanted *peace.*

I wanted *love.*

I wanted *freedom.*

They took that all from me twice, now—once as an orphaned little girl and again as a woman who found her strength. This time, I won't run or hide. I'm staying until they all pay.

My shadow splits into dozens of rope-like arms, surging into open mouths and snatching air from people's lungs before they can react. I look away, not wanting their faces burned in my memory. My gaze snags on a crowd of servants and the butler from earlier. They huddle together in the corner by the bar.

One of them turns toward me, crippling fear in their pale face. A dark, jagged line sits on their left cheek.

"Shite," I mutter, just as one of the tendrils reaches for them. "No!"

I carefully rest Rainer on the ground and jump to my feet, ready to bolt toward the group. But shockingly, my shadow halts. It wavers before careening in the opposite direction toward an escaping noble.

"Run!" I shout to the group of Tradelings. "Get out of here!"

They don't hesitate, sprinting toward the exit. My shadow leaves them unscathed, and I exhale a heavy, shaky breath.

"Don't touch the innocents," I say weakly. "No Tradelings. Save them…"

The ground beneath me grows unsteady as my legs wobble and my head swims.

My body goes limp as I collapse beside Rainer. Darkness clouds my vision, but I fight to stay awake, not wanting to relinquish my shadow's deathly feast. A woozy lightheadedness steals my focus. I try to shake it off, but it's too much. Too heavy.

"Save the innocents," I whisper again.

Only those who deserve it will pay.

I'm too weak to respond, but I hope my shadow feels the gratitude in my heart. For once, we understand each other. I will give the darkness what it wants if it lets me keep my heart soft when it counts.

The screams haunt me as the exhaustion of using so much power threatens to take me under, but I refuse to succumb. I will not crumble. And I certainly will not feel guilty for those who die today.

It's *their* fault they must die like this—choking on terror and burning in the shadow of my anger—for *they* are the complicit ones who built this realm of fear and fury.

THIRTY-NINE

I Shall Dream of You

Alessia

"*Na tromluithe is binne,*" *a young, soft voice says. "I know good dreams are too much to ask for, so I pray to the goddess for the sweetest nightmares instead.*"

I blink a few times, letting my eyes adjust to the dim light. I'm in a room I've never seen before, but instinctually, I recognize it as Rainer's castle—the dark, mahogany wood screams of Umbra Court. A massive bed with black sheets matches the dark, billowing curtains framing balcony doors. The crescent moon peeks in, its pale light slicing through the room.

But I barely pay any attention to the furniture. Instead, my gaze is drawn to the little boy perched on his knees beside the bed. His back is to me, and his dark, wavy hair falls to the back of his neck. His hands are clasped in front of him, resting on the mattress.

He continues his prayer, mumbling something indecipherable.

When he turns, the moonlight dances across his face, catching on his pale blue eyes. They fill like a well after a rainstorm. He sniffles, using his sleeve to swipe at his cheeks as the tears fall.

"I miss you, mama," he says softly, striding toward the balcony. He doesn't notice me as he passes me, reaching for the doors. He pauses for a moment, tilting his head toward the sky. He can't be more than ten years old, but the weight in his gaze mirrors centuries of pain. "Na tromluithe is binne. Goodnight, moon."

With one swift gesture, he tugs the doors shut. Then, he turns and runs to his bed, his little feet slapping on the hardwood floor. He dives onto the mattress, burying himself in the sheets and tugging them up over his head.

"He's why I wanted to be a better male," a soft, dark whisper comes from behind me.

I whirl around. Rainer stands there in identical dark pajamas as the young boy—as the younger version of himself. Now a grown man, his haunted expression still lingers but is complemented by a chiseled jawline and prominent eyebrows. Gone is the small, fragile frame; in its place is a robust and muscular body exuding strength.

I launch myself at him, throwing my arms around his neck and peppering his face with kisses.

"Mo róisín," he says softly. "You are normally much more reserved with your love."

I squeeze him tighter, not knowing how to respond. His words sink into my core, making me wish I'd been more open and free with my affections while I had the chance.

"We should've completed the bond," I mutter into his neck after a lengthy silence. "Wherever you're going next, I want to go with you."

Gently, he grips my waist and pulls me away from him. His hands rest on my sides, fingers splaying out and pressing into my skin.

"You can't die. Your purpose isn't complete," he says sternly. "Fate has other ideas for you."

"Feck fate!" I yell. Then, I wince, glancing over my shoulder to ensure I didn't disturb the little boy slumbering there. The quiet lump rises and falls with each of his breaths. The irritation slowly melts away from me. "That little boy would be so proud of the male you became," I add softly.

I don't know how much time we have together before our permanent goodbye. There's too much to say, and I don't want to waste it fighting.

"I know," Rainer says. He nods, and a sad expression creeps onto his face. "I know that because of you. All my life, I never felt good enough. I viewed myself as a monster, unworthy of love in any form."

"You are beyond worthy," I say, cupping his face.

With a soft smile, he gently places his hands over mine and says, "You've allowed me to see that I deserve love, flaws and all." He gives me a soft, reassuring squeeze. "I have so much love and generosity to offer, and I regret that it took me this long to admit that. If only I had recognized the truth earlier, I would have wholeheartedly given myself to you, unafraid."

As I try to speak, my eyes brim with tears, and a tightness grips my throat. I drop my hands, nodding as I start to pull away.

Rainer gently grabs my wrist, tugging me to him. He wraps his arms around my midsection, pulling me flush to his front and resting his head on my shoulder. We sway gently as we face the bed where the little boy sleeps, tucked away from sight.

"Another nightmare?" I ask softly, avoiding the reality of our situation. I don't want to talk about endings. I can't.

"Always," he whispers in my ear. "But that little boy's prayers came true. Now, I have the sweetest of nightmares." He kisses the tender spot behind my ear. "You are my sweetest little nightmare."

I allow my body to grow soft and pliable as I lean into him. "This is the last time I will feel your touch, isn't it?" My voice cracks, and I can barely speak through the heaviness in my chest.

His hand slides up to the middle of my chest, coming flat atop my heart. "You will always feel me here."

The words crack the dam, and my tears stream down my cheeks, staining my skin with the pain of our reality.

"I need you to know…" He sighs, and his breath tickles the side of my neck. "Alessia, it's effortless to love you. Don't guard your heart—let others fall for your beautiful soul like I have."

"No, Rainer—"

"You are easy to love," he repeats. "And you deserve love in its purest forms. Despite everything you've endured, you've thrived in the shadows. Don't let this—me—be an excuse to shut others out."

My heart spasms in an erratic rhythm. "I only want to be loved by you."

"I will always love you, and I will wait for you in the Otherworld and beyond." His arms tighten around me, and he lowers his voice. "But it better be a very long time until we meet again."

Ripping free from his hold, I spin around and glare at him through the tears obscuring my vision. "Just wake up! Stay with me!"

"It's not that easy." A tear streaks down his cheek, and he shakes his head. "I'm dying, Alessia."

"But you're not dead yet!"

He gives me an apologetic look, flattening his lips. "I—"

"No!" I ball my hands into fists, slamming them against Rainer's chest. "You wouldn't be here with me if you were dead!"

He doesn't even budge; he lets me pound him until, finally, he sighs and grabs my hands and pulls me to him.

"It's too late for me." His voice is hoarse, stained with his pain. "But it is not too late for you."

"I love you, Rainer." I sob, dropping to the floor and dragging him down with me.

My white lace nightgown flares out around me like the petals of a flower. Rainer moves with me, tucking a strand of hair behind my ear.

"I wish I said it sooner," I whisper, trying and failing to blink away the tears.

"You didn't need to say it for me to feel it," he says, his voice tender. His lip trembles, and it crushes me how much emotion is on this stoic male's face. "I love you, too. To the Otherworld and beyond."

I suck in a stuttering breath, a sob escaping. "Are you scared?" I whisper.

He holds my gaze for a beat. Then he murmurs, "I am a creature of fear and nightmares. I will be just fine."

"That's not what I asked," I say, sniffling.

Sighing, he hesitates. His head lolls forward, and he runs his fingers through his hair.

When he looks up and meets my eyes again, they shimmer with tears. "Yes," he whispers. "I am always scared, Alessia. My heart is filled with nothing but fear." He pauses. "Or it was—until you wiggled your way in, forcing it to make room for love."

Thunder cracks through the night sky, and the little boy in bed jolts up, a scream bursting free.

Panic strikes me like lightning. I'm not ready to go. Not yet.

"Stay. Just a little longer," I plead with Rainer.

Summoning my inner strength, I close my eyes and focus on changing the dreamscape. If I can at least gift Rainer one final good dream...

The sound of bubbling water reaches my ears, and the hardwood beneath me is replaced with a lush blanket of green.

Orange light bursts behind my eyelids, and slowly, I crack my eyes open.

"Our first dream together," Rainer whispers, gazing past me. He shifts from his haunches, planting his arse on the ground beside me.

I glance over my shoulder. A golden ribbon of water flows through the river—an impossibly beautiful liquid satin. On the other side, a dense forest stretches out. Birds sing tunes of joy, and the air is lighter here.

The midday sun warms my skin. Rainer leans back, gazing up at the clouds fluttering past overhead. Instead of doing the same, I hike my dress up my thighs and straddle him.

He chuckles, but I can hear the pain underneath it.

"It's not too late," I whisper, planting my lips against his. He kisses me back, pouring his heart into it as his fingers tangle in my hair.

Beneath me, he instantly grows hard. I grind against him, wanting him before it's too late.

Wanting to go with him, wherever that may be.

I lift my hips, reaching for the button on his pants, quickly undoing them. He sucks in a sharp breath as I pull him free.

Pulling my underwear to the side, I line him up with my slick entrance, rubbing his head against my clit. He groans, squeezing my waist tighter.

"Don't do it," he threatens, but he makes no move to stop it.

Every fiber of my being pulses with an overwhelming craving and urgency. It's as though the dormant bond within me has suddenly awakened, yearning to connect with him. No matter where he goes, I want to be right there with him.

My shadow stays still and quiet, and I don't know whether it's in deference of the bond or because we're entangled in a dream. Either

*way, I take it as a sign to continue—to chase the need eroding my
resolve.*

*"Do you want me?" I whisper, pausing with his flesh against mine.
My legs quiver as I hover over his hardness. All I would have to do is
sink down, and he'd be inside of me.*

We'd tie our lives to one another, solidifying our fate.

I wouldn't be without him ever again.

*"More than anything," he says breathlessly, staring at me with
reverence. Then he squeezes his eyes shut and makes a pained
sound.*

*Slowly, I begin to lower myself, but Rainer's fingers tighten, stop-
ping me before we merge.*

*"We can't." He growls, picking me up by the waist and depositing
me on the ground beside him. "I want you more than I've ever
wanted anything, but I'm not selfish enough to do this."*

*"I don't want to live without you," I say quietly, my hands trem-
bling with the gravity of what I almost did.*

*"This isn't right." He tucks himself back into his pants, sitting up
and reaching for me.*

*I collapse into his arms, sobbing. With care and patience, he
strokes my back in small motions.*

*"You are not selfish either, mo róisín, and so many people rely on
you now."*

*I shake my head against him, ready to argue. My hands tighten
around the fabric of his shirt, clutching him.*

*"Yes, they do," he whispers, cradling me. "Sheila and her brother.
The other little Tradeling. Fern. Das Celyn—they'll want to stay with
you. Ken, too. He might need you more than anyone. And—" He
sucks in a breath. "If Tynan didn't betray us, if this was all just a*

horrible accident, he'll need you, too. Be their leader, Alessia. Guide them through this."

It's too much. Too heavy and too real. I can only pour my emotions out through my touch, holding onto Rainer like I can't bear to part with him.

Because I can't.

But I have to.

"Sometimes, even the strongest roses wither and die," he says softly. "But new ones will pop up in their place. It's the cycle of life."

"I don't want a new rose, you idiot," I yell between sobs. "It's you. You or no one. Stay with me!"

He strokes lazy circles on my palm, staring down at it blankly. "Remember when I once said I'm cursed with malice while you are cursed with mercy?"

"Of course," I say, practically choking on the words. "I could never forget that."

He sighs, and this time, it's a sound of acceptance. "My curse isn't just malice—it's to destroy those I love. My mother, you…"

Shaking my head vigorously, I squeeze his leg. "That's a basket of shite, and you know it."

The sky darkens, and a loud crack resounds through the dream-scape.

"Don't you dare go, Rainer!" I cry. "I swear to the gods if you leave me here…"

The world darkens around us, and his voice rings out one last time: "Dream of me, mo róisín, and no matter where I go, I shall dream of you."

FORTY
REFILLS MY HEART
ALESSIA

"**D**earling?" a melodic, feminine voice calls. "Up with you now, dearling."

I stir in response, but my eyes feel heavy—sewn shut. Vaguely, I register hands wrapping around my arm and attempting to hoist me up.

Mustering up my strength, I force my eyes open. For a second, I sit dazed until everything comes flooding back to me.

"Rainer!" I scream hoarsely. I yank myself free of the stranger's hold, throwing myself over his limp body.

Sobbing, I squeeze him desperately against me, unwilling to make peace with reality. I shake him, my hands roaming every bit of his skin, trying to rouse him from his state of unconsciousness. He's not dead. He can't be.

"You've certainly left your mark here, little one," the stranger says.

"Go away," I yell without looking up. I push Rainer's hair back, peppering kisses along his forehead. "Rainer, baby, *please*."

She utters a dismissive *tsk* sound, then grips my arms again. This time, she's much more forceful as she yanks me to my feet.

I'm prepared to fight her off, to drop back down to the male at my feet, but the sight of her face turns my blood to ice.

For a moment, I stare at her, unbreathing and unblinking.

She drops her grip on me and steps back, inclining her chin with a smile that wrinkles her eyes attractively—highlighting the kindness found in a life of many smiles.

My breath catches in my throat as I take her in. We're practically twins, somehow, but the smile lines around her mouth and eyes tell me she's a few decades older than I am. Her mane of ashy-blonde curls are wilder and messier, and her grey eyes are sharp. We're about the same height, but she's thinner, her dirty, beige dress hanging off her. A small, black beauty mark dots the side of her chin.

"You," I breathe, taking a step toward her. She looks utterly familiar, more so than the shared features. I've seen her somewhere before. But I can't place it.

"Me." Her smile grows. "I am Enid. Pleased to meet you…"

My heart stops. "Enid?"

She laughs. "Yes. And you are?"

"Alessia?" I say it more like a question as it hits me—the *portrait* in Spiritus Court. She's the female whose journals I've been poring over. "*Enid Liadain Lírshadow.*"

"Well met, Alessia." She touches her chest reverently. "I was once known as a Lírshadow, indeed."

"But… how?" I blink, my body stiff and numb.

Am I dreaming still?

Am I dead?

My pulse thunders in my temples as I scan the room. The weight of the scene settles on my shoulders, pressing down like a block of iron. Horror and disbelief flood me, churning my stomach and threatening to expel its contents.

I did this.

I try to steady my breathing, but it comes in short, shallow gasps. The sight of so many lifeless faces etched with pain will eternally haunt my mind, but it's nothing compared to the male lying lifeless beside me. It takes all my strength to keep the tears from streaming down my face.

The sorrow turns to anguish—*rage*—and it squeezes my lungs with a vice grip.

"Look at me, dearling." Enid's voice is soft but commanding. I do as she says, forcing my blurring gaze to hers. "What you have accomplished is most admirable. You have done a truly noble thing here today."

A knot forms in my throat, making it impossible to reply.

There's nothing *noble* about losing the love of one's life.

"You bring pride to the Lírshadow bloodline," she says.

"I don't care about any of that," I croak. How could I possibly?

She sighs softly, her smile dropping as sorrow creeps in. "I was exiled from my land by Yvanthia long ago. I had made a life for myself here instead. Found peace, married a wonderful partner, and had many beautiful children."

The queen banished the bloodline... Char's story from many years ago comes creeping back to me—the tale of two powerful females—one born a queen and one who became queen.

Yvanthia and Enid.

With a resigned sigh and a twinge of curiosity, I ask, "What happened?"

"The humans and fae are not so different after all," she says, gently tapping my cheek. "Like Yvanthia, the humans are led by jealousy and desire to obtain power. Iron happened."

"But you're alive."

"A blessing." Her lips curve up slightly at the edges again. "They poisoned me, entrapped me, but they kept me alive to use—should they ever decide they need my magic."

I frown. "Your magic? Wait—how long have you been here?"

Her grey eyes shimmer. "Long enough to lose hope things would change. Long enough for every drop of magic to leech from my veins. Over time, the iron depleted me permanently." She shakes her head softly. "That does not matter."

My shadow begins to stir, waking back up after its temporary slumber. Despite the satisfaction deep within me—having fueled itself with many souls—it thrums excitedly.

Generations later, another new descendant was birthed, it says, reciting Char's story to me. *One who could challenge both queens and their cruelties... the old faerie queen had heard a prophecy about this child, so she had been secretly seeking the bloodlines she exiled, murdering them to prevent them from returning to the realm and rising against her...*

"The story was about me," I mutter. Enid cocks her head, taking me in. "Yvanthia—she's the one who killed my parents. Who tried to kill me," I say breathlessly as the pieces click into place.

Enid nods carefully. "I would not put it past her. There were whispers of Yvanthia sending fae into Dovenak to hunt my blood-line. I speculated that is partly why they kept me alive—to use me against her potentially."

Is that what Wyetta and her guards were talking about?

Did the fae genuinely attack first?

Dread consumes me as I realize the line between innocent and guilty is hazy. Like Char once said—the truth changes depending on what side of the Gleam you stand.

Now, I realize what she means.

Any of us can be seen as a hero or a monster, depending on the perspective.

"Yvanthia is worse than I thought," I say, returning to the faerie queen's cruelties. She killed my family and tried to kill me until she realized she needed me to save her own life. "So *she* is why the human queen wanted to go to war with the fae."

Enid nods, then glances over her shoulder toward the throne, where the elderly queen slumps, blood trickling from her mouth. "That human *queen* was merely warming my seat, dearling. She stole my name, my freedom, and my throne. It was never truly hers, and now, I shall reclaim what I built."

My veins vibrate as my shadow breaks free, surging toward Enid. The dark, wispy tendril coils around her leg, like a dog cozying up for pets. I swear it even makes a brief purring noise.

Enid's eyes crinkle at the corners as she reaches down, running her hand through its tendrils. "I never thought I would see the day..." she mumbles, her voice thick with emotion.

I'm tempted to ask what she means, but I feel her strokes through my hair, and the tenderness distracts me. I shudder, my eyes flitting shut under the show of affection.

After everything so dark, sharp, and brutal, it feels... soft like home.

Home.

A sinking feeling pulls at my gut, and I snap out of the delirium.

One who could challenge both queens and their cruelties.

Even if my shadow likes Enid, she isn't innocent in all of this. Just because we share blood, it doesn't mean we share values.

"The Trade," I snap. "That was you who instilled it?"

A horrified look crosses the female's face. "Certainly not!" She scowls, shaking her head. "That is *not* the ruler I strive to be. Not then and certainly not now."

I exhale in relief. Whatever cruelties or crimes she's guilty of, we can figure that out later, so long as she's willing to help me secure the iron and abolish the Trade.

My eyes flit back to the carnage in the ballroom. Dark crimson rivulets trail through divets in the tile, streaking through the room. The bodies strewn about are still *human*. Even if they were horribly complicit, they still had thoughts and feelings and families.

A lump forms in my throat, and I swallow it, averting my eyes again. It does me no good to drown in guilt, but it's a reminder that we are *all* capable of cruelties—even if it's in the name of the greater good.

"You plan to dismantle the Trade?" I clarify, meeting her eyes again.

"I would much like a bath and a meal first." She chuckles gingerly. "But yes, I will revert Dovenak to its former glory."

Something else strikes me as odd. My forehead scrunches with confusion. "You said the human queen—Wyetta Wessex—stole your *name*?"

A faraway look crosses Enid's face. "Wessex was the surname of the man I loved. I claimed it like I claimed the crown—the entire Wessex Peninsula. Wyetta's great-grandmother posed as one of my children, succeeding the throne after my purported *death*. Her lineage has been falsely ruling as Wessexes ever since."

"What happened to him? The man you loved?" My voice cracks, and I force my eyes shut so I don't look back at Rainer. I don't want to see him like this.

I *can't*. It'll break me.

Enid sucks in a slow, heavy breath. "The same thing that happens to all humans, I'm afraid, my dearling."

"Not just humans," I say bitterly, a tear slipping free.

An image of Rainer's beautiful face fills my mind. A tremor courses through me as I picture the enormous pool of blood around him. Any semblance of peace I had is ripped ferociously away. My chest cracks, and a pained cry bursts out.

"How am I supposed to go on?" I drop to my knees, burying my face in my hands and letting my tears soak my skin.

"One breath at a time," Enid says softly. She places a hand on my shoulder. "He needs to feed. But you know that, don't you?"

"What?" I croak, using the back of my hand to wipe the stream off my cheeks.

The violent brownish-red stain coating the front of my white dress turns my veins to lava. It's the last bits of him I have left—merely a muddy smear on a borrowed gown. It's so disrespectful, so unfair, that I want to rip the damn thing off and burn it.

"He's—he can't," I wail, clutching the dress in my fists. "He's gone."

Enid chuckles pitifully, her lips pinching together as she takes me in. "His body has gone still, but his soul lingers." She squats beside me, placing a hand on my heart. "Can't you feel it, spirit-caller?"

I wrack my brain, desperately sifting through the pages and pages of journals I've read. Of *her* very journals. But nothing about bringing back lives or saving the dead crops up.

"I don't understand," I say weakly.

Her eyes flit to my hair, her fingers dancing over the messy tendrils that have loosened from my braid. "You look so much like I did at this age, even with many generations between us. It is rather magical in its own way."

I snap into action, jerking away from her mundane conversation and whirling around. Quickly, I drop my head to Rainer's chest and pause. At first, I don't feel or hear anything. But when I place my fingers against his neck, a faint, sluggish pulse twitches against my fingertips. It's barely there, but he's *alive*.

"Enid," I say, my voice cracking. "What can I do to save him? The iron—" My eyes flit to the dagger protruding from his side, and panic surges through me again. I lift my head and hold Enid's stare. Despite the fact we're both fae, I use the only words I know to convey my desperation. "*Please.*"

She studies me and offers me a soft smile. "You love him with everything you are, don't you?" But she doesn't wait for an answer. She points toward Rainer and then leans in toward me. "As long as he is *still* breathing, he will live," she whispers. "Take care of him."

Reaching into her dress's pocket, she pulls out a small glass jar and places it beside me. The substance inside is a cream color with a glittering quality to it.

"What is this?" I open it and smell it. It has a vague hint of lemongrass and mint, reminiscent of the healing salve Char used to make me, but different...

"It is strong," she says. "You need less than you think. Use it sparingly—the sorceress who made this is rather elderly."

"But... the iron!" It will render the magic ineffective.

"Remove the iron first," she says patiently. "After you feed him—he needs strength."

"How is he even alive?" I ask as my shaking hands reach for his shirt to inspect the wound. "The iron is *in* his bloodstream."

"As it is in yours."

"I don't understand," I murmur. Forget the iron—the dagger is embedded deeply into his side. If it hit an organ, there's no way this salve will help.

"You have human blood in your system. Is it a farfetched assumption to say he has fed on your blood?"

"Yes... I mean, no." I pause. I think of Fern and the human assassins he'd feed on when they crossed the Gleam... then I think of his face buried between my thighs as he— "Yes, he's fed on human blood." I cough awkwardly, my cheeks heating.

She leans forward, lowering her voice conspiratorially. "There is iron in human blood."

I only frown harder. "Wouldn't that... poison him?"

"Does the dose make the poison? Or does the dose make the poison *resistance*?" Then she pats me gently on the shoulder and stands, turning away.

"Wait!" I yell after her. "Where are you going?"

She turns back, raising a sharp brow. "To get fresh air. But first, I want my goddess-kissed crown back."

Shaking off the strange interaction—I can process it later—I turn to Rainer.

Enid said to feed him.

I search desperately for something to cut myself with so I can force him to drink. Starting there is my best bet. He's sharper and healthier with my blood coursing through him. That might help combat the blood loss and give him a fighting chance when I remove the weapon.

It's worth a chance.

My skin vibrates, and a heat overtakes me. Before I know what's happening, my shadow whips toward me. It morphs into the shape of two fangs, similar to a vampyr's, and thrusts into my wrist. I hiss, trying to stay still. The pressure is sharp, and blood wells up, dripping down my arm right away.

My brows flit up. That'll do.

Quickly, I situate myself behind Rainer, propping his body up with a grunt. My shadow helps lift him up, placing him carefully against me.

I tilt Rainer's head back, resting it on my shoulder. Blood spills from my fresh wound, and I shove my trembling wrist against his mouth. "Drink, you broody bastard."

Warm crimson rivulets trail down my arm, and I smear it all over his lips in an attempt to lure him back to life.

My shadow wavers around his side, inspecting his wound. It wraps around the blade, tugging it free.

I gasp. "No—he can't lose any more blood."

But it's too late. The iron-infused weapon slides out with a horrifying squelch. I wince, slamming my eyes shut. It clatters to the floor.

When I reopen my eyes, I catch my shadow ripping Rainer's shirt off. I clench my teeth at the sight of his bare skin. His dark, swirling tattoos are stained rusty-brown and red, like a violent piece of art, and an angry, vicious gash oozes at his side. Nausea burns the back of my throat, but I don't look away this time. Now that I've seen it, I can't.

A piece of my shadow wads up his undershirt, stuffing the fabric against Rainer's side while another tendril reaches for the jar of salve. It opens it, scoops a healthy dollop, and returns to his wound, slathering the cream around. Right before my eyes, the wound begins to heal, and my shadow removes the fabric carefully, applying more cream.

A tiny bit of relief flickers through me, but not nearly enough.

It won't be enough until I hear Rainer say my name again—until I feel his soft lips against mine.

"*Drink*," I demand, shoving my arm more aggressively against his lips. "I swear to the gods, Rainer. If you don't drink right now, I will bring you back to life just to kill you again myself."

Something soft and warm flicks against my wrist, causing me to gasp. I go still, desperately waiting for more movement.

"Violent little rose," Rainer mutters in a raspy, barely audible voice.

My heart stalls, forgetting to beat at the sound of his voice.

"Rainer," I whisper.

His tongue flicks out again, and he groans in satisfaction. In an instant, his teeth clamp onto my wrist, and he eagerly sucks. A surge of intense pleasure courses through my veins.

And as he gradually drains my blood, he steadily refills my heart.

FORTY-ONE

WHAT'S ONE MORE DEBT?

ALESSIA

A cascade of emotions gushes through me. My heart races, pounding with a mix of anticipation and desire. Each forceful beat churns the blood through my veins, feeding Rainer the life force he needs.

He's alive.

He's alive!

With each sip from my wrist, his fingers dance along my arm, creating a pleasant tingle that spreads throughout my body. His feverish touch overwhelms me, leaving me in blissful surrender. Our desire for each other is insatiable—he hungers for my blood and flesh, just as I hunger for his heart and soul.

Tears of euphoria stream down my face as his bite reminds me of his miraculous existence.

"I thought I lost you," I cry. As he drinks, I pepper kisses on the top of his head, running my free hand through his onyx waves. "You scared me."

"You saved me," he murmurs against my wrist. His tongue tenderly laps at my minor wounds, and he groans. "You taste... so good. So thirsty."

"Rainer," I whisper his name, throwing my head back with a moan.

He shifts between my thighs as he drinks. One of his hands stays on my wrist, holding it against his mouth. The other drops to my thigh and his fingers bite into my exposed skin. My nipples harden beneath his touch. With each caress, a wave of pleasure courses through me, heightening my senses.

It should be inappropriate. It should be wrong.

But it's never felt more *right*.

After almost losing him, I can't risk waiting another moment to give myself to him completely.

"I can't wait anymore," I gasp out. "I want the bond. I want you. I *need* you."

He chuckles darkly against my skin, his hot breath causing me break out in anticipatory goosebumps. Pressing himself up to all fours, he crawls toward me. His expression is hard as stone, and his hand is firm as it reaches up to cradle my face. He tugs me forward, and our lips find each others with a searing intensity, both of us giving into the emotion.

He shifts onto his haunches, tilting me back as he devours me with a fevered, primal need. My nails rake down his back, drawing blood as I pull him as close as possible. It's as if our kiss can anchor us forever in this moment. The kiss turns salty as tears pour down my face, but we don't stop. We continue to express our feelings with our lips until we're both out of breath.

I pull back, gasping as Rainer studies every corner of my face. His hands roam my body, his fingers memorizing my flesh. His bare chest heaves, and I reach up, tracing the lines on his skin. He shudders, gripping my wrist and pulling my hand to his mouth, where he plants a gentle kiss on each of my fingers.

"I'm not stopping," I whisper breathlessly—it's a warning. A plea.

My shadow explodes upward, stretching and expanding to form a wall around us. It blocks out the rest of the room, giving us an illusion of privacy.

It wants this as much as I do.

He shifts back, leaning down to my inner thigh again, his eyes locked on mine the entire time. His mouth brushes my skin as he says, "Nothing can stop us ever again, Alessia Lírshadow. I give my soul to you—from now until forever."

His teeth press into my skin once more, and my body goes limp with desire. Rainer drinks my blood, pain, and pleasure—it intertwines into an intoxicating blend made just for him. I lose myself to the high, floating in a fog of lust. After a little while, he slips his fangs free of my wrist and tilts his head back to gaze at me. His wavy hair is attractively mussed up, and his beautiful, sharp ears point through. Blood trickles from the corners of his mouth, and my attention lingers on his deadly fangs. The fact he can be so delicate and tender with me even while lost to bloodlust is a testament of its own.

"My little rose," he mutters. His eyes flicker from cobalt to sky blue before darkening again.

With a growl, he flips himself around and presses his lips to mine, his mouth possessing me with a hunger that mirrors my own. In a rush of passion, he pulls me to his chest and lowers us to the ground, lying me on my back.

His hands release me, moving lower. They find their way back into the slit of my dress to my exposed flesh. His fingers bite into my bare thighs, squeezing, and then they travel upward.

The sound of tearing fabric reaches my ears as he rips off my underwear, leaving a sharp band of pain around my waist. I gasp, propping myself up onto my elbows to watch him.

Greedily, he inhales my panties. As he shoves them into his pocket, his eyes lock with mine, darkening with both a warning and a promise.

A surge of anticipation fills the air as he lowers his face to my inner thigh and sinks his teeth in. Another sharp sting followed by an airy delirium fills my veins. I moan, throwing my head back and reveling in the feel of his fangs deep inside my skin.

He draws more of my essence with each gentle suckle, causing a delicious ache to build in my core. He pulls back, licking the wounds he's created while staring up at me through his lashes. His tongue dances along my skin, igniting a fire within me. I grow wet with desire as I spread my legs further, begging him to taste me *there*.

The cool air caresses my intimate bits, and I throb with need.

Slowly, with his eyes locked on mine, he licks a trail from my inner thigh to my apex.

"I love you," he whispers against me, the heat of his words hitting my skin and my heart just right. "From the moment I shared air with you, I knew I'd never be able to breathe on my own again."

Before I can reply, he descends on me, his tongue swirling around my clit. He sheds the tenderness he possessed while drinking from me. Instead, he lets his monster free as he presses his entire mouth against me, sucking and licking like a starved male. His reckless abandon turns me on insanely. I entwine my fingers in his hair, keeping him firmly in place while my hips instinctively move against him, overwhelmed by his passionate attentiveness.

The pressure between my legs builds, reaching a high in record time.

"I'm going…" I cry out his name, gripping his hair as I arch my back.

He pauses, pulling back to sit on his haunches. The wave recedes all too soon, and I groan angrily. There's a twinkle in his eye as he stares down at me, his irises back to their pale, icy coloring.

"Wha-why?" I gasp.

He smirks, looking like a beautiful nightmare with my blood and juices smeared across his lips. His hands move carefully to his trousers, and he unbuttons them. Gracefully, he slides them down his muscular thighs. They flex as he kicks off his boots. He removes his pants and undergarments, leaving himself entirely bare before me.

My eyes focus on his thick cock. It's almost painfully hard, and he grips it, tugging it in slow, corkscrew motions. He sucks in a heavy inhale.

"The next time you come, I need to be inside of you, mo róisín," he says in a low, demanding voice. "I need to feel you squeezing me."

A thousand things flit through my mind, but all I can say is, "*Please*."

Hiking up my dress, I allow my knees to fall open, granting him access.

Swiftly covering me with his body, he hovers over me, propped up on his forearms. My head tilts to the side, taking in the way his veins pop and muscles bulge as he cages me in. I reach up, running my hands over his chest. Tracing one of the swirl tattoos, I follow the ink to his back. I grip him tightly, allowing my fingers to dig into his back.

He groans, and his hips jerk. With the motion, the head of his erection prods against my opening, begging to be let in. But in a show of immaculate self-control, he pauses.

"You are *it* for me, Alessia," he whispers against my lips. He pulls back just enough to study my face with a pure, unrestricted expression of love. "I'm done denying myself your love. After the hell we've been through, the prices we've paid, we deserve something beautiful."

"I want all of you, Rainer." I wrap my hands around his neck. "You are mine, and I am yours, from now until the Otherworld."

He leans forward, kissing gently the corner of my mouth. Nibbling gently, he trails kisses along my Tradeling tattoo up to my temple.

"Without you, my life is filled with fear and nightmares," he says, voice filled with emotion. "You are my confidence—my heart and soul—my beautiful, sweet dream."

Emotion clogs my throat, and my eyes tear up. I'm done waiting. The time will *never* be right, and we will always find excuses if we look hard enough. I almost lost him. I nearly missed my chance to give him my soul.

Reaching between us, I grip him and line him up with my entrance. Rubbing him against me, I ensure it's nice and slick to accommodate his size.

"Are you sure?" he whispers, body going rigid.

"I've never been more sure of anything in my life, Rainer."

He nods, then slowly, gently sinks the tip of his cock into me. As my walls stretch almost painfully around him, stars alight in my vision. My chest flutters with an ethereal joy, my pulse pounding with euphoria.

The weight of the world slips away as he fills me. Once he's all the way in, he pauses, dropping his head to my shoulder. His body shudders as he groans.

"You feel like a gods' damned dream," he whispers. "I could happily live here forever, buried inside of you."

I wiggle my hips, inviting him to move. He lifts his head, using a hand to push the hair off my forehead. Planting a kiss there, he begins to move in and out of me.

I surrender to his touch, taking each of his thrusts with hungry anticipation.

"More," I plead, tilting my head back and shutting my eyes.

"Look at me," he demands, his voice husky. "Keep your eyes on me, little rose. Be here with me in this moment."

My eyes whip back open, connecting with his. An intensity passes between us.

"I am," I say on an exhale. "I promise—I am."

Satisfied with my response, he picks up his pace.

"You're so wet for me," he mutters, thrusting so hard against me that my body jerks. "So snug and soft."

He hits me in the right spot, and a tingling sensation builds low in my core. With each plunge, fire shoots through my veins. Every nerve ending awakens, memorializing this moment.

Without delay, the climax builds.

I wrap my legs around him, locking him in place as the wave comes crashing down over me. A scream of pleasure rips from my throat as my orgasm wracks violently through every part of my body. My pussy pulses, spasming on his cock.

He groans, pressing his lips to mine and swallowing the noise. His body jerks against mine, and he pushes deeper. The blissful sounds he makes will be the everlasting melody accompanying my pleasure. He grunts as he spills inside of me, imprinting a piece of his essence into my body, soul, and mind, forever intertwining our fates.

A surge of love and connection expands within me, stretching and expanding the limits of my body.

An invisible rope tangles our souls, and I can no longer distinguish where I end and he begins. In a split second, my sensations become more intense, as if confirming the presence of magic.

Suddenly, the brightness of the overhead lights makes me wince. The strong scent of copper, sweat, and salt overwhelms my nose—a potent mix representing life and death, pain and love. The weight of Rainer's body pressing down on me causes every nerve to come alive, and combined with the warmth of our connection, it's deliciously asphyxiating.

And then my senses settle, coming down from the euphoric high and leaving me in a state of deep contentment. It's not merely a moment of pleasure but a sensation of finality that transcends satisfaction. Rather than an end, it's a beginning.

As our eyes lock, a rush of emotions crash into my chest, and I gasp for breath. The blood rushes to my cheeks, spreading warmth across my face and betraying the intensity of my feelings. The vulnerability and awe in Rainer's pale eyes as he gazes at me tell me he feels the same way. It's as if he has the power to unravel me with just a look.

Time seems to slow down, stretching each moment into eternity as we share breaths. Our unspoken connection transcends words, allowing our shared emotions to communicate the depths of our love.

"I love you," he whispers breathlessly, although I can *feel* his love within me now. With a trembling hand, he reaches between us, grips himself, and slowly slides out.

Instantly, I mourn the loss of him.

The warmth of his seed slips from me, coating my inner thighs.

My legs tremble as I lie there shell-shocked, simultaneously ruined and repaired by our consummation. The intensity of my love for him is palpable, as my heart seems to expand physically, pulsating with amplified emotion.

Rainer runs his fingers along my arm, watching me with tender curiosity. After a moment of comfortable silence, he reaches for his pants, balling them up and using them to wipe me dry. The entire time, he keeps his eyes locked on me. Briefly, I fear he might lock up and push away—afraid of the strength of our love—but his expression remains open. There's a lightness to him, a softness to his lips that's not always there.

Unfazed by our pleasure staining his pants, he slips them on. Then, he kneels and slips his boots on, quickly lacing them without breaking our stare. His top is long abandoned, ruined entirely.

My eyes drop down his torso, stained with dark brown blood, finding the spot where he was injured. Air catches in my lungs as I take in only a faint hint of a minor, jagged reminder of what almost killed him.

My vision goes blurry with tears, and I blink rapidly to hold them back.

"I don't normally cry this much," I say hoarsely. "It's just... a lot."

He opens his mouth like he's going to say something, then clamps his mouth shut and shakes his head. Reaching for me, he helps pull me to my feet. I wobble to the side, and his arm shoots out, wrapping around my waist.

"That was..." My head spins, not knowing how to put it into words.

"Everything," he whispers.

I glance up at him, cupping his cheek. "Everything."

"Do you feel it?" he asks quietly.

Nodding, I know immediately what he's asking because I do. A part of his essence courses through my veins, as if his very being has merged with mine, creating a connection that transcends the physical realm.

His pleasure intertwines with mine, amplifying the sensations coursing through me. And though I'm trying not to focus on it in this beautiful moment, I share his pain, feeling every ounce that lives in his heart as if it's my own.

Which means he can feel mine, too.

I'm so full I can't fathom how my shadow will find space to squeeze back in.

The dark, shadowy wall around us begins to thin out as if it can hear me. The darkness merges into a tendril, shooting back toward me and slithering beneath my skin.

Rainer jerks, his eyes widening a fraction. I chuckle.

"Does it always feel like that?" he asks.

My laughter grows, brightening, until the scene around me registers. All the happiness dies away as my heart stops for a moment.

"Look at *me*," Rainer growls, placing his hands on either side of my head. "Come on. Let's get cleaned up and find the others."

I nod, swallowing the lump in my throat. We're not done yet. We still have to get the iron from the mines in Illynor, hopefully *before* word of what happened here today spreads. If the soldiers find out their queen is dead and fae are in their realm, they will strike against us.

We need to get ahead of them.

"I need to get out of here so I can thoroughly ravage you again, little rose," Rainer says.

"Oh, it's a *need*?"

"I need you more than I need air and blood." He flashes his dimple, winking at me.

This lighthearted, thoroughly satisfied Rainer makes my stomach flip. Just like that, the weight slides off my shoulders, allowing me to breathe again.

I can do anything with him by my side—and in a part of my soul.

"You know," he says as we exit the ballroom and stride toward the bathrooms. "They say when you share your joy, it's doubled, but when you share your pain, it's halved. *Thank you*—for trusting me with both your joy and your pain." Jerking to a stop, he tugs me to his chest and leans down to kiss me. "Thank you."

"You're not supposed to thank the fae," I tease with my own smile.

"Does it look like I give a feck?" He chuckles. "I already owe you everything, Alessia. What's one more debt?"

FORTY-TWO

LOVE OF FAMILY

ALESSIA

After cleaning ourselves up, Rainer and I stride around the ground floor, searching for Ken and Tynan. The place is hauntingly empty—the ballroom transformed into a somber morgue. Only the array of tacky floral decorations lingers, silent witnesses to today's horrors. Their cheery presence is a jarring juxtaposition to the events that transpired.

Rainer sniffs the air. "Both of their scents are here. Fairly fresh. I don't think they left."

I give him a worried glance. After the chances we've given Tynan, the fact that he likely betrayed us and set us up hits doubly hard. Rainer was finally trying to make peace with the only blood family he had left.

But something doesn't sit right with me.

"What would he gain by betraying us?" I ask, thinking aloud.

Rainer reaches out and picks at a piece of curling floral wallpaper, tearing a chunk off and letting it flutter to the floor. "Does it matter? He'd turn his back on us at the first sign of something better."

"What if he didn't, though?"

"How else would the glamour drop, Alessia?" Rainer's tone is defeated, as if he's already accepted the fracture between him and Tynan. "Everything he does is for self-gain. This is no different."

"And when you find him?"

He sighs. "I don't know."

We reach the back of the estate. Enormous glass pane doors spread open, the lacy, flowered curtains billowing in a slight breeze. I step through to find a patio stretching out toward the sea, with only a small strip of sand separating the wood and water.

Tiki torches light the path from the house to the coast.

It's just before dawn, and the sky has a dark, eerie glow. The night passed by so quickly, but the adrenaline carries me forward.

On a bench, with her back to me, Enid sits. For a moment, it's like seeing myself from a different lens. The likeliness is uncanny.

"I'm going to talk to her," I tell Rainer softly.

He nods, stuffing his hands in his pockets. "I'll check upstairs."

"Be safe." My eyes flick down his bare chest, taking him in shamelessly. The wound on his side is fully healed, nothing more than a jagged, pale scar. If Enid hadn't given me that salve...

I can't even bring myself to think about it.

"Hey," he says, reaching for me. He plants a kiss on the back of my hand. "I am *fine*. I have more reason than ever to take care of myself now."

I flush, my body feeling warm with his implication. That we are *soul-bonded*.

Gripping the back of my neck, he leans forward and kisses my forehead, muttering, "*You* be safe, mo róisín."

I can't help but smirk as he releases me, and we pull away. "I've got my shadow. I'll be just fine."

And surprisingly, for the first time, I mean it. I feel less like I'm housing an enemy inside my skin and more like I'm... complete.

A newfound strength and comfort thrums through my veins. My shadow-self doesn't feel as unsettling as it first did. Whether it's the souls it feasted on or the love of the soul-bond placating it, I don't know. Perhaps both.

Or maybe I've finally stopped fighting it and started to accept it for what it is.

Despite the wreckage in the ballroom inside and the impending, impossible journey stretching out before me—in both realms—my heart feels lighter.

Rainer gives me one last, long look, then turns and reenters the house, leaving me with Enid.

My pulse kicks up as I draw closer to where she sits on the bench. She turns, greeting me with a smile. Her spine is straight and rigid, but her features are relaxed. Wyetta's golden crown, adorned with sapphires and diamonds, sits atop her head, fitting well.

Then again, I suppose it was Enid's crown all along.

"It has been much too long," she says with a sigh, tilting her face toward the dim sky.

Fresh sea air caresses me, and I suck it in greedily. The salt and seaweed lighten me further, and for a brief moment, I think I might miss this when I return to Spiritus Court.

The sun begins to rise behind us, gold-kissing the sand and water. It sparkles lightly, a small sample of what's to come once day truly hits.

There's a different sense of serenity here.

Or perhaps that's just a post-orgasm illusion.

A smile ghosts my lips, and I shake it off, focusing instead on Enid. The crow's feet and smile wrinkles give her the illusion of wisdom, but it's the keen, quiet intellect hiding behind her sharp grey eyes that alert me to her old age.

How long exactly was she locked up?

How old is she?

I'm tempted to ask how she looks so young despite being centuries old. But then I think of how fae—especially powerful ones—age slowly. Yvanthia, for instance.

Will I grow old and die one day while Rainer stays young and healthy? The thought is too much to bear, but I must ask anyway.

I clear my throat. "Enid?"

She turns, gazing serenely at me. "Yes, dearling?"

"Do half-fae… like me, age like you? Or like humans?"

She chuckles and gently beckons for me, patting the bench beside her. I join her, perching stiffly on the wooden seat. "Of all the questions I thought you might ask…" She shakes her head, smiling at me. "A love like yours is rare," she says reverently.

"A soul-bond?"

Another chuckle falls from her lips. If she's surprised by my admission of being bonded, she doesn't show it.

She grabs my hand, squeezing it tightly. My brows fly up at her grip strength. "The way you and your bonded care for each other. It is always worth fighting for."

A humorous laugh escapes me as I think of the mayhem in the ballroom. Even if I didn't start that fight, I indeed finished it.

It wasn't even really a fight—it was a slaughter.

"I'm tired of the violence," I admit.

"That is not the fighting I am referring to. I mean not the external carnage, but the little internal fights." She releases my hand, patting it, then places it back on her lap as she stares at the horizon.

"I will not pretend to be family if that makes you uncomfortable, Alessia. I understand we are far removed. However, I would like to be a part of your life if you will have me."

I bite my bottom lip, unsure of what to say. There's much to sift through, so I only nod. I hope that's enough for her, for now.

It must be because she takes a breath to continue speaking.

"Then consider this a piece of grandmotherly wisdom: fighting for love is often quiet and personal. The battles are often tiny, but they add to the whole war. Sometimes, you must lose battles, but it does not mean you lose the war. Know when to fight and when to back down, but never give up on your love."

I squint at a bird sailing above the water in the distance. Her words are a puzzle, yet they somehow make perfect sense. Rainer and I are a team. Especially now that our bond is completed. We've been through so much in half a year, and it's only the beginning.

Despite solidifying the bond and choosing to be together, it doesn't mean things will be perfect. We're still two flawed beings with much personal work to complete. Rainer is still the broody, wounded male he was when I first met him—a traumatized little faeling deep down—just as I still carry the wounds of *my* past.

Enid is right. Sometimes, we fight for love in quiet, meaningful ways, like staying when we want to flee the discomfort or speaking honestly when we want to hide the words behind our hearts.

"The darkness calls to you, does it not?" Enid's voice draws me out of my thoughts. A line forms on her forehead, yet her eyes glisten with pride. "From within."

"Yes," I admit.

She tucks her feet onto the bench, resting her head on them. For a moment, she appears so tiny and… normal. *Human*

"Did it call to you, too?" I ask. Perhaps I will finally learn the truth of my power. The one I searched for in the journals to no avail.

She shakes her head. "It is rare." She exhales, her shoulders softening as she hugs her legs tighter. "It is a power of its own, separate from being a spiritcaller."

"*Power*?" My blood heats at how she says it, as if it's some advantage and not a terrible, vile hindrance.

She chuckles. "You are blessed with great power, my dearling, even as a half-blooded fae."

"It's awful," I whisper, furrowing my brow. "It's not great at all."

Though there's no sharpness to my tone, it still causes Enid to sigh. Slowly, she turns to face me. Her expression is unreadable as she studies me.

"Your shadow-self is part of you. It may be your soul's deepest, darkest part, but it is a part of you nonetheless. It works alongside you, offering you a second strength."

I shake my head. "No. It says awful things. It wants to do awful things. I've never had such thoughts until encountering it."

"Is that the truth? Or did you never acknowledge such thoughts until you started *believing* in your strength?"

I am not weak.

I am strong.

The voice is loud and clear, and I hear it for what it is this time. A mantra I've always heard echoing in my mind—words I've always wanted to believe but never did until Rainer.

Until he called me *his* and convinced me I was the girl who fights.

My spine goes rigid, and my skin prickles with surprise at the connectedness of it all.

The voice—those thoughts—they *have* always been there, en-couraging me to find my inner strength. I've just never seen it for what it is. Not until now.

"But I don't want to hurt anyone," I whisper, confused.

Enid reaches for my hand, and I let her take it. She squeezes it, offering me a sympathetic look.

"Your shadow-self is made of the parts you repress. Perhaps they are feelings of shame, or fear, or simply unacknowledged desires, but they are the parts we often frown upon." She pats my hand and then releases me. "It is normal to feel at odds with your shadow-self, but truly accepting that part of yourself is how you gain control of it."

Shame and disgust roil inside me. What she's saying can't be true. I can't be as vile as that little voice. I've never wanted to hurt anyone, even when they've deserved it.

But then again… I *chose* to kill Edvin and Nilda.

I chose to burn Edvin's house down.

I unleashed my shadow in the ballroom, even knowing the con-sequences.

And none of it broke me like I once imagined it might.

Because you are strong, you are capable.

I am capable of darkness just as I am goodness.

"No," I snap, squeezing my eyes shut briefly.

Enid makes a tutting noise. "It is speaking to you now, yes?"

I swallow the lump in my throat and turn away. "It's been… quieter lately. Less demanding, but yes."

"Because you are making peace with yourself. This is a beautiful thing." I can hear the smile in her voice.

Perhaps *that* is why I bled when I hurt it—I was only hurting myself. Deep down, I think I knew the truth of it all along. I just wasn't ready to accept it—I wasn't prepared to accept myself.

With a deep inhale to steady myself, I face her again. "Why did I need to sacrifice a life on Spiritus Court's land to accept my power if I already had it?"

"Dearling, there is always a price to pay. We pay in souls. It strengthens our magic."

"But I've..." I can't bring myself to speak the word *killed*. "Paid with mostly humans."

"A soul is a soul," she says, squinting at the glittering horizon.

I lean forward, planting my elbows on my knees and hanging my head in my hands. "If you didn't have a shadow-self, what was your power?"

"Soulmancy," Enid says softly.

I let the unfamiliar word sink in. "What could you do with that?"

She frowns at the sea. "Bring souls back to their body." Her gaze shifts to mine. "The last of my magic was in that salve."

My spine tingles at the implication. If it weren't for her salve, Rainer might truly be dead. My eyes brim with tears and my tongue—for the first time in so long—burns with a thousand thank yous.

"Is that why Yvnathia feared you?" I ask instead, not wanting to get swept away in the panic of how close I was to losing Rainer.

"It does not matter." Enid's features harden briefly, her eyes narrowing. Then, with a sigh, she shakes her head. "It is long gone, a piece of the past left to rest, and I am better for it."

I blink away the annoyance at the nonanswer, trying not to get caught up on irrelevant details. I don't bother asking about spiritcalling—I've read plenty about that power. All the matriarchs in our lineage wield that power by default, keeping the court alive.

"Stifling your shadow-self down and ignoring it will only worsen its demands," Enid adds. "Perhaps now that you truly embrace who you are—the *truth* of who you are—it will settle down. Do not abandon the parts of you bathed in shadow, my Alessia."

My Alessia. The words remind me so much of Char—a woman I haven't seen in much too long. A woman who, at this point in my life, almost feels like a figment of my imagination.

This time, when I study Enid carefully, I see a tiny resemblance to the woman I once loved. It's not in her features but in how she speaks and moves. As if... as if Char, somehow, for some reason, modeled her demeanor after this ancestor of mine.

Something comes back to me—about how the hand of Fate presents herself differently depending on who she is appearing to.

Is that what Char did for me, too? Did she present herself as my ancestor, preparing me for this introduction one day? Was it so I would be inclined to find comfort in Enid, drawn to the familiarity?

The answer sits raw and honest on my chest. It's bittersweet but beautiful in a way. I could be resentful of the manipulation, but it's wasted energy. Especially since I wouldn't be here now, filled with so much hope, love, and freedom, if it weren't for Char's invisible guidance.

"Enid?" I say.

"Yes, my dearling?"

"I would very much like to be in each other's lives."

She scoots closer, wrapping an arm around my shoulders and hugging me tight. The faint smell of that lemongrass and peppermint healing salve reaches my nose, and a pang of longing tugs at my chest. Wherever Char is now, I hope she's happy. Something tells me the pieces she placed fell perfectly in line—the thread of fate she tied me to held firm. She's likely moved on to her next task, saving the realm silently from the shadows elsewhere.

And she might be done with me, but I recognize why she did everything she did now. For this moment right here: a moment of peace at the sea's edge, with my soul-bond in my heart and my ancestor at my side. A moment of silence before the Trade finally comes to a halt, and liberation is found for all Tradelings.

Char's words come back to me, and this time, as they replay, I smile to myself: *I am not your family… One day, you will experience what a true family is.*

She was wrong—she *was* my family. She'll always be in my heart as such. But now, I hope she's right, and I will finally experience the true love of family.

FORTY-THREE

A LIFELESS BODY

RAINER

I stand vigilant beside the open doors, keeping an eye and ear out for any movement. Alessia doesn't *need* me to watch after her, but I can't help it. I thought I was protective before, but it's incomparable to how I feel now that our bond is completed.

There's no way I'm going to leave her alone out there with that… I don't even know what she is. Not quite a human, not quite fae, not quite a queen, and not quite family.

But whatever she is or isn't, I don't want her negatively affecting Alessia after how far she's come.

If Alessia saw me standing here, peeking through the sheer curtains every few seconds, she'd hate it. The thought makes me chuckle.

A dull, throbbing ache steals my attention. I glance down at where I was stabbed. The skin is merely dirtied with my blood, but there's no longer a visible indication that I was injured. Despite that, my body is still working to heal the internal damage. It's taking longer than my skin took to recover.

Even so, the healing is happening much more rapidly than I could've hoped because of Alessia's blood and the healing salve.

I shouldn't be alive right now.

But I am.

Because of *both* of them.

My eyes narrow suspiciously on the back of Enid's head. Her hair is a little greyer than Alessia's ash-blonde, a little messier with larger, knotted curls, but there's an obvious similarity between the two. But I find it hard to believe the older female is genuine in her affections toward my beloved. So, what does she want?

What the hell was in her healing salve to make it as powerful as Eoin's magic once was? And why give it to me?

Alessia might trust her, but I don't.

Looking over my shoulder, I scan the hallway. Straining to listen, I don't catch the thump of pulses or nearby shuffling. It's as silent as the dead. I inhale deeply through my nose but quickly realize that's a bad idea. The scent of rich, sweet, coppery blood floods my nostrils, causing my stomach to swirl with a feigned ache of hunger.

I've drank plenty, but the fragrance of *human* blood is decadent. Shaking my head, I focus my attention back on Enid and Alessia. I can't let the physical pain or enticing scents distract me. It's a mental game to push it all aside and stay vigilant.

The two females pull apart from an awkward side hug. They sit silently on the bench, staring at the sea for a few more moments, and then Alessia rises. She says something to Enid, but I focus elsewhere to block out her words. Watching them is one thing, but I don't need to eavesdrop on their conversation too.

I'm a protective, possessive bastard, but I have to set boundaries to give Alessia her space and freedom.

Besides, I can feel everything Alessia does to some extent. Right now, a warm, peaceful vibration pulses from my connection to her. Whatever is happening between her and Enid, it's bringing her a sense of joy.

That's all that matters to me—her happiness. And her safety. And right now, she has both.

She meets my eyes as she begins striding toward the house, and her face lights up. My lips lift automatically in response, my joy a mirror image of hers. She looks like a deadly dream in that form-fitting white gown. The front is stained rusty brown with my drying blood, and her slit is ripped a little higher than it should be because of our bonding event.

My smile transforms into a smirk, and a bolt of heat shoots straight to my cock.

"Gods, you are the most gorgeous rose of all," I mutter once she's close enough to hear. Her pale cheeks light up with a pink tint, and I love how sweet she is when I compliment her. As if she's a little embarrassed, a little bashful, despite being the toughest fae I know.

She glances down, frowning at her dress. "I'm a mess."

I reach for her hand, lifting it above her head and twirling her around. She obliges me, laughing freely.

"Even in chaos, you're the most stunning thing I've ever seen," I tell her earnestly. "Curated roses are charming, but it's the wild ones that radiate with untamed beauty."

The flush on her cheeks deepens, and she bites her lips. Those big, grey eyes sparkle with love that's all my own.

She is all mine.

Behind her, Enid rises from the bench. I go stiff. My smile melts away, leaving a hard, blank shell. Instinctively, I step around Alessia to put myself between her and the other female.

She sighs, then chuckles, planting her dainty hand on my bicep. "You don't have to worry about her."

"I will worry about everything when it comes to you, mo róisín," I say over my shoulder.

Enid approaches me, a broad smile forming on her face.

I scowl harder at the flashy crown atop her head. She wasted no time. "Who do you think you are?"

"Rainer," Alessia says exasperatedly, stepping beside me. "She saved your life."

"Great." I narrow my eyes at Enid. I abhor owing debts. "You started the Trade?"

Her smile drops. "I was exiled from my own home, forced to watch my kind oppressed—my bloodline hunted down. You cannot possibly think I would be responsible for such an atrocity."

I cross my arms, standing tall and looking down at her. Clearly, Alessia's short stature runs in the family. "Nobody is ever what you might *think* they are."

She tilts her head up, narrowing her eyes right back at me in a ferocious gaze that reminds me so much of the female at my side. "The Trade never should have begun, and I will ensure it ends with a swift, meaningful death."

We hold each other's stares, neither wanting to back down first.

"They're going to need support," Alessia blurts out. "They won't have anywhere to go or anyone to turn to."

I glance at her, unsurprised by her forethought and kind heart. Enid's expression softens into pride as she nods in agreement. Some of the tension in my shoulders alleviates, and I unfold my arms, shoving my hands in my pockets instead.

"You truly are a Lírshadow," Enid says, beaming. "I have been walking the realms long before you were even a whisper of air in your great-grandmother's lungs, dearest. I assure you, I can handle the situation here."

"Yeah, look at how that ended," I mutter. "How the hell did you even get free?"

Alessia stomps on my toes, and I hiss.

"Violent little rose," I mutter, raising a brow at my bonded.

She shrugs, mouthing, "Be nice!"

Enid throws her head back in a laugh, then she turns to Alessia, with a twinkle in her eye. "Your shadow released me from the cell the humans kept me in. A small, thin bit wove into the lock and popped it free."

The female smiles easily and freely despite the atrocities around us, even after being imprisoned for generations. Though I naturally tend to be skeptical and apprehensive, I try to follow Alessia's lead, giving her the benefit of the doubt.

I won't trust *her*, but I will try to trust that her intentions are not inherently harmful. I suppose.

"Want to prove your intentions?" I say, turning back to Enid. "Then help us. We need the iron from the mines. All of it."

"*All* of it?" Enid questions.

"Yes. There's no chance we're leaving you with weapons to potentially use against us."

Amusement twinkles in her eyes as she glances at Alessia. "He is a good male, you found." Turning back to me, she adds, "I have no intention of using it against my own kind."

"Then you'll give it to us."

She hesitates, then draws in a long, slow breath. "Now, how do I know *you* will not use the iron against *me*?"

"Because we need it for the woods," Alessia jumps in. "And you don't have magic anymore, anyway."

"The woods?" Enid scrunches her forehead in confusion.

A flicker of embarrassment courses through me. The last thing I want to do is explain my incompetency to this female. I clench my teeth, thinking of how to explain succinctly but thoroughly enough for her to understand our needs.

Alessia reaches for my hand, gripping it tightly in hers in unity. She squeezes it almost in reassurance, and when I glance down at her, I see the understanding in her soft smile.

Feckin bond. No doubt she can *feel* what I just did.

However, instead of being annoyed or resentful, there's a relief that settles inside me. I no longer have to do this alone or hide the things I'm ashamed of. She loves me for *me*.

And when Alessia speaks up so I don't have to explain, that love expands into a warmth, caressing my previously cold heart.

"The woods back home—they're cursed," Alessia says. "We have a sorceress who can use iron to help us nullify the magic and fix things."

"She has done this before?" Enid asks.

"Well…" Alessia shifts her weight, pausing as she contemplates her answer. "Kind of? Admittedly, she needs some practice."

"I know of a sorceress who can aid you." A brief pity flickers across Enid's face. "She also owes you a debt for what you did here today—earning her freedom as well." She plants a hand on her chest. "She is a dear friend of mine. I will send her to help your sorceress break the curse."

Alessia lets out a heavy breath. "Than—"

"You're giving us the iron." I quickly cut her off before she can finish thanking the female. "Just to clarify."

Enid cocks her head, scrutinizing me with approval. Her eyes flit between me and Alessia. "You are good for her."

"Not what I asked."

Enid bursts into a short laugh. "If this is what will keep the peace between our realms, it is a small price to pay."

Our realms. She considers Dovenak her home. Perhaps this could be a good thing, a new chance to make peace with the humans and protect both sides of the Gleam.

"All we want is peace," Alessia says. She elbows me.

"I am inclined to agree with my bonded." Sweat glistens on my bare chest, and I squint at the bruised sky. The humidity here is brutal, and the heat will only worsen once the sun comes up. It makes me miss my court.

I've always been a creature of shade and darkness. It makes perfect sense why I'd belong to Alessia and her shadows.

"Iron is heavy," Enid challenges, interrupting my rumination.

"My problems are heavier, and I carry those just fine," I shoot back. "We'll figure it out."

Enid's lips twitch as if holding back another laugh. Glad she finds me so damn amusing. Can't say I feel the same.

"You will need help getting it back to Avylon, will you not?" she asks.

"Yes," Alessia says before I can disagree.

My lips twist with disdain. "Perhaps," I admit.

"All right then." Enid strides past us, heading into the house.

"Wait," Alessia yells after her. "Where are you going?"

"To secure your iron."

"How?"

Enid waves a hand over her shoulder. "The God of War owes me a favor."

"The what?" Alessia gives me a confused look. I shrug at the insanity.

Stopping and turning back to us with a look of pure force, she says, "Lexyll, God of War, can help. I have called on him in need, and something tells me he can assist here in more ways than one. We might need an army with what is to come."

"But..." Alessia starts, chewing her cheek nervously.

"No fear, dearest." Enid strides back to her, gently patting her cheek in a motherly manner. "Despite his name, the God of War desires peace, too—not violence. We are on the defensive, not the offensive here, but we must still be cautious and protect ourselves." Her eyes flit to me. "And you must always protect *her*."

"I don't need you to tell me that," I mutter defiantly. Unable to swallow *all* my skepticism, I ask, "Why the hell are you helping us with all this?"

"Two reasons," Enid says. She points to Alessia. "First is that pretty little thing right there. She is my family, and family sticks together."

They share a tender moment, and a shock of pure appreciation pulses from the bond. I squeeze Alessia's hand in acknowledgment, just as she did for me earlier, letting her know that I feel her and that she's not alone.

I nod in respect because it's one thing we can agree on. "And the second?"

"You have both done much for me here today. My freedom is because of you both. One might say I owe you." She winks. "And a Lírshadow always pays their debts. Now, you must excuse me. There is much to do. I will send for you in Avylon once the details are ironed out."

Alessia snorts at the pun. I scowl harder.

This time, Enid leaves us, and Alessia and I share a long stretch of silent relief.

Now that the iron situation is sorted out, I'd like to return to Avylon immediately. I'm going to kill my feckin brother when I find him—he's lucky everything worked out.

"We need to find Kenisius and Tynan," I mutter, scrubbing my brow.

Alessia presses her lips together, giving me a nod of under-standing.

We head back inside, striding to the front of the house. The sound of familiar footsteps reaches my ears, raising my hackles. I speed up, practically bolting to the foyer, keeping Alessia safely at my back.

The hallway dumps me beside the grand stairwell, and my gaze shoots up to the figure slowly descending.

"There you are!" Alessia yells. She blows past me excitedly, charging toward him.

"Wait," I call out, my voice cracking.

Something's wrong. It's written in his somber expression and the faint scent of fae blood.

First, my heart drops. Then, my gaze drops to his arms—to where he carries a lifeless body.

FORTY-FOUR
T'll Be Home
ALESSIA

I screech to a stop at the bottom of the stairs, my breath catching in my throat. The floor beneath my feet feels unsteady, and I reach for the railing. Rainer is at my side instantly, gripping me so I don't topple over.

"Is that..." His name sticks in my throat. I glance at Rainer, gauging how he's feeling, because the body in Ken's arms is *his* brother, clad in only his underwear. "Rainer?"

Pain flickers across his face before he goes blank. "Where was he?"

Ken jerks his head up. Blood streaks his face, and his hair is in messy waves around his shoulders. "From what I gathered, he was engaging in... adult activities with a human." He sighs. "A guard—dead now—walked in on him biting the woman and stabbed him in the back. I found him like this." His voice cracks. "Ty won't wake up."

Ty. It's the first time I've heard Ken use the nickname, and it's done almost reverently. A show of respect from the bear shifter.

My eyes flit to Tynan's face. He's unnaturally still, paler than usual. Despite the scars marking his face, he seems at peace. It's the softest I've ever seen his features. I round the shifter, and my eyes search Tynan's back. Ken shifts him so I can see better. An ugly, gaping wound stretches. A new cut that will never have the chance to join the others as scars.

It's stained with the color I am downright sick of seeing.

My stomach pitches, and I turn away, heaving. A violent anger courses through me, causing my shadow-self to buzz like bees beneath my skin.

"Gods *dammit*, Tynan!" Rainer slams his hand down on the banister, causing it to quake under the force.

"The salve," I croak, taking deep breaths to keep my shadow down. "Get the salve."

"Little demon," Ken says softly. "It's too late for that."

"But… but this one is different. Trust me!"

He makes a soft sound in his throat. "No salve or magic will bring him back."

"Yes it will!" I yell, balling my hand into a fist and slamming it down on my thigh. "It worked for Rainer!" Focusing inward, I direct my plea toward my shadow-self. "Get the feckin salve."

The males stay silent as a coil of smoky darkness heeds my command, evaporating from my skin and shooting down the hallway. Every second that drags by is a second too long, until finally, the tendril returns and drops the container of salve in my hand.

I open it, and step toward Ken. His face is grim as he adjusts Tynan, lifting him up so I can see the wound.

"You shouldn't have removed the blade," I say hoarsely, even though I know it's unfair. I smear the remaining bit of salve on his wound, forcing myself not to recoil at the cold feel of his flesh beneath my fingers. His skin knits together before our eyes. "He needs to feed."

Before Rainer has a chance to respond—or stop me—I hold my fresh wrist wounds to Tynan's lips in offering, trying to lure him from his slumber. The blood no longer freely flows, but I just fed Rainer from the same spot.

It should work.

But Tynan remains lifeless. Ken shakes him, trying to help, while Rainer paces beside me.

"He's gone," Rainer mutters.

"If he was dead, he wouldn't have healed!" I say, my voice cracking. Rainer has lost too much—he can't lose his brother, too. I refuse to let him shoulder this guilt.

Closing my eyes, I hover my hand over Tynan's body. I think of what Enid said about us being spiritcallers. We can feel the spirit—the soul—right?

Perhaps not *now*, but Enid was a soulmancer. Could she have brought him back? If only the humans hadn't stolen her power. If only they hadn't slit Tynan's throat. All of the *ifs* weigh heavily on me.

Quelling my mind, I focus on the energy emanating around me. When I block out the typical five senses, I'm left with a pulsating feeling. It's similar to the sensation of my shadow-self, except it wavers around me instead of within.

I can sense the various energy threads. Rainer's is apparent—because it's tangled with my own. It's powerful and impossible to ignore. Then, there's another sturdy pulse of energy. Ken's. I recognize it instantly.

Beneath them, if I focus very carefully, I sense another faint vibration. It's barely there, but it *is* there.

"He's alive," I whisper, my eyes whipping open.

"Little demon," Ken says sadly. "I'd hear his heartbeat if he was."

"I *knew* he was going to feck this up." Rainer begins to pace, gripping his hair angrily. "I warned him about this shite!"

My chest hurts so bad I can barely breathe. It takes me a moment to realize my visceral response to Tynan's death isn't all mine—it's *Rainer's*. This is why it's so intense.

I try to summon my love and gratitude for all the good, sending them down the bond to Rainer—anything to ease his pains.

I grip Rainer's arm, giving him a pleading look. "Trust me, Rainer. He's not gone yet. I can't explain it, but I can feel his spirit."

He sucks in a sharp breath and goes still, but he doesn't face me. His face is scrunched in turmoil, the muscle in his cheek popping.

"At least he didn't betray us," I whisper. If he was knocked out, that explains why the glamour dropped. "He was loyal to you, Rainer. To us."

Slowly, he turns to me. His eyes glisten, and wrinkles line his forehead. "Yet somehow, that's worse." His voice cracks.

A puff of air whooshes past us, and I turn. Ezamae drops into the space wearing a thick, fluffy, blue and silver robe with bare feet. His pale hair is a mess, and there's a flush on his cheeks.

"Hello, friends," he says, smiling. He glances at Rainer, and his smile drops. "What in the clouds happened to you?" He looks past us to where Ken stands on the stairs, holding Tynan's limp frame. "Oh, *no*."

"I am not in the mood," Rainer mutters, putting his back to the Aer Prince.

"What happened?" he asks carefully.

"What didn't happen?" I give a sarcastic laugh. "Rainer almost died—we finally bonded like you wanted—but now Tynan isn't waking up. I murdered an entire ballroom of humans." An awkward silence stretches out. "Wait, I almost forgot. An ancestor of mine from *centuries* ago was kept prisoner by the human queen, whose own ancestors stole the throne from my ancestor, but it was really because she was kicked out of—"

"Alessia." Rainer clears his throat. He holds out a hand for me, his rings glinting in the chandelier's light.

My cheeks burn as I clamp my mouth shut to keep from stress-rambling. I place my hand in his, and he squeezes it. Just as I have his back, he has mine.

Ez studies us. Instead of celebrating like I expect him to at the mention of the consummation, he gives us a somber look. He places a hand on his chest and bows his head.

"Your brother was... not awful," he says. "May he rest in solace."

"He's not dead," I murmur. "We need Sera."

"Why her?" Rainer asks, heaving a sigh. "She can read auras. She'll tell you I'm right—he's not dead."

"You have the energy to take any of us back?" Ken says, hoisting Tynan over his shoulder. With the adjustment, Tynan's limbs flop, his body still loose and limber.

I wince, glancing away in discomfort.

"I can take you all back," Ez says.

"Her first." Rainer jerks his chin toward me.

"I can take you *all* back," he repeats, clarifying. "Together."

"Wait... at once?" My brows shoot to my hairline. "To *Avylon*?"

A small smile touches Ez's lips. "I do recall telling you my power is much stronger than it had been. Now that I can come again, I—"

"Do *not* talk about your orgasms with my bonded," Rainer snarls, lunging toward Ez.

I jump in front of Rainer, planting my hands on his chest. "Hey," I say softly.

Ez sighs, adjusting the sleeves of his robe. "One might think he'd be a little nicer after draining his testicles."

"His brother just *died*," Ken says exasperatedly.

"He's not dead," I whisper, but no one acknowledges me.

"He was not even fond of said brother," Ez says.

Rainer growls, stepping around me. "Shall I disembowel you and send you back to *your* brother, air-twat?"

"Whoa," I quickly side-step to block Rainer again. "What has gotten into you? Ez is here to help." I rub my forehead, as if I can rub away my exhaustion.

His gaze latches onto mine, and an apology crosses his face. He shakes his head, backing up.

"It's the bond," Ez says heavily. "I can personally attest to how it provokes strong emotions in the first few days."

"Gods save us all," Ken says. "It's a damn good thing two fae can't have the same bonded. Could you imagine what a bloodbath that'd be?" He chortles. "Laisren would love that shite."

His laughter is cut short as he descends the rest of the stairs, shifting Tynan over to his other shoulder. A heavy silence fills the space again.

"Let's just go," Rainer mutters.

"What about the iron?" Ken's confusion reminds me that he has no idea what transpired with Enid. "We're not going to the mines? Our whole purpose—"

"I'll fill you in back home," Rainer says, setting his jaw. "I need to deal with my brother first."

Ken nods as he steps up to our side.

"Grasp hands," Ez says, gesturing toward us.

Since one of my hands is already in Rainer's, I reach for Ez with my open one. Rainer huffs in annoyance, and I raise a brow at him. He shrugs, grabbing onto Ken's hand. Since Ken has one arm around Tynan, Ez grasps his elbow instead.

"Hold on to your tallywackers," Ken mutters, squeezing his eyes shut.

I do the same, readying myself for the jarring shift as gravity disappears and we soar through the ether impossibly fast. The next time I open my eyes, I'll be home.

FORTY-FIVE
LOVE FOR HIS BROTHER
ALESSIA

As soon as our feet hit Spiritus land, I bolt to the tree door and descend into my court.

This time, the grand, gothic hallways are warm and welcoming, with golden light from the sconces bouncing around the walls. New pieces of furniture—sitting chairs, tables, and random decorative artifacts—decorate the nooks and crannies. Faint chatter echoes from various rooms.

My tense muscles melt with relief as I take it in, grateful for what my friends have done for me while I was away.

It's not nearly as lonely as it was when I found it.

"Alessia!" A high-pitched voice calls, followed by the thud of slippered feet on the stone floor. "She's back!"

Sheila flies into view a second later, her braided ponytail swinging behind her as she runs toward me.

Instinctively, I open my arms and catch her.

"Thank you, thank you, thank you," she mutters into my neck. She sniffles, squeezing me tight.

I release her. "What did I tell you about—"

"Yeah, yeah." She pulls back, rolling her eyes and smiling despite the tears tracking down her cheeks. "I'm not thanking the fae—just *you*." Reaching for my hands, she gives them a tight squeeze. "You brought my brother back."

"No, she kidnapped us, Sheila," Zephyr's voice reaches my ears. I glance up to catch him striding cautiously toward us. His gaze drops to my dress, and he freezes. "Is that *blood*?" He turns to his sister. "Go take a bath! Now!"

She rolls her eyes. "It's dried. Stop making a scene."

"But that's blood, and…" Zephyr's eyes flit over my shoulder to the large males at my back, and he halts, his bravado deflating. "I mean—it could be worse, I guess."

Rainer steps forward, tilting his head up and looking down his nose at the man. "You owe her for what she's done for you. If it were me?" He pauses dramatically, then shrugs. "I wouldn't be as nice to share *air*, let alone my home."

Zephyr's cheeks turn deep red. "Yes, sir."

"Rainer," I hiss. "Leave him alone. You don't know what he's been through."

Rainer turns, stuffing his hands in his pocket. He quirks a brow at me. "Doesn't give him an excuse to be an arse to you."

I sigh, tenderly cupping his jaw. "Go, my love. Take Tynan to Sera—she needs to find a way to get him blood."

Leaning forward, he kisses my cheek, then hovers there, whispering, "I trust you, little rose."

"Find me when you need me," I say softly.

"I will *always* need you." He pulls away, pausing as his eyes dance around my face. The haunted look on his face eases slightly when he gazes at me, and my heart flutters.

"Awww," Ken says.

I scrunch my nose, trying not to blush at having an audience for the tender moment. At least Zephyr and Sheila are human, so they likely couldn't hear.

Rainer jerks his head toward Ken. The bear shifter cradles Tynan's body in his arms as they stride toward the heart of the court and out of sight.

"Is th-that another dead body?" a shell-shocked Zephyr says, blinking rapidly. "Gods save me."

Ignoring his question, I say, "You can leave soon—once Dovenak is safe. I won't stop you."

"Oh my gods," Zephyr repeats, staring at Ken and Tynan's lifeless frame.

Sheila scowls at him, crossing her arms. "And go where, Zeph? Home? We have no home. Stop ruining this for me."

He grips her elbows, shaking them gently as he pleads with her. "We can make a home of our own."

"Or we can stay here. Yeah, you know what? I like it here!" She jerks away from his touch and storms off, stomping her feet the entire way.

"Wait! Sheila!" Zephyr chases after her, leaving Ez and me alone in my grand foyer.

I glance up, taking in the carved ceilings overhead. All the edges are soft and curvy. There's not really anything sharp or violent to the architecture. It gives me a sense of comfort.

Inhaling a deep breath, I take in the scent of soil and wood. It smells clean and fresh without all the dust.

"Well, now what?" I ask Ez.

"I need to inform Yvanthia of your bond now that you're back in the realm," Ez says. "Ensure she doesn't try to replace Rainer."

"It's a good thing though, right?" I swallow the thick lump in my throat. "She won't be able to hurt him now?"

He shakes his head. "The inability to eliminate him without simultaneously eliminating you would return her to her original predicament." Before I can reply, he smirks at me and says, "Besides, she won't be an issue for much longer."

"How are you going to... you know?"

"Leave that to me." He winks. "I have a plan."

"And... what exactly is this plan?"

"With everything you have going on here—" he gestures around my court, his smile growing "—you have enough to worry about."

"Can I do anything to help?"

"Alessia, darling, you have helped more than enough." He steps forward, checking over my shoulder before reaching for my hand and planting a chaste kiss on the back of it.

I blush furiously, pulling my hand out of his clasp. Rainer would lose it if he saw. "You're going to get us killed!"

He throws his head back, laughing. "No, no. I would only get myself killed."

"Get on with it then, go see Yvanthia." I give him a gentle shove, shooing him.

He glances down, chuckling at his robe. "I should probably find my trousers first."

Shaking his head, he strides past me, tightening his robe.

"Wait—your pants are *here*?" I ask with a furrowed brow.

Tilting his head, he gives me another smug smile over his shoulder.

"Gross!" I call after him. As much as I love Ez and Fern, the thought of them together is... actually, maybe it's not awful. "Hold on a second."

I jog after him, catching up before he goes too far. He continues to walk, and I keep pace with him as we turn down a residential hallway.

"How are you bonded to a *human*," I whisper, my eyes widening conspiratorially. "She *is* human, right?"

He laughs, side-eyeing me. "Yes, Alessia. She is."

"So you confirm! It's Fern!" Despite my hunches, the confirmation sends a bolt of surprise through me.

The grin on his face grows. "That woman is a... *wow.*" He whistles. "Too bad she hates me."

We reach a door, and Ez raps out a rhythm. It swings open, revealing Fern. Her burgundy hair is thrown up into a messy bun, and she's dressed in a modest tunic with leggings.

"Oh, it's you." She slams the door in his face.

"Darling, wait," Ez says, placing his arm on the doorframe and leaning into the door. He uses the back of his pointer knuckle to leisurely rap on the wood again. "Alessia is with me."

The door swings open. Fern narrows her eyes at Ez, crossing her arms, and then gives me a half-smile. "Hey," she says. A storm brews behind her eyes, but I know it's not reserved for me. "Glad you're back."

I nod, looking between the two of them. "I think he needs his pants."

Fern sighs, glancing over her shoulder into the room. She kicks the door open with her bare foot, rolling her eyes. "You left them on purpose."

"Perhaps I knew you'd abandon me after our passionate love-making." Ez winks at me before entering the room. "I needed a reason to see you again."

Fern huffs a breath, her eyes shooting to the ceiling as she mutters something inaudible. "Once was enough. Twice was a mistake—"

"And the third time's a charm?" Ez offers coyly.

"Oh my gods," I say, stifling my laughter into my palm. "Fern, I will see you later. Good luck." I glance at lovesick Ezamae, shaking my head. "Aren't you supposed to be an enchanter?"

He frowns at me. "Using my power on my own bonded would be in poor taste."

"I'm not your bonded, you freak," Fern grumbles. "Get your pants and get out." She shoves at his chest, and his robe falls open, revealing more skin than I care to see. She eyes him, licking her lips while pouting.

"Bye!" I avert my eyes, quickly trotting down the hallway.

Fern and Ezamae... disbelief and humor pour out of me as I laugh, wondering how that's even possible.

Love and fate don't play by the rules, my shadow-self says.

"I don't think they're in love," I mumble, my lips twitching.

Said as if you and Rainer never had your obstacles.

The memories of first meeting Rainer flood my mind, warming my body from the inside out. I always thought he was ethereally handsome, even if he was a complete bastard. But he was so much more than an arse. He was an enigmatic prince, tending to his flowers and secretly caring for those around him. He was—*is*—a tender soul who protects those he cares about.

Even if it's sometimes done a little aggressively.

Love for him floods my veins, and I send it down the bond toward him. It vibrates back like an invisible cord wrapped around my heart, infusing me with affection.

As I walk, I continue to process everything, trying to make sense of what comes next. Ez says he'll take care of Yvanthia, and I trust he can do so. He's more equipped than I am to murder the faerie queen, after all. At least, for now, Rainer is protected by our bond.

And in the meantime, Enid is rounding up her friends to bring us the iron. I also trust that she will keep her word and do what's right—dismantling the Trade and providing us with the iron. She's been around a lot longer than I have. Maybe I can have Seraphina read her aura when they meet.

After we receive the iron, the sorceresses will make the concoction to neutralize the magic. Sennah and Ez will use their elemental and air power to spread it throughout the forest. Despite the obstacles, our plan is proving fruitful thus far. We're close to achieving what we set out to do.

All of this is great, it's what I wanted to accomplish, but these are all the next steps for everyone else. What's next for *me*? How do I fit in here in Spiritus Court?

What about Rainer and Umbra Court?

The question is like a heavy boulder perched atop a hill, ready to come crashing down.

Sucking in a deep breath, I keep walking—one step at a time. I'll deal with everything one second at a time. My feet move on their own accord, and soon I recognize the door to the muniment room looming before me. I came here mindlessly, as if I knew it was the one place I could truly be alone.

The hallway is cold and narrower than the others. My gut sinks with every step. After Eoin's name, I didn't ever want to add another.

At least it's not Rainer.

This time, the shadow-self's voice—*my* voice, I suppose—is soothing. Reassuring.

"You're right," I say aloud. "At least it's not Rainer, but I'm not adding his brother's name either."

My heart squeezes tighter and tighter at the prospect of writing Tynan's name in the ledger. Once I'm in the muniment room, I close the door behind me, sink to the ground, and let the tears burst out. I cry until I'm a dehydrated husk, emptying every bit of my sorrows into the vacant space.

Somehow, I know it's not only my pain but mostly Rainer's. I *need* to be right about Tynan—he can't be dead.

As detached as he acts, the Umbra Prince truly does possess love for his brother.

FORTY-SIX
FOLLOW HIM ANYWHERE
ALESSIA

After composing myself, I bathe and change into a soft, simple dress. It falls to my knees and has a modest neckline. It's reminiscent of a nightgown save for the light pink color and little roses sewn onto the thin straps. After pulling an all-nighter, I can't wait to crawl into bed. But first, I need to speak with Sera.

I quickly locate her in the apothecary. Candlelight flickers, highlighting Sera's profile as she crushes herbs with her mortar and pestle. The herbs smell floral and a touch spicy. She wears a deep, forest-green dress with moss around the hem and a plunging neckline. Her braids are tied back in a neat bun decorated with small twigs and leaves.

I smile at the sight, preferring to see her in her element like this rather than as the façade she put on in Terra Court.

"Hey," she says softly, forcing a smile. Her usually spirited eyes are dull, her shoulders slumped. She wipes her hands on a rag and turns to me, leaning her hip against the table in the center of the room.

"How is he?"

"Not well, Alessia." Her tone is severe, but even so, I perk up at her words as she confirms my hopes. "But he's alive."

I close my eyes and pinch the bridge of my nose, trying to keep the emotion at bay. "Thank the gods. Is he awake?" She's silent for far too long. My eyes flick back open and lock onto her. "What is it?"

She clears her throat and inhales slowly. "He's on a nasogastric tube right now."

"What does that mean?"

"He's not waking up." She shakes her head. "It's a tube that goes through his nose, down to his stomach, feeding him the blood he needs since he can't drink it on his own."

"When will he wake up?" I whisper, knowing it's a stupid question.

Sighing, she grips the counter and hangs her head. "I don't know, but the longer he's unconscious, the more unlikely his chances are. We're just lucky I had that barrel of blood on hand."

"And what if it runs out?"

She sets her jaw and gives me a hard look. "It won't. We won't let it."

I nod in solidarity. "He needs to survive, Sera." His death will destroy Rainer. It'll destroy *me*. He only went to Dovenak to help me, after all.

"You have one win today—you retrieved the iron. Let's focus on that."

"Well…" I sigh exasperatedly. "Not exactly."

Her brows draw down. "Oh?"

"It's a long story."

"You say that as if I don't have all the time in the world." She forces a laugh, but it's stilted. Gesturing to the rows of dried herbs lying before her, she says, "It'll take me hours to crush all this, and I could use a distraction, so…"

"What're you making?" I squint. "And why did Ez need you so badly?"

"The first was a synthetic drug for Fern—if she faces withdrawals, it's not only her life on the line anymore." Her face shutters, and she glances down, toying with a bundle of lavender. "He also needed me to make a potion for Yvanthia."

"I thought you didn't like the queen?"

Sera smirks. "I don't." She reaches for a small amber vial with a dropper and holds it up. "It's to kill her libido."

My confusion must show because Sera's smile fades, and she scrunches her nose.

"It's not my place to share details, but Yvanthia enjoys Ez." A dark shadow crosses her features. "He tolerates her since he's used to the price of his magic. But now that he's found his bonded…" Her voice cracks, and she sets the vial down.

Sympathy swells inside of me. "He doesn't want to engage with the queen anymore."

Sera nods, gripping the counter. "But if he rejects her, she will know something is amiss, so I created something to stifle her desire."

A heavy weight settles in my stomach as I realize what it all means—the sacrifices Ez has made to help us and use his magic so freely. I've seen those flickers of unease underneath his good-natured demeanor. My mouth floods with a bitter taste, and I hate the queen even more.

Now that Ez has found his bonded… well, no wonder he's so thrilled. Except that Fern doesn't seem to share his joy. Another wave of pity washes over me. The Aer Prince can't catch a break.

"I thought Yvanthia had wards up to prevent magic?" I ask, redirecting the conversation away from the discomfort of Ez's truths. "How can you use a potion on her?"

"It's alchemy," Sera explains. "It works a little differently than soul magic, since it's a creation rather than a part of me."

"Why not just poison her then?"

Sera lets out a bitter laugh. "She has poison tasters. It would never reach her, and even *if* it did, who do you think would be blamed? Ez is the only one allowed *close* to her while still having the freedom to come and go."

"Because of their bond," I surmise. "She's complacent in thinking he'll protect her or else he'll die alongside her."

"And *that* is what we're using to our advantage."

"So you'll still help him, even though he's... bonded?"

"Of course I'm still going to help him!" She smiles sadly. "He's my best friend, and he deserves happiness. Even at the cost of my heartbreak."

"Did you tell him how you feel?" I ask softly. "I might've, uh, spilled the beans when he visited me the other day."

Her lips tighten, and she glances away, a stoic look working its way onto her face. "He asked me, but I couldn't tell him the truth, Alessia. There's no point. Not now."

"But Fern doesn't even like—"

"I won't interfere with a *soul*-bond," she says quickly. "Especially not a consummated one. Absolutely not. It's best to let it go." The hardness in her voice punctuates her words, and I nod numbly, letting it drop.

Perhaps Sera is a better female than me because I don't know if I could give Rainer up in the same situation. Then again, it's not the same situation because Rainer *is* my soul-bond.

And Ezamae can never be hers.

I place a hand on her shoulder, squeezing gently. "I'm here for you. If you need a friend."

Her eyes shoot to mine, and she nods almost imperceptibly. "There's a good chance I might."

"Well, that makes two of us."

She exhales a short laugh, and we share a comfortable silence. Afterward, I tell her about Enid and the sorceress she knows, who can help her with the iron.

"What's their name?" Sera asks curiously.

I shake my head. "Enid didn't say."

Sera hmms to herself, but she shrugs. "There's not many of us left."

"I guess we'll find out soon enough." I study her as she works, plucking the flowers off a bushel I don't recognize. "How are *you* doing? Really?"

She purses her lips, blinking slowly as she tilts her head up. "How do you think?"

I shake my head. "I think you present as strong and unbothered but that you're hurting inside."

"I *am* hurting, Alessia." She turns to me, pain etched into her face. "I'm in love with my best friend, and he's bonded to someone else."

"Do you want to talk about it?" I ask.

She laughs, but it's dry and full of hurt. "Not really. Like I said, there's not much to it."

A masculine cough comes from the doorway and both of our heads shoot up. Ken stands there stroking his beard, a cocky smile on his lips. His dark brown eyes are latched on Sera, and there's a definite spark of interest there.

"There ya are, little demon and little witch."

"I'm a *sorceress*, not a witch." Sera rolls her eyes, but her lips twitch with a small smile.

"Same thing, no?"

She pauses, setting down her tools and planting a hand on her hip. "That's like calling you a walrus."

Ken snorts. "I'm a bear."

"Exactly," Sera says, staring him down.

Ken hovers awkwardly, as if he's unsure of what to say. It's rare to see him without his confident swagger. "How's Tynan?"

Sera groans, throwing her arms up. "He needs rest and blood. I'm doing everything I can for him."

"I know you are. I just—" Ken huffs, scratching the back of his head. "I want to help you, Sera."

My gaze ping-pongs between the two of them, and I come up with an idea. "Ken, I think Sera could use a break. Fresh air. How about you take her for a ride?" Ken gives me a toothy smile. The tension immediately lightens in the room. I can practically hear the dirty retort before he even makes it, so I cut him off. "In bear form. Through the woods."

Sera gives me a pointed look. "I'd almost rather the other kind of ride at this point," she mutters quietly. "Might help me get over—"

"He can *hear* you," I hiss back, pointing to my ear.

Sera sizes him up, shrugging. "Let's go, bear." She strides past him out the door, wagging a finger for him to follow. "There's not much we can do around here right now anyway."

Ken glances at the ceiling, muttering something. Then, he turns his smile on me and gives me an exaggerated double thumbs up. Spinning quickly, he darts after Sera.

I glance at the mess on the table, shaking my head with a laugh. Even after all the shite that's happened, the fae have a beautiful ability to find joy in small moments. They rebound well from even the worst of life's disruptions.

Desperate for fresh air myself, I head above ground. The brightness makes me squint. With the adrenaline gone and the exhaustion creeping in, the sun intensifies the pain in my eyes.

I've spent weeks in my court alone, but after being back in the world and in my friend's lives again, I find it harder to appreciate the underground space. Many of my friends might be in my court right now, but how long will that last? How long are they staying?

Worse, Rainer will return to his court—the thought of having a whole forest between us stings.

"Little rose blooming beneath the sun," my favorite voice says. "I was about to come find you."

I whirl around. Rainer stands a few paces away with his back against a tree. His ankles are crossed, and his hands are stuffed in his pockets. He tilts his head, taking me in with a soft expression.

My pulse quickens, and a warmth seeps through my body. I take a quick inventory of the bond and find a calmness there. There is no anger, no remorse, and only a tiny glimmer of pain.

He kicks off the tree and striding toward me. The pain pulsing down the bond intensifies. "Life has a funny way of taking everything from us."

"Not everything," I say, reaching for his hand.

"No," he whispers back. Slowly, the hurt shooting down his side of the bond subsides, and tranquility returns to our invisible connection. "Sometimes it gives us the most beautiful gifts, too."

"I'm glad we didn't wait any longer. Even fae lives can be much too short, Rainer, and I want to spend every second with you." I suck in a deep breath, preparing for what I'm going to say next. "I want to come live with you—at Umbra Court."

Surprise flashes across his face, and his spine becomes rigid. Slowly, a smile curves upward until his dimple pops out. "You mean it?"

I nod.

He pulls back abruptly, running a hand through his hair. "I can't let you, Alessia. After everything, I won't let you give up your court."

My own smile blooms. "I'm not going to. That's the thing. I want to use Spiritus Court to create a sanctuary for fae—and humans—who need a safe, clean space to live or recover." Perhaps that was another seed Char planted in my mind all that time ago when she mentioned the rumor of a sanctuary in Avylon. Maybe I was the one meant to create such a space. I blow out an exhale. "I'm not prepared to run a *proper* court, anyway. This way, the court will be lived in, and I can ensure I'm serving the land, but I can still be with *you*."

His eyes soften as he studies me. "You'd have to return often…"

"The curse on the woods will soon be broken. I can learn to ride a horse properly."

He tilts his head up, gazing at the clear blue skies. "There's better sun here."

"I won't see it below ground anyway," I retort.

"We could build above ground, give you a bright space to—"

"Too much work." I step toward him, quirking an eyebrow. "Or is this your way to try and convince me not to stay with you?"

He shakes his head, whipping his gaze to mine. "I don't want you to make any more sacrifices for me, mo róisín."

I can't help but laugh. "That's what love is—sacrifice. It's finding a balance between honoring your own needs and selflessly caring for your partner. *This* is a sacrifice I can make. It feels right."

He shoves his fingers into his hair, pushing it off his forehead. I reach for his hand and grab it. He lets me pull his hand away and then faces me fully.

"You are my home," he says. "Wherever you are, I will be. Wherever you go, I will follow. Whether it's here or Umbra Court, or both." His face lights up. "We will reside in *both* courts. Deal?"

I chuckle, swatting at his chest. "I'm not making any more deals."

He grabs my hand, tugging me to his body. "If you think about it, our relationship started with a bond—"

"And it will end with a bond, too," I finish, realizing the poetic irony of the situation.

"Who said anything about ending?" He scoffs playfully. "We're just getting started." Leaning his head down, he plants a chaste kiss on my lips. Then, he hovers there and whispers, "Follow me."

When he turns and strides into the trees, I obey without question.

Our loyalty is mutual, and I will also follow him anywhere.

FORTY-SEVEN

DESTINED TO BE RAINER

We navigate through a thick part of the woods—still on Spiritus land but away from the entrance—stopping in a small clearing of wildflowers. At the edge, I pause. Wordlessly, I spin toward Alessia.

"I'm sick of *waiting*." I stalk toward her and then cup her face.

Her brows draw together in confusion. "Waiting for what?"

"This." Without wasting another breath, I press my lips against hers, savoring the sweet taste that lingers there. With a gentle yet firm touch, I coax her lips apart, and our tongues intertwine.

She moans, sliding her hands to the back of my neck and tugging me closer.

My cock is as hard as iron, desperate to be between her glorious thighs again. Nothing in this cruel world feels as divine as nestling into her pussy.

The urgent need to feel her body against mine drives my hips forward. She gasps, breaking the kiss and staring up at me.

"I need you," she whispers, her fingers clutching my hair. "*Now*."

"You are not in control right now, mo róisín." I chuckle darkly, pressing her against the tree. She gasps as the rough bark scrapes her backside.

With one hand, I hold both her wrists above her head while my other finds her thigh. I work my way up her soft flesh, silently thanking the gods she's wearing a short dress.

My fingers trail up until they hit the fabric of her panties.

"I want these off." My vision flickers, darkness encroaching.

Without releasing her hands, I tuck my fingers in her waistband and tug her underwear down. They slide down her legs. She steps out of them, squeezing her thighs together. Her heart beats frantically, sending her blood surging through her veins. It causes my cock to throb, begging for more.

"Rainer." She whispers my name, and it's half a moan.

I lean forward, running my nose up the side of her throat. Inhaling deeply, I groan. My gums ache as my fangs begin to descend. I nudge my boot between her feet, kicking them apart.

The scent of her arousal reaches my nose, and I have to focus on my breath to keep from spilling in my pants.

Gods save me.

This woman ruins me.

"Wait," she says, her chest rising and collapsing with her vigorous breaths. "Not like this."

I draw back, frowning.

Is it too much for her?

Too fast?

"Do you want me to stop?" I say, releasing her hands.

I focus carefully on her face, not allowing the many tempting sensations to distract me from what matters most: *her*.

A wicked smile curves up on her lips. Her eyes sparkle with mischief. She lifts a hand, and I freeze as a dark tendril bursts free of her skin. She pushes off the tree and circles me like a predator as her shadow wraps around me. Quickly, it flips me around and presses *my* back against the trunk so our positions are reversed.

Delight flickers to life inside me, and a disbelieving laugh crawls up my throat.

Her shadow rips my pants down—quite literally ripping the button free—until they lay around my ankles. My erection springs out, hard and wanting. Precum leaks from the tip without her even having touched me.

The dark tendril yanks me back violently, wrapping around my legs and midsection, effectively tying me to the tree. The bark bites into my skin, undoubtedly leaving its mark there.

I raise a brow.

Alessia's eyes stay locked on my cock. She licks her lips.

Tilting my head back against the bark, I close my eyes and groan. "What are you doing to me, little rose?"

"Experimenting," she says coyly.

My eyes flick back open, and this time, there's a hint of color on her cheeks. She bites her lip, and I'd give anything to feel those soft lips on mine right now.

Instead of commanding her like I want to, I relax against the shadow's grip and allow her to dictate. The dark, cool shadow branches off, coiling around my shaft. My heart nearly stops. Its tantalizing grip is firm yet surprisingly gentle. A tingling sensation slides down my spine as the tendril dances along my length. With each stroke, the shadow's grip grows more assertive—tightening and tugging, bringing me closer to release.

I hiss, trying to fight the intensifying pleasure until my legs are trembling.

"Alessia," I warn. My voice is barely a whisper. Sparks burst behind my eyes as the pressure builds in the base of my spine. "If you don't stop, I'll come."

Suddenly, the shadow releases its hold on me. The tension in my body simmers as I focus on breathing, letting the wave of intensity subside. The sensation leaves me slightly disoriented, my body yearning for more stimulation.

The rest of the shadow refuses to release me. Instead, it branches off toward Alessia. She pauses, reaching for the hem of her dress and pulling it off over her head. My breath stutters as I watch her step toward me, fully nude. The meadow acts as a colorful backdrop, framing her impossible beauty.

She's a rose in a field of wildflowers—beautiful, untamed, *mine.*

A breeze kisses her skin, and she shudders. Her dark, rosy nipples harden. Pale hair marks the place between her legs, and I ache to bury my face there and suffocate.

The shadow lifts her carefully by the thighs, forming a swing as it carries her toward me. The tendril holding me releases its grip, allowing me to touch Alessia as we're brought together. I grip the backs of her thighs, prepared to support her full weight, but the shadow doesn't relinquish its hold.

I give Alessia a questioning look and she smirks. Even with the confidence, she blushes, bashfully chewing her lip.

"Use it," she whispers. "Use *me.*"

It's all the encouragement I need. I release her, trusting the shadow-swing to hold her for me. Gripping my shaft, I slide my tip over her slickness. She wiggles, spreading her legs wider. Pressing a little firmer against her clit, I move in small circles. She throws her head back, enjoying the sensation.

The shadow holds her in place with ease.

How else might it accommodate us?

A dark delight sparks inside me.

"Flip over," I command.

Without hesitation, the shadow grips Alessia and flips her onto all fours, hovering her in the air before me. It holds her at precisely the right height, with her soft, round arse lined up with my tip. I squeeze her arse, then bring my hand down, slapping her cheek.

Her body jerks and a soft gasp escapes her. She glances back at me with her lips parted in surprise. I rub the ache away, smirking at her.

"Do it again," she says, her voice husky.

She arches her back, temptingly wiggling her arse. I slide a finger through her wetness, then plunge it inside of her.

"Don't tell me what to do," I order. With my finger inside her, working in and out, I bring up my other hand and spank her again.

My naughty little rose moans, squeezing my finger.

"I need you inside of me," she says breathlessly, writhing again. "*Now.*"

I don't have the chance to tease her any further because her shadow splits off again, wrapping around my wrist and yanking my hand away from her. I chuckle darkly as it grabs my penis and places it at her entrance. Neither of us has to move because the shadow does all the work.

I stay pressed against the tree, watching eagerly as the shadow swings Alessia backward. Her glistening lips devour my shaft, her round arse framing the sight so beautifully. Each bit of skin is slowly swallowed down until she's pressed flush against my base.

"So… big," she gasps. Clenching around me.

Reaching up, I grip her hips to hold her in place. My vision wavers, and lust suffocates me—so hot and heavy that I fear for a second I might explode.

My entire body vibrates with love, passion, and *need*. The tether between us goes taut as we send the same feelings back and forth—an unspoken language of emotion.

I can feel her pleasure as acutely as I feel my own. It's too potent, too powerful, that I can't move for a second. She writhes, trying to instigate me. My fingers bite into her flesh, begging her to stop.

"Hold still," I hiss, shutting my eyes.

She's too warm, wet, and soft. My cock twitches, threatening to burst. Finally, I exhale the pressure sitting on my chest and slide her off of me. Then, I sink back into her. She whimpers, arching her back further. The shadow moves like a swing, finding a mellow pace as it rocks Alessia back and forth against me.

Releasing her hips, I grip her hair, gently tugging her head back. My other hand finds her breast, tweaking her nipple between my fingers. The shadow picks up its pace, faster and faster, until her bare skin slaps against mine.

The sky darkens briefly, followed by an unfamiliar flapping noise, but I ignore it, continuing to revel in pure bliss.

Alessia moans, taking me like a champion.

Then, her body tightens. "What's *that*?" She points toward the sky.

I glance up in time to see a set of enormous white wings disappearing over the trees.

"Doesn't matter," I mutter, drowning in the feel of her skin against mine. It looked like an Angelli—probably Uriel. Unimportant. "I want you to ride me. I want to look at you while I come, baby. I want to kiss your pretty little mouth while you take all of me."

The shadow responds immediately, pulling Alessia off of me and planting her on the ground. Her legs shake, giving out, but I'm there to steady her. I sit before her, my back still against the tree, and pull her down on my lap, with a knee on either side of my thighs.

I'm covered with her juices, slick and ready to slide back into her. She reaches between us, gripping my hardness and holding it steady as she sits on it—right where she belongs.

The pleasure bursts through me again, spreading like wildfire, and my vision goes spotty. My gums ache as much as my balls—one desperate to be filled, one desperate to be drained.

"Bite me," Alessia whispers against my lips. "I can feel it in the bond—bite me."

I grip her chin, forcing her head up for access to her throat. "I love you. With everything I am, everything I've been, and everything I will be," I whisper, and then I press my fangs to her skin.

The next time she sinks onto my cock, I sink my teeth into her throat, breaking the skin. She yells in pleasure, gripping wildly at my hair. I keep my palm planted on her back to steady her. The other cups her chin to lock her in place.

The sweet, metallic taste of her blood washes over my tongue, and I moan as I sip from her. Her inner walls squeeze around me, and my eyes flutter shut.

With each pull from her veins, her muscles pulse, and her fingers tighten in my hair.

"Rainer!" she screams my name, and it's the most incredible sound I've ever heard.

My hands find her hips, and I jerk her back and forth in small circles, grinding her clit against me. Her throat vibrates against my tongue as she whimpers, finding her climax with me inside of her. I pull my lips from her throat, slamming them against her mouth to stifle her cries.

My balls tremble, and the second most glorious orgasm I've ever had blows through me. I roar, tightening my grip on her as I explode, letting every drop of my pleasure fill her up.

"That's it," I mutter, meeting her eyes. "Take my cum like a good girl."

She gasps for breath, her face flushed and sweaty. Her shadows must've recoiled at some point because they're no longer in sight. The creative use—and control—impresses me greatly.

"That was..." Instead of finishing her sentence, she drops her forehead to my shoulder and blows out a long exhale. Her body begins to shake with laughter. "Holy shite."

She lifts herself onto her knees, sliding off of me. I reach for her, pulling her back down on my thighs. I wrap my arms around her, cradling her. As my seed drips from her center, down her thighs, I use a finger to swipe it back up inside of her where it belongs.

Her cheeks pinken again, and her eyes fill with lust when she turns to face me. Instead of saying anything, I press my mouth to hers and kiss her lazily.

My fingers dance in small circles on her spine. I break the kiss and lick my lips, loving the taste of her lingering there.

"I love you," she says, wrapping her arms around my neck. "I love you Rainer Rohan Iorworth."

"Marry me," I say quickly. The words fall from my lips before I can second-guess them.

Pulling back, she searches my eyes. "But we're already bonded."

"Yes, but I want a ceremony. I want to declare my love for you in front of the realm. Marry me—complete the monogamy ceremony with me, and let me claim you publically."

She laughs, cupping my cheeks and bringing her forehead to mine. "I'm *yours*. I will marry you a thousand times over, and it would still never be enough, my beautiful nightmare."

The nickname sends warmth through me, kicking up an emotional storm. We sit together beneath the tree in the meadow, entwined in each other's arms for what feels like hours. We fall asleep, meet in our dreams, and consummate our love repeatedly.

Our bond deepens with each encounter, solidifying that we were *always* destined to be.

FORTY-EIGHT
WELCOME TO AVYLON
ALESSIA

The days go by as we wait for Tynan to regain consciousness. Nothing really changes as we stay put in Spiritus Court with everyone around us. Any day now, he will wake up, and everything will be okay.

But with each passing day, Rainer makes peace with the idea of losing Tynan.

Rainer and I continue to sneak away to the meadow, losing ourselves to bliss under the open sky. The likely death of his brother impacted him more than he says with words—I can feel his guilt and sorrow through the bond. They vibrate down our invisible cord, hitting me in the chest at the most random of times.

Even with all the horrible things that have transpired around us, it's not enough to steal the joy of being in love—and having that love returned.

"There you are," Ken hollers, waiting for us one afternoon. He stands next to the massive tree door, tapping his foot anxiously. "I started to look for you, but when I caught a scent of—"

Rainer growls, narrowing his eyes. "Don't finish that sentence."

"Well, I figured it'd be best to wait here for you." Ken clears his throat, grinning. "Guess broody prince *is* the little demon's type after all, eh?"

Embarrassment washes over me, but when Rainer gives me a private smirk, I can't help but return it.

"Why were you looking for us?" Rainer asks.

"Oh—you have visitors." He jerks his thumb toward the door. He pushes it open, gesturing for us to enter first. "They got here a little while ago, but they seem a little impatient."

Ken leads us to one of the receiving rooms that I never thought would actually be used. He pushes open the double doors with dramatic flair, turning to grin at us.

I expected to see Enid, but instead, an unfamiliar group sits on couches around a table, playing cards and drinking wine. I count six of them.

"Squid!" The blond one yells, throwing his cards down on the table. He turns to us with a crooked grin and jumps to his feet. He kicks the female next to him in the shin. "Lo, they're here."

"Asshole!" she yells, and I can't place their accents.

Most rise, eyeing us with various levels of wariness and intrigue. A curvy female about my height with olive skin and a dark pixie cut separates from the pack. She steps forward, inclining her chin and narrowing her teal eyes on me. There's a stern expression as she scrutinizes me, and I'm not sure I like it.

"You're her," she says thoughtfully. Like the others, her accent tells me she's not from Dovenak or Avylon. "Hm. Not what I expected."

I frown. "Who are *you*?"

We hold each other's stares for a second, then she laughs.

"I'm Aife." She points to the tall, stunning male with long, dark hair pulled into a low bun standing beside her. "This is Lex." He nods but doesn't smile. Then, Aife gestures at a brown-haired male in suspenders, wearing a teasing smirk. "That's Dash."

"Hey." He waves.

"Way to forget about us." The blond one says. "I'm Callan." He throws his wine back and slams it on the table. "That's good wine. And that's Lo." He jerks a thumb at the female with long, white-blonde braids and upturned eyes. "The asshole behind us is Sora."

The other dark-haired male with narrowed, angled eyes stays planted on the sofa, refusing to look at us.

I squint at Callan, wondering why he looks so familiar. Then I shake it off.

"Lexyll," I murmur, my eyes latching onto the one whose name I recognize. His bright green eyes are equally alluring and haunting. His shapely muscles beneath his all-black ensemble as he crosses his arms. "God of War?"

He arches a brow as he stares me down blankly. "Indeed."

"You're really a god?"

The male chuckles, and Aife appears amused.

Rainer steps closer to me, and I feel his jealousy radiating down the bond. Whatever expression is on his face causes Aife to laugh again. Her ocean eyes twinkle with amusement.

"Easy, killer," she says to Rainer. "They're *mine*." She rolls her eyes, then turns to me. "Males, am I right? Always having a motherfucking pissing contest."

I frown in confusion at the strange turn of phrase.

"What the feck is going on?" Ken mutters loudly. He strides past the group, snatching the wine bottle and plopping down next to the glowering arse on the sofa. Ken angles the bottle toward him. "Sláinte." Then, he brings it to his lips and downs the whole thing.

"Holy shit," Callan says with a laugh, clearly impressed by Ken's shenanigans. "You're crazy."

"We came to help you," Aife says, ignoring the males.

"Enid contacted me and requested assistance," Lex says, his deep voice booming through the space and commanding attention. The lilt to his words is slightly different from the others—still unplaceable to me. "I brought others."

"It means a lot that you'd come to help," I say, nodding my head. I hope they can read the *thank-you* between my words. I'll say it to Rainer, but there's no way I'm saying it to strangers.

"How the feck do *you* plan to help exactly," Rainer challenges, stepping forward toward Lex.

Lex sighs, as if he's tired, and his eyes shoot to Callan.

A whooshing sound cuts through the air as white wings shoot from Callan's back. I gape, stunned by the sight up close. I've only seen wings like these twice before. Once at Ostara and once in the—

"*You*," I breathe out. "I saw you! Up on Mount Altum in the moonberry field." Right before I went into the Cave of Reflection and my entire life changed.

"Probably." His grin grows, and he shrugs his shoulder. "I can't resist returning home for my favorite snack now and then." He winks at Aife, who chuckles.

"Hey, I love moonberries!" Ken roars, clapping his hands.

Callan reaches into his pocket. "Want some? I have a few ex-tra—"

"Can we hurry this the *fuck* up," Sora snarls from the sofa. "I have things to do."

"You can shut the fuck up, how about that?" Aife snaps back, rolling her eyes. "Sorry about that one. And Callan—now is not the time to get high."

"But it's always a good time to get high," Ken protests.

Rainer sighs, rubbing his forehead.

Callan laughs, stepping over to Ken to give him a high five. "I like this guy."

"Share your berries, and I'll say the same about you," Ken says, reaching a hand out.

Sora slaps it away, scowling at them both.

I'm still caught up in the strangeness of it all. The casual apol-ogy, combined with their unfamiliar accents and word choices, confuses me.

"Where are you from?" I ask Aife.

She glances at her companions. "A few different places."

I scrunch my nose at her non-answer. "You're human?" I ask, trying to understand these strange… beings in my court.

"Sort of?" Aife offers. "I identified as human for a while, if that counts."

"Don't let her downplay it," Dash says, wrapping an arm around her waist and pulling her to his side. "This gorgeous woman here is a—"

Aife snorts and slaps his arm away. "Sora's right. We should move things along."

"Where would you like your iron delivered?" Lex asks calmly, getting down to business.

"Uh, here is fine?" I look to Rainer for confirmation. He's busy sizing up the males as if he's readying for a fight. I step closer to him, leaning up toward his ear, and I lower my voice. "They're here to *help*."

"I don't trust them," Rainer responds loudly.

"But Enid sent them to—"

"And I don't trust her," he adds.

His icy blue eyes narrow, sending a chill down even *my* spine. The strangers are no more intimidating than Rainer. The thought that Rainer could fit in amongst a *god* has me biting down a smile.

"You don't trust anyone."

"For good reason."

"Okay, I'm hungry," Callan says, cutting through the tension.

"Me too!" Ken stands, slapping his thighs. "Let's talk this out over a meal, how bout that?"

"Good idea." I nod, striding to the door. "I'll let Das Celyn know we have visitors, so they can prepare something. In the meantime, I'll show you to the guest rooms so you can make yourselves comfortable."

Rainer grumbles, and I shake my head as I chuckle to myself.

I pause at the door, turning back to the teal-eyed woman right behind me. "Wherever you're from, Aife and friends, welcome to Avylon."

FORTY-NINE

Wicked Sense of Humor

Alessia

"There are more Angelli here than I've ever seen in my entire life," Ezamae says with wonder.

We stand in the great hall, watching the dozens of folk come in and out. Inside, they appear almost human—albeit ethereally beautiful, impossibly strong humans. But once they reach the ground level, feathered wings shoot from their backs as they explode into the sky.

They drop off iron by the bucketload—some in rock form, some already forged as weapons. The mound grows as the day goes on.

Lex wasn't kidding when he said he brought friends.

"Who is that?" Ez asks, pointing to Aife.

She stands on the opposite side of the room with Dash, a hand planted on her hip as she barks orders to the Angelli. Dash watches her with a smirk, like she's the most fascinating thing he's ever seen.

"I'm not really sure, but she makes a great leader." I shrug. "And she has multiple lovers."

"Interesting." Ez makes a face of approval. "I do see the appeal in that lifestyle."

I elbow him, and he chuckles.

"Speaking of. How are things with Fern these days?" I ask.

His smile fades. "I would rather talk about *your* love life, how about that?"

"How about no."

"Where *is* your broody bonded anyway?"

"He's up top tending his roses." Shortly after we decided to share courts, he began a garden here, taking full advantage of the sunlight. "He's not fond of our visitors—despite their help—so he's keeping busy."

Ez laughs. "He's come a long way."

"What do you mean?" I ask, studying Ez's profile as the Angelli grunt and groan around us, dropping piles of iron off.

He glances at me, lifting a brow. "I hadn't seen the Umbra Prince in *years* before you came along, and now I see him almost daily. Even when he hosted Ostara, he rarely made appearances. He was a prisoner to his own mind—locked in a tornado of self-pity. You helped him find his freedom, Alessia."

My chest warms as I smile to myself.

"After all that nagging for us to consummate the bond, and you still haven't killed Yvanthia," I say.

"Sh, not so loud." Ez looks around, then flicks his wrist, and a brief blast of air washes over me. "Now we can speak freely."

"What's holding you up?"

He sighs, kicking at the stone floor with his silver boot. "There was a slight miscalculation on my part… a minor hold up. However, I am reevaluating and have devised a new plan to remove her."

"You mean *kill* her?" The casual reference to murder is so absurd that I want to laugh, but Yvanthia has been a menace to two realms for hundreds of years. It's time for her to go. The era of change is upon Avylon, and Ez would make an extraordinary king.

"If you're concerned about your bonded, don't be. Yvanthia's attention is focused elsewhere these days—you and Rainer are two tiny rainclouds in a sky of storms."

My brows flit up. "Should I be worried about you?"

"I've got it under control."

"And if you need help, you *will* come find me, right?"

"Right..."

"Promise?"

He chuckles, turning his sharp silver eyes on me. "I must go now, Alessia. I will bring Laisren from Ignus Court, and then I must return to Yvanthia."

"You can't stay?" The thought of him returning to that wretched queen turns my stomach.

"No," he says sadly. "But best of luck to you. I will see you sooner rather than later."

My forehead wrinkles. "Wait. What do—"

He disappears before my eyes, leaving a slight breeze and a faint shimmer where he stood. I sigh, tossing my braid over my shoulder and striding out of the great hall.

A pixie flits toward me, nearly crashing into my face. "Spiritus Princess!"

"Yes?" I chuckle as the fist-sized creature tumbles in the air, doing excited backflips.

"The old princess from the portraits is here! She's here!"

My nerves come alive. "Enid? She's here?"

"Yes! In the foyer!"

My heart thunders in time with my footsteps as I jog to the entrance of my court. What will Enid think, being back home after all this time? Does she still consider it home? Should I be worried that she wants her home back?"

No no no, my shadow-self says. *This is* your *home now. You* are *the Spiritus Princess. Beside, she's magic-less. Much good that'd do for the court.*

I let the words wash over me, finding power in them. Ever since I accepted the darker side of me, things have gone much more smoothly. In fact, admitting the primal urges are mine has helped me control them better than trying to ignore them.

"My dearest!" Enid bellows, opening her arms the moment she sees me.

Dressed in a regal teal gown that's snug around her top and billowing out around her as it sweeps the floor, she looks every bit a *queen*. Her ash-blonde hair is tied up in a smooth bun, hiding away our shared curls.

Awkwardly, I move into her arms and let her embrace me. Her lemongrass and peppermint scent is soothing, so familiar that I can't help but melt in her arms.

"Welcome home," I mumble.

She chuckles, patting my back tenderly. Then, she pulls away, holding me at arm's length.

"This has not been my home in a very long time." She smiles. "I am very pleased to see you breathe life into these abandoned halls once more."

An old female with dark, wrinkly skin and shaking hands peers at me from behind Enid.

"Who is that?" I whisper to Enid.

She chuckles, turning and waving the female over. "This is Deidre. The sorceress I was telling you about."

"Welcome," I say to Deidre. She stares blankly, her lips tugging into a frown.

"She is rather old—and tired," Enid says, patting my cheek. "Introduce us to your sorceress so we shall get on with it."

Everyone works tirelessly for the next few weeks, and my heart fills with love and relief. We can achieve so much more when we combine our resources and skills.

I pass the great hall, peeking my head in. A blast of heat hits my face as I take in the enormous, controlled fire in the center of the room. Chunks of iron sit in a fireproof container, slowly melting beneath the flame's impossible heat. Though I can't see him because he's on the other side of the fire, I know it's the Ignus Prince's flameweaver power responsible. Quite frankly, the male scares me with his spiky collar, tight leather, and chains. His dark eyes are smudged with kohl and he wears an unwaveringly stern expression.

I shudder, backing away from the doorway before he finishes. My elbow bumps someone as they pass.

"Princess," an Angelli says as she bows her head, shuffling quickly past with two more buckets of iron.

She's gone before I can say anything.

"It's hot as hell down here," Fern's voice calls from down the hall. "They're not done yet?"

I turn as she strides toward me. Her face is expertly made up, but her eyes are bloodshot, and I can't tell if she's been crying or using.

My chest tightens with empathy. Soon, Sera should have an elixir made with just enough iron to neutralize Fern's addiction without harming her. With Ez's life tethered to Ferns, I know Sera will take it more seriously than ever.

I offer Fern a friendly smile, knowing she needs the kindness more than she lets on. "They should be done today."

She grimaces. "Have you seen the damn Aer Prince?"

"Not since he brought Laisren." I study her reaction, trying to figure out if it's good that she's looking for him. "Is everything okay?"

Her nose scrunches, and she flicks her silky, burgundy hair over a shoulder. "Forget it."

"Sera might know where he is."

"Why would *she* know?" Fern's lips harden. In jealousy? Frustration? Something else? "I'll see him when I see him."

She turns and practically stomps away. I watch her go, shaking my head. I'm not getting involved with her and Ez—that's their business to work out.

Instead, I head to the apothecary to see how things are moving along with Sera.

Enid, Dedire, and Sera work in tandem around a makeshift cauldron in the corner of the room. Deidre's eyes are narrowed in focus as she watches Sera pour in melted iron, using a trembling hand to encourage her to add more and telling her when to stop. Enid stirs, ensuring everything mixes well.

"They're bringing the last batch of iron soon," I say in lieu of a greeting. They finish what they're doing and glance up at me.

Enid smiles. "My dearest. Deidre and I will be returning to Dovenak this afternoon. I am not comfortable leaving the throne unattended another day."

I nod. "I understand." *Thank you for coming*, I want to say. "It means a lot that you came to help.

She steps away from the cauldron, gripping my hands in hers and giving them a squeeze. "That is what family is for." Releasing me, she steps back to her position and resumes stirring with the steel spoon resting in the cauldron.

I approach Sera's side. "Princess Sennah is coming to help soon."

Sera doesn't meet my eyes. She bites her lip, keeping her gaze down. We both know what I'm not saying: Sennah doesn't forgive Seraphina for killing her brother. The moment she killed Eoin—accident or not—she sealed her fate. The other fae won't stop Sennah if she tries to kill Sera—it's a debt owed.

Finally, Sera sighs and looks up. "I'm going with them."

"Who?" I ask, confused.

"Deidre and Enid," she says.

As if on cue, the two older females nod to each other and step out of the room to give Sera and me space.

"You're going to Dovenak?" I tilt my head, and my brows draw together. "For how long?"

She shrugs. "I've never had a mentor before, and Deidre has much she can teach me. Plus, she's..." A long exhale comes out of her mouth. "She's sick. Old. She can't use her hands much. I can *help* her, Alessia. I can help Enid and the Tradelings. I can put my skills to use somewhere where it matters."

"But you matter here, too."

Sera laughs softly. "There's nothing here for me, and you know it. Ez has a soul-bond now. Sennah wants me dead, and I don't feel like running."

"Going to Dovenak is exactly that," I say."

She shakes her head. "No. It's moving on with my life."

"Tynan needs you," I say.

Her brows pinch together as she gives me an apologetic look. "Alessia," she says softly. "I don't think he's waking up. His aura isn't growing any stronger, and we've given him more than enough blood *and* time."

Sorrow grips my throat. I shake my head.

The look of pity she gives me forces me turn away.

"You have to accept it," she says. "Everyone else has."

"Are you sure you don't want to stay?" I ask one last time, returning to the original conversation. "I like having you here, Sera."

"I'm sure." Her tone leaves no room for argument. "I can rectify my past mistakes and contribute to a positive future. I have numerous debts but am unwilling to sacrifice my life to settle them. This is how I absolve myself."

Scrutinizing her, I try to read between her words and look for any doubts or insincerities, but find none.

"Okay," I say, nodding softly. "You deserve to find your peace and happiness. Even after everything." And I hope she finds it. We've all made mistakes, and Sera's stemmed mainly from looking out for others. "You deserve to put yourself first for once."

She smiles sadly. "Now who's giving the good advice." A soft chuckle leaves her. "I told you we'd be friends in another life."

"No. We *are* friends. In this life, Sera." I'll be back to Dovenak. How could I not visit? I have family there now. There's so much I have yet to learn about my bloodline and my court. Like Deidre can be a mentor to Sera, Enid can be a mentor to me.

Plus, I will personally ensure the Tradelings find their freedoms. I'll do anything to help their transition, including opening my home as a refuge. In a way, despite my horrible past there, Dovenak will always be a piece of me.

"So, this is goodbye," Sera says.

"For now," I add. "I'll see you soon, though."

Her smile widens. "I'd like that."

"Maybe I'll bring Ken, too," I tease.

This time, when she laughs, she throws her head back. It's a beautifully untamed sound. "That bear is no good."

"He means well."

"Yeah," she mumbles. "I think he does. Do you… know where he is? I want to say goodbye."

I press my lips together, fighting the grin trying to break free. "He's sparring with that Angelli—Callan—and the two Tradelings we brought back—Zephyr and Luis."

"Do you think he'd mind if I interrupted?"

This time, I have to turn my back on her because my smile wins out. "I don't think he'd mind at all."

I head to the door. Pausing at the threshold, I turn back to her. "Speaking of looking for folk—do you know where Ez is?"

She shakes her head. "Haven't seen him. Why?"

"His bonded was looking for him."

Sera sighs, but she forces another half-smile. "A human…" She shakes her head. "That one is a handful. She might be just what that damn enchanter needs."

Unsure of how to reply, I share a look of understanding with her and then head out of the apothecary.

Sometimes, fate has a funny way of giving us just what we need before we realize we need it.

Other times, I swear Fate—the god—has a wicked sense of humor.

EPILOGUE

ALESSIA

Above ground, I pass the newly planted sunset roses. Sennah brought them as a gift of friendship, and Rainer was more than pleased. Together, we planted them around the entrance to my court. The light and soil conditions are right here because they're thriving.

Their orange, red, and yellow colors blend, offering a beautifully bright contrast to the abundance of black roses sprouting throughout my land.

Finally, Rainer has his mother's favorite roses.

And finally, the curse on the woods is broken after all this time.

Sennah and Ez successfully combined their elemental and air powers to create a rainstorm with the sorceress's crafted potion of melted iron. It was a beautiful sight, really—dark clouds the color of steel and onyx hovering above the trees. And when it rained, the drops that streaked through the sky were metallic.

It was hauntingly beautiful and the start of something new for Avylon. Once Ezamae completes his task of succeeding Yvanthia's throne, things will truly be as close to perfect as they could possibly be. It's more than I could've ever imagined. More than I dared hope for, even back when Char was my only friend—the one who initially encouraged me to *dream*.

I glance up at the sky, giving a silent thanks to Fate's hand—wherever she may be.

My steps are light, and I smile as I stride deeper into the woods. Soon, I come upon Tynan's old dwelling. The vampyr remains in my court without change, and even I am beginning to accept the truth of his fate. A flicker of grief sparks inside me, but I focus on the positive changes instead. Rainer didn't want it to sit empty, so he turned it into a beautiful memorial for Tynan.

Morning glories and ivy crawl up the side, bringing some life to the old, rotting wood. The door is wide open, revealing the many pots and gardening tools scattered within. Rainer kneels in the dirt beside the shack, packing down dirt with his palms.

"Mo róisín," he says softly without turning around.

Joining him, I lean against the side of the building to watch him work. He's shirtless, and the lines of his muscles bulge and flex as he digs through the dirt. Beads of sweat drip from his collarbone, trailing down the dark ink on his chest and torso.

My mouth dries out as I'm lost to his beauty. Heat builds low in my core, burning me up from the inside.

Rainer chuckles, sitting back on his haunches. He removes his gloves and uses the back of his hand to wipe the moisture off his brow.

"Am I distracting you?" I tease, knowing he can very well sense the temptation within me.

"Never." His pale eyes glint with mischief as they drag up my body. Even though I'm fully covered in plain leather pants and a form-fitting tunic, his eyes blaze with lust.

I toe the abandoned gardening gloves. "These are new."

He smirks. "They are."

"You've never used them before."

"I've never had a reason to keep my fingers clean before," he says huskily, slowly rising. He stalks toward me, and in two steps, he's hovering above me. He plants his forearm on the wood above my head and leans toward my ear.

"I prefer to dirty my fingers other ways," he whispers, toying with the waistband of my pants.

My skin pebbles, and I suck in a sharp breath, tilting my head up to face him. His lips hover above mine, and for a minute, neither of us talks. We simply share air.

He pops open the button on my pants, slipping a finger into the top of my underwear.

A dark shadow flits over us, then another. The rhythmic sound of flapping reaches my ears. I glance up to see a dozen Angelli soaring high overhead.

Lex and Aife said they'd be back to check on us. They were kind enough to offer their army should we need it. Avylon and Dovenak are undergoing significant transitions, and with change often comes unrest. I appreciate that Lex's army is trained in defense first—and offense second. We have the shared goal of minimizing harm. But I declined, not wanting to send the wrong message.

Until Ezamae said that today was *the* day. Then we decided it might be best to have additional support and sent for Lex as backup. The Council of Elders and some other courts might not respond well to their queen being assassinated.

But we're prepared to do what it takes for both realms' greater good and long-term peace.

Rainer sighs, slipping his hand from my pants and resting his forehead against mine. "I suppose now isn't the time."

Gripping his hand, I slide it back down my stomach, planting it where it was.

"It's *never* a good time." I tangle my fingers in the back of his onyx hair, pulling his lips to mine, whispering, "Which means we need to make it the right time."

Pouring out my passion through my lips, I kiss him frantically.

A loud, hoarse cough startles us. We jump apart, searching for the source.

"You didn't even have the decency to wait for me to die fully before fornicating on my sacred property, little brother?" A dry voice says slowly, as if straining to talk.

Hope and relief swell within me like a rising tide, surging higher and higher until it can no longer be contained. It bursts, flooding my chest and spilling into my limbs—a mixture of both mine and Rainer's emotions. We share a look, and his eyes glisten with moisture.

At the same time, we take off, tackling Tynan to the ground. He wheezes trying and failing to push us off of him.

"I thought I lost you, you feckin bastard," Rainer yells, punching his brother's shoulder affectionately as they tumble beside the flowers.

"Try harder next time." Tynan chuckles, and the sight and sound of him here alive is overwhelming. We climb off him, offering to help him up. He wobbles, but swats Rainer's hand away. "What the hell did you do to my home?"

"You mean this old shack?" Rainer asks, his lips twitching with humor.

Tynan glances at me, and I exhale, smiling up at him. "You're more than welcome to stay in my court, Ty," I say affectionately.

"You'll have much of the space to yourself, actually." I turn my smile to Rainer, reaching for his hand and squeezing it. "If you'd like, of course."

"The feck did I miss around here?" He runs a hand over his hair—which has grown out a touch since he was last awake. "There's a bunch of weirdos with wings over there." He jerks his thumb over his shoulder.

Laughter bubbles out of me, and I turn my face to the sky, soaking up the joy of the moment.

Like the roses, we all need water, light, and nutrients to survive—but unlike the roses, it's *love* that allows us to truly *thrive*. Love for ourselves and others—romantic, familial, and platonic.

There, beneath the expanse of blue sky and the soothing touch of the sun, I'm blessed to recognize that love touches my life in all its forms.

From a curse of malice and mercy, a love story took root—one that continues to flourish and bloom eternally.

DEAR READER

Thank you so much for coming along on Alessia and Rainer's journey with me. Concluding their trilogy is bittersweet. Though it is the end of what we see of their story, it's just the beginning of their Happily Ever After. There's a very good chance you might see more of them in the future. In fact, they have a few friends who are quite loudly demanding I tell *their* stories next. You never know who you might see again. ;)

In the meantime, are you interested in seeing more of the mysterious guests that helped Alessia and Rainer with the iron?

Check out the *These Wicked Lies* series!

You might recognize a few faces. Keep reading for the blurb.

THESE WICKED LIES
BLURB

When a princess with the ability to absorb and transfer life force energy discovers her mother, the queen, is manipulating her, she works with unexpected allies to steal the throne, battling magic-induced anxiety and unexpected attractions along the way.

Astrid is a vygora—a rare being that can absorb one's life force energy and transfer it to another with a touch. Only two people know what she's truly capable of: her best friend, Ilona, and her mother, the Queen of Hakran, a powerful myndox.

When foreign royalty and their handsome guard, Dashiel Dargan, show up unexpectedly with the ability to mute myndox manipulation, Astrid discovers she's been a prisoner to her mother's power her entire life, and she's not the only one. Faced with a lifetime of memories built on lies, she's caught between the story she thinks she knows, and the one she doesn't remember.

But when she can't trust anyone, how can she figure out which story is true?

Also by Miranda Joy

These Wicked Lies Series:

These Wicked Lies

These Wicked Truths

These Wicked Gods (Coming Soon)

Courts of Malice Trilogy:

A Curse of Malice & Mercy

A Dream of Fate & Flesh

A Realm of Fear & Fury

Silver City Series:

Shades of Silver City

Made in United States
Troutdale, OR
12/20/2024

26989714R00278